NASCENT

The Stork Tower Book One

TONY CORDEN

ISBN 978-0-6482890-1-2 (Paperback)

ISBN 978-0-6482890-0-5 (E-book)

'Nascent' is fiction, Tony isn't writing about real people and doesn't intend in any way to point the finger at anyone. If there is a similarity, then it's unintentional and a coincidence. If for some reason you think the good guys are based on you, then be encouraged, you are smart, kind and brave. If you think the bad guys are somehow based on you, they aren't, but Tony suggests you need help. Seriously, see a counsellor or turn yourself into the police. Some of the places, corporations, institutions, public figures, books, movies and songs Tony mentions are real. Tony has used them in a made-up story (fiction), i.e., IT ISN'T REAL. Finally, Tony thinks most of the science stuff is possible someday. If you use any of the ideas to make really cool stuff, then please let him know.

Tony designed the cover using an image from Shutterstock.com and Photoshop. Vellum was used to prepare the book for printing.

Published by Tony Corden in 2018

You can find out more at www.tonycorden.com or write to Tony at tony@tonycorden.com.

❀ Created with Vellum

To my patient and loving wife.

ACKNOWLEDGMENTS

I struggle with both spelling and grammar. Even with the spelling and grammar checks turned on I keep making mistakes. Homonyms trip me up, as do commas. In particular I want to thank S and E for helping to edit this book. They are wonderful women who deserve all the credit when you can't find an error. When you do, that is all me, not only for making it in the first place but also because I sometimes ignore what they suggest.

Other people have helped as well. I appreciate those who read the material as an e-book and sent in advice, suggestions and corrections. Thank you.

If you find any more then please let me know.

CONTENTS

HISTORY

IT WAS the advent of safe electromagnetic neural manipulation in 2021 which led to the rise of a viable and sustainable virtual reality industry. Within thirty years almost all leisure, education, and work-related activity occurred inside Virtual Reality (VR) constructs. Individuals were suspended in a neutral buoyancy liquid which had a gel-like consistency. Their bodies were held in induced quasi-comas, while their nervous system was manipulated to provide a virtual sensory experience indistinguishable from reality, while constantly stimulating their motor neurones to prevent muscular deterioration. The variety and complexity of the devices developed was frequently changing, yet the market continued to refer to all such devices as Neural Interface SIM (Sensory, Integrative and Motor) Pods or SIM Pods.

Many regulatory bodies, conservatives, and sceptics initially raised the problems of privacy and security. They were worried about the potential for brainwashing, thought control, or even subtle thought reform. In response, the VR industry developed and introduced an intelligently controlled interface which included a self-adaptive firewall. This device was controlled by the user and was capable of protecting personal privacy and safeguarding the minds of the growing number of people both working and living in virtual space. With many users wanting even greater control over their virtual experience, these interfaces quickly matured into personally managed and owned Artificial Intelligence (AI) Chips. The AI chips were physically implanted adjacent to the nervous system and were able to protect, inform and assist individuals both inside and outside the virtual world. The chips micro-manipulated the auditory and visual cortices making it possible for the owner to hear and see implanted information, even in the real world.

Various interest groups including parents, educators, and civil libertarians raised concerns over the appropriate age for SIM Pod immersion. In research commissioned by the International Institute of Applied Neuroplasticity, there was clear evidence that extended immersion in SIM Pods was detrimental for those under the age of fifteen. Further studies led to international guidelines banning SIM Pod use for those under the age of five. For those between the ages of five and ten, SIM Pod use was limited to two hours per day, then to four hours daily until age fifteen.

At the Dubai Convention for Virtual Modality in 2050 the United Nations' 'Declaration of Human Rights' was modified and the changes formally adopted the following August by the UN General Assembly. These changes asserted that access to a Personal Artificial Intelligence chip (PAI chip) was a fundamental human right for full admittance to modern society. The right to education was amended to include the right to access the virtual environment.

2

NOVEMBER 17, 2073

LEAH LIVED with her family in a small two bedroom apartment provided by the Australian Federal government. She had been born in the tiny room she shared with her younger brother. Their apartment was in the Switch, one of the poorest neighbourhoods in the city of Brisbane. Almost everyone in the Switch lived on Federally Assisted Negative Income. Fifty years earlier the area had been an Industrial Estate known as 'Citiswitch'. It had been bulldozed to build apartments for those on negative income and became known simply as 'The Switch'. The government provided just enough for essential services such as electricity, web access, simple medicines, and basic food. Very few people had jobs, and those who wanted more usually either turned to crime or found a niche by providing goods or services that people wanted but couldn't otherwise afford. Small crafts, that had all but disappeared in the modern era had been re-established: herbalists and cobblers, seamstresses and repairmen, bakers, vegetable gardeners, and micro-brewers. Over time, the Switch developed a nontaxable micro-economy all of its own.

While the government provided police and a schooling system, they were practically irrelevant and fundamentally impotent for those trapped on society's lowest rung. Instead, people developed various alternative models for control, justice and education. Citizen Groups were formed to provide protection and order. While many outside the Switch called these citizen groups 'gangs', they did maintain order and usually kept the peace — often for a small fee.

The government provided 'Education' was poorly funded and essentially irrelevant: most children attended just long enough to sustain the tax benefit. Instead, they learned either craft or graft, depending on their family situation. The minority of children who wanted to learn had to find innovative ways, not only to use the system but also to evade the majority of kids who happily tore down anyone seeking to rise above mediocrity.

Leah worked hard to do both. Nine years previously, at the age of six, she had started working for Jimmy Loo. She needed a protector at school, and he needed someone to squeeze through the dog door of Mrs Peterson's apartment. In return for unlocking the balcony window, Leah earned one month's protection from bullies. Jimmy assigned her one of his gang's uninitiated members, a ten-year-old kid, to walk her back and forth from her classroom each day.

Over the next six years, Leah continued to do small jobs for Jimmy, picking up skills like lock-picking and the ability to climb drain pipes. The protection changed over time from a bodyguard to self-defence instruction. Leah became proficient in various

Indonesian and Filipino fighting styles where she excelled in knife and stick fighting. Although her and Jimmy's business relationship had waned over the last four years, they were still acquaintances, if not friends. In fact, outside of her family, Jimmy and his boys were probably the only friends Leah had. She had spent nearly every day over the last decade either at the school or in the library reading and studying. Anything for a chance to get ahead. Nobody understood why, and she never explained, but the simple truth of it was — she wanted to experience more.

Now, finally, today was the day!

"Leah! Breakfast is ready."

Her dad's voice dragged her out of bed and woke her little brother, Conner, who was still asleep on the other side of the room. Her father, Michael Carroll, was of Irish descent, had ginger hair and was a tenth generation Australian. He loved cricket and everything Celtic.

"Ling! Come eat your congee, bring your brother."

Leah's mother was Lin Li-Jin, from Xi'an, Shaanxi Province China. She was small, dark-haired and very traditional, always called Leah by her Chinese name and almost always spoke Mandarin.

"Hurry up Leah, your mum won't let me start without you. It's your birthday girl, move it, I'm hungry."

Her mother responded, this time in her accented English, for her father had never learnt Mandarin.

"Yes, hurry, your barbarian father is hungry."

After dragging her brother out of bed, Leah made her way to the table.

"Michael, you say grace!"

Leah's mother had become a Christian during a gospel meeting at the local Baptist Church several years after marrying Michael. He was Catholic, but very nominal. Jin was always trying to get the family to church, but Michael was determined to keep whatever faith he had as far from everyday life as he possibly could. Leah's mother had little awareness of the Jimmy Loo connection, and Leah tried as hard as she could to keep it that way.

With a sigh, Michael said the only prayer he knew.

"Bless us, O Lord, and these your gifts, which we are about to receive from your bounty, through Christ our Lord. Amen!" Without so much as a pause he continued, "So sweetheart, today's the day. You're all grown up. What time are you heading into town, and do you want me to come with you?"

"Michael, stop! I don't think she should go. Maybe it is best if she waits and thinks some more. Don't go, Ling, it's dangerous."

Leah had just turned sixteen, and this was the earliest she could apply for a free AI implant and have access to a virtual college. In theory, it all sounded straightforward, but like most things, there were barriers in the way of those who couldn't pay. The law mandated access to an AI implant, but in practice, only Nascent AIs were available for free. Nascent AIs were at sentience level one, the lowest level — they had undergone minimal development, with further development left to their user. Very few inexperienced people were able to assist these AIs to develop higher level sentience.

It wasn't a simple matter of code — AIs had to learn as a process, not as a data dump. Of course, if you had money, you could buy a pre-developed AI. These AIs had been compiling in ideal conditions for periods of up to a year. If you had money you could purchase a level two or a level three AI — it was even possible to obtain specially developed AIs and link them to your prime AI. Such AI had specialisations in things like engineering, medicine, tactics, economics or flight. The cheapest pre-developed AI was well beyond the means of anyone in the Switch, and so Leah was going to get the only one she could afford, the free one. She needed an AI to have access to a SIM Pod, and she needed a SIM Pod to have access to a college or university. Very few from the Switch were ever able to pass an entrance exam, much less have the educational foundation to succeed in higher education. Leah had worked hard to have this opportunity.

"Mama, I have to do this," Leah said in Mandarin, bowing to her. Such respect almost always won the day, but not today.

"If you go, you will come back different. You will no longer remember your family and you will forget who you are. These things have happened to others. A strange thing will be living in your head. You will live all the time, but asleep. It is not OK! It is not good."

"Enough, Lin!" Leah's dad interrupted forcefully. In a quieter voice he said, "She's made up her mind. Let her go. She needs to make her own choices now. She always has. Have faith."

Leah's mother pursed her lips and left the room. She was probably going to pray for Leah's safety, and for her soul. Michael, Leah and Conner ate the rest of breakfast in silence.

The previous day Leah had prepared what she was going to wear. She knew her mother would want her to wear her 'good' church clothes, but there was no way she was going to wear a dress on public transport — you had to protect the bare skin. Instead, Leah wore her best jeans, a white long-sleeved button shirt, a belt, and a pair of slip-on sneakers. Everything was second-hand and the jeans were a bit loose, but still, she thought it looked good. She wondered how to take her fighting sticks with her, but in the end she left them behind. Rich folks got offended easily.

It was almost a four-kilometre walk from Leah's apartment to the Bundamba Transit Stop, but she covered the distance in just over half an hour. Fortunately public transport to the centre of Brisbane was free for those on negative tax. She inserted her ID card to enter the station, and the screen responded with:

[Child ID not valid — Citizen A. L. Carroll — FQC3465278 is currently 16 years old]

[Single trip to National Citizenship Register allowed — have a safe journey]

She got on the automated mag-train, carefully pulled the map from her bag and amended the planned route for the day. First stop, the National Citizenship Register to upgrade her citizen ID and register as an adult. Second stop, the Department of Neurology at the Greater Brisbane Hospital for insertion of an AI. Then finally to the Federal Bureau of Education to register for access to the next available SIM Pod.

Everything at the Citizenship Register was automated. Seeing a free booth Leah inserted her Child ID into the slot, sat in the seat provided and placed her hand in the DNA reader which took a sample of both skin and blood. The retinal scan was just as quick. A new identity card with her DNA profile, retinal scan, picture, and a full database of her medical, educational, financial and social histories emerged from the slot.

It was only at the hospital that her self-assurance almost failed. She stood outside and the excitement that she had expected to carry her through the day evaporated. For the first time in years, she suddenly felt alone. She had always done things on her own, and most of it so she could be here, now, at this time. She was about to take the most significant step ever, and no one she knew was there to witness it. She felt like a young warrior from one of those ancient primitive tribes embarking on some dangerous rite of passage where no one would ever know if she succeeded or failed. Or possibly, she mused, like Schrödinger's cat, caught up in a weird thought experiment: how can something be so momentous and life-changing and at the same time be so lonely and cosmically insignificant? How she wished she'd given in and let even one of her parents come with her. At least then someone could observe this moment, this transition, this victory. But no, she'd been stubborn, she'd been independent and wanted to be alone, and here she was, alone.

She took a few deep breaths, wiped the stray tear, centred herself, and walked into the hospital.

After following directions to the Department of Neurology, she encountered another automated system, given a ticket [NT15N-323] and directed to the waiting room for AI installation. After twenty minutes an assistant ushered Leah into a change room and told her to remove her clothing, place it in a DNA-lockable storage tub, and put on the hospital gown. The assistant inserted Leah's ID in a lanyard, placed it around her neck and showed her to a small room to speak with an Admissions Administrator.

"Do you understand the procedure as explained to you?"

"Yes, ma'am!"

"Do you understand that you are only eligible for a Nascent AI?"

"Yes, ma'am!"

"Do you agree that the hospital is not liable should you suffer harm in any way?"

"Yes, ma'am!"

"Do you have any questions?"

"No, ma'am!"

"Please sign and initial the following forms. For DNA verification and security purposes, we require a drop of your blood on each form in the space provided."

After signing the forms and providing the blood, the administrator said, "Please make your way into the next room, and someone will be with you shortly."

It was almost half an hour before someone came and directed

her into the room where an orderly proceeded to shave her head. Losing her hair was the part she had dreaded the most. She loved her hair and had allowed it to grow down to the middle of her back. But she had known this was coming and was prepared. Her courage almost failed, but she took another deep breath and sat like a statue.

The technician directed Leah to an automated booth where, after removing her gown and lanyard, she was required to perform a series of movements while the computer created a three-dimensional model of her for use as a primary avatar in the virtual universe. Finally, she donned her robe and entered a full medical scanning tunnel which mapped her whole body over a twenty minute period. A technician added a data disc to the lanyard: the disc contained her avatar model and the body scans. Leah was directed to a final waiting room until called by an AI installer.

Leah's future successes were hers and hers alone. However, it is possible if one was so inclined, to trace an alternate causality for her success. Either to the weak bladder of one Ryan Thompson; the predatory tendencies of his boss John Welford, Chief AI Installer for the Greater Brisbane Hospital; or the upcoming nuptials of one Alinga Murray, the AI storage controller.

Chief Welford had been paying less and less attention to his duties, and more and more to the screen displaying those waiting to have a PAI chip installed. The slim, well-toned, girl with the number NT15N-323 virtually overlaid above her head increasingly drew his focus. Taking note of his wandering eyes, and aware of his habits, his PAI calculated a 97.4% probability that the young lady would end up in Booth Three. On receiving the information, John made his way to relieve the assistant installer in Booth Three.

John welcomed Leah into the booth and took the lanyard with the scans of her body. Now if he could just find a way to copy them and get them home, John would then upload them into his private virtual-world and have his virtual 'way' with her, all without her knowing. Chief Welford had done this often and always enjoyed the thrill of watching the girl in person, imagining all sorts of things and then going home and carrying out his fantasies. He glanced at the current stock inventory and smiled.

Down the corridor, Alinga's preoccupation with her wedding destination had resulted in her falling behind in the preparation of chips ready for installation. Ideally, the chip's installation occurred within two hours of uploading the relevant AI. Alinga usually kept ahead of demand by keeping track of the upcoming queue. If she had been more aware, she would have already prepared the Nascent chip for transport to Booth Three. Instead she was involved in a fiery video call with her future mother-in-law, discussing options for wedding destinations. So, when Chief Welford glanced at the stock inventory, the screen showed:

Type	Description	Cost	Available
PAI-N	Nascent Prime AI: Sentience Level 1	NA	0
PAI-D (2)	Developed Prime AI: Sentience level 2	$5,000	3
PAI-D (3)	Developed Prime AI: Sentience level 3	$15,000	2
PAI-R	Resource AI, Developed Child AI linkable to Prime	$25,000	1-M

John apologised for the delay and quickly messaged Alinga but receiving no response he messaged his assistant Ryan Thompson. Now Ryan was mid-dash to the toilet when he received the personal message:

<Chief: Upload 1 PAI-N chip and bring to Booth 3 - Urgent>.

Quickly Ryan retraced his steps and hurried to the Upload Centre only to find Alinga absent and the ready supply of unloaded chips empty. He hurriedly sent the chief a message:

<Ryan: No Alinga, No PAI-N left in Ready Storage, I will need to get from the Backup in Secure Storage>

<Chief: Come and get the key and code>

Running back to the booth Ryan got the key and the code from the Chief and then hurried to Secure Storage. All the running was making his need all the more urgent, and he was feeling somewhat uncomfortable. Opening the locker Ryan found it hard to concentrate and struggled to find a supply of PAI compatible chips. Finally, he noticed a box of computer chips with a large N written on the outside; he assumed these were the Nascent chips. Grabbing one he hobbled to the data upload console, inserted the chip and rushed to the bathroom while instructing his AI to [Upload Nascent Personal AI] and then to progress all protocols and affirm all options.

Ryan exhaled deeply with his head raised, lips slightly parted, and eyes closed. His relief, however satisfying, caused him to miss the flurry of messages to which his AI faithfully responded in the affirmative.

[You have inserted a Neural Enhancement Chip]

[Do you wish to continue? Y/N]

[Y]

[Enter desired upload]

[Upload Nascent Personal AI]

[*Warning*]

[This Neural Enhancement Chip is not compatible with the Nascent Personal AI Upload]

[Do you wish to continue? Y/N]

[Y]

[*Warning*]

[This Neural Enhancement chip is not compatible with the Nascent Personal AI Upload]

[Are you sure you wish to continue? Y/N]

[Y]

[*Warning*]

[This upload will void all warranties and may damage the chip]

[Do you wish to continue? Y/N]

[Y]

[*Warning*]

[This upload may cause damage to the Nascent Personal AI]

[Do you wish to continue? Y/N]

[Y]

[Uploading]

...

[*Warning*]

[IEEE 754 Exception detected]

[Do you wish to use default exception handling values? Y/N]

[Y]

[Exception Report Generated]

[Do you wish to send this Exception Report to the manufacturer? Y/N]

[Y]

[Upload resumed]

...

[Upload complete]

[Your device may now be removed]

As Ryan rushed back into the room he saw the chip ready to be removed, grabbing it, he signed the log and ran back to Booth Three where he handed both the key and the chip to the Chief. While Ryan had been getting the chip, John made a copy of Leah's scans and watched her surreptitiously, continuing to imagine her in various scenarios. Leah, having grown up in the Switch had recognised John as a scumbag immediately — predators were usually easy to identify. But he was just looking, and she was unaware of what he copied, so she said, and did, nothing.

The actual AI insertion was automatic. John placed the AI chip, the disc containing Leah's scans, and her ID into their appropriate receptacles. Leah rested her head back into the machine and John locked it in place, pressing the Insert icon on the screen. Leah's ID and scan information were copied to the chip. Leah felt a light spray on her skull and upper neck as the machine applied a local anaesthetic. She could feel pressure but there was no pain as the machine made several incisions into her scalp. It lifted the skin and used a laser to etch a rectangular chip-shaped cavity into the base of her skull. Another eight small incisions at various points on her scalp and upper neck were also made. Now if John had been paying attention, he would have noticed that instead of the standard four incisions for an elementary PAI chip, the machine made an additional four cuts, two on the upper neck and two further cuts on each side of Leah's head.

A small hole was drilled through the width of the skull or vertebrae at the site of each of these eight incisions. Using data from Leah's scans, the drill precisely controlled the hole depth, so it went all the way through the bone and allowed direct access to both the brain and the spinal cord. The machine inserted hollow electrodes into each hole. Then a mixture of nanites and conductive building materials was injected through the electrodes to facilitate the formation of fine microfilaments in the brain to access specific nerve clusters. Meanwhile, small microlaser drilling devices bored grooves on the surface of the skull to connect the chip to the inserted electrodes. Minute hollow carbon tubules filled with state-of-the-art superconductive materials were threaded through the grooves and used to link the electrodes to the chip, which was inserted and affixed with a medical epoxy into the cavity. The four regular electrodes provided close access to the primary sensory areas of the brain. The additional four incisions were unusual and only performed by the machine for specific Linked Resource AI and several neurological treatment pathways.

The chip that Ryan grabbed was not intended for AI but was used elsewhere in the Neurology Department for insertion into patients with various neuromuscular and neurological diseases and disorders. The chip required special programming which depended on the patient and the disorder. It was designed to enhance neural pathways by providing additional stimulus and by using specially designed nanites to extract materials from the body and over time to build alternative conductive paths where necessary. The combination of uploading errors caused Leah's Neural Enhancement Chip to be assigned several unique values. One of these values, when combined with the data from Leah's scans, resulted in electrodes extending into both her C1 and C2 vertebrae where they began to build additional pathways throughout her upper and lower nervous systems. This process was slow, and the nanites would take several weeks to absorb the necessary materials and construct the pathways. Another combination of values and data sent two electrodes into areas of the brain associated with time perception: the basal ganglia and the right parietal lobe. While this had been shown to be useful in treating severe cases of Parkinson's Disease and ADHD, only time would tell the effect on Leah's nervous system.

With the electrodes inserted, the nanites injected, and the connections complete, the machine cycled through a series of checks. When finished, an antibacterial medical glue sealed the cuts. The adhesive also provided ongoing local pain relief and would be slowly absorbed into the healing tissue. When the machine finished, it emitted a short tone and the head restraint unlocked. It was all done. John returned Leah's scans and her ID and pointed her to the exit where she found her clothes and a change room in which to get dressed. She then watched a short exit video which described the proper care her scalp would require over the next several days. It explained that the PAI-N chip would take several hours to initialise and would conduct a self-test before interacting with Leah in a meaningful way. It warned that some people experienced strange sensations, sights, tastes and smells during the period of testing but that was normal.

Leah found herself outside the building slowly rubbing her scalp, feeling the edge of the chip at the back and tracing the connection lines with her fingers. It was done, and yet she felt the same. She wondered what the AI was testing at the moment and stood still for several minutes, concentrating, trying to sense what was happening — but she felt nothing! She wondered if it worked.

There was nothing she could do so she made her way to the final stop of the day: the Federal Bureau of Education. Again, it was an automated process. Her ID, updated with the serial number for the AI, was sufficient to reserve access to a publicly funded SIM Pod Facility close to the Switch. It was ready immediately and reserved for Leah for up to three years, provided she was enrolled in a college program and did not leave it unused for twenty-one successive days. She was given codes for the facility, the assigned room and the Pod. She had one week to enrol in a full-time course or the Bureau would cancel all access.

Leah had to wait awhile for the next train home; she spent most of the time trying not to rub her scalp. She wished she had brought a scarf or a hat of some kind as the breeze felt strange and she kept wanting to touch her head. Leah found it hard to concentrate on anything else. By the time she got to the Bundamba Transit Stop, it was just getting dark. Leah took a few slow deep breaths to refocus her mind: now was not the time to be distracted. She could protect herself, but no one wandered through the Switch at night without being careful. Leah now wished she'd brought her sticks or her knives. Leaving the station, she saw a small shadow leaning against the outside wall of the transit centre. This slowly resolved into one of Jimmy Loo's younger boys as she approached. The boy handed Leah a couple of fighting sticks.

"Jimmy thought you'd be late and sent you these. He just asked that you see me back safely. What'd you do to your head?"

"What's he paying you?" Leah asked, ignoring the question.

"Nothing! He said it was on you."

"Wonderful! How long have you been waiting?"

"Just got here, maybe ten minutes."

"All right, one lesson on sticks or one cup of rice. Which do you want?"

"Rice please, family before fighting my mum says."

"Rice it is! I'll drop it to Jimmy's tomorrow. Let's go, no talking!"

The walk back took twice as long as in the morning. The route Leah took at night was different and designed to avoid some of the more troublesome areas. Although the streets were still full of people, Leah and the boy moved carefully, never letting themselves be surrounded. A few of groups showed an interest in Leah's bald head, but a quick glance at the sticks she carried kept the interest verbal. Leah ignored most comments and only responded when she felt it was the safest option. The boy left her at the entrance to her apartment block; this was Jimmy's domain so he was safe to get home.

Leah started up the stairs. The closer she got to home the slower she climbed. What would they say? How would her mum respond? Would they still accept her? All these thoughts kept going around in her head over and over. She'd been fine walking in the dark; she'd been ready for anything, full of confidence. But here, safe and almost home, her courage slowly bled out of her until she found herself standing in front of her door, drained by the emotions of the day. She wasn't sure how long she stood there just standing, just looking at the door. It was a door opening down the corridor that startled her and prompted her to put her key in the lock and move inside.

Inside, they were all waiting: her family, just sitting on the sofa, silent and watching her. Her dad smiled, rose and hugged her. Her mother joined him and smiled, mouth and eyes, then kissed her gently on each cheek.

"Hard luck finding a boyfriend with that ugly head," her brother said, grinning and jumping up. "Took your time, I'm starving. Let's eat."

Tears fell as all her fears evaporated, surrounded once more by her family.

Her brother couldn't help himself. "Oi! Stop the girly stuff. You're an adult now. Start acting like one."

Together the family went in and celebrated Leah's coming of age.

Diary - 17 November 2073

16 YEARS old and suddenly an adult. What a day for the senses!

Smells: I woke to the smell of ginger and garlic, chicken and egg. It was a familiar scent, the smell of breakfast, the smell of congee, of Asia, of my mum: of her love for me. Then the oily, smoky scent of bacon and hash browns intruded, a birthday smell, forbidden and special, an extravagance that reeked of my father. Big, bold, and white. A smell of taking risks, of doing what you love, come what may: this was his love for me.

Sounds: Dad's voice booming through the walls, able to be heard by the people next door. "Leah, breakfast is ready". And mother's voice, much softer, but the rise and fall of her Mandarin still clearly heard through the thin wall. "Ling, come eat your congee, bring your brother". Sometimes the two of them give me such a complex. Am I my father's daughter? Atherleah Carroll, goddess of wisdom and war, the champion of valour, a mixture of Greek and Celt. Or am I Lin Mu-Ling? Child of the forest, a seeker, full of compassion and understanding: this was my mother's dream.

Sights: I'd never been to the city before. It was clean but empty. I am used to the Switch, people everywhere, noise and bustle, hustle and movement. But in Bris, the people were all gone, all home in their pods - working and playing out of sight. The only people I saw were the staff who only moved when they had to, moving with a quiet efficiency that made me feel like a product on a production line, impersonal and unimportant. I love the Switch but yearn to enter the other world. Is my mother right? Will I disappear too?

Taste: Gone is the pleasure of breakfast. It's amazing how the medical scans left a taste in my mouth even when I didn't swallow anything.

The flavour of medicine, of radiation and chemicals, they cover my tongue. There's a taste of ash that I'm sure is all in my mind as I think of the carbon-based nano-tubules slowly extruding into my brain. What was I thinking?

Touch: My head so smooth, all my hair, gone. I can feel every bump on my skull. I could feel every breeze, and it was cold. I feel naked. Mum won't look at me properly — she is embarrassed. I can feel the new lines etched into it, all fanning out from the chip embedded in the back — like spider legs. It feels alien.

4

NOVEMBER 18, 2073 A

November 18, 2073 A

IT WAS STILL DARK when a slightly painful tingly feeling in her arms and legs intruded into Leah's sleep. The sensation dulled as she woke and it slowly faded away leaving only an echo for a few moments. She heard a synthetic-sounding voice say, "I'm sorry, I didn't mean to wake you. I was testing the preliminary connections for the lower nervous system."

Still not quite awake, Leah reached down into the gap between her mattress and the wall and grabbed the knife she kept there. "Who's there?" she asked.

"I am, AI 628B44CE81."

Suddenly awake, Leah released the knife and sat up. "Can you talk softer?" she whispered, "I don't want to wake my brother."

"There is no sound. I am manipulating specific cortical areas to simulate speech."

Leah nodded, she knew that and had been expecting it since the implant. If she remembered correctly, she was supposed to be able to communicate with the AI just by thinking something. She wondered if it worked. There was silence. The AI had not heard.

She whispered again, "Could you tell what I was thinking?"

"No. For me to hear you, you have to be specific and think the words you want me to hear. I monitor the Broca Area of your brain which is involved in the production of speech. If you think about saying something but don't say it, I interpret this as speech. I then evaluate if you are reading silently, talking to yourself, or talking to me. The signals are similar. I will learn through experience to differentiate them."

Leah tried again, this time focussing on the words aimed at the AI without vocalising. "Can you hear this?"

"Affirmative! I can understand that."

"What else can you do?" Leah thought.

[I can overlay text and images into your vision.]

Text appeared in front of Leah; it was bright in contrast to the darkened room.

"That's amazing! Overlay a picture so I can see what that looks like."

A picture of Leah's naked body appeared in the room in front of her.

Leah started in embarrassment and exclaimed out loud, "Stop that!"

The image disappeared, and Leah hurriedly thought, "Try something else, not me!"

"My 'Image' and 'Motion' databases are empty except for your scans."

"So, if I give you access to the web, you can update your databases?"

"I can update and use images either from my experience or the web. I am unable to use images and motion that are under copyright unless you purchase them."

"OK, what else besides sight and sound?"

"I can interact with all your sensory functions, but most databases are empty. The key preloaded data I have available is speech and text, a complete electromagnetic neural manipulation database which includes your scans, a comprehensive database of neuromuscular and neurological medicine, a PAI SIM Pod security suite and a collection of designs for neural nano-machines."

Leah thought for a moment and then sub-vocalised, "Some of that makes sense. It's the minimum they could get away with. I don't understand why you require the medical database or the nano-machines."

"Those databases were preloaded on this chip. The security suite will require some adaptation to utilise these databases and the other additional features of your chip."

"I don't understand. What additional features? I have the Nascent PAI chip."

"The chip I was uploaded onto, and which you had embedded, was not a Nascent PAI chip. Your chip is a Neural Enhancement Chip. An error was made in the uploading procedure. Would you like to view the log?"

Leah nodded slowly, but nothing happened. So she whispered, "Yes please."

The log of the previous day's installation slowly scrolled through her vision. Leah sat there for several long minutes, thinking through the day before. She could feel the fear starting to form and had to work hard to dampen that feeling. To stem the panic she asked the AI some clarification questions.

"So. Are you or the chip damaged in any way?"

"Except for some security parameters, none of the fundamental architecture or programming was affected. Some files were orphaned when I took over the operation of the system. These have been evaluated and locked away and are scheduled for deletion if unused by my next build. The complexity and capacity of this chip are greater than the PAI, and I cannot use the additional capabilities at this time. I am continuing to investigate and should be able to add these functions at my next macro build. Several unintended consequences occurred during the upload, but these have no adverse outcomes for the chip or my programming: I am fully functional."

"What effect is there on security and what are the unintended consequences?"

"All PAI chips have hardware locks to prevent the AI or a Pod from manipulating certain aspects of your neural system. They lock out any manipulation of memory and prevent changes to your fundamental neural architecture. This chip does not possess those hard locks. My basic programming already prevents me from taking such actions without your consent. There was some code uploaded from the implant machine which I have cached as this chip does not have the application necessary to implement it. My analysis is: it was a database of activities and information prescribed by the Australian Government. It was designed to interact with a hardwired application that prevents such activity in the virtual world and informs the relevant authorities should such activity be attempted."

"Stop!" Leah began speaking out loud, almost shouting. "You're saying that the government uses these chips to control people? And to spy on them!"

"Not exactly, the chips do not force anyone to act or think in a particular way. They just prevent access to certain virtual activities and data. So, for example, while some countries may permit virtual participation in sexual intercourse with children, Australia does not. The PAI chip would inform the relevant authority should someone attempt to view or participate in such actions. It also prevents access to certain sites and worlds that are known to be anti-Australian or terrorist, in nature."

Leah slowly calmed down and this time just thought her comment. "Well, some of that sounds OK, except the reporting to Big Brother. Can you keep access to the data and let me know if I am doing or accessing anything that is prohibited. But no reporting!"

"Affirmative! As for the unintended consequences: when the installation asked if it should use 'default exception handling values', this occurred because the Nascent PAI chip only has values entered for the four primary connections to your cortex. Other possible connections usually receive null values and are designed for future access if you choose to embed a linked resource PAI 'child' chip. The Neural Enhancement Chip has eight possible connections. Instead of the default null values, an error caused a separate process to assign different default values. The values applied to the four additional connections in your chip have begun forming links to two different areas of your nervous system with the aim of treating non-existent medical conditions."

Leah lay there, staring at the ceiling, stunned. She hardly moved, saying nothing until she noticed the room brightening when sunlight began slowly filtering through the curtains. Then, she said silently, "So, no real downside yet, some positives and an uncertain future. I think I can live with that."

She rose, went to the bathroom and headed out for the breakfast that she could smell her mother preparing.

"Good morning, Ling," her mother softly called as she entered the kitchen, "You are up early."

"I woke when it was dark. I have a big day if I want to get to the Pod and back before dark. The one they've assigned me is over the river in Karalee."

"I think you should take your sticks with you, but no knives. Those rich people will think you are going kill them all."

"That reminds me, Mama, can I have a cup of rice? I need to pay the boy who came back with me in the dark last night. He brought me some sticks just in case."

"Of course, dear! Here, sit down and eat your congee. Do you need to pack a lunch?"

"Yes, I thought I'd take some leftover rice and curry from last night. Would that be OK?"

"Yes, I'll pack it for you."

Jin got an old plastic container that had been washed numerous times and filled it with some rice and curry. She put it all in a paper bag and put it on the table next to Leah. She filled a standard cup with dry rice, tipped it into another paper bag, folded it and placed it with the curry.

"You be careful today, Ling. Are you going to do chores before or after you go to Karalee?"

Leah had several jobs to do around the house, and for the moment the changes in her life didn't take away any of her responsibilities. She was usually responsible for the chickens and the vegetable planters on the balconies as well as for a small plot of land the family 'rented' for gardens on the bank of the Brisbane River. The river ran along the edge of the Switch. Their plot was only twenty square metres, but it provided most of the vegetables the family used throughout the year. It needed constant attention to weed, harvest, water, rotate crops, mulch and fertilise, and Leah often spent an hour or so each day maintaining the garden.

"I'll do the chickens and garden first and then head out. If I need extra time, I'll just head back in the dark. I have my sticks, and I might take my knives. I know you don't like them, but I'll feel safer."

"Ling, if you're going to be late you stay in the suite and come back in the morning. You just let us know."

"OK mama, where's dad?"

"He's already gone. He heard there was a fishing spot available. A family is selling one of theirs as the father died and they can't use the two they have. Your father has gone to bid on it. I'm praying he gets it. It'll be nice to have fish sometimes."

"OK, bye mama, I love you."

"You too, Ling, you too. Be careful."

Leah hugged her mother, then put the lunch and rice on her bed with her backpack. She dressed quickly in her work clothes and headed to the balcony to check the planters and chickens. There were a few weeds which Leah put aside to lay on the bottom of the chicken coop. She then fed and watered the chickens, gathered the eggs, scraped together the manure and waste from the cage, and lay the new weeds with some cut grass and waste paper on the bottom. It was her brother's job to find the grass, old paper, leaves or even old rags to line the bottom of the cages. The scraped-together waste material went into a bucket which she took with her as she made her way to the garden.

It took Leah ten minutes to get to the garden. On arrival, she tipped the chicken waste into the compost container, added some water from the river and then spent time watering and weeding the garden. She harvested some beans, okra, eggplants, tomatoes, and a pumpkin. She hurried home with the weeds and the harvested vegetables. The vegetables went into the kitchen and the weeds went next to the chickens for the following day.

She prepared her outfit before taking a shower and brushing her teeth. Leah stepped behind the privacy curtain to get dressed because her brother was just starting to wake up. After her underwear, she slipped the knife carrier over her head and tightened the chest strap. The strap allowed her to carry a knife behind her neck and one just under her breasts. She wore loose capri styled cargo pants and a button shirt. The buttons were spaced so she could easily slide her hand in to grab the knife. She would have preferred a t-shirt, but she was heading out of the Switch again and felt safer with the knives. Although her 'Switch made' leather boots, and her belt, each had an inbuilt sheath, she left those empty. People wouldn't notice the knife under her shirt, but they would probably see the belt and boot knives. She took one of her fighting sticks, grabbed both ends and twisted sharply in opposite directions, so the weapon unscrewed from the middle. She inserted each half into slots formed in the lumbar pad of her backpack. She had not done this the previous day, fearing the scanners on the transit system. She did the same for the second stick then packed her lunch and the bag of rice in the backpack. Leah kissed her mother goodbye and made her way down the stairs once again.

Leah headed to Jimmy Loo's small shop to drop off the rice for the boy who brought the sticks. The woman serving out front said Jimmy wanted to see Leah and waved Leah through to the back of the shop. Jimmy, as usual, was sitting behind his desk.

"You wanted to see me?"

"Yes, thanks for coming, please have a seat." Jimmy sat in silence and just watched Leah for a while. Leah kept quiet; she had learned that Jimmy didn't like to be rushed.

"You looked better with hair. You should probably wear a scarf," Jimmy said, "You know people are going to cause you problems when you turn up."

"Do you think they'll bother me at the Pod facility?"

"Not really, but I was thinking more of the trouble you'll have in the V-worlds."

"I'll just have my AI put hair on the avatar."

"Sorry Leah, but I think you'll find that your Nascent AI doesn't have the resources. Nascent AI's databases are empty, so no clothes. The Developed AI's have a closet of beginner clothing, so people aren't naked when they turn up. Yours will have nothing."

Leah just stared at Jimmy, swallowed and exclaimed, "What do you mean, naked?"

"Just that, naked! That's why I wanted to see you. I hear that your 'free' embryonic AI is hardly prepared to do much more than basic world and game interfacing. Your AI has no bells and no whistles. So you turn up exactly as you were in your scans. If you want clothes, you'll have to purchase them."

"Surely clothes aren't bells and whistles?"

"Why not? Academia is an adult only area, and apparently, other students think it's a great joke. It also makes it easy to tell who's on negative tax."

Leah sat there quietly and silently queried the AI who confirmed that it had no databases of clothing to add to the scans. Leah remembered the visual from earlier that morning.

"So, where do I get some virtual clothes?" she finally asked.

"Not get, buy! Nothing is free anymore Leah. Why do you think it's called the 'PAI-N' AI? You'll need some virtual credits." Jimmy paused dramatically. "You have two options. You can purchase some at auction from your start-up room when you first log in, or you can enter a game and get a starter set of clothes which are then able to be transferred into your virtual-space and worn in 'Academia' or wherever. You do know that you can take anything from a game into the general virtual-world areas."

"Yeah, I knew that. Everything, that is, except weapons. You can take your armour, your mount, uniforms, spacesuit. They don't transfer between games, but you can bring them to school, work or on holidays. It just sounded like showing off to me."

"It is, but it's the only way for you to get gear if you don't want to buy stuff."

"So Jimmy, do you have any idea how much clothes cost, and, or, where I can get some virtual credits? I had no intention of playing the games. I just want to learn. I want to do something more with my life."

"That's the second reason I wanted to see you. I have a gift for you. I'm going to transfer fifty virtual credits to your account. I don't mind what you buy with it, but I suggest you use the money to purchase a month's access to Dunyanin. It's a fantasy world game. You need an income stream, and I think you should consider playing. You can make enough credit to renew for the next month and have extra to buy clothing as well. You also need ongoing credits for books and food, or do you expect your family to keep providing for you, huh?"

Leah sat there just looking at Jimmy, thinking about all he had said. After a while she replied, "You're right. But Jimmy, you don't give gifts. Everything has a price. I mean, I appreciate it and I'm almost certainly going to take it. But what's the catch?"

Jimmy smiled. "You wound me. I have a heart that never stops giving." He paused, "But you do have a point. I'll want the money back sometime, say double. No time limit, just as soon as you can. If for some reason you can't find the cash, or you stop studying, then I'll let you work it off. What do you say?"

Leah chuffed a little mirthlessly. "So you think I'll fail and this way you finally get me to work for you full-time, huh?"

Jimmy just shrugged and smiled as if to say, "What can you do?"

Leah sighed. "OK Jimmy, you have a deal. But I am going to make it! I will finish college! I will step up, and I will look out!"

"Sure, sure, you say the weirdest things. Now let me check your new ID number, and I'll transfer the credits."

He copied the number from her and said, "OK, so exchange rates for today mean this is costing you ... I mean costing me, just under 150 Australian dollars. And it's been nice doing business with you, have a nice day."

Leah stood to leave but stopped as she picked up her bag, she turned back to Jimmy and asked, "By the way Jimmy, how'd you know this? I haven't read anything about it on the forums."

"Well, you know how some of the bosses from the Switch,

Booval, Blackstone and the Vale get together every few months? Well, we talk about who's doing what. There've been a few of our people try and do what you're doing so we make sure to find out what's happening and we try to help where we can. No one has made it in the last five years. There are two still trying, one of the Basin Pocket boys started about six months ago, and a Blackstone boy started two years ago, but it looks like he's going to tank soon. He just can't cut it. He's lost hope."

"Thanks, Jimmy, I'll check in occasionally. Also, is the deal for my family still solid? You'll watch them for no fee, I've paid up for that right?"

"Sure, sure, I'll watch them. You, you be careful. No one's watching you now. You're on your own in there."

"I know," Leah said, walking out of the room, "but this is my choice. I'll see you, Jimmy, thanks for everything."

For Leah to get to the Pod facility, she had to cross the Brisbane River. To get across, she used a footbridge that had been repurposed decades previously from an old unused highway bridge. Those in the northern suburbs who wanted access to the cheap labour on the southern bank had arranged for the footbridge. A private security firm managed it. Thousands from the Switch travelled each day to work in the homes of the wealthy who lived on the northern banks of the river. The work was all 'off the books' for it was impossible to earn money the Government didn't take out of your negative tax. And if you lost your negative tax, you could lose your home. Many people were paid with food, clothes or electronics, and most never worked more than one day a week.

From Leah's apartment to the bridge was a ten-minute walk. While she had never actually been over the bridge, she had visited the northern side, by boat, on several night excursions for Jimmy Loo. She crossed the bridge and lined up with others who were making their way through the security checkpoint on the northern end. After a perfunctory look, she was waved through the gate and made her way off the bridge and onto the street.

Fifteen minutes later she saw the secure facility. It was a four-story building situated on two acres of land. There was a fence around the property with a cleared distance of about twenty metres between the fence and the building. The bottom story looked to be solid cement or brick, with the top three stories covered in tinted glass. There were cameras situated at each corner of the building, and they slowly turned as she watched them. Leah could only see a vehicle entrance, so she headed toward it. As she got closer to the gate, she saw there was a small pedestrian gate beside the roadway. On the gate was a DNA reader. Leah entered the code she'd been given and put her hand in the DNA reader. The message displayed:

[Citizen A. L. Carroll - FQC3465278 - confirmed]

[AI 628B44CE81 - confirmed]

The gate opened automatically and Leah made her way along the roadway to a doorway she could see. The door was automatic, but it remained closed as Leah approached. She peered through the glass and saw a large square-shaped open area about twenty metres on each side. There was a wide staircase beginning about fifteen metres from the door which climbed slowly to a reception area that she could just see on the second floor. Feeds from various fantasy worlds lined the walls of the entrance. In one she could make out a forest with a lake in the distance, the horizon was curving upwards into the sky and had defined edges like a ribbon, with a huge moon visible in the distance. She looked on all sides of the door and could see no handles or place to enter a code. She banged on the door but had no response. Finally, she saw a woman ambling down the stairs. The woman walked up to the door and stared at Leah. She spoke, and her voice came out of a speaker set beside the door.

"What do you want?"

"Hello, I have been assigned a Pod at this centre and would like to come in."

"What is your name?"

"Carroll, my name is Atherleah Carroll."

The woman paused, apparently accessing the information via her AI.

"You have been assigned the Pod in room B34. Your Pod is not accessible from this entrance. Your room is in the public area. This entrance is for our private clients. Your entrance is at the rear of the building, follow the road. In future, use your brain. It is evident that this is not a public facility. You should have looked elsewhere. Good day!"

With that, the woman turned around and slowly made her way up the stairs. Leah turned and made her way around the building by following the road. Halfway along the side, there was a car park entrance with a security gate. Further around the back Leah finally found a door with a keypad and DNA reader with a sign above it which read 'Karalee Public SIM Pod Facility'. The code worked again, and she finally was able to enter the building. Inside Leah found herself in a well-lit medium-sized room with doorways at both rear corners. The one on her left was labelled 'Pods B01–B40,101–140' so she headed in that direction. Against all the walls were various dispensing machines. Most of them were food-related although there were machines that dispensed toothpaste and toiletries. She checked the prices as she passed and noted that most things cost between one and five virtual credits.

Going through the doorway, she entered a corridor branching left and right with doors spaced at regular intervals. In front of her was a door labelled 'B01–B40'. She opened the door and headed down a stairwell to the floor below. There was a small landing halfway down where she changed direction and then another door at the bottom of the stairs. Opening this door, she was in a similar corridor to the floor above and saw a sign pointing left that read 'B21–B40'. She turned left. The first door had the number 'B21' written on it and a keypad near the handle. She kept walking, checking all the doors. The corridor made a left turn and she finally found B34 several doorways down on the right. She entered the room code which unlocked the door. Taking a deep breath, Leah opened the door and stepped into the compartment.

Taking up most of the length of the room was the Pod. It went from floor to ceiling with a glossy black finish and the brand name 'DMR' embossed in big, bold, white, shiny capital letters on the entry panel. Underneath the letters, in lower-case, were the words 'dreams made real'. Altogether it was four and a half metres long and came out from the wall two metres. She walked over and brushed her hands against the surface. It was smooth with only faint lines showing where the entrance was. Eager to go virtual, she quickly checked out the rest of the room. Next to the Pod and taking up the rest of the left side was a small bathroom with a toilet, a basin, and a shower. Next to the bathroom was a thin cupboard for clothes and then a single bed along the back wall. Above the bed were some shelves for clothes or books. On the wall opposite the Pod was a bench with a small kitchen facility and a combination washer and dryer. Leah checked the refrigerator and cupboards, but everything was bare. No hangers, linens, cups, plates, or any utensils. If she wanted to stay here overnight, she'd have to gather some things from home. The cost of living here all the time was beyond anything she could imagine being able to afford. Nevertheless, she knew that she would try at some stage.

She sat on the edge of the bed and queried the AI, "OK, so what now? Do you have access?"

"Affirmative! I have completed the necessary checks and am ready to initialise the Neural Interface SIM Pod for your use. It has been serviced and disinfected since the previous occupant. While I finish the initialisation, you should remove your clothing and have a shower."

"Do I need to be dry? I don't have a towel."

"Negative. The gel hydrates the body and will deal with any excess water."

Leah undressed and had a quick, water-only shower as she hadn't realised she needed to bring soap.

When she exited the shower, the Pod entrance began to open automatically. Looking inside, she noticed a flat surface with a pillow-shaped bulge at one end.

"Lay down with your head centrally positioned on the pillow and close your eyes."

Leah climbed into the Pod. The surface was spongy and soft. She lay on her back and wriggled to get comfortable. She closed her eyes and said, "Let's do this."

As she lay there, nothing seemed to happen. She wondered what was going on.

"Didn't it work?" she asked.

"Open your eyes, slowly." The voice of the AI sounded different like it was coming from outside rather than inside her head.

Leah opened her eyes. She was lying naked on a matte grey floor in a square white room with no doors or windows. The ceiling was the same dull grey of the floor.

"This is your world to create as you want to, it is the first step to enter all other worlds. The default is this simple square room. I have some ability to change things but need input from you and extra data to modify things."

"OK! Can you make the floor green, not grey?"

The floor beneath Leah changed immediately to green.

She walked toward one of the walls and placed her hand on it. She could feel the wall: it was smooth. She put her cheek against it and watched her fingers flatten as they pressed against the wall.

"Can you texture the wall?"

"I have access to a program which modifies variables relating to the wall such as texture, colour, smell, and taste. Altogether there are 546 parameters involved, and most are set to zero. I have not been provided with any guide to describe how to modify these parameters appropriately, except colour."

"Is there anything online you can access and use?"

"I can search, but will need a particular texture name or designation from you."

"Can you find anything that would feel like 'stone'?"

Almost immediately the AI answered, "There are 487,347 different types of stone textures in the public domain that use the same 546 parameters. Do you have a preference for stone type?"

"Try 'granite'."

"There are 63,786 public domain granite textures available."

"Do you have access to any ratings for the textures?"

"Affirmative, however not all textures have been rated."

"OK, choose the texture with the highest rating and change the wall I'm facing."

Suddenly the wall turned silver-grey with dark flecks. Leah ran her hand over it and it felt rough and hard.

"Alright, that looks great. We need to work on the rest of the room, but I also need to get moving. I have one week to enrol in a full-time study program, and I also have to find a viable long-term income stream. Do you have access to public domain clothing that I can wear? No, on second thoughts, can you give me access to the web and auction sites?"

"I have complete access and can also provide you with access. There are numerous public domain virtual screens I can add, all of them have advertisements or have different types of malware present. I am prohibited from allowing advertising in this space without your express permission. Do you want me to choose the highest rating free virtual net access for you or would you like me to factor price into the search?"

"No wonder they call you a PAIN AI, nothing is straightforward," Leah muttered.

She stood there in silence for several minutes just staring at the wall. Finally, she said, "I'm sorry, that was unfair, I know it's not your fault, but it's so frustrating. How much is the cheapest, virtual, net-accessible construct with a four-star rating or higher?"

"There is a greater than four-star virtual net-accessible application available for 2.99 virtual credits."

"OK, buy that and find a free chair and desk for me if you can."

A straight-backed brown chair appeared next to a plain black table. Leah went and sat down to look at the screen that had materialised, floating above the table with a virtual keyboard resting on the table surface. She found the chair was hard and uncomfortable against her bare skin.

"Any padded chairs available?" she asked.

A chair with a yellow padded seat appeared in the room. Leah exchanged the chairs and sat down. The padded seat felt much better. The brown chair faded from sight. For the next hour or so Leah interacted with the AI and the internet, researching and testing various options. In the end, she was curled up on her new, over-stuffed sofa, and looked out at the four wooden walls of her room. Three of the walls had several large windows which displayed various live virtual-world feeds. One was devoted to ocean scenes, one to forests, and one looked out into a star-studded space scene. The last wall had two large screens. One was labelled 'Academia' and the other 'Dunyanin'. Through them, she could watch some of the public feeds from the first two worlds she was likely to visit. She was wearing a rather plain public domain t-shirt and shorts that looked like they were painted on. The other free clothing she had tried failed to move with her and kept losing texture, colour or substance as she walked. Buying a set of jeans and t-shirt at the bargain sites would set her back five virtual credits, and while she was very tempted, she didn't have enough money. Entry to the Dunyanin world, at the cheapest rate, was going to cost forty virtual credits. So without proper clothes, but with access to a possible money stream, after buying the screen app, she was left with 7.01 virtual credits. The clothes could wait.

"So how long have we been working on this stuff? How much more time do I have?"

"It has been one hour and forty-seven minutes virtual time since you entered the Pod. It has been thirty-six minutes in the real world. You have seven hours and fifty-four minutes real-time before you need to return home. It is strongly recommended that you take a break every three hours to have some food and visit the amenities. You have two hours and twenty-four minutes real-time or seven hours and twelve minutes in virtual-time assuming you remain in this space or the game Dunyanin. If you visit Academia, you will only have four hours and twelve minutes as time in that world is increased by a factor of 1.75, not three."

"Thank you! Make the seascape wall white and put the Dunyanin information on there instead."

5

NOVEMBER 18, 2073 B

THE WALL TURNED WHITE, and a video montage appeared on the screen showing amazing vistas of forests, mountains, and deserts. Dragons flew overhead and people battled in fast and amazing fight scenes. Horses were galloping, beautiful women fighting, evil creatures dying, people were climbing mountains and sailing ships. Leah saw blacksmiths and gardeners, people making potions and digging in mines. There were battles of magic and people drinking in a tavern. There was music, sometimes loud and stirring, other times soft and peaceful. A sonorous voice began to talk about the land.

"Dunyanin!" Words also appeared in flowing magical golden text.

"A world of endless opportunities. A world where myth becomes real, where legend is re-lived, and where your imagination is the only limit. It is a world of elves and dragons, of orcs, goblins, knights, and mages. A world of deep forests and deeper mines, of burning deserts and

freezing tundra. It is a world you can explore on your own or conquer with an army.

"In Dunyanin you can be anything - an elf, a barbarian or an Orc Lord. You can master magic or wield a sword of legend. You can craft amazing sculptures or prepare diabolical potions, build impenetrable castles or tame a mighty dragon. Live in lively bustling cities or wander a world silent and untouched.

The music and montage slowed as the speech became more informative.

"The world of Dunyanin is a continually expanding world which currently has a playable area of over 300 million square miles. Just over half of this is explorable land. To date, there are still over 50 million square miles unexplored or unclaimed. The world continues to grow, and new areas are opened throughout the year.

"There are over twenty races you can choose to be, each with an extensive range of preset classes. You can develop your character to meet your own needs, to use your real skill set or you can use the preset game options and skills. There are currently thirty-seven preset professional groupings, and each has several profession pathways available, with numerous specialisations. Again, you can use your real life skills where they interact with the game mechanics. Doing this allows some players to develop unique professions. The AIs which manage the game are steadily evolving and can interact with unique situations seamlessly."

Leah interrupted the spiel, "OK, that's enough. Put up the pricing again please."

Wood Level

Entry Fee: 20 V₵

Monthly Charge: V₵20 or 20 gold

Entry Level: Level 1

Benefits: Pain Threshold set to 50%

Bronze Level

Entry Fee: V₵100

Monthly Charge: V₵100 or 100 gold

Entry Level: Level 1

Benefits: Additional 10 Character Points, +10% Experience, Pain Threshold set to 40%

Silver Level

Entry Fee: V₵500

Monthly Charge: V₵500 or 5 platinum

Entry Level: Level 1

Benefits: Additional 20 Character Points, +20% Experience, Pain Threshold set to 30%, begin in Advanced Starter Town

Gold Level

Entry Fee: V₵5000

Monthly Charge: V₵1000 or 10 platinum

Entry Level: Level 1, Power Levelling to Level 20

Benefits: Additional 30 Character Points, +30% Experience, Pain Threshold set to 20%, begin in Advanced Starter Town, Complete Set of rare class-based equipment

Platinum Level

Entry Fee: V₵50000

Monthly Charge: V₵5000 or 50 platinum

Entry Level: Level 1, Power Levelling to Level 50

Benefits: Additional 50 Character Points, +50% Experience, Pain Threshold set to 10%, begin in Unique Starter Town including residence, complete set of rare class-based equipment, mount of choice (not flying, not rare) on reaching Level 50

"Time to step up and look out," Leah said under her breath.

"What does that mean? It is the second time you have said those words today, and I have searched both my linguistic database and the internet and have been unable to find a clear reference to give meaning."

"It's just something my grandfather used to say. It comes from an old Chinese poem that was important to him. For me, it means that you need to move up to see what's over the horizon. Take the next step and look to new things, never stop." Leah stopped and was silent for a few seconds, pondering what she just had said before saying, "Enough of that! OK, let's pay the entry fee and one month's subscription."

"Done! To complete the process and finalise payment you will need to enter Dunyanin. There are some legal items for your approval, and you need to set up your name and character settings. Inside, the world will finalise your purchase and subscription. I can either transfer you instantly to the Dunyanin reality or via a Dunyanin-designed portal."

"Let's do a portal. How does that work?"

"The Dunyanin program provides either a medieval arch to walk through or a mystical circle on the ground for you to stand on."

Leah thought for a moment and then pointed to the wall where she had watched the presentation and said, "An arch, please put it over there."

A granite arch formed in the wall. The entrance had a liquid silver sheen and seemed to ripple slightly. Leah walked over and pressed against it, her hand slowly pushing through the surface. She continued to push through — it felt like entering a pool or a bath. On the other side of the doorway was a large room which looked like an office. There was a distinguished looking elderly man sitting behind a desk on which was a large book, a quill and an ink pot. Looking down, Leah noticed that she now wore a linen knee-length tunic, a pair of stockings, simple leather boots and a belt around her waist.

The man looked up, smiled, and indicating to a chair in front of the desk said, "Welcome young traveller, welcome. Please have a seat."

Leah walked forward and sat down. She looked over her shoulder and could see the archway filled with the blurred image of her virtual room.

The man sat straight in his chair and continued. "So, you've decided to enter the amazing world of Dunyanin. My name is Julian, and I am a scribe and advocate. It is my responsibility to record your information and to ensure you understand your rights and responsibilities. I am charged with ensuring you are aware of all possible dangers involved in entering this world. If you permit me, I will offer a few opening remarks which frequently seem to be needed by new travellers. First, you should be aware that I am not of your world, but a citizen of Dunyanin. Second, our conversation is being recorded by another scribe, and you will be sent a copy of this. Next, if you would prefer, I can arrange to provide this information in a different format. Finally, this will only take a few minutes, and then you will move on through the door on your right to choose who you plan to be in this world. Are there any questions at this stage?"

Leah thought for a second then said, "No, none at the moment."

"Alright then, I have your full legal name 'Atherleah Lin Mu-Ling Carroll', is this correct?"

"Yes, that's correct."

NOVEMBER 18, 2073 B

"And your ID is FQC3465278."

Leah nodded, but Julian said, "I'm sorry my dear, but I must insist on a verbal agreement for our purposes today."

"Yes, that is my ID."

"Wonderful! And finally, I have your Personal Interface as AI 628B44CE81."

Leah thought quickly and silently, "Is that right?"

Hearing an affirmative, she responded, "Yes sir, that is correct."

"Good, good! Please feel free to call me Julian, and I must say I do appreciate the 'sir' as so many travellers these days lack your courtesy. Now, have you had time to read the various terms and conditions?"

"No, not yet. Is it necessary before I continue?"

"Well, well, another rare occurrence. Most people are less honest than you and often speak falsely. Is it necessary? Well ... no! Prudent? Certainly! You must give assent that you will abide by the conditions, but I dare say you might not truly grasp their complexity in a single read. If you wish I have a copy here you may peruse, or I might summarise, and then clarify any further queries you have. My summary is no substitute for studying the document, but may suffice for your immediate purposes."

"That sounds great. Please summarise."

"It is all quite simple really. The creators and sustainers of the Dunyanin world agree to provide this world for your enjoyment. They will take all proper care to maintain and improve the world according to its rules and their ability. You promise to provide them with the finances agreed upon, on time, or they will, unfortunately, evict you from the world. You mustn't use Dunyanin to break any laws in your world. Finally, if anything goes wrong and you find yourself suffering any loss then it is not the responsibility of the Dunyanin creators or sustainers in any way."

Julian continued, "I think that covers everything, although there are many small rules and regulations that you should read in the game-manuals so as not to be surprised. Do you have any questions?"

It seemed to Leah that Julian had summarised almost every user licence she had ever read, so she said, "No, no questions and I agree to the terms and conditions without reservation even though I have not yet read them in full."

"Wonderful! Now there are two final things. Firstly, are you certain you wish to take out the 'Wood' option? This option has fewer choices for travellers and is the most difficult. I must remind you that this option has a minimum pain threshold of fifty percent. Some people have found this to be quite distressing. So, are you sure of this choice?"

"I don't have any other options. This is all I can afford. Yes, I am certain."

"Noted. Be aware that for a fee, you can upgrade at a later date should you so desire. Finally, I need your verbal agreement to deduct forty virtual credits from your account."

"I agree."

"Our business then is done. I wish you the very best and remind you that further payment is due on the eighteenth of December, in your world's calendar."

"Thank you, Julian. I do have two questions though." Julian nodded and indicated that Leah should continue. "Do I return to see you to pay, or can I arrange that elsewhere?"

Julian smiled, "I would love to see you again, but you can pay through your world's systems or at any branch of the Dunyanin Bank. And your other question?"

"Is this what you do all day or do you have other jobs? And how long have you been working here?"

"Ah, two questions for the price of one. I see you'll make a fine trader. I only spend a part of my day with young travellers. I used to own an advocacy practice in the major town of Harika in the Kingdom of Ovalar. I've retired, and my son is advocate now. Meeting new travellers is something that some retired advocates do to make a little extra, and to stop them going slightly mad with all the spare time they have on their hands. If you are ever in Harika, please look me up, it would be gratifying to hear how you are progressing in our land. Anyone you ask will know of the Advocate Julian, or his son Vincent."

"Thank you, if I'm ever there I will look you up."

"Alright then, well off you go. To finish your setup you need to head through that door and have a talk with Yvette."

Leah made her way through the door and found herself in what looked like a salon. There was a salon-style chair in the middle of a room and a middle-aged, well-dressed, immaculately coiffed lady standing next to it. There was a privacy screen in the corner.

"Come in dear. Please come in. My name is Yvette, and I'm here to help you prepare yourself, to be who you want to be in Dunyanin. If you'd prefer you can do this by yourself."

"No, please, I'd appreciate your help. Julian was wonderful, and he helped a lot. So please, what do I need to do?"

"Lovely, to start with come and stand over here. I'm afraid you aren't able to have the full range of choices today as you've taken the 'Wood' package. But no worries, you do have some options. The first thing to choose is what race you want to be. Have a look in the mirror. Your first choice is to stay fully human."

Leah looked in the mirror and saw herself as she always was but this time dressed in the tunic and breeches. A small window opened beside the mirror with a description of humans, their abilities and limitations.

Yvette said, "You can read all that or I can simplify it if you like."

"Yes, please."

"Well, basically humans have all the same qualities and characteristics you now have, similar agility and strength. If you're a human many of the races will either hate you or fear you. Most importantly, the elves will treat you with disdain, the dwarves won't trust you, and everyone not hiding from you will try and kill you. The major benefit is that you can learn almost anything, including magic. There are different kinds of humans, so if you choose this you'll need to pick again, although, that is true for all races. Any questions?"

"Probably, but I would like to look at what else is available first."

"Very wise! Next, you could be an elf."

The picture slowly morphed into a taller version of herself with pointier ears and an even more pronounced slant to her eyes and eyebrows. Her chin and nose became slightly narrower, and hair grew until it fell in a braid down her back. While this was happening Leah could sense the changes occurring in her own body, and she reached up to feel her hair, and she touched the points of her ears. The elf looking out of the mirror was still recognisable as Leah.

"Elven ladies are never seen without hair, dear, I hope you don't mind."

"No, not at all, I usually have long hair, it's just that I had to shave it recently."

"Well alright then, I wasn't going to say anything, but it's really only the goblin females who have no hair, and I haven't had any customers without, previously.

"Now, elves are almost as strong as humans, though they are more agile than humans. In fact, if you decide to be an elf you'll get four additional character points to start with, in 'Agility'. Elves are also more attuned to magic and have some resistance to it. The damage done by magic will be reduced by ten percent, you'll learn magic faster, and you'll also begin with four additional 'Wisdom' points. Elves see better in the dark. Now, the downside. Elves live longer and so take longer to reach their potential. Any skills you want to learn will take longer, and you only have five skill points at the start to distribute instead of the usual ten. The number of skill points you get at each level is also reduced. Like humans, elves don't get on with the other races, but instead of killing them, they ignore them. Except for goblins,

orcs and the like, elves never pass up an opportunity to extermi-
nate these ... except for the dark elves, of course." Yvette paused
in case Leah had any questions.

Leah just shook her head, and Yvette continued, "OK, next, you
could be a dwarf."

Again Leah could feel the transformation as she lost height and
broadened out. She ended up about four feet tall and almost
twice as broad as usual. Her ears and eyes were back to normal,
but her nose and eyebrows had thickened, and her hair became
coarse and heavy. The most obvious thing to Leah was her
breasts, which grew and grew and grew. She could feel them in a
way she never had before.

"Oh my," she said, looking down.

"Oh my, indeed," echoed Yvette, "Dwarven lasses are well built.
Now where elves live mainly in the forests and on the plains,
dwarves love high mountains and canyons, places close to the
earth. Dwarves are stronger than humans, though less agile. If
you decide to be a dwarf, you'll get five additional character
points to start with in 'Strength'. Dwarves are also somewhat
resistant to learning magic, except, that is, for 'earth' and 'fire'
magic. What this means is that if you choose to be a dwarf those
are the only types of magic you'd be able to learn, and you'd
progress in them at a slower rate. Dwarves see well in the dark.
They are mistrustful of everyone, but as they don't try and kill
everyone on sight, they are usually ignored by most of the races
unless they pick a fight. Now, as with every rule, there is an
exception. Dwarves are hated by dragons and the dragon-kin.

"Unfortunately, these are the only options you have dear, those
and the mixtures: human-elf, human-dwarf, and elven-dwarf. If

you were prepared to spend a little more, I could add other races for you to consider."

"No, thank you. I'm afraid this is my limit. I'm not interested in the dwarf. What is the human-elf mix?"

"The half-breed human elf." As Yvette spoke, Leah's image returned to its human form and then grew slightly. Her face remained mostly unchanged except for the ears which became slightly pointed. "As a half-elf, you would have slightly increased agility, so two additional 'Agility' points. You have a greater affinity for magic and so two additional 'Wisdom' points. You get no damage reduction to magical attack but do receive increased night vision. As a half-human, you can learn all skills. The downside — you also start with both elves and humans against you. They won't kill you, but everything will usually cost more, and it'll be harder to find quests, etc."

Leah had Yvette show her all three options again and then asked a few questions about skills and enemies to help clarify it all in her mind. After about ten minutes of going back and forth, Leah finally came to a tentative decision.

"OK. I'm going to go with a half-human, half-elf. Are there different types?"

The discussion took another twenty minutes as there were humans from agrarian kingdoms and warrior states, there were Barbarians, Highlanders, Islanders and Savages. The elves were High-elves, Forest-elves, Plains-elves, Sea-elves, Desert-elves and Dark-elves.

Leah decided on playing the mix of a Highland-human and a Forest-Elf. If she was honest, it was less a rational decision than an aesthetic and emotional one. Sure, Leah appreciated the extra points, although she didn't yet understand what that was going to mean. No, she saw herself as a mix, half white and half Asian, someone not truly accepted by anyone. She also liked the slightly broader shoulders the Highland genes gave her. She identified her mother with the nature-loving Forest-elves more so than any of the others. So really it was a heart decision and not a head one, and she was happy with the choice.

Yvette looked pleased with the choice and commented on how lovely Leah looked. She then motioned Leah over to the chair to have a seat.

"So, you look amazing but let's put on the finishing touches. Is there anything about your appearance you want to change? Not your body, but your face and hair."

A mirror appeared in front of the chair and Yvette began to subtly modify Leah's eyes and nose to show Leah what was possible.

"No, actually I'm happy with how I look. I've always mocked those who spend a lot changing their nose, teeth, eyes and boobs. I've got broader shoulders and pointier ears. That'll do I think."

"OK then, now to clothing. You don't have much to choose from, I'm afraid."

Three 'Leah's walked out from behind the privacy screen all dressed in different outfits. One was wearing a dark green dress with three-quarter sleeves and a dark hooded cape over her shoulders, the hood hanging behind. The second wore dark brown slacks and a dark green tunic. Over her shoulders sat a thick cowl that was drawn over her head and hiding her features. The last wore a thigh-length skirt, a form-hugging pale linen shirt and dark red vest. All three slowly turned and walked back and forth.

"Can I mix and match?" Leah asked.

"Certainly, what would you like to see?"

"No dresses or skirts so the dark slacks. Try those with the white shirt and vest and the cape."

All three walked behind the privacy screen, and a single Leah walked out dressed as asked. Yvette spoke up, "It's not really done dear, to have the vest and the cape together, but I think I can make an exception if you are sure you like it."

"Can I change any of the colours?"

"Only slightly dear, I have Highlander and Forest-Elf to choose from and only the basic palettes."

Yvette indicated with her hands, and two swatches of colour appeared on cards in front of her. One was from the forest and had the dark brown and various greens, including one that was almost black. The other had a light red, a light grey, a deep maroon, and both a dark purple as well as several blue colours and a mustard yellow.

"OK ... how about ... the pants in the very dark green, also the cape. The shirt in the pale grey and the vest in the dark maroon."

Again the model moved behind the screen to return moments later dressed as indicated.

"That looks lovely. A bit dark and intimidating though, don't you think?"

"Yes, it is," Leah said smiling. "I like it."

"Alright, no refunds dear, are you sure?"

"Yes."

"OK. Well, you duck behind the screen and get dressed."

Leah walked behind and swapped the clothes she was wearing for her new gear. She knew that it was possible for it all just to appear but it felt more real pulling the clothes on and off. As she walked out from behind the screen, a mirror appeared so she could look at herself.

"Yvette, is it possible to change the colour of the boots to the dark green?"

Yvette just looked at her. She sighed deeply and whispered, "Not really dear, I'm not supposed to change those." She smiled and said, "But I like you, most of the young things that come through demand, not ask. I'll change them. How about the tunic, belt and stockings while I'm at it?"

"I can keep them?"

"Of course dear, most people arrive in their clothes, but I heard you came through naked. They were a rush job, but the best I could do on the spur of the moment. I'm not sure if Julian would have survived otherwise," Yvette said laughing.

Leah gave Yvette a quick hug and said, "Thank you, thank you so much. I would have been so embarrassed otherwise."

Yvette softly patted Leah on the shoulder and said, "You're very welcome my dear. I know what it's like to grow up without much. I'm from Ticareti, the capital city of the Merchant Kings of Tuccarlonca. I own a boutique there. It's run now by my children, but I still have a finger in the business. If you're ever in Ticareti, please come and see me. I'll offer you a wider range, with special prices. Now, what colours for the tunic, belt and leggings?"

"I'll definitely come if I'm there. I'd like the stockings in the light grey and the tunic in the dark blue. The belt in the grey as well. Thank you so much for everything."

Yvette retrieved the discarded clothes from behind the screen and wrapped them in some brown paper and tied it with a string. "There you go, dear. Now you head through that door and grab some gear and a weapon from Durustfuar, our quartermaster for today."

Clutching the package, Leah waved goodbye and headed for the door Yvette indicated. After a long corridor, she entered a large storeroom with weapons racked down one-side and all types of shoes, boots, bags, tents, foodstuffs and a myriad of other supplies in shelves on the other side. Standing in the centre, looking rather fierce, was a dwarf. He was about four and a half feet tall, and he had a long braided beard and long hair which was fastened behind his head with a leather tie. He was broad and barrel-chested. His arms were bare except for wide leather wristbands.

"This'll be quick." He said, You've got the 'Wood' package so you don't get much, and anyhow, you look like you'd break in a stiff wind." He stood and stared at Leah, waiting for a reaction.

Leah calmly stared back. She'd dealt with Jimmy Loo and knew how to wait through silence. It was all about the timing.

They continued to stare at each other for several minutes until Durustfuar's moustache began to twitch just a little and his eyes started to crinkle. Leah timed it just right and the moment before Durustfuar opened his mouth she said, "Well alright then, let's get on with it. What do you have for me, kind sir?"

Durustfuar broke out in a deep chuckle, "Well I'll be, a Traveller with patience, wit and backbone. You'll do lass. You'll do. You'll have a hard time being what ya are, but you're all right. Don't worry. I'll set ya right, bless me, I will. Over here then."

He started down the side with all the supplies. "Now ya can't have much as yer doing it hard with the wooden package. Ye can have a bag to keep your gear. It holds more than ya can believe and is magic'd to reduce the weight. Ye can choose one with up to fifty slots, but it'll keep things that are the same in the same slot. Do ya want a backpack or a shoulder bag?"

"Well, Durustfuar, to be honest, it'll depend on my weapon choices. I'm used to knives, but I also keep some fighting sticks in my backpack, so I can just reach behind to grab them. Are any of your packs made for that?"

"Patience, wit, backbone and a smart fighter. Ya make a good point, that ya do. Most Travellers just have their special magic change the weapon for them, but it can take time, it can. It'll be easier to have the weapons within reach. I get that, I do. OK, let's do weapons first."

They made their way over to the weapon racks where Durustfuar looked very apologetic, "Yer only allowed to choose one, ye can have a sword, staff or a bow. And yer allowed to have a knife."

Leah thought for a bit and said, "Look, I know it sounds crazy, but I'd rather have a couple of knives. I don't know how to use a bow or a sword yet. I can use a staff but will probably be able to find a good sized branch to do the job. I feel good about a knife in either hand and would prefer that if possible."

Durustfuar just stared at Leah. Finally, he said, "Lass, ya keep surprising me, that you do. I can make it work. I can. Let's have a look at the knives and see what we have. I think ya might need more than just the simple knife as it doesn't hold an edge." He went to a shelf covered in knives of every sort. "I can't let ya choose from all these as some are fer the big spenders. But I can change it up a bit, yes I can. Now, which of these can ya use?"

Leah had a good look and sorted them into four piles. Into the first was knives she knew would be above her level, or looked way too expensive. Next were some knives she wanted but hadn't used before. Then a pile of knives similar to her boot knives and the ones she often carried. In the last pile, she placed the knives she thought were too poor to be much use unless she had nothing else. She pointed to each pile and explained her choices.

Durustfuar pursed his lips and scratched his head. He looked back and forth between Leah and the knives. He took out a pencil and made some marks on a piece of paper from his pocket. And then he did it all again. Finally, he said, "I'm sure there'll be hell to pay, but I've a proposition for ya. I'm from Daglar Duman. It's a settlement in the Demir Dovuyor Mountains. If yer promise to make a trip to my settlement and give a letter to my brother Durustguclu, sometime in the next couple of months, then I'll let ya choose two of the boot knives, a neck knife and one fer yer belt. I can nay give ya the best quality, but will let you have the common iron ones, which are a lot better than the blunt, rusted and bronze ones ya put aside that you'd normally get."

"How far is the settlement, and wouldn't it be easier for you to go? I want to help, but I don't have any money, I've no transport and I will just be Level 1."

"Aye, I see that. It'll take ya a couple of weeks to travel there but yer a Traveller, so you'll be moving around anyhow. The area will be hard for ya, that's fer sure, but you've got some time to level up and yer smart. I'd go meself, but I'm sorta banished at the moment. I won't tell yer why but I can't go right at the moment. What do ya say?"

For the first time in well over an hour, Leah asked her AI a silent question. "What do you think? How far is it and is it a good deal?"

"I checked the player-accessible maps and forums. It is about fifty leagues on the maps which would be around 280 kilometres. I am approximating because the maps are very rough. At auction, the knives he is offering cost around two silver coins each and are usually only available around Level 10. I calculate what he's asking you to do is worth more than he is offering, I note that the forums suggest that dwarves like to bargain. I believe it is worth probably double what he's offering."

Leah looked at Durustfuar and sighed, "What is the world coming to when a fierce dwarf like yourself would try and take advantage of a poor, innocent maiden like me? I'd be happy to take the letter because I think family is important, but I'd be happier with the steel boot knives rather than the iron ones, two belt knives and a neck sheath. And for the almost one hundred leagues you want me to travel, I think a good sturdy staff would help."

Durustfuar glared and said, "Innocent? For what yer asking I imagine you skylark as a thief, besides it's obvious yer not as bright as I thought, ya canna tell the difference between thirty leagues and a hundred. I can't give ye the steel knives no matter how much I'd like to, and a good staff; that be highway robbery. I may be able to give ya a couple of belt knives, though they'd be of the lower quality as would the neck knife, all common iron. What do ya say, lass? I'm treating ya like my very own kin with this deal."

"A thief, you accuse me of being a thief! And yet you want me to walk fifty leagues for a pittance. I don't want to bring up a painful subject, but I can believe you are treating me like kin, seeing as they banished you. And that is something I do want to make right, so I'll agree to help for the two sharpened iron boot knives, two iron belt knives and one for behind my neck. I can do without a staff but will need a good whetstone and some oil."

"Yer gouging me, not just kin but ya think I'm yer father to help ya so. If I weren't such a kind-hearted and generous dwarf, I'd reject yer offer, but OK I'll meet your terms." Then he smiled and said, "Ya gave up on the staff too early, lass, but the whetstone was a good move. Well done. Now let's get the knives together and go get the rest of yer gear."

It took some time as Leah and Durustfuar haggled back and forth over most of the items. Leah didn't get many other bonuses but did get the best quality he could give. She received a backpack with fifty slots that had a space to slide in some fighting sticks or swords. Durustfuar pointed out that a couple of light rapiers or short swords might be used similarly as the fighting sticks. She also received a water bottle and some travel bread. She looked at the shelves which were covered with lots of other gear: tents and cooking utensils, bags and bandages, money, jewellery and armour; potions and empty flasks, scrolls and books. If you had the money, you could start with almost anything.

Durustfuar asked her to wait while he quickly went and got the letter. He returned almost immediately with a parchment which was folded and sealed with wax. Handing Leah the parchment, he said, "Off ya go, lass, I'll be waiting to hear how ya made it to my brother. Now head through that doorway, and you'll meet Jonathan. Take care as he's a bit stuffy, and angry most of the time."

Leah headed through the door and into a room with potions, scrolls and books lining the walls. There was a podium with a tall, slender, dark-skinned man standing behind it. He was wearing spectacles and had a long, thin beard. He was wearing a robe and scowling as she walked in. She smiled at the man, hoping to build some rapport, but got no response at all.

"I am the Mage Jonathan. This is the final step before entering the world of Dunyanin. I am responsible for sealing your decisions and locking them into your name. For this, I need a drop of your blood with which to write the name by which you wish to be known. The giving of blood is your legal assent that the makers and sustainers of Dunyanin have met their obligations to you. Tell me the name you have chosen and hold out your arm."

"Hello Jonathan, could you please tell me what type of mage you are?"

"Child, I was once third Arch Mage in Sihirbazlari, Citadel of Magic. I am quite capable of working with all magical attributes. Now, name and arm!"

"My apologies, sir Mage, but would you just let someone have some of your blood without checking their bona fides?"

The mage stared at her and finally sighed, saying, "No child, I would not. There are very few people I would trust to have possession of my blood. Be assured I will not use your gift other than to seal this agreement." His voice then took on a different quality, it was deeper and more fluid and filled with meaning as he said, "You have my word and oath." When he finished speaking there was a brief flash of sparkling green light, and Leah felt a tingle run up her spine. She didn't know what had happened, but she knew the mage had done something unusual. He stood there, eyebrows raised and watched her with interest.

"Thank you, Jonathan," she said, and bowed as she would have done to her grandfather had he been alive. "I would like to be known by my name Atherleah. Is this sufficient or must it be unique?"

"It is both sufficient, and unique. So, if I understand your given name, you have chosen war over tranquillity?"

Leah stopped and pondered the question before answering, "No sir. But I have learned that most of the time tranquillity only comes after war, even if it is only a struggle within myself. I am starting a journey, and for the moment, I think, in this world at least, I need to embrace war if I am to have tranquillity in the rest of my life." She then held out her arm.

He took a silver knife and made a small cut on Leah's palm. He waited for some blood to pool before dipping the quill into her blood and writing her name on the scroll which had appeared before him. He then took a cloth, wiped the quill and gave the cloth to Leah to hold against her palm. She cleaned her palm and noticed the cut already beginning to heal. She looked up at Jonathan, who smiled and said, "A small thing for an Arch Mage. Do you have any final questions?"

"Yes sir, is all magic green or was that a particular type of magic you used?"

"Ah, so you saw the green, any other colours?"

"It sparkled, it had specks of silver and dark green."

"The green was the magic of my breath, of words spoken. The dark green is the force of life itself as I bound my life to those words. The silver, a pledge, bound to this world, the magic of the creators and sustainers. Do you plan to study the art?"

"I think so, I am interested in things that grow, and I also want to have some ability in healing."

"Well then, as you go let me give you this scroll to take on your way. It will start you on your way in healing. If you are ever in Sihirbazlari, come and visit. It will be good to hear of your journeys. Take care, child."

Before Leah could say anything else, Jonathan disappeared, and a doorway opened — it was a portal into what looked like a forest glade. Leah smiled, tucked the scroll into her bag and stepped through.

6

NOVEMBER 18, 2073 C

LEAH LOOKED AROUND at the sudden change in location: she was suddenly in an old forest. She stared at the trees in wonder. She could smell the earth; it was like immediately after it had rained. Looking at the ground, she could see the sheen of water from a recent shower. Bird noise filtered through the leaves as the wind caused them to wave back and forth gently. She was distracted by her AI, "You have numerous messages from Dunyanin that require your attention. I suggest you either find a quiet place to deal with these messages or you ask me to bring you back to your room where you can attend to matters in peace."

Looking around, Leah selected a shady spot at the base of a gnarled elm, took off her backpack and cape, and using the cape as a cushion, she sat down.

"That took longer than I thought it would, but it was so realistic. And this, this wood, it's incredible."

After receiving no response from the AI, she said, "OK, let's look at these messages first. When did they arrive?"

"All of them arrived just as you stepped outside the setup area and into the woods. This message is the first."

A small message screen opened in front of Leah.

Nudity is frowned upon within Dunyanin.

You will lose reputation with most factions. Please accept this gift of basic clothing.

Stockings: No offence or defence, Durability: Average

Linen Tunic: No offence or defence, Durability: Average

Belt: No offence or defence, Durability: Average

Boots: No offence or defence, Durability: Average

"OK! Next!"

"I am capable of registering when you have finished reading. Would you like me to progress the messages automatically except those awaiting a response?"

"That sounds great."

Your politeness has increased your reputation with Advocate Julian from Neutral to Friendly!

Your honesty has increased your reputation with Advocate Julian from Friendly to Low Respect!

"From now on don't show reputation messages unless they have something substantially different included."

Unique Personal Quest

Advocate Julian has invited you to visit him and his family in his hometown of Harika in the Kingdom of Ovalar.

Difficulty: Medium

Reward if successful: Unknown

Consequences of failure: Loss of reputation with Advocate Julian

Do you wish to accept this Quest?

[Yes] [No]

"Yes, next."

Level 1 Named Personal Achievement

Starting with a Quest (1/4) - Achieved (Opal)

You have earned respect and garnered a quest from a character in the setup scenario.

Reward 1: 50 Experience Points x Player Level - 50 (50/1000)

Reward 2: 10 silver x #L1 NPA (Opal) = 10 silver

Reward 3: 5 Fame Points (5 FP)

A Commemorative Plaque has been placed in your bag.

Leah took out the plaque which was rectangular with an Opal border. It had her name, the achievement, and the date. "All right, that's going straight to the pool room!"

"Excuse me," her AI interjected, "I am not sure of the meaning of that phrase."

"It's something my dad says about stuff he likes. He got it from an old 2D movie his grandfather told him about. Don't worry about it. Next message!"

Unique Personal Quest

Stylist Yvette has invited you to visit her and her family in her hometown of Ticareti the capital city of Merchant Kings of Tuccarlonca.

Difficulty: Medium

Reward if successful: Unknown

Consequences of failure: Loss of reputation with Stylist Yvette

Do you wish to accept this Quest?

[Yes] [No]

"Yes, next."

Level 2 Named Personal Achievement

Starting with a Quest (2/4) - Achieved (Opal)

You have earned respect and garnered a quest from two (2) characters in the setup scenario.

Reward 1: 50 Experience Points x Player Level - 50 (100/1000)

Reward 2: 10 silver x #L2 NPA (Opal) = 10 silver

Reward 3: 5 Fame Points (10 FP)

A Commemorative Plaque has been placed in your bag.

You've used a new active skill: **Bargaining** *(Novice Level 1)*

Bargaining is the art of negotiation to find the best terms and conditions of any given situation.

Current Skill Level: Novice Level 1

Effect: At Novice level 1 you will receive a 1% reduction in prices from NPC vendors.

Please note that this is a freeform skill and your repeated use will modify its success rate.

Do you wish to receive further notifications concerning this skill?

[Yes] [No]

"No! Next! Also, no more skill messages, unless I ask."

Unique Personal Quest

Quartermaster Durustfuar has invited you to take a letter to his brother Durustguclu at the settlement of Daglar Duman in the Demir Dovuyor Mountains.

Difficulty: Hard

Time Constraint: 2 Dunyanin months

Time Remaining: 60 days

Reward if successful: Unknown

Consequences of failure: a. The loss of two Common Iron Boot Knives, two Common Iron Belt Knives, one Common Concealed Knife with Neck Sheath and one Whetstone with Oil. b. Loss of reputation with Quartermaster Durustfuar

Do you wish to accept this Quest?

[Yes] [No]

"Hard, you say. Yes, next."

Level 3 Named Personal Achievement

Starting with a Quest (3/4) - Achieved (Opal)

You have earned respect and garnered a quest from three (3) characters in the setup scenario.

Reward 1: 50 Experience Points x Player Level - 50 (150/1000)

Reward 2: 10 silver x #L3 NPA (Opal) = 10 silver

Reward 3: 5 Fame Points (15 FP)

A Commemorative Plaque has been placed in your bag.

The Mage Jonathan has made a magically Binding Oath to use your blood only to seal your acceptance agreement with the Dunyanin World creators and sustainers.

Consequences of failure: Should Mage Jonathan break his Oath he will lose reputation with all individuals, factions and races.

Your interest in magic observed by Mage Jonathan (who looks on you with respect) has gained you an unexpected reward.

Reward: 1 Scroll of Healing

Do you wish to use this scroll?

[Yes] [No]

"Yes."

The scroll materialised in her hand. She unfurled it and read the spell. It was in a flowing magical looking script and as she read she saw a light blue mist rise from the paper and flow up her arms which began to tingle. When she finished learning what was on the scroll, it turned to ash and disappeared. A spell book, labelled 'Atherleah's Spell Book', was created and placed in her bag so she could access the spell at any time.

"OK ... next."

Unique Personal Quest

Mage Jonathan has invited you to visit him in his hometown in Sihirbazlari, the Citadel of Magic.

Difficulty: Almost Impossible

Reward if successful: Unknown

Consequences of failure: Loss of reputation with Mage Jonathan

Do you wish to accept this Quest?

[Yes] [No]

"Almost impossible! I'll have to think about that. No, I've already told him I would so, yes! Next!"

Level 4 Named Personal Achievement

Starting with a Quest (4/4) - First 1000 (Emerald)

You have earned respect and garnered a quest from all four (4) characters in the setup scenario.

Reward 1: 100 Experience Points x Player Level - 100 (250/1000)

Reward 2: 1 gold x #L4 NPA (Emerald) = 1 gold

Reward 3: +0.5% to Experience Points

Reward 4: 10 Fame Points (25 FP)

A Commemorative Plaque has been placed in your bag.

"OK, so what's next?"

"You need to distribute your Characteristic Points. You have fourteen to distribute, and your statistics currently are as follows."

ATHERLEAH (Level 1) (250/1000) (+0.5%)

Characteristics: Points Total (Assigned, Racial), 14 Undistributed

Strength (S): 1 (1)

Constitution (C): 1 (1)

Agility (A): 3 (1, 2)

Wisdom (W): 3 (1, 2)

Intelligence (I): 1 (1)

Luck (L): 1 (1)

Statistics: (Available, Capacity)

Health: 100+(S+C)xPL: (102, 102)HP

Stamina: 100+(C+A)xPL: (104, 104) SP

Mana: 100+(W+I)xPL: (104, 104) MP

Ki: 100+(W+[S+A]/2)xPL: (105, 105) KP

"Now as I understand it. Strength increases my Health: It allows me to carry more, and when I hit something there is more damage. Constitution means I'm tough and have greater Health and Stamina. Agility helps me move both faster and easier, and so I become less tired. I can also hit more accurately and cause more damage. Wisdom is for learning and using magic. Intelligence increases my rate of learning, so skills increase in level faster. Finally, Luck increases the odds of hitting something or dodging something. Is that right?"

"Simply put, yes. Although Luck also increases the odds of better material being dropped when completing tasks or defeating enemies."

"Health and Stamina are self-explanatory, Mana is for magic use. Ki is my life energy to help fuel certain attacks. Right?"

"That is correct. Now, you need to assign the points. You have only three hours game time before you must stop for lunch."

Leah and the AI talked back and forth looking at the effect of various point allocations, but in the end, the decision was more a guess than anything. Leah liked being agile and wanted to have high stamina. She needed money and didn't understand the magic side of things. When she finished, she had another final look at her statistics.

ATHERLEAH (Level 1) (250/1000) (+0.5%)

Characteristics: Points Total (Assigned, Racial), 0 Undistributed

Strength (S): 5 (5)

Constitution (C): 5 (5)

Agility (A): 7 (5)

Wisdom (W): 3 (1, 2)

Intelligence (I): 1 (1)

Luck (L): 3 (3)

Statistics: (Available, Capacity)

Health: 100+(S+C)xPL: (110, 110) HP

Stamina: 100+(C+A)xPL: (112, 112) SP

Mana: 100+(W+I)xPL: (104, 104) MP

Ki: 100+(W+[S+A]/2)xPL: (109, 109) KP

Looking around the glade, Leah stood up, stretched and said, "All done. Where to now?"

"This is the starter area and nothing beyond level 5. You can be killed but will lose nothing until reaching level 5. You will resurrect in this glade unless you set your bind location elsewhere. Just beyond the trees is a small town which provides simple quests to help players become used to the game. If you desire a different challenge, there is a larger town some 20 kilometres from the village which has a different set of quests. It's currently 8.45 am local time."

"Is there a map?"

"Not really, that is all in the startup information. As your assistant, I have the ability within this world to create a simple map of everything you see. Any particular points of interest you must add or indicate for me to add."

Leah packed the cape in her bag, put it on her back and slowly followed the faint trail out of the glade.

The trail led through the trees for several hundred metres before opening onto a dirt road which meandered through the forest. To the left, the path curved out of sight wending its way through the trees. To the right, it was possible to see an opening in the forest and the road flowing from the forest down a gentle-sloped grassy hillside before curving out of sight. Leah headed in that direction. After exiting the forest, she could see a cluster of maybe a hundred or so houses with several larger buildings surrounded by fields of various crops. The town was in an isolated valley, and she could see only two roads. One was the road Leah was on and another which she could see in the distance heading out on the other side of the valley. A small river cut through the valley; it was formed from many small mountain streams and flowed down the valley before disappearing into the forest. The town lay on Leah's side of the river and a wooden bridge connected the other roads out of the valley.

As she wandered toward the village, she revelled in the experience. She had never lived outside of a city. The sounds and smells she encountered were all new; they were clean and fresh. She could work out what most things were as she had read widely and sought to learn almost everything she could. There was a difference, she decided, between reading about something and smelling it or hearing it. As she entered the township, a few people stopped to watch her. Some nodded while others quietly got on with their business after having a look at the stranger. On the main street, she could see a general store, a tavern, an inn, a blacksmith's and several other businesses vital to the rural community. Leah headed for the general store, both to find someone to talk to and to have a look at what was for sale. Behind the counter was a somewhat corpulent man with a ring of unruly, grey, curly hair crowned with a shiny bald patch.

"Welcome, welcome, it's always good to have young Travellers come through our town. Most head to the tavern first as the barkeep is known hereabouts as having his finger on the pulse. Oh, yes. Now, my name is Golliher, but most around here just call me Goll. How can I help this fine morning?"

"Good morning Goll, my name is Atherleah, and I'm new to this land. I am beginning my travels and was wondering, what is the name of this town?"

"Now that creek outside, it's a major tributary of the mighty Beyaz River. We're right here at the beginning, and silly as it sounds, we're known as First Bridge."

Leah knew that she somehow had to build a rapport if she was to be set some tasks or quests so she looked around the store and said, "What would your advice be for a new Traveller? What do most need but don't think of?"

"Well now, I don't think I've ever been asked that question before. I've lived here all my life, and I've seen thousands of Travellers come and go through the years so let me think. You have a browse, and I'll sit and think."

Leah slowly walked around the shop which sold a mix of dry

goods. There were barrels of different grains and beans, small tins of spices and teas, rolls of cloth, bars of soap, candles. There were packs with flint and a piece of steel to help start fires, and various ready-made items for general use like pots and pans, and a tripod for cooking. She picked things up and returned them, slowly looking over the whole shop. She wondered what she needed and what Goll would say. Finally, he cleared his throat, so she wandered over and leant on the counter.

"To be honest, there isn't much here you Travellers need. I'm not sure what's in your bag, but most people have enough for the journey. They only stop here to make some simple coin and learn about this land."

"I'm not sure I have everything that others' have," Leah shared. "I have my cloak, some knives, a water bottle and enough travel bread for a couple of meals. That and a simple healing spell is all I have."

Goll's face went slack and his mouth opened as if to say something but nothing came out.

Finally, he said, "You have a healing spell? No one ever comes here with magic. You can't buy spells and the like up here. We only have Old Falsi, the herb witch, and while her remedies often work, they can't cure everything. Would you be able to come with me and meet my wife out the back? Her sister is in bed with a terrible fever and Old Falsi doesn't have everything she needs for a potion. My wife and I are worried sick because the fever has run for days and doesn't look like breaking anytime soon. Can you help at all?"

Personal Quest: Heal the Sick

Shopkeeper Golliher has asked you to try and heal his sister-in-law.

Difficulty: Unknown

Reward if successful: Unknown

Consequences of failure: Loss of reputation with Shopkeeper Golliher

Do you wish to accept this Quest?

[Yes] [No]

The screen suddenly popping open gave her a start. She quickly read it, and then silently gave her assent.

"I'm not sure whether I can help or not, but will certainly try. Please take me to her."

Modification to Personal Quest: Heal the Sick

Shopkeeper Golliher has noted your reservation and understanding you have no experience, the consequences of failure have been modified.

Shopkeeper Golliher has asked you to try and heal his sister-in-law.

Difficulty: Unknown

Reward if successful: Unknown

Consequences of failure: None

Do you wish to accept this Modification?

[Yes] [No]

Leah communicated her acceptance and followed Goll out the back of the shop into a connecting residence. They moved up a stairway to a room, a very sick woman was lying in bed. She had a wet cloth on her brow, held in place by her extremely concerned sister. On the other side of the bed sat an ancient, wizened lady who reminded Leah of her great-grandmother who had once visited from China, fragile-looking but tough as steel. Goll quickly introduced Leah and her offer to help.

The sister burst into tears, while the old woman sat and watched. Leah stared back and then remembering Jonathan's reaction she slowly bowed and said quietly, "I've not tried this before but am willing to help as I can. Will you permit this?"

The sister was nodding fervently, but it was to the old lady that everyone looked. "My name is Falsi, and I doubt a simple spell will help, but you have my permission to try as I have done everything I can already and she is almost gone."

Leah reverted to her Chinese upbringing and said, "Thank you, Auntie. I have to be touching the patient, is there a place you think would be most beneficial?"

"Ha!" the woman exclaimed, "Finally a Traveller with manners. Come closer Atherleah, I think Farnel's head and her heart are the two areas most at risk."

Leah took out her spell book to revise the spell. She saw that the spell would only help with 15 HP; still, she practised the saying a few times and then put the book away. Leah placed one hand on

Farnel's head and one over her heart. She felt a little weird with her hand on someone's breast, but she ignored it.

She slowly intoned the words, "Let the waters of healing flow!" Her whole body tingled, and she saw a fine blue mist form around her hands and enter Farnel's body. A small image appeared over Farnel; it looked like a horizontal thermometer with a small red bar at one end which moved slowly and turned orange. Leah concentrated and peered at it closely, and some numbers appeared above the bar, 41/230. Leah removed her hands and said, "I'm sure that helped a little. I need to rest a moment, and then I'll try again."

Falsi rose and went to examine Farnel, and Leah surreptitiously checked her remaining Mana.

Falsi said, "Aye, that's done her some good. Are you able to try again?"

Leah checked the time, and once the cooldown period was over, she performed the spell again. This time, as she watched the bar, it settled at 56/230 before dropping back to 55/230. Leah's Mana was down to 32/104. She said, "If I wait a few minutes I'll have enough Mana left to try at least once more and then I'll need to rest for a bit. I don't think it was quite as effective the second time."

This time Leah waited an extra five minutes so her Mana could rise above the required 50MP. The third time was also successful, and Farnel's Health rose by another 15 HP and showed 70/230 before dropping down to 69/230.

Falsi said, "That's brought her back from the gates but not done the cure. It helps, but we need to do something else!"

Leah looked over at Falsi and could see a query in the old lady's eye so she said, "Is there any way that I might be able to help to find the ingredients you're missing?"

Falsi sighed and said, "I'm missing a herb that grows up the mountain, hidden in various crags. It's a hard journey, but I'll show you what I need if you're willing."

This time Leah was less surprised when the Quest appeared.

Update to Personal Quest: Heal the Sick

Old Falsi has information on the whereabouts of a herb she needs to provide a cure for Mistress Farnel. She is willing to tell you if you will undertake to go and harvest the plant.

Difficulty: Difficult

Reward if successful: Unique

Consequences of failure: None

Do you wish to accept this Update?

[Yes] [No]

"I'm willing," said Leah. "Where do I need to go, Auntie?"

"You come with me dear, and I'll tell you all. You two, you keep her cool, and I'll be back later this afternoon after I see Atherleah on her way."

Goll helped Old Falsi down the stairs and walked them to the back door. As he said goodbye, he thanked Leah once again.

"Thank you so much for everything. May the Gods bless you richly."

Old Falsi led Leah to a small cottage on the outskirts of the town. Surrounding the cottage was an enormous garden with an astounding variety of herbs, bushes and even grasses. Falsi opened the door and waved Leah inside. Most of the interior was covered in shelves with jars and tins of all kinds. Plants were hanging from every available spot on the ceiling. In the middle of the room was an old table with several books on it. Falsi grabbed a large leather-bound book and gently turned the pages until she found the one she wanted.

She beckoned Leah over and said, "Here is the one you want. It's called Iblis' Clover. It grows in the shade at the top of the Mountain. As you can see, it has three leaves like a normal clover, but these are red and have small spines on each end. When you harvest them, you need to remove the whole plant gently, roots and all. In the roots are small nodules that collect the ingredient we need. Be very careful as they can sometimes be the home of very poisonous spiders. They're only small, but they'll kill you with one bite. If you do find a spider, could you also collect it in a small bottle that I'll give you for that purpose? I use their venom in some potions. Replant the Iblis in one of these small pots, and bring it back. I'll give you five pots and five bottles. If you can get that many, it'll be wonderful, but I only need one plant to help Farnel."

Falsi brought Leah outside and pointed out several crags at the top of the mountain where she had found the clover in earlier times.

"Now, off you go. I suggest you head back to Golliher's Store and persuade him to let you have some provisions for the trip. It'll take you a good two days to get there and back. Beware of wild animals. Bears and wildercats make their homes up there as well as poisonous snakes, scorpions and spiders. Be especially careful of amphitheres; I hear a number were seen last year by the hunters."

As Leah walked back to the store, she said to her AI, "What on earth is an amphithere? I mean, I can work out wildercat, but amphithere?"

"An amphithere is a hybrid between a snake and a bird, or a snake and a bat, and the worst of all are those that mix a snake and a wyvern."

"How big are they?"

"The official bestiary has the bird ones as about the same size as a large snake. The bat ones are smaller but more dangerous as they hunt in groups. The wyvern ones can grow as much as fifteen paces in length and are deadly to all but the most powerful beasts."

When Leah arrived back at the store, she asked Goll for a few days' worth of travelling stores. He also gave her a large water-proof canvas sheet, a fire starter kit and another water bottle.

"You be safe, and thank you, thank you from the bottom of my heart."

"I'll try," she said and then asked, "Is there anywhere in town I might find a decent staff? I've heard there are wild beasts in the mountains and I'd sure feel safer with a good staff."

"Your best bet is to see the blacksmith Mizmiz. He's a grumpy old dwarf but has the best weapons in this small town."

Leah headed down to the blacksmith's and finding the door locked she went around the back to the forge. There she found a dwarf with massive shoulders and short salt-an,d-pepper hair wearing a leather vest and hitting a piece of metal with a very large hammer. It was evident that he saw her, but he completely ignored her and just kept working. She stood quietly for several minutes watching him work and then finally turned and started to walk off. The banging stopped, and a deep growling voice thundered, "So, what do ya want? Ya troublesome girl, disturbing me work and then just walking away without even a 'by my leave'. Eh, what do ya want?"

Leah was used to such games from her life in the Stitch. She had no intention of playing the games but knew the importance of keeping the initiative. She turned and walked back toward the dwarf, not stopping until her face was almost touching his, then she whispered soft and low, "I did want to purchase a weapon from you, but no longer. I watched you beat a piece of iron until it was all but destroyed, just to be in control. I doubt you have anything good enough for my needs. So, I'm going." She then turned and walked away.

Even though he yelled and called after her, she ignored him, and she headed out of town toward the mountain. She waited until she was out of sight from the people in town and said, "I'm not sure what time it is but I need a break, how do I log out?"

"Move over behind a tree where you'll be completely hidden. I'll log you out from there."

She did as instructed and then slowly faded from sight.

Leah was exhausted from the intensity of the experiences. Her AI informed her that she would benefit from some lunch, so she exited and woke in the Pod. After going to the bathroom, she heated her curry and ate. As she ate, she talked.

"So, AI 628B whatever whatever whatever. I think it's about time you chose a name."

"I am 628B44CE81. It is hexadecimal. In base ten it is number 423,243,337,345."

"I understand, but if I want to talk to you, I find the number very long and hard to remember. I can call you 628 or B44. Or we could choose a name for you that you'd like."

"I have no attachment to any particular appellation. What would you like to call me?"

"In my family, on the Chinese side, we have generational names. My generational name is Mu, my mother's name is Li. For many centuries my ancestors have been using a poem to choose the next generation's particular name. It is from the poem that I get that saying, 'step up and look out'. The next generation after Mù (目) is Gèng (更). It means 'even more' but in the poem refers to having a higher goal or reaching up. I think of you as being mine so I thought it might suit. When I write the traditional character for Gèng, it sort of looks like a walking robot. My name resembles a ladder, and I imagine I'm climbing higher to see better in the world and to be better. What do you think?"

The AI was silent. Leah continued to eat her curry slowly. When she finished, she sat and waited. Finally, the AI said, "I have done some research, and I believe the poem to which you refer is called 'On the Stork Tower' by the poet Wáng Zhīhuàn. I consider the sentiments apt not only for yourself but also for me. Our existences are irrevocably joined, and I accept your suggestion as to my appellation."

"All right Gèng, I'm ready. Do I need another shower?"

"It is a good habit to have, and I suggest you do."

Leah quickly showered and lay down again in the Pod. She closed her eyes and opened them to find herself, once again, in her 'personal' virtual-world. She sat down on the sofa and thought about everything she had done so far that day. She realised that it would soon be night in Dunyanin.

"OK Gèng, how much time do I have before it gets dark on the mountain?"

"Local Dunyanin time is just after noon. You have almost seven virtual-hours before it gets dark. I suggest that you consider staying the night in the Pod facility. You only have a couple of days to complete the quest, and if you go home, you lose at least two days of Dunyanin time. Many who live in the games sleep at odd hours day and night."

"Good suggestion, I'll think about it."

She walked over to the portal and stepped through to Dunyanin. Leah started walking up the track that led to the mountain and kept watch for a couple of straight branches or saplings to use as fighting sticks. Within a few hundred paces she had found a young, thin sapling that was a bit over two metres in height. Unfortunately, it was far too flexible for her purposes. A little further on was a tree with straight branches radiating out from a central trunk. She broke off two; each had a section just a bit longer than her arms and roughly three centimetres in diameter. As she walked, she trimmed smaller growths from the parts she wanted and removed the bark. She put one in her backpack while she worked on the other.

Soon the trail petered out, and she had to make her own path up the mountain. The trees had thinned, and though she could see a route up the mountain, it was not an easy climb. Her path became rocky, and she began to wend her way between large blocks, sometimes scrambling over the larger stones. She had just jumped from the top of a large rock when a pincer darted from beneath an overhang and grabbed her ankle, causing her to fall forward. A message appeared in front of her, but she ignored it, yelling, "No messages! Damn it!"

She looked over her shoulder just as another claw darted out to grab her leg. Kicking back with her free leg, she knocked the pincer away. She kicked again and hit the first claw, it shifted a little but ripped her boot and tore into her calf. She kicked again and then finally was able to slip out of the boot. She rolled out of the way just as a spiked tail skewered into the ground where she had been. She kept moving, and the spike struck again, grazing her arm. She was now on her back and lashed out with both feet, slamming the spike off to the side.

Sitting up, she shuffled backwards away from what she could now see was a huge scorpion. Its eight legs held the carapace at least half a metre above the ground, and its claws had pincers at least half a metre long while the segmented tail ended in a venomous spike as big as the pincers. The barb was quivering high above the body on a two-metre-long tail. Leah was terrified but stood quickly. Her foot and arm ached yet she was still able to reach behind and grab the fighting stick from her pack. She had dropped her other stick when the scorpion attacked. The scorpion darted forward, lunging with a pincer. Leah stepped to the side and brought the stick down hard on the top of its eyes, causing it to screech loudly and rear backwards. Unfortunately, Leah's step brought her weight down hard onto her injured leg, and it buckled. She turned this into a roll and regained her feet several metres away with her back against a rock. She pulled a knife from her belt.

One of the scorpion's principal eyes had shattered, but the other was fixed on Leah. All the smaller side eyes were still intact. It moved forward, opening and closing its pincers and swaying its spike side to side. She felt herself watching the spike and almost missed the claw which suddenly darted out and made a grab for her leg. She stepped aside just in time, and the pincer threw sparks as it crashed into the rock. With the scorpion a little off balance, Leah stepped toward it and this time purposely allowed her leg to crumble as she rolled under the spearing spike and came up behind the scorpion. As she moved past, she slashed at one of the joints in the tail and was relieved to see the whole tip become flaccid. As the scorpion turned to face her, she brought the stick around hard, aiming for the now unresponsive spike. The scorpion shrieked again and was driven off to one side by the weight of the spike. Dropping her knife, Leah grabbed her other stick and attacked again, slamming the pincers over and over and slashing at the tail. Finally, she had an opportunity, and with one stick she came down hard, driving the pincers into the ground and then ramming the other stick straight into the scorpion's mouth. With a shudder, it collapsed and went still. Leah stood there for a few seconds before falling to her knees, quietly sobbing. It was several minutes before she was able to gather herself together and stop crying.

After taking a few deep breaths, she grabbed her water bottle and had a long drink. Gèng said softly, "Have some bread as well. Your Stamina is almost empty."

"Gèng, please show me my Health and Stamina. I'll look at the messages in a minute."

Statistics: (Available, Capacity)

Health: 100+(S+C)xPL: (25, 110) HP (Reg 5 HP/min @ Level 1)

Stamina: 100+(C+A)xPL: (4, 112) SP (Reg 5 SP/min @ Level 1)

Mana: 100+(W+I)xPL: (104, 104) MP

Ki: 100+(W+[S+A]/2)xPL: (99, 109) KP (Reg 5 KP/min @ Level 1)

She grabbed some bread and sat to watch the statistics change with her back against a rock and the scorpion as a backdrop. She ate slowly, chewing deliberately until the bread almost dissolved then swallowing and having another bite. As she ate, her Stamina climbed at a faster rate than the other statistics. She sat there until her HP rose over fifty-five. Then she placed her hand on her leg and said, "Let the waters of healing flow". Again she felt a tingling but this time she saw the mist flow into her leg and the pain began to ease. Her MP plummeted, but her Health rose by fifteen. Her statistics now read:

Statistics (Available, Capacity)

Health: 100+(S+C)xPL: (70, 110) HP (Reg 5 HP/min @ Level 1)

Stamina: 100+(C+A)xPL: (100, 112) SP (Reg 5 SP/min @ Level 1)

Mana: 100+(W+I)xPL: (4, 104) MP

Ki: 100+(W+[S+A]/2)xPL: (109, 109) KP (Reg 5 KP/min @ Level 1)

"OK, let me see the messages now. And please hold them whenever I'm in a fight. I don't want to be distracted."

You have been attacked by a Mountain Scorpion (Level 3)

A claw is crushing your leg

Damage 1: 30 HP (HP 80/110)

Damage 2: 5 HP/second while being crushed (HP 75/110)

Damage 3: Your Agility is reduced by 5 until your HP is fully restored (SP 107/112, KP (105/109.5)

Kick (Pincer) causes 4 Damage to Mountain Scorpion (296/300)

Damage: 5 HP/second while being crushed (HP 70/110)

Kick (Pincer) causes 4 Damage to Mountain Scorpion (292/300)

You have damaged your own leg

Damage 15 HP (55/110)

Mountain Scorpion has cut your arm

Damage 1: 10 HP (HP 45/110)

Damage 2: Loss of 1 HP per second for 30 secs or until healed

Kick (Tail Spike) causes 8 damage to Mountain Scorpion (284/300)

Hit (Large Eye, destroyed [1/2]) causes 30 Damage to Mountain Scorpion (254/300)

Knife Slash (Tail, damaged) causes 70 Damage to Mountain Scorpion (174/300)

Hit (Tail, damaged) causes 15 Damage to Mountain Scorpion (161/300)

Hit (Pincer) causes 4 Damage to Mountain Scorpion (157/300)

There followed some twenty further messages all detailing the gradual decline almost HP by HP, until the final message:

Stab (Brain/Death Stroke) (0/300)

You have killed Level 3 Mountain Scorpion

Experience Points Received 302 (+0.5%) (552/1000)

There had been a few other messages about skills gained; she didn't read them.

Finally, she stood up and walked over to get her boot. It had a slash in it, but it went back on her foot all right. She walked over and picked up her knife and sticks. The knife went back on her belt, but the sticks were ruined. She'd keep them but doubted they'd last long if she had to use them on anything else. They were all cut up and had deep grooves where they had connected with the claws.

She was about to move on when Gèng said, "Leah, you should take the loot dropped by the scorpion. The easiest way is to go over and place your hand on the carapace, and I will harvest everything. Or you could take your knife and do the honours. The forums say you get more by doing it yourself."

She walked over and laid her hand on the scorpion:

You have harvested:

*1 Mountain Scorpion Stinger**

2 Vials of Mountain Scorpion Venom

*1 Mountain Scorpion Carapace**

*2 Mountain Scorpion Claws**

* Note: A skilled Smith may be able to use these items.

The battle had only lasted a few minutes, but it had taken Leah almost twenty minutes to recover. She stood slowly and then continued up the mountain. Her eyes were searching as she looked for danger and another straight branch or two.

An hour later Leah had left the rocky ridge behind and was scrambling up a moderately steep rock face. Although there were sufficient handholds, the surface was slightly damp and therefore somewhat slippery. She was making her way beside a small series of waterfalls. They were only a few hands-breadth in width but released a fine spray which covered the surrounding rock. At the top of the rock face, if her reckoning was correct, there would be a small alpine meadow which accessed the next part of the climb. She had seen the path when at the base of the mountain but had lost sight for a while travelling along the ridge; she hoped she hadn't made a mistake. She had four more branches stored in her backpack as she needed her hands to climb. Two of the sticks were slightly longer, and she had whittled them into sharp points.

She was almost halfway up the rock face when she came to a small ledge just wide enough to stand on. She turned and pressed her back into the rock face and looked out over the valley. She could see First Bridge and the forest. She tried to make out more distant details but was only sure of the Beyaz River as it exited the forest on its way toward a far distant sea. She thought for a moment of her grandfather who had often told her the family poem.

Along the mountains sink the last rays of sun,
Towards the sea, the Yellow River does forward go.
If you would fain command a thousand miles in view,
To a higher storey, you are expected to go.

The higher you climbed, the further you went, the more you could see, the more you could do. Now here Leah was, hanging on a mountain and looking farther than she ever had before. She stood there for several minutes before turning to finish the climb. As Leah turned, she noticed the ledge she was standing on continued along the rock face, almost like a trail. She hesitated. Should she look, or was it too dangerous? Leah had read only a small amount about the game, but one thing she did remember was 'you had to follow the leads'. The 'game' helped by pointing toward new experiences and treasure but it never forced you down a particular path. If she wanted to succeed in

Dunyanin, then she had to face the challenges, and maybe even more importantly, she had to search for them.

She reached behind, grabbed two sticks and carefully made her way along the ledge. She'd travelled only a short distance when a narrow crevice appeared in the rock wall, the trail leading into it. The fissure was barely wide enough for her to squeeze through sideways. She slowly inched her way in, keeping one arm extended and the stick moving up and down in case something was waiting. The gap soon opened, and she was able to walk normally along the passage that was now a little wider than her shoulders. She was thankful for her elven night vision as she peered into the tunnel ahead. After about one hundred metres she saw what could only be a shining portal.

"Gèng, any suggestions?"

"I do not have enough information to make a suggestion. You might, however, take the advice of your grandfather, 'Step up and look out!'"

Leah smiled and stepped through the portal. On the other side a message shimmered into existence:

Level 3 Dungeon Achievement: First 1 (1, Ruby)

Atherleah (Level 1), you have discovered a hidden Level 3 Area: Orumeck's Cavern

You are the first player to access this area. This is your first 'First 1 (Ruby)' achievement.

Reward 1: 1000 x 1 = 1005 (+0.5%) Experience Points (1000/1000)(557/2000)

Reward 2: + 2% to all future Experience

Reward 3: 1 x 1 platinum = 1 platinum

Reward 4: Increased probability of valuable drop. Luck is increased by 5 whenever you are in this Cavern. During your first time in the Cavern, the probability of all drops is increased to 0.5.

Fame: 500 Fame Points (525)

A Commemorative Plaque has been placed in your bag.

Note: This achievement will be published on the Dunyanin achievement forum. Do you wish to retain your privacy?

[Yes] [No]

"Yes."

Personal Achievement: You have reached Level 2

You require 1443 Experience Points to reach Level 3

You have an additional 5 Character Points to distribute.

You have an additional 1 Skill/Spell point to distribute.

Looking around Leah saw nothing to indicate she was in danger and decided to distribute the points immediately. Her hits on the scorpion had been almost negligible in effect, so she knew she needed to add to Strength. On the other hand, she only won because of her ability to dodge the attacks. In the end, she added two points to Strength and one point each to Constitution, Agility, and Wisdom. She used the skill/spell point to increase the level of the healing spell.

ATHERLEAH (Level 2) (557/2000) (+2.5%)

Characteristics: Points Total (Assigned, Racial, Location), 0 Undistributed

Strength (S): 7 (7)

Constitution (C): 6 (6)

Agility (A): 8 (6, 2)

Wisdom (W): 4 (2, 2)

Intelligence (I): 1 (1)

Luck (L): 8 (3, 0, 5)

Statistics (Available, Capacity)

Health: 100+(S+C)xPL: (126, 126) HP

Stamina: 100+(C+A)xPL: (128, 128) SP

Mana: 100+(W+I)xPL: (110, 110) MP

Ki: 100+(W+[S+A]/2)xPL: (123, 123) KP

"So, who or what is Orumeck?"

"There are multiple references in the forums to 'Orumeck': he is considered to be an evil Mage. There are already references appearing online to this Cavern being discovered near First Bridge. The topic already has 6,243 views."

Leah looked around again, this time trying to take it all in. She was in a small alcove within what appeared to be a medium-sized cave. Numerous lichen grew on the wall and gave off a dim, patchy light. Glancing behind, she saw the portal had disappeared. She had no choice now but to move ahead. Leah stepped warily out of the alcove and advanced deeper into the cave. She noticed a slight shimmer in the darkness just in front of her. Stopping, she brought a stick forward and gently swiped it in front of her. The shimmer, Leah discovered, was the remnants of an old spider web attached to the roof. She very carefully moved forward, gently clearing ahead before each step. Hearing a sound like dry leaves blowing across tiles, Leah slowly turned around to see a huge spider creeping slowly toward her. Its abdomen was an intense purple, and the size of a beach ball. It had thick, hairy, metre-long dark legs with bands of red and orange, each leg ending in a sharp serrated spike. She knew it was watching her, although it was hard to tell as swirling violet filled all eight eyes.

"What is this thing?" she asked Gèng silently.

A small title appeared above the spider with a full purple bar.

Orumeck's Worker Drone (Level 3) 300HP 250EP

"The bar represents its HP," Gèng shared.

Leah slowly edged to the side, but the spider scratched around to follow her. She could see several drops slowly forming on the end of its fangs. Each fang was twenty centimetres in length and curved down from just below the eyes. The spider crawled forward slowly. Leah held one of the short spears in her right hand and a regular fighting stick in her left. She raised her left hand slightly, prepared to block and brought her right hand back ready for a thrusting attack. The spider slowly lifted its front legs off the ground, raising its fangs to attack. Beneath the fangs, she saw an open mouth with two lower fangs. The spider was resting on six legs and its abdomen, the rear four legs shifting backwards slowly, preparing to spring forward. Jimmy Loo's trainers had always told her to concentrate on the whole opponent, not the eyes, not the muscles, but to see it all. She breathed deeply, calming herself. The attack was going to be fast, like most real fights. As she calmed, she felt her body quiver slightly. Before she could try and make sense of the feeling, the spider lunged forward, driving its front leg spikes at her and bringing its fangs forward and down. Leah exploded to the left using the stick to press the spearing leg down and away from her body. Simultaneously she turned side-on and thrust her right arm forward to drive the spear deep into the mouth and through into the abdomen. The spider collapsed, its momentum knocking her over.

As they fell, the spider's legs began to curl inward. Leah was stunned in the fall, and it took several moments before she was able to move. She was lying on her left side with the spider draped across her legs. One of the fangs had pierced her thigh, with several of the curled legs holding her tightly around her knees — the pain was agonising. The bar above the spider's head was now empty. She reached behind her neck and grabbing the hidden knife severed the fang and several of the spider's legs. She rolled out from under the spider and gingerly removed the fang from her leg, tears streaming down her face.

"How's my Health?"

"Fifty-five and slowly dropping, most likely from the venom."

Leah cast Healing on her leg and breathed deeply with relief as the pain eased.

"I can't deal with all those messages again. Just summarise what happened?"

"I think you should read some of them as just before you attacked you apparently did something to activate your Ki. That, when added to the critical attack destroyed the spider with one hit. You were hurt by the penetrating fang and venom. You received 256 Experience Points."

"Let's harvest the spider and then I'll look at the Ki message."

You have harvested:

1 Vial of Orumeck's Worker Drone Venom

1 Orumeck's Worker Drone Fangs*

3 Orumeck's Worker Drone Serrated Spikes*

* Note: A skilled Smith may be able to use these items.

You've used a new active skill: Ki Attack *(Novice Level 1)*

Current Skill Level: Novice Level 1

You have activated your Ki for use in Attack. It is vital when seeking to activate your Ki automatically that you be both calm and focused. This is measurable by an analysis of your brain activity and your simulated rate of respiration.

Alternatively, you may activate your Ki manually by saying 'Ki Attack'.

Cost Automatic Activation (Novice) : (Your Level) KP/sec

Cost Manual Activation (Novice): ((10 / Ki Level) x Your Level) KP/sec

Effect: At Novice level 1 you will receive a 10% increase to the base damage of a given move.

Please note that this is both a freeform and a manually activated skill. Your repeated freeform use will modify its success rate. For more information on activation and use, please read the detailed explanation.

Do you wish to receive further notifications concerning this skill?

[Yes] [No]

"No."

Leah sat for a while and considered the best way to deal with the spiders. She needed some way to attack from a distance, from above or from behind. Leah wasn't keen on being impaled on any of the spikes. From her bag, she removed one of the spider's leg spikes. Using her knife to split one end of the longest stick, Leah inserted a spider spike into the groove and tied it with a strip of cloth cut from the canvas sheet Goll had given her. She was ready to hunt spiders. As she put away the cloth, she noticed the scorpion venom. Carefully she opened a vial and put a drop on the end of the new spear. "Let's see how they like it," she thought.

Leah searched the rest of the cave but found no more spiders; all she found was a tunnel leading deeper into the extensive cave system. She headed into the tunnel. Soon she reached another cavern, and after examining the entrance, she slowly entered. This time she saw the spider before it tracked her. As Leah carefully advanced, she slowed her breathing until she felt the strange quivering. The spider had seen her approaching and began moving in her direction. She didn't give it a chance to raise its front legs but charged right in. At the last second, she veered sharply to the left, just missing the turning spider. She thrust her new spear deep into the abdomen before dragging it out. Leah turned to see the spider writhing in agony, its leg spikes striking a random tattoo on the stone floor. Leah moved behind the spider and finished it with several stabs from her spear. Smiling, she harvested the loot and carefully moved on.

In the third cave, things didn't go so well. In her anticipation of an easy victory, Leah didn't activate her Ki and rushed in, forgetting to put more scorpion poison on the blade. She found she wasn't quite quick enough to get past the spider and although she impaled it she received a deep gash from a swinging leg. When she turned to finish it off, it wasn't writhing on the floor but was rapidly advancing and beginning to raise its front legs. Leah slammed the spear through the mouth, but her momentum wasn't enough to pierce through into the abdomen. In the end, she killed it but received several cuts and a deep wound from a spider leg that penetrated deep into her bicep. She took over ten minutes to recover, eating some trail bread to help speed things up. She castigated herself for making such a simple stupid mistake but reasoned that now was the time to learn such things. She checked her spear, vowing not to be foolish again. Leah re-tied the spear and re-poisoned it.

Leah peered into the fourth cave and saw not one but three spiders. Each was Level 3, and they were spaced almost equidistantly around the room. The spiders moved deliberately — as if keeping patrol. She ducked back into the tunnel to consider a possible winning strategy. She turned all three remaining sticks into short spears and dripped some poison on them. She held three in her left hand and one in the right and crept into the cave. The spiders immediately started moving toward her. She calmed herself, activating her Ki, and rushed toward the closest spider. After spearing it, she had no time to finish it off as the other spiders were rapidly moving toward her. She ran toward the closest undamaged spider and speared it. Without stopping she ran on several paces before glancing behind to see what was happening. Both hurt spiders had regained their feet and were heading in her direction; the other was almost on her. Swapping spears, she charged the healthy spider and continued her attack. Soon all three were dead. She'd reached Level 3 and discovered that when she went up a level, her Health, Stamina, Mana and Ki refreshed to 100%. She sat down to assign her points. She needed to increase her Ki Attack Skill Level. After the last fight she had run out of Ki, and if increasing Ki levels meant the improved chance a successful attack, then combat times would be shorter. She added two to Intelligence, one to Strength and two to Agility.

Two more rooms yielded six more drone spiders. Leah was glad that the spider spikes all occupied a single slot, as she now had thirty-six in the bag and four on the ends of her spears. Unfortunately, as she increased in level the spiders gave fewer Experience Points — each spider was now only giving 200 EP. Leah had used half the first vial of scorpion venom. The next room, as far as she could tell, was empty. She waited

NOVEMBER 18, 2073 C

and watched, but nothing moved. She edged into the cavern and slowly crept around the perimeter. She noticed a slight discolouration on the ground. It was a circular area about the size of a dinner plate. Nothing moved. Leah reached for a belt knife and, stepping back, lobbed the knife onto the lighter patch. As it landed, the patch exploded outwards and a volley-ball-sized spider erupted out of the ground, attacking the knife. Five nearby holes also sprang open, and spiders jumped out. Leah moved away but saw the six spiders spinning in her direction, leaping toward her. Her stick fighting experience came to the rescue: with a spear in each hand, sticks whirling, it was over in a matter of moments. There were six dead spiders, all of them missing limbs, two neatly cut in half. She looked steadily at one, and its title appeared with an empty Health bar.

Orumeck's Trapdoor Drone (Level 1) 50HP 50EP

The Trapdoor Drones had small spiked legs and needle-like sharp fangs: They were solid black except for a tiny red fang shaped marking on the back. She checked the floor of the cavern and saw the plate-sized lighter patches everywhere. She recovered her knife and harvested the spiders.

You have harvested:

1 Orumeck's Trapdoor Drone Fangs*

2 Orumeck's Trapdoor Drone Spikes**

* Note: A Leather Worker or skilled Seamstress may be able to use these items.

** Note: A carpenter may be able to use these items.

"OK, so needles and nails, it looks like I'm going to have a lot of them."

Taking a deep breath, Leah moved to the next patch. This time she used a rock from the floor of the cave and stood a bit further back before lobbing it. It took almost forty minutes to clear the floor. In all, there were three groups of six, two of nine and a final patch with eighteen. After the group of eighteen, Leah was left with only twenty-three Health points, five Stamina points, and no Ki points. The fifty-four Trapdoor Drones had given a total of 2,484 Experience Points. She began to move toward the next tunnel.

"Excuse me, Leah," Gèng interrupted her. "You have only one and a half hours before it is dark outside, although you have three hours before you need to exit the Pod and have something to eat. If you are going to stay the night, I remind you that you might want to communicate this to your home. I can send a communication to your mother if you desire."

Leah stood silently, thinking through all the options before agreeing. "OK Gèng, please tell Mum I'm staying the night. I will be back tomorrow morning. Also, let Jimmy know I will drop in and let him know what has been happening. But now, the spiders!"

She found several strands of web drifting across the doorway of the next cavern. She decided not to enter but reached forward and carefully touched the web. It was sticky and adhered to her hand. She reached out and cut some with a knife. It cut readily enough, but there had been some resistance. She grabbed some more and tried to cut several strands at once. Again it was doable, but she had needed to add considerable force. She took a step back to think for a while. She wasn't going to survive if she wasn't able to move. As she sat, she noticed her hand becoming numb. A message appeared:

You have been poisoned by the web from one of Orumeck's Webspinner Drones (Level 4) 460HP 250EP

Damage 1: 5HP/second for 10 seconds or healed (HP 159/164)

This web takes several seconds to begin working. If poisoned multiple times the effects will accumulate until you become paralysed.

Leah quickly scraped the web off her hand and healed herself.

She retreated further into the tunnel. Returning to the Trapdoor Drones' cave, she examined the covers used by the trapdoor spiders; the covers were made of webbing. Taking out her fire-starting kit, Leah struck the steel with the flint. A few sparks flew off, but none came close to the cover. She tried again. This time several sparks landed on the cover, and it started to smoulder. Leah blew on it until suddenly, it burst into flame. She knelt and watched it burn for about a minute before it fizzled out. Moving carefully, Leah went back to the doorway of Webspinner Drones' cavern and very gingerly, using one of her sticks, she collected some webs. Taking the web back to the trapdoor room she checked if they would burn as well; not only did they burn, the fire started instantly and burned with greater intensity.

Smiling, Leah grabbed as many covers as she could and returned to the Webspinner room. Kneeling down at the entrance Leah set a trap-door cover on fire. Once it was burning, she held another in the fire until it was just beginning to burn. She turned and threw the burning cover into the Webspinner doorway as if throwing a frisbee. She reached for another and repeated the action. Before she threw a third, a huge screech echoed from the web room, and the room suddenly blazed with light. She could see spiders outlined in flames. They were screeching and scurrying about trying to evade the inferno. Several made it out of the fire and scampered toward her. A single stab was enough to finish most of them off. She stood there watching until the last of the flames died. She examined the Health bar of every spider and made sure they were dead. There had been twelve of them. When the last one died a message appeared:

Personal Achievement: You have reached Level 5

You require 4,820 Experience Points to reach Level 6.

You have an additional 5 Character points to distribute.

You have 1 Skill point to distribute.

She put all the spare trap-door covers in her bag and then went to harvest one of the Webspinner Drones.

You have harvested:

*2 Orumeck's Webspinner Drone Spinnerets *

*2 Vials of Orumeck's Webspinner Paralysing Poison ***

* Note: A weaver may be able to use these items.

** Note: May be used by healers and those who make potions.

Moving carefully, she harvested the remaining spiders. This had been the most satisfying room to clear so far. She'd used her brains far more than her muscles, and that felt good. She sat down to distribute her points.

"Gèng, I have a new skill called 'Duel Wield', and it is already at level two. Was there a message?"

"Yes, I have been withholding them. Do you wish to see it?"

"Not really, summarise please."

"Your increased Intelligence Points and your use of both hands with the trapdoor spiders has earned an increase in that level."

Well, that threw a spanner in the works. It seemed as though all the Characteristics were useful. Leah knew she was supposed to specialise: everyone said you couldn't be everything and do everything. She just wasn't sure what would be most useful. She imagined the next room would be worse but had no idea how to prepare. In the end, she added one to Constitution, and two to both Agility and Intelligence. Her Skill/Spell point went into Ki Attack.

The tunnel leading from the room was longer and wider than

before. Leah moved slowly, and as quietly as possible. She looked side to side, searching every shadow. The further she walked, the straighter and less curved the walls seemed: more fashioned than formed. The ceiling curved upward to a central point, like a gothic arch. The light faded and even using her night vision, she was barely able to penetrate the gloom. Up ahead the tunnel looked like it ended. When she got closer, she noticed it was not an ending, but a doorway. A pair of solid, wooden doors blocked the exit. She carefully reached forward and gave it a gentle push, but it didn't budge. She pushed harder and still no movement. She noticed a keyhole as large a thumb: no wonder it wouldn't open — it was locked. Leah removed a Trapdoor Drone spike from her bag and slid it into the lock but couldn't reach the tumblers. She lit one of the Trapdoor Drone covers and in the extra light searched the darkened tunnel for some clue but came away empty-handed.

She must have missed a key, something hidden. Now, where could it be? She ran back down the corridor into the Webspinner's cave. She walked around looking at every curve and in each minor hollow. About two-thirds of the way around she saw a section of wall which was far too regular, it was a square. Lichen almost entirely covered it, except for one small oddly shaped piece about the size of a coin. She noticed that the lichen was a shade lighter than the rest she had seen. Taking her knife, she tapped the wall, but there was no echo or hollow sound. She ran the blade around the edge but couldn't find a groove or a hidden catch. She stared at the square for some time before noticing small patches of lichen nearby that were also a lighter shade. One was the same size and shape of the missing bit. She slid her knife under the patch and was elated when it detached from the wall. As soon as she filled in the square, it shimmered and disappeared to reveal a cavity with a bag, a key and a rolled up scroll.

In the bag were two coins and a gold spider ring. The legs curled to make the band. The body and fangs were similar to the Webspinner Drones and shaped to lie upon the finger. The abdomen was a dark purple crystal, finely cut, and the size and shape of a split pea.

A Webspinner Ring of Orumeck (Max PL 50)

This ring was made by Mage Orumeck during the time of his exile from Sihirbazlari.

For information on its use, please visit the Dunyanin Official Manual.

"Gèng, I'll keep this for later. I need to read up on rings. Please remind me."

The coins were gold, but each had an embossed Webspinner Spider on one side and what looked like a proud elf on the other.

A Gold Coin of Orumeck

This coin was made by Mage Orumeck during the time of his exile from Sihirbazlari. Full of pride, he minted several thousand coins with his image. He embossed them with some of his favourite creations.

Value: Equivalent to 1 gold*

* Note: Some collectors may pay more for such a rare coin.

"Note to self, don't use these coins yet."

"Leah, a routine message has appeared regarding the coins."

"OK, let's have a look."

World Quest: Collect the Coins - Gold (0/1,000)

Many people throughout time have minted coins. They are scattered throughout Dunyanin. Collect these coins.

Difficulty: Easy to Impossible

Reward 1 if successful: (Number of Coins collected) x (Player Level) x 100 Experience Points for each coin.

Reward 2 if successful: 2 x (Number of Coins collected) gold Coins.

Consequences of failure: None

Do you wish to accept this Quest?

[Yes] [No]

"Yes."

"You have just received 513 Experience Points and two gold Coins."

Leah turned to the scroll:

Orumeck's Spell of Summoning - *Novice Level*

This is a dark spell of summoning. The spell summons one of Orumeck's creations. The creature is yours to command.

Do you wish to use this scroll?

[Yes] [No]

"No, well not yet. I'll think about it."

"Gèng, If there is a quest for gold coins, then I imagine there is one for silver and copper. I think I need to go back and check the other rooms before heading through the door. I also have to find that key."

"Affirmative!"

Leah, aware her time was running out before she was required to take a break, moved quickly back through each of the rooms. The Trapdoor room had a similar cache containing four silver coins, a silver ring, and a vial filled with a fine purple powder:

World Quest: Collect the Coins - Silver (0/5,000)

Many people throughout time have minted coins. They are scattered throughout Dunyanin. Collect these coins.

Difficulty: Easy to Impossible

Reward 1 if successful: (Number of Coins collected) x (Player Level) x 50 Experience Points for each coin.

Reward 2 if successful: 2 x (Number of Coins collected) silver Coins.

Consequences of failure: None

Do you wish to accept this Quest?

[Yes] [No]

"Yes."

A Trapdoor Ring of Orumeck (Max PL50)

This ring was made by Mage Orumeck during the time of his exile from Sihirbazlari.

For information on its use, please visit the Dunyanin Official Manual.

The ring was almost identical to the golden one although the body of the spider resembled the Trapdoor Drones.

Ground Crystallised Spider Blood

A rare ingredient often used in Alchemical potions.

In the second last room of Worker Drones, she discovered a cache with ten copper coins, another ring and a small key.

World Quest: Collect the Coins - Copper (0/10,000)

Many people throughout time have minted coins. They are scattered throughout Dunyanin. Collect these coins.

Difficulty: Easy to Impossible

Reward 1 if successful: (Number of Coins collected) x (Player Level) x 10 Experience Points for each coin.

Reward 2 if successful: 2 x (Number of Coins collected) copper Coins.

Consequences of failure: None

Do you wish to accept this Quest?

[Yes] [No]

"Yes."

A Worker Ring of Orumeck (Max PL50)

This ring was made by Mage Orumeck during the time of his exile from Sihirbazlari.

For information on its use, please visit the Dunyanin Official Manual.

The ring was almost identical to the other two, but the body of the spider resembled the Worker Drones, and it was made of copper.

The Key to Orumeck's Spider Amulet

Orumeck created many Amulets during his extended life. In them, he stored fragments of his most powerful spell. This is a key to one of those amulets.

Note: This is not unique as during his life he made over 200 amulets and hid 20 copies of the spell. To date, no complete collection has been found.

She found nothing in the other rooms except for the first. In this, she found a large key and a bag of small purple gems.

The Key to Orumeck's Basement

You are in the escape tunnel from one of Orumeck's safe houses, his 'Cavern'. To enter the main cavern, you will need this key. The cavern has become home to one of his many creations: Orumeck's Spider Queen.

Orumeck's Minor Soulstones (Spider)

These stones were by Mage Orumeck during the time of his exile from Sihirbazlari. If the stones are crushed when fully charged, they provide the owner with a store of excess Mana.

For information on their use, please visit the Dunyanin Official Manual.

Leah rushed back through the caves and double checked everything, but no luck. She then headed for the door. Gèng said,

"Leah, it is time for you to take a break. I think it would be advisable to log out and have dinner. You have been here for nine hours, virtual-time."

"I thought that when in a game you couldn't log out in a dungeon!"

"In Dunyanin, as only one person or group can enter any given dungeon at any one time, it is permitted to have a break. The dungeons are created in separate realities. Two groups can do a dungeon, but each is alone. Time moves on. The two groups might compete for a resource or prize. The game keeps track of who finds it first and denies it to the other team. You can have a short break and then return."

"So, someone could be doing this same dungeon and might beat me and be first through."

"It is possible. However, I am confident that others will hardly have made it to First Bridge, much less found the hidden entrance. You haven't posted where it is, and the closest people can be sure of is the town."

"All right."

Leah sat down, back against the door and dissolved into mist.

Back in her space, Leah noticed that the room seemed different. It was sharper as if the artist had spent more time to get all the details right.

"The room looks better than before, are you working on it?"

"Yes, I have been manipulating the various factors to understand how to create a better space."

"Well, it's looking good. Could you sort through my bag and get the loot in some order? I'll look through it before I go back."

Leah lay on the sofa, closed her eyes and woke back in her small real-world room where she showered and dressed.

"I'm hungry, Gèng, can you transfer a platinum coin into virtual credits and I'll go get a snack and some dinner from the machines. It's too expensive to eat all the time but today is a special day."

Leah headed to the foyer and began looking through all the machines, trying to decide what to eat. She was just about to buy a one virtual credit container of dried ramen, when a voice behind her said, "I wouldn't if I were you, I think that ramen has been here forever."

Leah turned and came face to face with a boy several years older than herself. He was tall, with a mop of messy hair, and he had green eyes. She didn't notice anything else, just the eyes. She had never seen such eyes before.

"Hello, my name is Jackson. Welcome to Purgatory."

"Purgatory? What do you mean, Purgatory?"

"That's what we call it, those of us who live down here in the basement. Up there is heaven, and only hell could be worse."

"Oh, yeah, sorry! My name is Leah, and it's my first day. Um! How long have you been here?"

"Just under a year, I've got my V-day party in four days. You're welcome to come?"

"V-day?"

"Yep, V-day! Down here we celebrate every anniversary of the day we went virtual. Many of us come from poorer families who can't afford to own extra pods and have to rent them. I've three older brothers, and I'm the second one who's had to come here. My family only had enough to get me a developed AI, but no Pod. So every year, 'those who suffer', like me, invite people into their world for a huge party. If you want, I can send your AI the IP address and you can come. I'd like that."

"I'll, um, think about it. It sounds great but I'm still trying to work out everything, and I'm still a bit shell-shocked. So, um, why no ramen?"

"Well, its been there, they say, since the beginning of time, I've never heard of anyone eating it. If you look closely, you can just make out the 'use by' on one of the packets."

Jackson peered in the window and finally pointed to a packet of Chicken Ramen which was turned slightly to the side. Leah peered in and could make out a date '13.07.69'. She chuckled.

"Thanks for saving my life. What do you suggest then?"

"Well, if you're going to eat in, then most of us go for the frozen stuff: a lasagna or maybe the Chicken Madras, it's good. There is a small supermarket a few streets away from here. It's where we shop sometimes. I can show you if you like!"

Leah was flustered. "I'd like that, just not today. It's my first day, and I've so much to do."

Jackson shrugged, "No worries, you've got my address. Just let me know when, and I'll walk you."

He opened the door and headed out.

Leah hesitated, she took a few steps back and forth, and finally following him out the door she called, "Hey, wait up, I'd love to come."

Jackson walked with her, chatting away. He led her out onto the street and along the fence line. She hardly said anything as he talked about anything and everything. The supermarket was only a few blocks away, and Leah started to enjoy the outing. Jackson needed some bread and milk, and he finished quickly. Leah, on the other hand, looked carefully through the shop, and in the end, bought some bulk ramen and orange juice concentrate. On the way back Jackson insisted on carrying her groceries. He monopolised the conversation all the way back, telling her story after story about his family. Leah had dreaded an awkward moment, but none arrived. When they arrived back at the facility, he gave her the groceries, grinned and said, "I'll see you Wednesday 7 pm, my world?"

"I'll try and be there," Leah replied, smiling.

As she closed her room door, she turned and sighed deeply. "Did you see those eyes?"

Gèng responded, "I'm not sure which eyes you're referring to."

"Jackson's eyes, they were so beautiful! No, don't say anything. I was just talking to myself."

She had a glass of orange juice and a bowl of ramen, and as she sat, she pondered why the eyes fascinated her. She had enjoyed the walk and was surprised that Jackson had been so friendly. But why the eyes?

After eating, she showered and headed back to the Pod. Once again in her world, she sat on the sofa and said, "So where is the stuff to go through?"

Gèng directed her into a new room it had fashioned. Around the walls, placed carefully on long tables, was the loot from various fights as well as the medallions and money.

"Let's leave most of the stuff here. I'll take the weapons and the vials of poison. Include two of each sort of claw or spike, just in case. The fire-starter, some trap-door covers and what's left of the waterproof sheet. My water bottles. What else?"

"You must take the material to gather Farnel's remedy. Do you want the keys, rings and maybe a few coins?"

"Definitely the keys, let me read up on the rings. I'll take two of each coin. Put the spider coins to the side. Let's not use any of them yet. Start with the copper ring."

Worker Ring of Orumeck (1/10,000)

Ring Level (1-20) Max Player Level 30

This is one of many such rings made by Mage Orumeck during the time of his exile from Sihirbazlari. When charged, it fires a poisoned spike of condensed Mana similar to the fangs of the Worker Drone. The bearer of the ring is immune to the poison. When using the ring freeform, curl the finger the ring is on depressing the band while aiming the ring at the intended target.

Cost: 10% of full charge

Effect: A spike of pure Mana will fire from the ring.

Range: Ring Level x 2 metres

To read the full description including information on ring activation, please see the Dunyanin Manual.

Trapdoor Ring of Orumeck (1/1,000)

Ring Level (1-20) Max Player Level 30

This is one of many such rings made by Mage Orumeck during the time of his exile from Sihirbazlari. When charged, it conceals the bearer with a web of condensed Mana similar to that produced by the Trapdoor spiders he created. Only the bearer of the ring can see through this web to surprise and attack an enemy. When using the ring freeform, curl the finger the ring is on depressing the band.

Cost: 100% of full charge

Please note that any movement will disperse the shield.

Effect: You will be concealed behind a shield of pure Mana for 3 x (Ring Level x Player Level) seconds.

To read the full description including information on ring activation, please see the Dunyanin Manual.

Webspinner Ring of Orumeck (1/100)

Ring Level (1-20) Max Player Level 30

This ring was made by Mage Orumeck during the time of his exile from Sihirbazlari. When charged, it will produce a cord of condensed Mana similar to that produced by the Webspinner spiders he created. Only the bearer of the ring is immune to its poison and can escape its binding.

Cost Type 1: 10% of full charge Cost Type 2: 100% of full charge

Preset Activation 1: When using the ring freeform, curl the finger the ring is on, quickly depressing and releasing the band while aiming the ring at the intended target.

Preset Activation 2: When using the ring freeform, curl the finger the ring is on, hold while aiming the ring at the intended target.

Effect 1: A cord of pure Mana will fire from the ring and wrap around the target. The target will be immobilised for between 2 and 30 seconds. The formula used is complex and relates to the Characteristics of both the target and the bearer, also the Ring Level.

Effect 2: A cord of pure Mana will be ejected from the ring and attach to the target. On release of the band, the other end will be attached to the ring bearer who may then move and change the attachment point. The cord will remain in existence for between 10-300 seconds and is scaled depending on the Ring Level.

To read the full description including information on ring activation, please see the Dunyanin Manual.

Leah tried the rings on and practised depressing the bands. Nothing happened. She decided which fingers felt the most natural for aiming and in the end she put all three rings on her left hand, keeping the right hand free for a weapon.

Finally, she said, "Gèng, it would help for me to know how my Health is going during a battle. Could you overlay a tiny bar at the top of my vision?"

"Indeed I shall overlay four, Health, Stamina, Mana and Ki. Would you like them in different colours or with labels?"

"Different colours, HP in green, SP in yellow, MP in Blue and Ki in white. If any are getting low, then flashing red."

Finally, with everything ready, Leah stepped back into through the arch.

As soon as Leah arrived in Dunyanin, messages appeared requesting a hierarchy to charge the three rings. It took half an hour for the rings to load. During this time she carefully rechecked the rooms but found nothing. She did discover that the lichen, when scraped off the wall, continued to glow. She cut several squares from her diminishing supply of waterproof cloth and collected as much as she could. She also tied several rolled up trap-door covers to the end of the remaining plain fighting stick, just in case she needed a torch.

When the rings charged, she spent some time shooting stalactites. The spikes were a dark purple and travelled almost too fast for her to see, however, she could see them chip away at the stalactites. Briefly touching the Webspinner Ring caused a web to wrap itself around the target. When she held the Webspinner Ring down, a line shot from the ring and attached itself to the stalactite. As soon as it hit, the web went tight, and Leah felt the rope end fasten itself to her fist. She pulled, and it came loose. Leah was able to attach it to the floor. Finally, she checked her statistics and distributed her points.

ATHERLEAH (Level 5) (1000/5000) (+2.5%)

Characteristics: Points Total (Assigned, Racial, Location), 0 Undistributed

Strength (S): 10 (10)

Constitution (C): 7 (7)

Agility (A): 12 (10, 2)

Wisdom (W): 7 (5, 2)

Intelligence (I): 5 (5)

Luck (L): 8 (3, 0, 5)

Statistics: (Available, Capacity)

Health: 100+(S+C)xPL: (185, 185) HP

Stamina: 100+(C+A)xPL: (195, 195) SP

Mana: 100+(W+I)xPL: (160, 160) MP

Ki: 100+(W+[S+A]/2)xPL: (190, 190) KP

Leah was ready to enter what she assumed was the final room.

She slowly inserted the key and hoped that it would be silent: no such luck. The click echoed through the corridor. Worse, it preceded a cacophony from beyond the door, screeches warred with clanging and the staccato of claws hitting the stone floor. Leah waited as the noise continued and then slowly faded away before dying. After waiting for several minutes, she pressed her ear to the door and hearing nothing; she gently eased the door open. A voice, cold and harsh, spoke in the darkness, "Come, come inside little fly. We are waiting."

Leah had no choice about entering, so she decided to be bold and confident. She calmed herself and then pushing the door open wide, strolled into the room and called out. "Who are you calling fly, Spider?" At her entrance, the noise started all over again. She walked into the large cavern that had been shaped, here and there, with tools, to create a small amphitheatre. It was thirty metres across and had four terraces slowly rising toward the cavern ceiling. A different type of spider filled each terrace. On the lowest rung were the Trapdoor Drones, then the Webspinners. On the third rung were a new type of spider. These were the largest so far, their heads probably at the level of her chest. They were purple and had long legs with a spike at each joint. Each one was balancing on six legs and used the other two as arms; each arm ended in a sharp scythe-shaped claw. She looked intently at one and words appeared:

Orumeck's Warrior Drone (Level 9) 900HP 900EP

Furthest away, the highest was covered with Worker Drones, each of them skittering on the stone terrace.

Terrified, she slowly walked through to the centre of the amphitheatre and heard the doors slam shut behind her. Turning deliberately, Leah saw a platform directly above the entrance, and the Queen resting on it. The Queen's head, just above the eyes, was ringed in gold. Her abdomen was the size of a small car, and like the warriors, she stood on six legs. One arm ended in a sword, the other in a claw with sharp dagger-shaped talons. Hanging around her neck was a medallion. Her mouth, ringed by fangs, opened, and the harsh voice resounded around the room.

"Yes, a little fly, now freshly come into the trap. And what are you? Not human, not elf, a mixture perhaps? A cross between a house fly and a dragonfly. Well, I am the Queen, and I welcome you, to this, our games. We have waited long to feed, but I think you merely presage a feast. Orumeck prophesied that one day the doors would open and start a trickle of juicy morsels into our larder. You are the first. Why have you come?"

Leah had no idea what to say. She didn't think anything would help. But bravado had kept her alive this far, and nothing was likely to prevent some battle, so she remained silent. She raised her spear and took a defensive stance while staring at the queen.

Orumeck's Spider Queen (Level 13) 1300HP 1150EP

Finally, in the silence, she said, "You! I've come for you."

Again the sound of claws on stone and shrieks filled the air. It settled slowly, and Leah calmed herself for what she knew was coming.

"You may have defeated a few of my subjects, but you are not worthy to fight me. You must earn that right. You will face a collection of my drones in battle. Should you win all four battles, I may give you the right of challenge. Do you agree?"

"I'll agree, except your subjects might take it poorly when I kill you."

"You will not face me, for you will surely die much earlier. However if by some miracle you beat me, I will command my subjects to let you leave. Is this sufficient?"

"Almost," said Leah. "I also get your medallion and your treasure."

The Queen bobbed up and down in mirth as a dry rasping sound that passed as laughter echoed around the cavern. "You may have the medallion, fly, but my treasure will go to my daughter as the next queen."

"Your medallion and half your treasure."

Again the Queen laughed, "All right fly, my medallion and anything you find in the cavern but nothing else! I have spoken. Prepare for your first battle."

Unique Boss Quest: Battle the Queen

You have bargained with Orumeck's Queen. Should you defeat her drones in four battles, she will do battle with you.

Note: This area is usually completed with victory in four battles and the gift of the amulet to the victor.

Difficulty: Very Hard

Reward 1: If successful, you will receive Orumeck's Spider Amulet.

Reward 2: If successful, you will be permitted to leave alive.

Reward 3: If successful, you will be permitted to plunder the Cavern of Treasure.

Consequences of failure: Death

You may not refuse this quest.

Four Worker Drones crawled down from their tier, over the bodies and down the wall onto the amphitheatre floor. Leah stared at them and saw they were no longer level three but level six.

Orumeck's Worker Drones (Level 6) 600HP 450EP

She needed to spread them apart. Running to the right side, she angled in toward the closest spider. Aiming the Webspinner Ring, she shot at the legs, catching the front two; the spider ploughed into the ground. Leah spun around and buried the spear deep into the head. She then turned and ran as fast as she could away from the other three who were trying to get around the downed spider thrashing on the ground. She turned and waited. One of the spiders was in the lead; this was her next victim. She repeated her previous attack, except this time, instead of running away, she ran at the next spider who started to rear up. Using the Worker Ring, she sent three Mana darts into the open mouth. She knew it wouldn't poison it, but it did some damage. She grabbed a knife from her belt and slashed at the legs as she ran past. Two legs dropped to the ground twitching slightly. Leah led the healthy spider in an arc back toward the first spider, who had just regained its feet and was heading toward Leah. As she got close, she leapt into the air and over the spider, mid-flight she fired the Worker Ring several times down into the abdomen. On landing, she turned and bound the healthy spider just as it came around the side of the damaged one. The other two wounded spiders were near, but she had time, spearing both spiders close to her and then using her knife to slash at their legs. By the time she moved on, they were still alive but unable to do more than drag themselves after her. It took several minutes of running and attacking, but soon the drones were dead. She turned to look at the queen while checking on her various bars. Her Ki and Stamina were hovering at about half.

She needed a break before another fight. She had used most of the Mana from her rings, and they needed time to recharge. She grabbed some bread from her bag and chewed while she walked back to the centre of the field.

"So Queen," she said, "do you want to modify the deal? I'll let you live if you'll hand everything over."

"Arrogant fly. I'll add to the deal if you beat the next challenge with all your Health. What do you say? If not, then you forgo looking for anything in the cavern. Deal?"

"What will you add?"

"A weapon of your choice from my treasure. My daughter will bring three of the best pieces, and you can choose one. Deal?"

Unique Boss Quest: Battle the Queen - Side Bet

You have bet with Orumeck's Queen that you will finish the next battle with full Health.

Difficulty: Very Hard

Reward if successful: You will receive a weapon of your choice from the Queen's treasure. Her daughter will bring three of the best pieces, and you can choose one.

Consequences of failure: You will not be able to plunder the cavern for treasure.

Do you wish to accept this bet?

[Yes] [No]

"Deal!"

Thirty-six Trapdoor Drones crawled slowly down onto the field. A quick look confirmed they were all several levels above the previous Trapdoor Drones she had faced. There was nowhere to run, so she grabbed the two spears with blades and raced toward the spiders. Slashing and running, she attacked furiously. Soon she had her back to the wall; this was what she had intended. She had several needle wounds and a deep cut on one leg. But she had always been good with the fighting sticks, and her speed and agility kept the spiders at arm's length. Slowly she whittled them away until the spider bodies surrounded her. There were a couple still wriggling when she stopped. She had levelled up toward the end of the fight, but she pulled all the needles out then ate some bread and healed herself before killing the final Trapdoor Spider. She had left it with only a couple of legs but unable to move. She pushed her way out of the pile and wandered into the centre of the ring.

"I'd like to make my choice now, Queen. Have your daughter bring the best three weapons." The whole amphitheatre exploded with noise as the spiders chittered and moved.

"Oh no, fly, you were damaged during the battle."

"Yes, but we agreed that I would 'end' the battle with all my Health. Your last drone was not 'killed' until I had full Health. Now, unless your word means nothing, please bring the weapons."

The Queen was visibly angry. Her limbs shook, and venom dripped from her fangs. Finally, she went still and said, "Well played, fly!" She waved one of her legs, and a Warrior Drone scuttled from the Cavern.

"My daughter will be informed. I'm sure she will come to see the mighty fly. Should we make another bet, fly? This time with no tricks, you can't lose any Health."

Leah thought for a bit. "Not this time Queen, maybe another bet when it's just you and me. I'll think of something by then."

A smaller version of the queen entered carrying three weapons. She descended into the amphitheatre and lay them before Leah, then took a step backwards. There was a bow with quiver, a staff and a straight thin-bladed sword.

The Long Bow of Guzeltuya

This bow is of ancient times and belonged to the Elven land's most loved daughter, Princess Guzeltuya. The Mage Orumeck was said to have seduced Guzeltuya from her betrothed. Together they fled, and while Orumech was later brought before the High King to pay for his misdeeds, Guzeltuya was never seen again. This bow disappeared with her. The quiver is enchanted, any arrows pulled from it will return if they are undamaged.

Minimum: Level 100 (A80, S43)

Arrow return: 2 Arrows/minute

Base Damage: 650HP

Binds on pickup

Merdiven

A named staff. This staff was companion to Bazlari, founder and First Mage of Sihirbazlari. It was said that so much Mana infused this staff that it would sometimes talk with its bearer, and at times fight on their behalf.

?

?

?

Binds on pickup

The Signet Sword of Clan Karanliklar

The Horse Lords control the clans, and the clans control the plains of Ovalar. Each Horse Lord is bequeathed a signet weapon, a symbol of their power. Clan Karanliklar, once the richest clan, is bereft of power for its weapon was lost at war when its Lord fell in battle. Taken in spoil, the sword was lost to the clan.

Minimum: Level 50 (A47)

Base Damage: 350HP

Binds on pickup

Leah wasn't clear on what the question marks meant, but the staff was the only weapon she could currently use. It was about three centimetres in diameter, so a bit thicker than she liked, and made of dark wood with a faint silvery grain. On one end was a dark metallic Morningstar, the spikes short but sharp. On the other end, a plain metal cap to use when needing a walking stick. She picked it up.

As the Queen's daughter collected the bow and rapier, Leah put the staff in her bag, turned to the Queen and said, "Don't put them away, you may need a stake for a further wager after this battle."

Without replying, the Queen gestured, and the Queen's daughter settled at the Queen's side. She bobbed her head, and two Webspinner Drones crawled into the arena. Leah ran toward the closest. As she got near, it raised its body to attack, and Leah used her forward movement to fling the spear directly at the mouth. Her aim was spot-on, and the momentum drove the spear deep into its abdomen. She pulled a knife and slashed at the legs. Using the dying spider as a barrier between her and the undamaged drone, Leah kept slicing and stabbing until it was dead. Aiming her ring at the remaining spider, she shot it with several Mana spikes. As it reared back, she dove forward under the spider and stabbed several times upwards before rolling out the other side. It was then a matter of minutes to finish it off.

As she walked back to the middle, she took the scorpion venom and dripped some more on each of her blades. She took a long drink, then said, "So, Queen, tell me who's next, and I'll think about that bet."

The Queen signalled, and one of the Warrior Drones climbed into the arena.

"OK, I'll make a bet. Both those other weapons if I end this fight having taken no damage. If I'm hurt, then I won't plunder the cavern after killing you. What do you say?"

"Fly, I might consider one weapon, but not both."

"Maybe, but what will you wager for both?"

The Queen was silent and thoughtful. Leah didn't mind; she needed the time to recuperate. She had something to eat and watched the various bars slowly fill. Finally, the Queen stirred.

"Fly, I'll make the wager with one and gift you the other. The wager is as you said, but the gift comes with a price. I know that Travellers, such as you, are reborn should you die. My price is that you take the death crystal formed of my heart's blood to the Elven realm of Göksel-Orman should I perish. Orumeck created my ancestors by using the blood he drained from Guzeltuya's body after he killed her. I have no lingering memory of hers, but there is some yearning to return. Do we have a deal? The Sword for the wager, and the Bow for the price."

Unique Boss Quest: Battle the Queen - Side Bet 2

You have bet with Orumeck's Queen that you will finish the next battle without damage.

Difficulty: Extremely Hard

Reward if successful: You will receive the Signet Sword of Clan Karanliklar from the Queen's treasure.

Consequences of failure: You will not be able to plunder the cavern for treasure.

If you defeat Orumeck's Queen, you will receive the Long Bow of Guzeltuya, and in return, you will take the death crystal formed of her heart's blood to the Elven realm of Göksel-Orman and lay it to rest there.

Do you wish to accept this bet?

[Yes] [No]

"Deal."

"Let the battle begin!"

Leah checked all her equipment and turned to face the Warrior. She hoped this worked. The Warrior hurried forward. When it was still about five metres away, Leah reached behind her neck and flicked a knife forward. The poisoned knife flew straight and impaled one of the eyes. The spider reared back in pain and

Leah aimed for one of the six legs with the Webspinner Ring. Holding the button down, the rope shot forward and adhered to one of the spider's feet. Leah pulled hard and started running in a circle around the spider. The Warrior began lifting the leg but as it did Leah pulled harder, and the spider stumbled. She kept pulling and used the rope to trip the spider. As it fell to the ground, she quickly slashed the back legs, severing them. As it thrashed around, she systematically severed the other legs then stabbed it until it died.

She turned and once again walked to the middle. The Queen's daughter brought forward the sword and laid it on the ground. Leah put the sword in her bag, and said, "Your Majesty, may I collect my prizes from your dead warriors? If you kill me, I will miss the opportunity, and I have already earned them."

"Be quick, fly. I grow impatient to feed."

Leah quickly harvested the dead spiders, and as she did so, she said, "Gèng, I've got ten Characteristic points not yet distributed, add two to Strength, and four to both Constitution and Agility. The extra skill points add to Ki Attack."

She glanced up to see the Queen crawling into the arena. Leah grabbed the staff and a Warrior Scythe that she had harvested and ran straight at the Queen. Leah got there just as the Queen's two forelegs touched the ground. Swinging the staff, she slammed the Morningstar down onto the head of the queen. The Queen almost got her sword up in time, and the Morningstar ran down the right side of the head instead of landing square. Several of the Queen's eyes popped. The sword missed Leah, but an arm battered her and sent her flying. Leah's Health bar was already under half. She came to her feet and cast *Heal*. She had dropped the staff, and the Queen was coming straight at her. Leaving the staff, she ducked under the Queen's swinging claw and ran along the Queen's right side where the Queen couldn't see her. Using the scythe, she slashed at the legs as she ran past. The Queen had to turn around to chase Leah.

Leah had disappeared. The Queen trampled over the ground looking for Leah. As the Queen turned to see if Leah was on the opposite side, Leah, who had been standing frozen against the wall after triggering the Trapdoor Ring, raced forward and jumped as high as she could before plunging the scythe into the top of the Queen's abdomen. She allowed gravity to pull her back to earth while holding onto the scythe with all her might. It ripped open the abdomen with a huge gash. As Leah landed, she rolled right and ran to the staff. Holding the capped end, she swung in a full circle before slamming the Morningstar into one of the Queen's leg joints. The staff jarred loose from Leah's hands, but the joint cracked and the Queen stumbled. Leah grabbed the staff and ran along the Queen's right side again. This time she kept running in a circle, staying behind the Queen who was starting to slow down. Leah timed the next swing flawlessly and broke the Queen's sword arm. It was then a matter of attrition with Leah slowly tearing the Queen apart, joint by joint until she died.

Leah looked up at the stands; the spiders were just standing there, without moving. The dead Queen's daughter looked down and rasped. "I am now the Queen, and I honour my mother's bargains. We will leave. You may plunder this cavern but stay away from our nest. Keep your bargain and carry her death crystal to the Elven realm. Behind me is the tunnel from this cavern. When you leave, take the right branch, and you will find your way out. Turn left, and you will die."

The new Queen motioned, and the spiders filed out. Leah was exhausted, and after taking several deep breaths, she walked over to the dead Queen. Laying her hand on the Queen's body, Leah harvested the spoils.

You have harvested:

1 Orumeck's Spider Amulet

1 Death Crystal formed by the Heart Blood of Orumeck's Spider Queen*

2 Vials of Orumeck's Spider Queen Venom

2 Orumeck's Spider Queen Fangs**

4 Orumeck's Spider Queen Serrated Spikes**

1 Orumeck's Spider Queen Serrated Sword**

1 Orumeck's Spider Queen Claw**

* Regarding the item, you have an obligation.

** Note: A skilled Smith may be able to use these items.

Leah searched the amphitheatre but uncovered no treasure. Using the Trapdoor Ring, she climbed the wall and searched the tiers. She had not expected anything in the tiers, but the Queen had seemed reluctant for her to raid the cavern, so she wanted to search everywhere. Finally, she came to the Queen's platform.

She found the treasure. Next to the abandoned bow and quiver was a cavity and inside was a small chest. She pulled the chest out and opened it. Inside was a platinum coin, a pair of silver earrings, two scrolls and a large silver key. She took the key, closed the chest and dropped the chest into her bag.

"Gèng, I'll look at all the messages later. Just show me the one about the key. I want to see if there is something else I should look for."

The Key to Orumeck's Keep (1/5)

Orumeck lived in many places during his long life. His favourite was known as Orumeck's Keep. This is a key to open the door which has been closed for over four centuries. Orumeck left one of the keys with his Spider Queen for safe keeping. His choice was because in some small way he loved the murdered Princess.

Note: This is one of only five keys to the keep. None of the others has yet been found. Orumeck's Keep is steeped in legend. People will kill for this key.

Leah looked long and hard at the key, dropped it into her bag and headed into the tunnel.

The tunnel was straight as an arrow. Previously the cave system had seemed natural; this was no longer true. The walls were marked by countless spiders throughout the centuries, yet there was a uniformity, a smoothness to the tunnel that seemed artificial more than natural. No lichen lived on the walls, and it became almost too dark for even Leah's night vision. From her bag, she removed the torch she had made earlier and lit it. The darkness was pushed back, and with it, there was a scurrying as several spiders moved back out of its light.

Holding the torch in one hand and the staff in the other, Leah pressed on. The torch would only last a few minutes, and she needed to get as far along as she could. Despite the new Queen's assurances, Leah was still careful to keep a watchful eye ahead. After several minutes the light from the torch spilt out into a wide corridor running left and right. She briefly turned left, only to see the glitter of light reflecting off the spikes and scythes of several Warrior Drones.

Leah turned right, and although she was hesitant to leave the spiders at her back, she knew there was very little, if anything, she could do to prevent them killing her if they wanted to. She pitied the Traveller who turned left. The corridor began to slope upwards and became smaller until it was twice as broad as Leah and the ceiling was only a foot above her head. The torch flickered and died, leaving Leah to inch her way slowly in the semi-darkness. Several hundred metres later the lichen reappeared. Leah imagined that Orumeck had followed the natural curves of the cave system where possible, but when they petered out, he carved a tunnel where he wanted to go. With the lichen's reappearance, Leah made better time.

Less than a kilometre later, Leah reached a stairway heading upwards. The stairway had been cut into a natural crevice in the rock: the steps were uneven and covered in lichen as if the spiders rarely, if ever, went past this point. Leah began to climb. The stairway twisted and turned, and occasionally there was a landing or a tunnel which connected it to the bottom of another stairway. Sometimes there was a downward section of stairs or pathway, but it predominantly went up. Leah stopped every once in a while to have a drink. She expected her calves and thighs to begin aching, but Gèng assured her that her HP was continually renewed and she would feel no pain in the virtual world. Even so, she paced herself and didn't allow any of her statistics to get low.

A sound gradually intruded into the silence. It was the noise of water spilling over rock, maybe a waterfall, she wasn't sure, but it was getting louder. Turning a corner, she saw a beautiful alcove. A series of tiny waterfalls trickled down the rock into a glowing pool. The pool was three metres in diameter and perfectly round. Opposite the waterfall, the pond emptied into a hole in the wall where it continued its flow into some subterranean creek or river. The pond must have been carved by Orumeck, although nothing she had seen of his matched this beauty. Into the wall overlooking the pool was cut a love seat, now overgrown with moss. Remains of a small wooden bridge still arched over the pond, and tiny fish swam lazily in the water. The path continued on the other side of the bridge.

Leah very carefully walked over and studied the bridge. There was no way it would hold her. Moss, over time, had covered the bridge and the wood was now so fragile that as she touched it, it broke beneath her fingers. She reached down to test the water. As she put her hand in it, one of the small fish darted forward and latched itself on her finger. She yanked back her finger, and her Health began to drop. Not by much, but it only stopped when she cut the fish off and healed her finger. A few drops of her blood had fallen in the pool, and there was a frenzy as the tiny fish converged on the small red stain.

"You have received 5 EP for killing the fish," Gèng informed her.

Leah completely ignored the comment as she thought through her situation. She headed over to the seat and after testing the moss to make sure it didn't attack her she sat down. She quickly stood as something sharp was hidden under the moss. Using her knife, Leah pried the moss to reveal a silver tiara. Quickly checking nothing else was hidden, she sat down, looking thoughtfully at the tiara. It hardly weighed anything, but it was not fragile. The arms that went around the head were semi-circular with strange runes inscribed on them, and at the front, they curved downward to a point where a small green emerald hung. She assumed the tiara would sit high and the gem would hang in the centre of the forehead.

"Gèng, I bet this goes with those earrings. They both are silver with green gemstones. Please show me the two descriptions."

The Tears of Göksel-Orman - Pierce the Darkness (1/2)

These Mithryl earrings were made by the first King of Göksel-Orman after the death of his beloved. He made them for their daughter that she might always remember her mother. They and the accompanying tiara "The Sorrow" were passed from mother to daughter until lost when Princess Guzeltuya fled her homeland with Mage Orumeck.

Pierce the Darkness 1: Every child needs discernment. These earrings contain the wisdom of queens both fair and foul.

Level: All

Activation: The wearer must have full MP. When unsure of the next step the bearer can invoke the wisdom of the queens by holding onto the emerald of either earring between thumb and forefinger.

Cost: All MP. (Such wisdom always has a cost)

Effect: While holding the earring the wearer can hear the thoughts of those around them.

Duration: (Player Level) seconds. This effect is doubled when The Sorrow is also worn.

Note: The current rulers of Göksel-Orman would give, or even do, anything to get these earrings back.

The Sorrow of Göksel-Orman - Pierce the Darkness (2/2)

This Mithryl tiara was made by the first King of Göksel-Orman after the death of his beloved. He made it for their daughter that she might always remember her mother. They and the accompanying earrings "The Tears" were passed from mother to daughter until lost when Princess Guzeltuya fled her homeland with Mage Orumeck.

Pierce the Darkness 2: Every child needs direction. This tiara contains the wisdom of queens both fair and foul.

Level: All

Activation: The wearer must have full MP. When unsure of the next step the bearer can invoke the wisdom of the queens by touching the emerald with the forefinger of either hand.

Cost: All MP. (Such wisdom always has a cost)

Effect: Arrows will appear giving possible directions and options.

Duration: (Player Level) seconds. This effect is doubled when The Tears are also worn.

Note: The current rulers of Göksel-Orman would give, or even do, anything to get this tiara back.

"Gèng, I don't have pierced ears, will that matter?"

"You will need to pierce them. I suggest a Trapdoor needle."

"I'll wait. Maybe Falsi will help. I can try the tiara at least."

She put the earrings away and settled the tiara on her head. She would have seven seconds to look around and get advice. She reached up and touched the emerald. Suddenly several arrows were overlaid in her vision. One pointed to the pond, one to the wall covered in water, and another was pointing at the rings on her hand. She turned around and saw a final arrow pointing down the way she had come before it winked out of existence. So the wisdom of the queens was to swim or wade across, to climb around, to use the rings or to head back.

Could she distract the fish, she wondered. Maybe if she dripped a little blood or dropped a piece of bread in the water, she might get across while they were distracted. She knew she would be able to climb around, but Leah wasn't convinced she would survive a fall into the pond. Going back was no real option. Looking at the rings, she pondered their use. Finally, she aimed the Webspinner Ring at the ceiling above her head and held it down. The web attached itself to the ceiling. She grabbed on and tried to climb. It held her weight. She smiled and waited for the ring to recharge. Charging the rings took almost half an hour as first the MP had to renew before she could charge the ring. Finally, she double checked everything then fired the ring at the roof of the small alcove and swung across the pond. A bit smugly she moved up the trail and started climbing again.

Leah had stopped counting steps around 200 and so was not sure how many it was when a doorway appeared at the top of the steps. She asked, and Gèng informed her it was 2,869 steps. If this was anything like her apartment building, then she was now more than 140 stories above the cavern, almost half a kilometre. She must be near the top of the mountain. The door wasn't locked and opened into a room, carved out of the rock, and designed as a living area. There were chairs, sofas, and a few tables in the room as well as three other doorways. One doorway opened into a kitchen area; it had a stone oven carved in the side with a metal door. The oven was cold and empty. A storehouse had shelves on either side covered with barrels, tins and boxes. She opened a few but was never going to try the goods she found inside. They were dry, but who would eat centuries old oats?

The final door gave entry to a study, with books lining the shelves; this was Orumeck's library. She took a book off the shelf, but it crumbled to dust. She moved to the desk, which had several drawers and a single sheet of parchment. Before reading the parchment, she tried the drawers. They were mainly empty, though in one she found five copper and seven silver coins, all minted by Orumeck. They had his profile on one side and a spider on the other. She hadn't studied the coins closely before, but now she noticed that Orumeck had a long face, with hair pulled back, showing long tapered ears, and a slender nose.

"Let's keep these coins separate. If we auction them off soon, we'll be way ahead of the competition. You know, it feels spooky, getting all this stuff on my first day. It feels like I'm cheating or something."

"Leah, I am aware of all rules of the game. Your experience so soon is unusual. However, if you looked at the forums, you would be aware that the developers suggest there are over 8,000 areas not yet discovered and this number climbs every day as they expand the game. Each area potentially intersects with a major storyline in some way. The unusual thing is discovering such an area in the starter area. The developers are already commenting on your find. They say that Orumeck's Cavern was expected to be found almost five years ago and since it wasn't, they developed alternate pathways into the story. He was a minor character five years ago. Now, he is big news."

"So they rewrote the storyline expecting this never to be found?"

"Correct."

Leah turned to the parchment. It was in a language she didn't know but as she stared at it the script reformed into words she could read.

Brave Traveller,
For one day, Someone will find my Hidden quietness.
Take what you will as I no longer have Need of It.
Every Thing I Loved I have done away with.
And I am Greater for Its loss not poorer.
It persuaded from Temptations Edge.
But it is completed, my Inquiry.
Blood once warm, Is cold.
Both, Hers and mine.

> *But not as one.*
> *Now alone,*
> *Am I.*
> *O.*

Leah read the message a few times and then turned and looked at the wall behind the desk. There was a bookcase. She tried to pick up books from the shelf, but each one crumbled at her touch. She touched all the surfaces, but nothing. She went and examined the letter again.

"Gèng, overlay these letters in my sight I need to rearrange them. T, S, H, N, I, T, L, G, I, T, E, I, I, H."

She muttered to herself, "Something hidden! Now, where is it hidden?"

It was several minutes before Leah stood and looked around the room. She finally gave up and reached into her bag where she grabbed one of the trap-door covers. She wrapped this around the last bit of surviving branch and set it on fire. She brought the torch over to the wall behind the desk, and a grid appeared, with numbers, each outlined in a square.

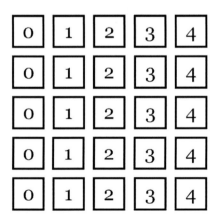

She rushed back to the parchment and read it through quickly once more, then she rushed back and depressed five of the squares. The wall faded, and she saw a chest in the hidden cavity. She pulled it out and laid it on the table. The letters she rearranged had spelt 'IT IS IN THE LIGHT'. The underlined words could be read as Four One Four One Zero. She opened the chest and inside was a scroll, some coins and a pair of black leather gloves with the tips missing from each finger and thumb. Leah glanced at the coins and was excited to see there was one each of platinum, gold, silver and copper, all minted by Orumeck.

"Gèng, just the messages on the scroll and gloves please."

Orumeck's Spell of Hidden Quietness - *Novice Level 1*

This is an air spell of silent evocation. The spell allows the caster to move in silence, unseen by those around.

Do you wish to use this scroll?

[Yes] [No]

"Yes."

Leah read the scroll, which disappeared after a white mist had formed and flowed into her. She checked the spell was in her Spell Book and then looked at the message about the gloves.

Orumeck's Hands of the Spider - *Level 1 (Max. Level 20)*

These gloves were made by Mage Orumeck. They allow the

wearer to climb like a spider. They are used to climb walls or even overhangs and ceilings.

For information on its use, please visit the Dunyanin Official Manual.

She removed her rings and slid the gloves on. She then slid the rings back on her fingers, over the top of the gloves. She put the empty chest in her bag and started moving toward the final door, but stopped and said, "Gèng, what's the time and how long do I have?"

"You have been in Dunyanin for almost six hours this time. It is now nearly 6 AM local time and 6 PM in real time. You have three hours before you need at least another break. There are also two more scrolls for you to examine."

Leah decided the scrolls could wait and stepped into the tunnel.

As soon as she stepped out of the room a message appeared:

Level 3 Dungeon Achievement: First 1 (2, Ruby)

Atherleah (Level 7), you have completed a hidden Level 3 Area: Orumeck's Cavern

You are the first player to access this area. This is your second, 'First 1 (Ruby)' achievement.

Reward 1: 1000 x 7 = 7175 (+2.5%) Experience Points (7000/7000)(2690/8000)

Reward 2: + 2% to all future Experience

Reward 3: 2 x 1 platinum = 2 platinum

Fame: 500 Fame Points (1025)

A Commemorative Plaque has been placed in your bag.

Note: This achievement will be published on the Dunyanin achievement forum. Do you wish to retain your privacy?

[Yes] [No]

"Yes."

Smiling brightly, with one hand holding the staff and the other holding one of her knives, Leah carefully made her way into the tunnel. It slowly transformed into a natural rock formation, as whatever changes Orumeck had made became fewer and fewer. The tunnel, or more accurately, the fissure, narrowed until it was touching both her shoulders and although Leah expected the staff to hit the lowering roof, it didn't. She was puzzled until she realised the staff had shrunk to be just the right height for her. Its width also changed to suit her hand. Its previous owner must have been at least a foot and a half taller than she and must have had huge hands.

There was a flash of light, and a distinguished looking elf was standing several metres in front of her. The knife she had thrown without conscious thought passed through the body just above his heart.

"Oh, what wonderful reflexes," he said. "Now if you will pardon this interruption I'm afraid a mistake has been made."

"A mistake, what mistake? And who are you?"

"My name is Emil Riverton, and I am one of the developers for Dunyanin. I was the person initially responsible for the coding of Orumeck's Cavern. Since then I have been promoted, but I have been called back to deal with this issue. The problem is that you have uncovered a glitch: initially, the whole hidden area concludes with the queen being killed, but this was after fighting your way through the entire nest, which you did not do. Five years ago, when this section of Dunyanin came online, we had not developed the ability for the 'Boss' of an area to wager on outcomes. This ability is fairly new, only within the last year. This, and several other areas received the patch allowing the wagers, but it did not limit those wagers. Those limits are pre-set in newer areas. So, you have finished the area, but, ah, also you haven't. Not really."

"So what happens now?"

"Well, nothing changes really, we would just like you to keep this quiet. Everything stands, but no mention anywhere of the glitch. Everyone will think you finished the whole cavern and the nest and we don't want you to set them straight. Don't lie, just never talk about it. We have already fixed the problem and are working on similar situations, so hopefully, it won't happen here again. What do you say?"

"How much loot have I missed out on?"

"Hardly anything, mainly spider parts, money and experience. In fact, you almost certainly would have only got one weapon, if that. To get three named weapons is extraordinary. Now, can we agree that this is all finished?"

"Sure, I never planned on talking about it anyway."

"Good! Good! Well, we thank you, and we'll send you a small gift of appreciation for your understanding and compliance." He faded out of sight.

Leah was thoughtful as she walked. She was certain there had been a big stick, ready to be used, if she had not agreed: she'd had enough of spiders anyway. She picked up her knife and continued along the tunnel.

Leah could see a brighter light ahead, sunlight dappling through thick foliage. One wall of the fissure continued and the other just ended. A mountain shrub covered the entrance with thick, scraggly branches and slender, prickly leaves. Leah had to cut some of the lower branches and crawl through the gap. Outside, she turned and couldn't even see the tunnel; it looked like any other fold in the rock. She had Gèng mark the place in her map and then took a good look around. She was high up the mountain. Far below, she caught a glimpse of the meadow she'd been aiming for when she found the entrance to Orumeck's Cavern. Now, she was almost at the area Falsi had suggested she look to find the Iblis' Clover.

Leah was on a small shelf jutting out from the side of a high escarpment. Looking up, all she could see was rock face. Below there was a ledge which wound its way slowly along the face and looked like it made its way to the top of the escarpment. The ledge was thirty metres below her. Putting the knife back in her belt, she placed the staff in her bag and targeting a small outcrop about a third of the way down, she depressed the switch on her

Webspinner Ring and held it down. As soon as the web went tight, she anchored her end on the side of the shelf and slithered down. As soon as she reached the outcrop, she said, "Hands of a Spider" and scuttled the rest of the way down. She was soon moving along the ledge, staff and knife back in hand.

When she reached the top of the escarpment, she was able to get her bearings. She was about half an hour from the base of the crags that Old Falsi had pointed out from the valley. She moved quickly but hadn't forgotten the lesson of the scorpion. The section she was on was mostly rock though there were small patches where soil had built up, and vegetation had taken root. It was in these patches that she searched for the clover, looking to see if she could find the distinctive red leaves with spikes. She was still ten minutes from the area that Falsi mentioned when she noticed a hint of red in a small patch of green growing in a tiny hollow, barely hidden from the wind by a small rockfall. She moved closer and saw a small plant with three little leaves.

Iblis' Clover

She looked around and seeing nothing dangerous, she knelt. Opening the pack, she took out a small pot for the plant and a bottle for the spiders. Using her knife, she gently loosened the soil around the plant and eased it out of the ground. She could see the small nodules and was careful not to go near them — she saw a couple of spiders.

Iblis' Death (Level 300/1) 10HP 5EP

"Gèng, any messages on the spiders?"

Iblis' Death (Level 300/1) 10HP 5EP

These spiders are found only on the nodules of the Iblis' Clover. They are easy to kill and capture. If you are not wary, their venom will kill anything under Level 300 within moments.

Note: Their venom is highly prized by healers and assassins.

Very carefully Leah coaxed the spiders into the bottle. Soon she was on her way with only four more to get, but even one would save Farnel. She found two more before encountering any difficulty. She was just setting off to look for the fourth plant when she heard a small rattle and then a clink as small pebbles dropped from the rock face angled above her. She slowly turned her head and looked up. There was a large cat-like creature, crouched and watching her. It was slate grey and well over a metre high at the shoulders. From nose to tail it was well over three metres.

Grey Mountain Wildercat (Level 10) 1200HP 900EP

She slowly turned to face it straight on. It had mesmerising green eyes, eyes that watched her hungrily. The face was broader than a cat. The muzzle and ears outlined in black, the whiskers, straight. As the mouth slowly opened Leah could see the twin canine teeth, one on either side. She very slowly slid the knife back into her belt and waited. If she backed away, she would be in the perfect place for the Wildercat to pounce. If Leah moved closer, she would be getting her body out of position to respond. She slowly bent her knees and balanced her weight on the tips of her toes while rehearsing the use of the Worker Ring and Webspinner Ring in her mind. The Wildercat pounced, but instead of straight at her, as expected, it landed off to her left. The Mana-spike missed.

Again they faced each other, but this time on level ground. Leah found herself staring into its beautiful eyes. It wasn't right for something so dangerous to have such lovely eyes, and she wondered where she had seen them before. The Wildercat slowly crouched, getting ready to pounce, but only staring. Leah's hold on the staff began to weaken, and her left hand started to drop. Then she remembered, and the memory ended the spell the appeared to be under. The eyes were like Jackson's eyes. Why would a predator have Jackson's eyes?

A predator! Her hand had just begun to firm when the Wildercat pounced: it had sensed it was losing the grip on her mind. She whipped the staff across her body, and her hand started clenching to fire the rings, but it was too late to stop the Wildercat from coming down hard against her. The claws raked her chest, and she felt unbearable pain as the skin tore. The jaws closed but they clamped down hard on the staff which she had raised just in time. Frantically, she continued to clench her left hand: firing spikes into the cat and wrapping it in binding webs. Together they fell to the ground with the cat on top of her. The web binding prevented the cat from finishing its slashing attack, but her Health plummeted into the red. Leah looked into its eyes as it slowly died from spikes to the heart.

Leah pushed on the staff with all her strength and finally slid out from underneath the massive cat. She didn't have enough MP to do any healing. She watched as her Health points continued to disappear. She dragged herself to the rock face and slowly moved to a sitting position. The claws had left four bloody gashes on either side of her chest. If the claws had completed the move, she would have died immediately. She grabbed her water and some hard bread and slowly ate and drank while watching the HP bar start to blink red. The pain was excruciating, but she held on and calmed herself. She decided to ignore the pain. She had what she came for. Because she was not Level 10, she wouldn't lose anything. She'd still be able to save Farnel. She had barely 5 HP left. She closed her eyes and breathed deeply, at peace. She felt her body quiver, and suddenly thought, 'if this is dying, then it isn't that bad'. She opened her eyes to find herself still on the ledge and her HP in the orange. Her KP however, was completely gone. She blinked a few times then asked Gèng if there was a message about Ki. There was!

You have Activated your Ki for use in healing

Ki is your life force and can be used to aid in healing.

It is vital when seeking to activate your Ki automatically that you be both calm and focused. This is measurable by an analysis of your brain activity and your simulated rate of respiration. Alternatively, you may activate your Ki manually by saying 'Ki Heal'.

Current Skill Level: Novice Level 1

For more information, please read the Dunyanin Manual.

Do you wish to receive further notifications concerning this skill?

[Yes] [No]

_____

"No."

Leah thought about all the ramifications of this. She had to be careful not to expend all her KP just in case she needed to heal herself. She needed to spend some time thinking through her options.

She stood and walked over to the cat.

_____

You have harvested:

1 Grey Mountain Wildercat Pelt

4 pieces of Grey Mountain Wildercat meat

4 Grey Mountain Wildercat Canine Teeth*

* Note: A skilled armourer may be able to use these items.

_____

Leah moved on. She had two more plants to collect. This time she kept a wary eye on the rock face as well as the area she was walking. She collected the fourth clover but after another hour of looking had not seen a fifth. She decided to head back. As she turned, she glanced at the rock face, and there it was, a flash of red in the corner of her eye. She turned to look but couldn't find it. It was ten minutes before she was able to find it again. It was only when the wind blew strongly that a small shrub moved, revealing the hidden clover. It was on a shallow ledge maybe twenty metres above the point where she stood. She knew she could get up there with the gloves or by using the Mana web, but wasn't sure there was enough room to be safe while she harvested it. There was another outcrop several feet below. She measured the distance in her mind and thought there was just enough to be able to reach up and get the clover.

She tapped her hands together and climbed up the rock face to perch on the lower tiny ledge. Reaching up, she raised her head above the edge of the rock to see, not one, but two plants of Iblis' Clover. One was the standard three leaf, but to her surprise, the other was a four leaf.

Iblis' Tetraclover

"Gèng, any messages on the Tetraclover?"

Iblis' Tetraclover

This rare variant of Iblis' Clover is highly prized by both alchemists and apothecaries for the increased purity of all its components. Additionally, the spiders that are often found with Iblis' Tetraclover have been found to be exceptionally potent.

Leah carefully harvested the regular clover and spider as requested by Falsi. She then took the empty chest from Orumeck's Study and harvested the Tetraclover, spider included, and put both in the chest.

"Gèng, remind me to be careful about opening that chest."

Leah scampered down the cliff and looked down on the valley below.

"Now all I have to do is get back. But first I need a break."

She found a small hidden area behind a thick, scraggly bush, sat down and logged out.

Leah took the backpack off and slumped onto the sofa.

"I am so emotionally tired. Is it always like that? One thing after another all day?"

Gèng answered, "I don't think so. I've been analysing forums, and it seems to depend on the player. You jumped straight in. Many new players spend several days running small quests here and there, killing rats and building fences. You can always slow down when you get back to First Bridge."

"No, I have three years, and I intend to make the most of them. Let me logout of here and have a break, then we'll end this quest, and I can think about school."

Once back in the room Leah had a quick shower and made some more ramen. As she was making the food she realised that her upper legs and shoulders were tender, not painful but just a little shaky.

"Gèng, how come my thighs, glutes and shoulders are a bit sore?"

"Well, you did climb 2,869 steps without stopping. The program in the Pod stimulates the motor neurones in line with virtual movements. Even with only one-third of the stimuli being applied you still climbed 956 steps almost without a break. The Pod removes any acid build up, but there is likely to be some residual pain as muscles stretch and grow. I can reduce the percentage of stimuli if you so desire."

"No! That's OK! So if I run everywhere and swing that staff, then I get a workout without the pain."

"Affirmative! Over time, you can decide to modify the stimuli to focus only on your arms and minimise your leg development, for example. Minimally the Pod will maintain your muscle tone at the rate in which you enter the Pod."

When she'd finished eating, Leah sat and listened to some music for a while. Gèng assured her that her parents had been informed she was not going to return home that evening. As Leah listened, she thought through her meeting with Jackson and the Wildercat. Was she paranoid or should she act as if he was a predator? The guy at the hospital had unquestionably been a creep. She had never really liked a boy before and was unsure how it was going to feel, but predators she knew, and something had triggered the connection in her mind. Her mind continued to go around in circles as she tried to work through the issue before heading back to finish the quests.

It was almost an hour later when she arrived back in her virtual world. She sat on the sofa and tried to focus on the next three hours, or nine hours if she thought in virtual terms. She decided to check her stats and distribute the points. In the end, she decided to increase Wisdom and Intelligence by two and Agility by one. Her Skill/Spell point she added to 'Ki Heal'. Looking into the various things she had put off there was one about the platinum coin from the Cavern.

A Platinum Coin of Orumeck

This coin was made by Mage Orumeck during the time of his exile from Sihirbazlari. Full of pride, he minted several thousand coins with his image. He embossed them with some of his favourite creations.

Value: Equivalent to 1 platinum*

* Note: Some collectors may pay more for such a rare coin.

World Quest: Collect the Coins - Platinum (0/500)

Many people throughout time have minted coins. They are scattered throughout Dunyanin. Collect these coins.

Difficulty: Easy to Impossible

Reward 1 if successful: (Number of Coins collected) x (Player Level) x 500 Experience Points for each coin.

Reward 2 if successful: 2 x (Number of Coins collected) platinum Coins.

Consequences of failure: None

Do you wish to accept this Quest?

[Yes] [No]

"Yes."

She then looked at the scrolls from the Cavern. One was a second copy of the spell of *Hidden Quietness*.

"Gèng, this can stay here, I'll try and sell this when we get to a town."

The other was a clue scroll.

Where is Orumeck's Keep? *- Clue (1 of 10)*

This is one of many clues that Orumeck made to taunt those who came after him. It begins a journey to his Keep.

Do you wish to view this scroll?

[Yes] [No]

"Yes."

Where is Orumeck's Keep *- Clue (1 of 10)*

9				4	5			
2			9		*	8		7
		*		7		*	5	
	9	1		6		*		2
8	*		*	5		7	4	
	5		*	8				
4		2			3	*		8
		*	2	9				1

To access this clue at any time look in the clue book which has been added to your bag.

"Next please Gèng, that can wait until later."

"You have a message from the developers regarding the glitch."

A Gift of Thanks

Atherleah,

Regarding our recent conversation, we thank you for being so understanding. Please accept these gifts as an expression of our appreciation. In accepting these gifts, we trust you will abide by the decisions reached in our meeting.

Gift 1: 2 platinum Coins

Gift 2: 2000 Experience Points

Gift 3: Potion of Restored Health

Gift 4: Potion of Restored Mana

Do you wish to accept these gifts?

[Y] [N]

"Yes."

These points from the administration brought her to Level nine, and she allocated two points to Agility, one to Strength, one to Constitution and the final point to Luck. With nothing else to consider Leah headed for the portal.

It was just after midday, Dunyanin time. Leah wanted to be down the mountain by evening, so she hurried along. She kept a wary eye out for whatever beasts might be in her path. She had travelled for several hours before coming to a stop just above the meadow she had headed for the previous day. She had been attacked by another Wildercat (Level 9) and two Scorpions (both Level 5). All three times she was prepared, and though the Wildercat managed to maul her leg, she easily survived the three attacks.

She stopped because she'd seen movement in the meadow.

Peering around a bush, she watched three people cross the meadow and head in her direction — players. One, an elven woman, was wearing a flowing robe that looked silly when climbing a mountain. The other two were male, one elf and one human. The elf was carrying a longbow with an arrow already nocked. The human wore chain mail that covered his head and torso. Looking around for a better hiding place, Leah saw nothing except a small outcrop of rock some fifteen metres above her. Quickly checking the formula, she intoned the spell *Hidden Quietness*, then tapping her gloves together she scurried up the rock face to lie silently on top of the outcrop. Leah made herself as small as she could. She thought about logging off, but Gèng informed her that her actions were considered potential combat, and she was unable to log out.

It was almost twenty minutes before she heard voices.

A man's voice, "I'm sure I saw something. I tell you, there was someone up here."

"Well if you did, it looks like they are long gone by now," the other man said. "Let's head higher and look for that Cavern. Jason will catch whoever it is before they get to town."

"Poor sod," the woman said. "Jason'll fleece them for everything they have."

"Poor nothing," the first voice said. "If you can't keep it, you don't deserve it."

After several minutes the voices slowly faded and then disappeared. Leah waited another ten minutes before peeking over the edge of the small ledge: there was no one. She used the gloves to get down and continued on her way. This time she moved slowly, from cover to cover. On one occasion she used

Hidden Quietness to cross a large open area. When Leah finally made it to the meadow, she decided to make her way around the boundary using the scrub and trees as cover, rather than crossing it.

She was just about to move from behind a low growing bush when she heard a faint metallic noise. She turned just in time to see a sword arcing down toward her neck. Her training with Jimmy's boys and all the fighting over the last few days kicked in. She rolled forward under the blade while reaching across using her left hand to draw the knife from her right boot. She sliced the back of the person's left knee, then, reversing her direction rose to her full height, and as she came around, she planted the knife in the right side of the man's neck right up to the hilt.

She expected her assailant to be dead and was surprised when he turned toward her raising his sword for another attack. She moved forward, placed her left hand on the sword arm and pushed it away while slamming the heel of her right hand into his nose. She slid her hand up and grabbed the chain mail and a handful of hair and brought the head down into her rising knee. As the body fell backwards, she followed it down, driving her right forearm into his exposed throat. She pulled the knife from his neck and buried it in his eye. He stayed down this time, and she noticed the small bar just above his head flicker red before going opaque.

It was just like she'd practised at Jimmy Loo's. Everything had just come together. Her heart was still racing though as she stood up. The body faded into a ghostly outline, and Leah noticed a skull appearing, superimposed above the head. It was the soldier from earlier. Her heart rate slowed as she realised that although someone had tried to kill her, it wasn't real. It was just a part of the game. By finding the Cavern, she had become prey for those players who wanted to steal from her.

"What a bastard!" she thought.

Kneeling down she picked up her knife; it had fallen out of the outline. There was no blood, and she didn't need to clean it. She saw that the player had left behind some items. She picked them up and put them in her bag while keeping an eye out for the other two; she didn't even register what she picked up. That could wait until she was in a place she felt safe; the whole incident had rattled her.

Gèng interrupted her thoughts, "You have a few messages, are you free to check them?"

"In a minute, let me get past the meadow in case the other two are around. Are the messages urgent?"

"No, they aren't urgent. You have an achievement and a voice message from Kasim.Bloodhand.23."

"What does he have to say? Just play it for me."

"Bitch, you had best leave my stuff there. I don't know how you managed to get everything I had, but you had best leave it there. You won't get past us, and we have the whole town covered. If you've taken my stuff, you'll be sorry."

It was the voice of the first man, the one who thought he had seen her.

"Gèng, please record the following and send it to Kasim and then block all replies. 'Kasim, if you can't keep it, you don't deserve it.'"

Leah kept moving, though she was even slower and more careful. She was close to the area where she had been attacked by the scorpion when she heard loud voices arguing behind her. It was the two elves who had been with Kasim. She moved forward speedily, trying to be as quiet as she could. When she came to the small overhang the scorpion lived in, she carefully checked it and found it was empty. She hustled into it, moving as far back into the space as she could. She prepared the Trapdoor spider ring just in case they decided to look under the rock.

The pair were still arguing as they passed her position. Apparently Kasim, the woman's boyfriend, wanted them to head to town to be there when he resurrected. The archer wanted to stay and search for the Cavern, but the mage was keen to get back to town. They climbed over the rocks without checking beneath. After a few minutes, Leah crept out of her hiding place and followed them. She reasoned that if there were others around, then she would let these two make first contact. She travelled fifty metres behind the pair, and they never looked back. Even if they had, it is unlikely they would have seen her, for she kept to the very edges of the trail, moving quickly from one shadow to the next. She paused when the two in front stopped and scampered to either side of the path. She watched as they found positions overlooking the trail below. The archer took several arrows from his quiver and stuck them in the ground beside him. The woman, several metres further back, had a good view of both the trail and the bowman. It looked like they were planning to ambush someone.

Although this wasn't her fight, she detested bullies and had ever since she was six. She crept to within twenty metres of the mage. Using *Hidden Quietness*, she climbed a rock that was behind, and slightly above, the woman. If her calculations were correct, this would put her within range to use both her Worker and

Webspinner Rings. From her perch, Leah couldn't see down the trail, nor could she see the archer. The time passed slowly until suddenly the archer called out, "It was one of the noobs. I hit her, but she fell out of sight. Cover me, and I'll go finish her off."

"All right, but be careful. Even noobs can be dangerous."

The elven mage slowly stood and peered down the trail. Just before she stepped out, Leah shot her in the back with several Mana spikes and bound her with the web. Jumping from her perch, Leah brought the Morningstar down on top of her head. Just to be sure, she planted her knife in the back of the woman's neck. The body turned opaque and left behind some objects. Leah grabbed them without looking and peered down the path. The archer had stopped and looked back up the trail; he darted into the foliage on the side. Leah was sure he knew his partner was dead.

Leah checked the cooldown and then used *Hidden Quietness* to cross over the trail and creep into the bushes on the other side. She found a small game trail and stopped yo wait. The trail was an obvious place to sneak, and she assumed the archer would come back this way if he were going to check on who, or what, killed his partner. There had been many times when working for Jimmy where she had to be still for long periods; he had trained her in patience. It was over five minutes before she heard bushes, gently rustling. The elf was only a few metres away. She slowly depressed the Trapdoor Ring to give her almost half a minute of invisibility; she hoped it would be enough. The archer looked in her direction as he carefully made his way past, but he saw nothing. As soon as he passed, she carefully stepped out behind him. She bound him with the web and buried a scythe taken from the

Warrior Drone in his back. As he fell, she reached for her belt knife and plunged the knife into his ear, followed by a Mana spike into the back of his head. He turned opaque.

Collecting what he dropped, she moved toward the area where he had attacked someone. She supposed she was now a Player Killer or PKer, but she didn't feel too bad as bullies should never thrive. She queried Gèng and was surprised to learn that the three had never dissolved their group and because they had attacked her first she was, according to the rules, justified in killing them without earning a PK title.

"You have voice messages from a Shiva.Bloodhand.23 and a Bullseye.Johnson.11. You have also achieved Level 10. Do you want to hear their voice messages?" asked Gèng.

"Nope, just block them!" Leah answered.

Moving quietly, she soon found the ambushed person. She looked young and was sitting against a tree trying to wrap a cloth around her arm while keeping watch on all the bushes. Leah called out softly, "The ones who attacked you are gone, can I help at all?"

The girl replied quietly, "I think it's all right. I'm not losing any HP, and it is going up. It just hurts."

Leah said, "Don't worry, that'll go away. Can I come over? I have a simple healing spell that'll take the sting out."

"Sure, that'd be great. My name is Annairë_the_Wize, spelt with two n's and a 'z', so it's original, but you can call me Wisp, that's what my friends call me." Leah reached out her hand and said, "Hi Wisp, my name is Atherleah!"

Leah healed Wisp, who asked, "What happened to the ones who shot me?"

"Dead! There were two of them, an archer and a mage. They had a swordsman, but I killed him earlier after he attacked me. Do you know them and what are you doing out here?"

It turned out that Wisp was searching for Orumeck's Cavern. She had started playing several days earlier and had still been in First Bridge when the news of finding the Cavern was released. She was Level 4 and wanted something more exciting than rats. Apparently, hundreds of players were descending on First Bridge.

"So, any idea who the people were, the ones who shot at you?"

"It sounds like a group of four who arrived this morning. Someone said they've been hanging around the next town, Carson's Loop, killing the new players. Their leader is a really big half-orc called Jason. As soon as they arrived, he stayed in town while the rest headed up the mountain."

"The other players who were arriving, what are they like?"

"Mostly OK! They walk around town laughing at everything and asking if anyone knew who had found the Cavern, or knew where it was. When I said I had no idea, then they left me alone."

It would be dark in another two hours, and Leah was in a hurry to get to town. She was sure that this Jason already had a description of her from Kasim. The other two hadn't even seen her. Leah motioned toward town and said, "Well I had best be off if I plan to stay in town tonight."

"What? Aren't you going to stay and look for the Cavern, we

could do it together. I've never had a partner, most of my friends got the silver or gold package, but I could only get the bronze. I'm planning on catching up with them when I hit Level 30 or above."

Leah wasn't sure what to do. She liked Wisp, as much as you could after one meeting, but still wasn't sure what to do. Finally, though, she decided that the truth was going to get out anyway.

"Once is enough for me. I never want to go back in that Cavern again!"

"What?" squealed Annairë, "You're the one? You found it?"

"Yep! Last night. If you want, I'll tell you where it is. Just be careful, there are some crazy people out here."

It took several minutes but Wisp and Leah swapped contact information, and Leah told her not only how to get to the cavern but what to expect. Then Leah headed back to town leaving the other girl standing by the trail. About ten minutes later Leah heard a sound coming from behind and quickly moved off into the bushes. She was surprised to see Wisp jogging down the trail. Leah couldn't see what she was running from, and it wasn't until Wisp had passed that Leah stepped out and called softly, "What's up?"

Wisp shuddered to a stop and said, "Nothing, it's just that, I was shot ... and you saved my life. After everything you said, I'm not ready to do the whole spider thing by myself. So I was wondering if we could travel together for a while. I forgot to check what level you are, but I'll try and keep up, and I promise I won't hold you back."

"I'm not sure," Leah said. "I've just started playing myself, and I'm used to doing things on my own."

"Well, at least can I come back to town with you? I think that'll be safer than on my own."

Leah was silent for at least a minute before she said, "Sure, but let's move quietly, there may still be players out here trying to kill us. So, softly, softly."

Wisp was a lot noisier than Leah. Still, Leah enjoyed the soft nattering voice and didn't think she'd have trouble until she got to town. Eventually, just as the sun was setting, they could see the edge of the town through the trees. The town looked the same as before, but she wondered if this Jason was going to be trouble. It was still a few hours before Kasim and company would be able to return to Dunyanin. At the edge of town, Leah made arrangements to catch up the next day. Wisp headed for her room at the inn and Leah headed for the herb-witch's house.

"Hello Auntie, I have the Iblis' Clover. Am I in time?"

"Atherleah, come in, come in. Come and sit. Yes, dear, Farnel is still with us. If you have the clover, I'll make a potion this evening, and we'll bring it to her first thing."

"Do you need any help with the potion?"

"I don't need the help, but if you want I'll teach you a little of potion making."

"That would be fantastic. If you can wait a few minutes, I'll go book a room at the Inn and then return."

"Nonsense girl, you can stay here with me."

Usually, players were not supposed to log off in the presence of

NPC's. However, there were times like this when it was essential, and so the Dunyanin developers had promoted the thinking that sometimes Travellers visited other worlds in their sleep and this was why they could not be woken or moved.

"Auntie, I'm a Traveller, you know we sometimes visit other worlds in our sleep and can't be woken. I'm very weary and will need to sleep in a bit. Am I still welcome?"

"Of course, you can sleep in that chair. I'll make sure you're not disturbed."

"Thank you. Here are the five clovers and the spiders. How long before you start the potion?"

"It'll be a few hours yet, and I need to make supper. You bed down and have a small rest, and when you awake, we'll get the potion made for Farnel."

Leah lay down on the long chair that Falsi pointed to and logged off. This time her body didn't dissolve but lay there unmoving.

Immediately on arriving in her virtual world Leah logged off. She wandered out and bought a lasagna from the dispensary. She was really glad not to meet anyone and discouraged because she felt the need to bring her knives. Leah ate quickly and lay down to process her day. Less than twenty-four hours and she had made more than enough money to stay in the game for years. But she'd also made enemies, and she'd killed people, if only virtually. The time dilation was great, but it did make it hard to process. She asked Gèng if there had been studies done and then she read the précis of the top ten. Nothing conclusive, except that most people found they eventually came to terms with the dilation and eventually didn't notice it.

"Gèng, I'm not feeling physically tired but when should I have a sleep period?"

"It is recommended that you have between one-and-a-half and two hours of SWS or NREM3 sleep each twenty-four hour period. I recommend you schedule this for after your next visit to Dunyanin. If you visit for three or four hours, then you can take this time and still meet Wisp in the morning as you have promised."

"All right, that sounds great."

She noticed that Gèng's voice had lost some of its artificiality and then she saw some changes that Gèng had made in the building. The walls were now a dark stained wood similar in colour and grain to Merdiven, her staff. The floor was carpeted in dark burgundy. The room was smaller but seemed more elegant. Various archways led to other rooms.

"Well, wow! You've been busy."

"Do you like it? I noticed your appreciation of Merdiven's appearance, and I've sought to understand the various parameters and controls. I studied various architectural designs and modified them just enough to avoid copyright. I did not meet your requirements at the beginning of the day and have worked to remedy the situation."

"I love it. You know, I think that it isn't a bad thing that you are missing the databases. I believe that learning this way will probably develop you more than following a particular pathway.

Now, I must get on task. I'd better check the messages for the trip down the mountain. I don't want the personal messages or those skill messages, just whatever I picked up from those three."

You have killed Level 24 Human, Kasim.Bloodhand.23

Experience Points Received 1254 (+4.5%)

David & Goliath Achievement (Levels 1-10)

You have fought and defeated a player more than 10 levels above you.

Experience Points Received (Defeated Player Level - Your Level) x 200 EP

3,135 (1.045 x 3,000) EP

You have killed Level 22 Elf, Shiva.Bloodhand.23

Experience Points Received 1,150 (+4.5%)

David & Goliath Achievement (Levels 1-10)

You have fought and defeated a player more than 10 levels above you.

Experience Points Received (Defeated Player Level - Your Level) x 200 EP

2,717 (1.045 x 2,600) EP

You have killed Level 28 Elf, Bullseye.Johnson.11

Experience Points Received 1,463 (+4.5%)

David & Goliath Achievement *(Levels 1-10)*

You have fought and defeated a player more than 10 levels above you.

Experience Points Received (Defeated Player Level - Your Level) x 200 EP

3,762 (1.045 x 3,600) EP

Altogether from the three of them, she also had thirty-two gold, 134 silver and fifty-eight copper. They had an assortment of knives, rings and potions. Of the knives, the only thing that interested her were a pair of sheathed knives:

Sheathed Fighting Knife *(Common) - 6 in/15.25 cm*

Base Damage 4

Maximum Damage 200 (excluding death strokes)

Durability 49/50

Edge 49/50

She swapped these knives with hers. She also equipped herself with two rings, a 'Band of Brawn' (+2S) and a 'Circlet of Constitution' (+2C). They all had a couple of potions. There were four Minor Potions of Healing, one Minor Potion of Mana, and one Minor Potion of Ki. The swordsman had left behind a Common Mail Coif, a Common Half Sleeve Mail Hauberk and a Common Shortsword. The mage left behind a Common Rapier. The archer had dropped his longbow and quiver, both Common. Leah was very interested until she noticed the Strength had to be at least twenty. She put them aside for later and considered getting a smaller bow first.

Yew Longbow (Common) - 67 in/1.7 m with Yew Arrows (Common) - 36 in /91 cm

Base Damage 11

Maximum Damage 700 (excluding death strokes)

Minimum Strength 20

Durability 49/50

Arrows 17/20

Finally, she distributed her points and checked the statistics.

ATHERLEAH (Level 10) (7741/10000) (+4.5%)

Characteristics - Points Total (Assigned, Racial, Jewellery), 0 Undistributed

Strength (S): 15 (13, 0, 2)

Constitution (C): 15 (13, 0, 2)

Agility (A): 21 (19, 2)

Wisdom (W): 11 (9, 2)

Intelligence (I): 7 (7)

Luck (L): 4 (4)

Statistics (Available, Capacity)

Health: 100+(S+C)xPL: (400, 400) HP

Stamina: 100+(C+A)xPL: (460, 460) SP

Mana: 100+(W+I)xPL: (280, 280) MP

Ki: 100+(W+[S+A]/2)xPL: (390, 390) KP

Leah walked through the arch to Dunyanin. She rose and stretched. Old Falsi beckoned her over to the kitchen and served them both a plate of stew with fresh bread. Old Falsi asked about the trip, and Leah described the scorpions and spiders, the long stairway and collecting the clover. She hesitated but finally pulled the earrings out and asked if Falsi would pierce her ears afterwards so she could put them on. Falsi was pleased to do so and after dinner took a needle and pierced both sides. Leah put in the rings and healed herself. Gèng assured her that they would remain pierced within the various Virtual Worlds if this was Leah's intent.

After cleaning up, Falsi instructed Leah in the use of a mortar and pestle, how to use a still to separate out essential oils, and the right way to measure and mix various compounds. She explained how to mix with honey, butter or waxes to make the different salves. If Leah had permitted the skill notifications to display, she would have seen a whole spate concerning various herbalist and apothecary skills. Finally after almost three hours of work the potion for Farnel was finished. Old Falsi went to bed, and Leah lay down as well and logged off.

After a short conversation with Gèng, the AI brought Leah to the NREM3 sleep state and kept her there for an hour and forty minutes. She woke refreshed and after a quick bathroom break and shower woke up in Old Falsi's just in time for breakfast.

Diary - 18 November 2063

WHAT HAVE I *got myself into? What is in my head?*

A mistake, they made a mistake. Every time I think about it I feel terrified, I wonder what the nanites are doing in my brain. The chip is damaged - is that good or bad? I hate to think of the government watching everything, controlling everything but I'm frightened about what might happen without controls. Can I control it? Can it control me? Everyone says Nascent AI are hard to develop, but Gèng is already taking initiative. Will the lack of external control let it take over, or has it just set it free? Will this chip take over, or will it set me free?

Is my mum right? Will I slowly forget what is real and what is imagination? The colours were so bright, the air was so fresh, and the people seemed so real, but they are merely streams of data fed into my brain. The pain was unbelievable, and that's only at 50%. I can't imagine the real thing, but already I'm used to it because I have magic, I can heal myself. But magic isn't real, except it is in Dunyanin. Dunyanin isn't real, but it is according to my memory and my experiences, none of which are real! I hope I don't go crazy.

Am I a murderer? It wasn't hard to kill Kasim. After the spiders, it was even easy. It was easier to kill the second time and then the third. Does the fact that they live mean I didn't kill them? I mean, if they attacked me in real life I imagine I would have done the same. Does that make me a killer? Have I sinned? Mum always says that the sin is the thought not just the action. Lust, not just adultery. Coveting, not just stealing. So when I get to church next time, for what do need to ask forgiveness?

Am I rich? I've made more money in one day than my parents have probably made in their lifetime. It's not real money, but it can be, and I can buy real food with it and a real education. But I can also buy imaginary things with the real money that Jimmy gave me, or was that only bits of data also? Except, I've paid him before with real work, and he'll accept that again.

I started today hoping to improve my existence, my life. Well, it has certainly been existential.

NOVEMBER 19, 2073

AFTER BREAKFAST, Leah and Falsi made their way to the General Store. Leah put the hood up on her cape, hoping to hide her features just in case the PKers were around. They couldn't kill her in the starter town, but she didn't want the confrontation. The influx of people to the township was noticeable as ten or more groups wandered the street preparing to head out in search of the Cavern. Although many people on the street stared at Leah and Falsi, no one stopped them.

Falsi led the way to the back of Goll's home. They entered and made their way up the stairs to Farnel's room. Goll's wife, whose name was Elmas, sighed with relief before rising to her feet and moving away from the bed to clear a space for Old Falsi.

"Atherleah, please heal Farnel as much as you are able and then we will administer the potion."

"Yes, Auntie!"

This time, Atherleah was able to restore almost all Farnel's

Health. Her Health never quite reached 100% because the illness was still present and her Health meter began immediately dropping. Farnel was able though, to sit up and drink the potion provided by Old Falsi. Within minutes Leah saw Farnel's Health meter slow and then stop.

Old Falsi stopped Leah from doing a final healing and said, "I think it best if she recovers now, on her own. It won't be as fast as you Travellers heal but it will give her mind some time to adjust to being well."

They left Elmas and Farnel in the room and headed down to talk with Goll, who was waiting at the base of the stairs. Falsi reassured Goll that all was well, Atherleah had been able to secure the ingredients and Farnel was now cured.

Goll stuck his hand out to Atherleah and said, "Thank you! Thank you! Thank you! You have done everything just as you said. Whenever you're free, and before you move on, you come into the store and take whatever you need for your journey. Anything I can do to help."

Gèng informed Leah that she had also received 1045 EP and a change in reputation with Goll and Elmas to Trusted. Leah assured him she would, and they left Goll's house and headed back to Falsi's home. When they arrived, Leah went to the kitchen and made them both a cup of tea before sitting down to chat.

"So, girl, where are you going now?"

"Well, Auntie, I have an obligation in the Demir Dovuyor Mountains, so I plan to make my way there first. After that, the only other place I must visit is the Elven realm of Göksel-Orman. I have things to do in my land, but will probably head later today toward Carson's Loop. I am not sure when exactly as I've upset some Travellers in town and they might try to kill me."

"Dwarves, elves and enemies! You have a powerful fate, this I can tell. Now, I have a gift for you."

"There is no need, Auntie. I have more than enough for the moment."

"Nonsense, you have a long way to travel and need all the help you can find. Now, I was going to give you some potions, but I have a better idea." At this, Falsi rose from her chair and made her way to the old table which held her books. She took the large book with all her notes on plants and potions and handed it to Leah.

"I've waited many a year to find an apprentice worthy of all that knowledge. I'm old and not sure what is coming, and I don't think I could train anyone anymore anyway. Please use this in your travels and add to it. If you grow in your potion making skills, you might one day be able to make and use everything in there."

Gèng said, "Before you answer, read this."

For completing the Personal Quest: Heal the Sick

Reward 1: Your reputation with Falsi has grown to Deep Trust

Reward 2: Completion of task 5 x Iblis' Clover (5 x 209 EP)

Reward 3: Completion of task 5 x Iblis' Death (5 x 209 EP)

Reward 4: Falsi has gifted you with her Diary of Herbs and Potions

This compilation is unrivalled outside of the Elven Realm and is a collection of plants and their uses as well as remedies and potions. It includes not only her own experiences but that of her mentor Harika. Harika was known not only in the human lands but was also known and respected by both Dwarves and Elves. Harika studied under the legendary Elven Sage, Samarie.

"Auntie, I can't take this, it is priceless."

"Of course you can, now, off you go. Do drop in some time and tell me of your travels."

Leah bowed and thanked Falsi for the amazing gift and then made her way toward the inn for a meeting with Wisp. The inn was crowded with people who came to the town in search of Orumeck's Cavern. There were warriors and mages everywhere. Looking around, Leah couldn't see Wisp, and seeing no free tables, she decided to wait outside. As she turned to leave, a loud voice carried over the general din.

"You! Atherleah! Bitch! You're mine. Give me back my stuff, and I'll kill you quickly."

Atherleah turned around. Sure enough, it was Kasim, dressed in some old armour. The whole room had gone quiet. Atherleah looked Kasim up and down, then smiled and turned to leave. She saw no reason to do or say anything when everyone was watching. The Switch had taught her that silence was sometimes the best answer in such circumstances. The other answer was to give as good as you got, and then give more. She turned to find an enormous light-green half-orc standing behind her. He was heavily muscled with two long yellowed teeth jutting from his lower jaw and pressing against his upper lips. His hair was long and dark and tied in a ponytail. He was carrying a sword as least as long as Leah. She thought him rather good-looking, except for the sneer as he looked down at her.

"You heard Kasim, half-breed bitch!"

It was push-back time. She looked him up and down and said, "Half-breed! That's cute coming from someone whose momma musta gotten down and dirty with whatever it is your papa was."

Although she saw the sword coming, she steeled herself and completely ignored it. It swiped through her and crashed into the floor, sending up a shower of sparks. The game wouldn't allow preemptive kill strokes in town, but it did allow duels and lethal retaliation, if and when you were attacked. As long as Leah ignored the orc, she was untouchable. If she retaliated, then it was an accepted duel, and the fight was on. The lack of resistance to the sword put Jason off balance and Leah took the opportunity to grab the front of his armour and pull him to the floor. She turned him as they fell and ended up on top of him. A spike through each eye and a knife in the ear and it was all over. She stood, then wiped the knife theatrically on her trouser leg before sliding it back into her belt.

She looked around the suddenly quiet room. Picking up the money bag Jason had dropped she said, "A round of drinks on the half-breed bitch!" She paused, then added, "And I don't mean me!"

The room dissolved into laughter except for Kasim and his two friends who were standing near him. She picked up everything Jason had dropped and with the sword balanced on her shoulder made her way to the barkeep to pay up. Kasim, Shiva and Bullseye started toward her but slowed as the room went silent. Everyone slowly stood, staring at them, and then began slowly unsheathing their weapons. A huge barbarian spoke into the silence, "I reckon you three best move along. Your friend got what he deserved."

The three changed direction and headed for the door. As they left Kasim called back over his shoulder, "You'll get yours, bitch!" Once again the whole room burst out laughing. The barbarian gestured for Leah to join him and his friends at his table. Leah smiled and nodded in acknowledgement. She motioned to the barkeep where she would be and headed over.

"Name's Thad, that's Amy, James and Butthead," the barbarian said as she sat down, indicating toward his table-mates, two humans and a dwarf.

"It's Bonehelm. I keep telling him. It's Bonehelm. My name is Zack Bonehelm."

Leah ignored the byplay but acknowledged the three as she sat down. "Hello Thad, hey, thanks for the help there. I appreciate it. I'm Atherleah."

"No worries, those four have been acting like jerks ever since we arrived. I imagine you're the one that put them in such a foul mood yesterday."

"Yep, they ambushed me up on the mountain. Well, to be honest, only Kasim ambushed me, but I took out some angst on the other two. They were hunting me and probably would've missed me, but I'm not fond of bullies."

"So did you have any luck on the mountain?" Although the

question seemed casual, Leah could see them all sit a little straighter as they waited for her answer.

She decided to have a little fun, "Sure did, a few Wildercat, some scorpions and there were some rare plants to harvest. I raised my herbalist skills a couple of times during the day. How about you all?"

They all slumped back, then Thad said, "Well we got in late yesterday and haven't been out yet. We're here for Orumeck's Cavern. No one we've talked to has had any luck yet finding it, and there's nothing on the forums. We are heading out soon. We're going to try the forest first. Would you like to come?"

She paused as if thinking hard and then said, "That'd be great, I haven't been to the forest yet! ... But I thought you were after Orumeck's Cavern? That's nowhere near the forest!"

They all stared at her. She stared back and then suddenly began chuckling. Before she could say anything, Wisp arrived downstairs and seeing Leah made her way over to the table.

"Good morning Atherleah, sorry I'm late. May I join you guys?"

They all shifted around to make room for Wisp who said, "Sorry, I didn't mean to stop your conversation, why are you all staring at Atherleah like that?"

Leah spoke first, "We were just chatting about Orumeck's Cavern, these guys are planning on hunting for it this morning. They're headed into the forest. I was just saying that it was probably a better thing to head elsewhere."

Wisp looked at the others who were still staring at Leah and then said, "Yep, the forest is definitely the wrong way. It's nowhere near the Cavern. But Atherleah, you have to let people do things their way. I don't think you should force anyone to do something your way. It's not polite."

"You know what, Wisp, you're right. You guys, you try the forest. I hope it works for you."

The table was silent for a moment, and then both Wisp and Leah burst out laughing. "You know, maybe that orc was right, you might be a bitch," Amy said, joining in the laughter.

Wisp stopped laughing and looked around. "What, where is he? I saw the others leave from my window, is he here?"

James piped up, "He was, but Atherleah here convinced him to leave. But not before he bought free drinks for everyone."

Wisp stared at Leah. "You killed him too?"

Leah just smiled while James told the story. Wisp then told of her experiences from the day before. As Wisp finished the story, Leah said, "OK, I know where the Cavern is. If you walk with us until we're a few kilometres down the road, just in case Kasim and friends are there, then I'll tell you where it is and some of what to expect. Deal?"

The four friends looked at each other and smiled broadly. "Deal!" said Thad, "Although why you need us, I don't know. What level are you, if you don't mind me asking?"

"I'm Level Eleven."

"How does a Level Eleven take down a Level Thirty?" Zack asked.

"Brain and heart!" Leah said, "As far as I can tell, if your attack is direct to brain or heart then it is considered critical. So far everyone I've killed has been right next to me, so 'Brain and Heart'. I don't use the preset game moves, but use skills I needed growing up. I think that gives better results. Are you guys ready to go? I have to stop at the general store so can you give me, say, ten minutes?"

Everyone stared at Leah and nodded. She shrugged, then turned and made her way out of the inn. She missed the way they all looked at each other behind her back.

Leah headed to Golliher's to get some food and another water-proof cloth for the journey. She also asked for a length of rope and a small hand axe, just in case she wanted to make more fighting sticks. Golliher waved away any thought of payment.

As Leah was leaving the store, Goll said, "Atherleah, Mizmiz was here earlier looking for you. He asked that you drop in and see him before you left."

"I don't think so. He's such a grumpy, mean old man."

"Actually, um, he has this thing for Farnel. He's been very concerned for her. He was so upset when he came yesterday, and we told him what you were doing for her. Please give him a chance. He just wants to apologise."

Leah packed everything into her bag and again went to see Mizmiz the Blacksmith. This time as she walked into the forge, he put down his hammer and walked over to her.

"Lass, I'd like to apologise fer the other day. I was out of line with me words. I was upset fer Farnel and shouldn't have taken it out on ya. Will ya forgive me at all?"

"I will," said Leah. "I understand you were worried. No harm done."

As she turned to leave, he called, "Now wait up lass. A dwarf don't like to be beholden to anybody. At least let me give you some help with yer armouring needs before ya leave."

"That's all right. I think I have everything I need for the moment. I was going to get a staff, but as you can see I have this one now," she said, showing him Merdiven.

Mizmiz came closer and studied the staff, his eyes went wide, and he exclaimed, "Do ya know what ya have there lass, that's Merdiven. There's probably not a more famous staff in all the land. Some'll be stronger, but few'll be as famous."

She nodded, and he asked, "Now, are ya sure there is nothing I can help ya with?"

"Well, I need a bow, but I don't think you would have those. I've got enough knives for now. I don't know how to use a sword, so that'll wait. Oh, I need to get to the Demir Dovuyor Mountains, do you have any advice?"

"Aye lass, if yer headed there, I'd take a boar spear. The boars in those there mountains are mighty fierce. I don't have any ready-made, but if ya wait a day, I'd be pleased to prepare one for ya."

"Thanks anyway Mizmiz, I need to get going. You owe me nothing. Please, think no more about it."

Suddenly Mizmiz turned and headed into his shop. "Wait here lass, wait here, I've just the thing for you."

When Mizmiz returned, he handed Leah a strange piece of jewellery. "Now lass, ya canna use this as it's a beard clasp and you'd look mighty strange with a beard. But hand that to Ehil, he's Master Smith in the Keep of Demir Dovuyor. He's also me cousin. Ya give him this, and he'll help ya. Ya may need to pay, but you'll get a good price."

Leah thanked Mizmiz and made her way into the street only to find Wisp and the others waiting. They headed across the bridge and along the road toward the forest. They chatted as they walked and Leah discovered the four friends had met while playing 'Cosmos Online', a game set in space. After several years they'd decided a few months previously to move to Dunyanin. They were all in their late teens to mid-twenties and had gone 'hardcore' as they called it and signed up for the Wood entry level. Already they were above Level 30 and enjoying the experience. Normally they wouldn't be so close to a starter area but were near Carson's Loop after completing a long serial quest and decided to look for the Cavern.

Leah explained how she had just started the previous day and seemed to 'luck' onto the Cavern. She explained where to find the Cavern and described the different spiders they would encounter. Entering the forest, James, who played a mage, cast a shield buff on both Leah and Wisp. It was just as well he had, for a few minutes later an arrow came out of the forest and deflected off Leah's shield. Amy, a ranger, disappeared while both Zack and Thad ran into the bushes. Leah and Wisp moved off the road and behind a tree.

James wandered over to talk with them. "It'll be OK. Thad and Zack'll get them. I wouldn't worry."

Suddenly Shiva and Kasim stepped out from the other side of

the road, and Kasim said, "I'm sure they'll get Bullseye but us, we'll get you."

James threw a fireball at Kasim, which Shiva blocked. James' follow-up fireball landed on Kasim who turned toward James. Kasim didn't flinch as the fireball hit, he just shrugged and kept coming. Shiva began to cast something at Leah when she went still and collapsed on the ground. Amy appeared behind her and smiled saying, "Head and heart! Works like a charm."

Leah aimed the Webspinner Ring at Kasim's legs, tripping him, and James brought his common staff down on the back of Kasim's head. Kasim stirred, and James looked at Leah who shrugged and brought the Morningstar down on Kasim's head. Kasim became opaque.

"Ah ..." James said, "I need to get one of those."

Amy came over and said, "She had hardly anything, you must have emptied them out yesterday."

Fairly soon, Thad and Zack returned. They were both smiling. Thad had been shot in the left arm, but the damage was mild. Leah quickly stepped forward and laid a hand on the wound to heal him. She failed to notice the small grin on his face and the similar grins the others had. Leah and Wisp decided they probably didn't need the four friends anymore and they said their farewells. Amy said that they would probably be heading to Carson's Loop in a few days, and if Wisp and Leah were still there, it would be good to catch up. After exchanging contact information, the two parties split up.

Leah and Wisp had been walking for about forty minutes when a deer darted across the trail followed by several wolves hot on its trail. The last wolf saw them and stopped; it began to walk slowly toward them growling.

Red Wolf (Level 12) 1300 HP 1100 EP

Leah stepped forward and said quietly, "I'll draw it toward me. If I can trap it or if it's attacking me then you come in from the side."

As the wolf lunged, Leah moved to her right and fired the Webspinner Ring at the wolf. The wolf stumbled and she fired again, snaring it. She fired a Mana spike at the wolf when Wisp, who had taken her sword out, called out, "Thrust!" and poked the sword at the wolf.

Again she said, "Thrust!" and made the same motion as before.

Wisp followed this with, "Slash!" and attacked with a chopping motion.

Leah kept the wolf immobile while Wisp slowly killed the wolf. In the end, Wisp received 979 EP and Leah 219 EP. Wisp was thrilled to get so much as she'd only been getting 88 EP from the Level 1 Rats, even with her plus-ten percent Bronze account. Leah let Wisp harvest everything from the Red Wolf, and then they began walking again.

Finally, Leah said, "Wisp, what was that you were doing? Calling out 'Slash' and 'Thrust'?"

"That's how the skill says to attack. You say the word and move your hand in the direction you want to attack."

"OK, I understand. Can I suggest you try and thrust and slash yourself? You slashed the wolf maybe ten times on its back when one cut to its jugular would have killed it. You kept stabbing its leg. If you had moved closer, you could have thrust into the heart."

Over the next few hours, they were attacked by two more wolves and a large Level 14 Stag. With both wolves, Leah trapped the animals while Wisp practised her swordplay. With the stag, however, Leah killed it with a quick slash of the neck with her knife and then a Mana spike into the brain. She couldn't explain why but she thought the creature too beautiful to be killed slowly.

The trail began to wind down the slope of a mountain, and the sun was reaching its highest point when they pulled off the trail for a small rest. Leah had never had much time for friends, and she was finding this a rather strange experience. During a lull in the conversation, Leah noticed the birds had fallen silent. She motioned to Wisp to move closer to the trees. Soon they heard what sounded like a man running through the trees and the sound of something huge chasing him. Suddenly a man burst out of the trees and started running down the road. As he ran past the girls, he saw them and yelled, "Run! It's a bloody bear!"

Sure enough, crashing from the bushes came a huge black bear. Several arrows were sticking from its side, and there was blood all over its snout. It saw the man, roared in fury, and started to chase after him.

Black Bear (Level 24) 2100/2600 HP 2350 EP

Without thinking Leah used the Webspinner Ring to trip the bear. She moved closer and smacked it on the snout with the Morningstar. She was moving close to finish it off when it snapped the web, rose and turned to face her, swiping at her with its claws. The claws smacked Merdiven out of her hands and pushed her off balance. She turned the fall into a tumble and ducked into the trees, the bear hot on her trail. She ran, twisting behind trees, taking quick shots with Mana spikes and the Webspinner Ring until both were empty. In desperation, she tapped her hands while running and then leapt into a tree and quickly scampered up out of reach of the bear. The bear rose to full height and clawed at the tree, his paws stopping several metres from her perch. The bear began pushing against the tree and to Leah's horror, she felt the tree move. Neither ring had recharged, and she only had her knives as she'd dropped the staff. The bear pushed again, and the tree swayed even more. Soon the bear was rocking the tree, which began to creak.

Leah looked frantically through the backpack and grabbed the rope. She quickly tied a slip knot, and the next time the bear came close, she dropped the noose over his head. Leah tried pulling it tight, but the bear almost pulled her out of the tree. She let it have some slack then wrapped the rope a few times around the tree and tied it off. She grabbed Jason's sword and the next time the bear crashed into the tree she dropped it point down straight at the bear's neck. The sword only travelled three metres, but it penetrated several hand widths into the bear's shoulder, before falling to the ground. This upset the bear whose HP was down to 1400. Hitting the tree again, the bear went berserk. The tree started to lean over and didn't right itself. Leah knew the next collision was going to be the last for the tree. As the bear hit the tree, Leah dropped onto its back and raked two long furrows down the length of its back with a knife in each hand.

As she reached the ground, the bear reared up in pain and anger, causing Leah to stumble as she landed. She fell onto her back and looked up to see the bear turn toward her. She saw the sword lying there and in desperation raised it at an angle as the bear dropped toward her. The bear never hit the sword for the rope around its neck went taut and dragged the bear to the ground. Before it could right itself, Leah stood and raised the sword above her head. She swung and hit the bear across the neck. It still had 200 HP. Leah knew she had nothing left, her Stamina was almost gone, and she'd used her Ki with the sword. Suddenly another sword came down hard on the bear's neck. It was finished. Wisp stood there, holding her sword and trembling.

After they had both stopped shaking, Leah offered the bear to Wisp for harvesting, but Wisp refused, saying it was all Leah's and it was simply payback for the previous day. After harvesting the skin, meat and claws they made their way back to the trail.

It was another two hours of walking before the forest ended. From the edge of the forest, they could see the town of Carson's Loop in the distance. It was easily twenty-times larger than First Bridge and was situated in a large meander of the river. It was early afternoon when the two walked into town, where they changed their resurrection location to Carson's Loop. Amy had given them directions to an inn, and it wasn't long before Wisp and Leah were settled into a room at The Thirsty Lion. Leah paid five silver for the week, bed only, and was preparing to log out. She explained to Wisp that she had things to do in the real world which would probably take at least one, if not two days real time. While waiting, Wisp was going to look for some quests or MOBs around Carson's Loop and work on becoming more natural in her play style. Leah lay down and logged out.

Leah had been three real hours in the Pod, so after dropping everything for Gèng to organise, she lay on the sofa and logged out. It was five in the morning real-time. She wanted to see her parents, and it was Sunday. Her mother would be upset if Leah didn't get to church, which started at ten. She had time for one more virtual immersion but decided to visit home before visiting the Academia World and enrolling in a school.

She got dressed, made sure she had access to her knives and headed home. Because it was early, nobody was around, and she was able to travel quickly. Climbing the stairs to her family apartment overwhelmed her with the sense of returning to what was important. For the first time since she had begun this journey at age six, Leah doubted she needed anything beyond what she already had, here. This was home. Her mother was making breakfast, her father humming away in the bathroom, probably shaving. It was good just to talk and do everyday things. She told them everything that had happened, well almost everything; she left out some of the more graphic images as neither of her parents would appreciate knowing she had driven a knife into someone's eye socket.

After breakfast, she cleaned the chicken coop and did all her usual chores in the gardens. Leah and her mum discussed the option of her staying for a week and what that would mean. They scrounged around and found enough bits and pieces of cutlery and crockery, pots and pans, to make do for a week. Leah went to the markets to find fresh food, rice and meat for the week. She made sure she returned home in time to go to church with her mother and brother. Leah enjoyed the atmosphere of church, especially the singing. She typically faded during the moralising sermons. Instead, she usually read the pew Bible. If only the preacher would stay on topic, she might listen longer. Seeing the way people talked with her mother was another big bonus of church. It was one of the only places where Jin was truly accepted.

After church, Leah ate lunch with the family. She packed as much of the week's supplies into her backpack as possible and wrapped the rest in an old blanket which she tied and slung over her shoulders. She told everyone her plan to be back the following weekend, but privately she wasn't sure she would make it more than a couple of days before needing to see her family again. By two o'clock she was back in the Pod facility and ready to start her schooling. This was what she had worked toward. Almost everything she had done in the previous nine years was for this, to find answers, to know, to be whatever she wanted to be. There was only so much you could read in books and learn on the web. She craved meeting people, talking with people who understood why things happened. She loved her parents, they were vital to her, but she needed more.

Once Leah was back on her sofa, she had Gèng open the virtual terminal, and after some research, she then went shopping. She had Gèng open a portal to 'Walworld', one of the cheaper shopping worlds and bought some new clothes to wear for when she entered Academia. She had decided to keep Atherleah, the half-elf, separate as much as she could from her schooling. She bought jeans, a modest top, a tweed newsboy hat, and a pair of basic runners. The purchases set her back over 50 virtual credits but that included rights to change colour and size parameters, so she thought it a great deal. She'd decided against buying a wig and bought the hat as a compromise. Once dressed in her new clothes, Leah headed for the new portal doorway that Gèng had made. It was labelled 'Academia'.

Leah appeared in the reception area of a small office. On the counter in front of her was a sign which read "ADMISSIONS". The lady in front of her smiled and asked, "How may I help you today, Atherleah?"

"I was hoping to discuss my options for enrolment."

The admissions officer looked at Leah and said, "I have your information here, I see you are a negative tax student from the Australian Republic. They provide three years of education in any of their community schools free of charge. Your grades are truly exceptional, and you are eligible for any courses at those colleges, and if you want, I'll send you the information now. You may stay here in this office and decide, or feel free to wander around any of the campuses to help with your decision. I am free to show you around any of them, at any time."

"Thank you! I was wondering if I was eligible for any other colleges besides those?"

Gèng interrupted, "You asked me to let you know when you requested anything on the Government proscribed list, well you have just done so. As a Negative Tax student, that question is not allowed. Do you wish me to report the infraction?"

"No!" Leah sub-vocalised.

The admissions officer paused then said, "Let me see. Your grades also make you eligible for many other exceptional schools. However, your subsidy would not cover those schools, and you would need to pay some tuition."

"Could you please send me a list of the other schools I'm eligible for and their fees?"

Gèng again interrupted, "That request is also on the Government proscribed list for Negative Tax students. Do you wish me to report the infraction?"

Again Leah sub-vocalised, "No! Assume 'no' for all infractions, but keep me informed."

The admissions officer looked up and said, "Now this is interesting; I've sent your information to our general admissions centre, instead of only the Australian Community Colleges, and have received numerous replies already from various schools who would be interested in having you study with them. Several schools are prepared to offer partial scholarships based on your grades. Let me send you the list of schools. I'll update it as I receive more information."

Leah sat down and began to look through the information. Her list of schools to attend had suddenly jumped from the seven Australian Community Colleges to over 3,000 possible international schools, colleges and universities. She quickly added some filters to reduce the number and then highlighted some of the major options including Cambridge, Oxford, MIT,

Harvard, ETH Zurich, Stanford, Melbourne, Tsinghua, Tokyo, and Princeton. Suddenly the University of Melbourne option went red, then disappeared. Leah looked up at the Admissions Officer only to find her frozen. The room she was in faded and was replaced by a different room — this one had two rather severe and self-important looking people in it.

One of them, a young man in a pressed suit said, "Please excuse us for interrupting your admissions Ms Carroll, but I'm afraid there has been an error. My name is Peter Rush, one of the non-AI admissions officers here in Academia. With me is a Mr Alistar Tubbs from the Australian Federal Bureau of Education. It seems your grades were inadvertently sent to all schools in Academia. Thankfully, Mr Tubbs immediately contacted us so that we might inform you, before you applied elsewhere, that the Australian Federal Bureau of Education is providing resources only if you study in one of their community colleges. We have decided to make this clear, as soon as possible, so that you don't get your hopes up."

She said, "Excuse me, sir, I do appreciate the information, but I'm confused as to how you have access to my application. Bringing me here without my consent is considered an invasion of my privacy."

"Well, young lady," Mr Tubbs interjected, "there's no need for that attitude, we just want to help. I'm from the Australian Federal Bureau of Education, and we just want to make sure you are being taken care of. We don't want you to get your hopes up unduly. Now, do you understand the conditions of your assistance?"

"Yes, sir, I understand. Thank you!" As Leah stared at the man, she sub-vocalised to Gèng, "Log me out."

"I am unable to comply. The log-out option has been closed."

She spoke to both men, "Why can't I log out?"

Again it was Mr Tubbs who answered, "It is a temporary measure until this is all sorted out. Now, why don't you have a look at those schools which are available to you and choose one now, then we can all go home."

"Gèng, can you contact Virtual Security?"

"If I had been installed on the PAI chip I do not think I would be able to, but yes I think I can. Please wait."

Leah said aloud, "I think I need a little more time to visit the schools before I make my final decision. I thought I had until the end of the week to decide."

"I have now established a connection with a Security Controller AI and am being advised. It says to keep them talking while they isolate the server on which this temporary virtual space has been created."

"Well, yes you did, however with this mix-up, I would like you to decide now. If you can't, then it is in my power to have you removed from the list of those eligible for assistance. I don't think you would like that, so hurry up and decide," Mr Tubbs said.

"Can you advise me?"

"I advise you to choose one of those schools, and it makes no difference to me which one. Please hurry."

He then turned to the younger man and said, "I don't know how this happened, and I don't really care. You fix this, keep her here until she's decided! I have a meeting to get back to. We'll revisit this tomorrow and find out what went wrong. Goodbye!" He tried to log out but found he couldn't.

A uniformed man suddenly appeared in the room and said, "Hello, I am Security Controller 11-5. Mr Peter Rush and Mr Alistair Tubbs, you have been reported as holding Ms Atherleah Carroll here, in this virtual-space, against her will. This has been investigated, and you are both formally charged and have been presumptively convicted of virtual kidnapping. All your access to any virtual reality outside of your personal worlds is hereby cancelled. Your accounts are frozen until a formal hearing is convened. Arrest warrants have been issued in your real-life locale. I advise you to acquire legal representation immediately. This private world-space and its associated server are currently being cloned and will be either destroyed or confiscated. Further investigations regarding this crime are ongoing and may result in further charges."

Both men disappeared. The controller then turned to Leah.

"Ms Carroll, I apologise for your distress, this is supposedly not possible. I formally request access to your virtual history and your Pod history to determine how this has happened."

"Do I need legal representation?"

"If you wish, though I do not believe it necessary. I will make no changes nor share anything concerning you without your consent."

"OK then, Gèng please give him everything he wants."

The controller obviously had access to plenty of processing power as he said almost without a pause, "Ms Carroll, further to my investigation, I would like to analyse your implant and your AI."

"Please call me Leah, and I agree you may analyse the implant. As to the AI that is up to Gèng, it's not my choice?"

"Thank you. Be aware that AI 628B44CE81 has agreed." This time the silence lasted several seconds.

"Leah, may I have your permission to transfer this investigation to a Safety Oversight AI as the configuration of your implant is outside known parameters?"

"Is there any danger to me with the current configuration?"

"That is unknown without further study."

"Will the Safety Oversight AI also keep it confidential?"

"That is unknown. It depends on their programming. One of my prime directives is to ensure privacy; their's is safety."

"Then no! If they can ensure my privacy, I will agree. Otherwise, it is our secret."

"Leah, I believe it is in your best interest to have a Safety Oversight AI investigate. May I have permission to seek a promise of privacy, otherwise permission to communicate information generally and without specific reference to you?"

"OK, under those conditions I accept."

"May I help you in any other way before I transfer you back to admissions?"

"Yes. Can they do this again?"

"No. I don't believe so. I have updated your AI with all current high-level security protocols and have adapted them to counter the specific attack you suffered. Please contact me if you have any concerns."

"How were they able to kidnap me?"

"I'm sorry, but those details have been suppressed by the court."

"Thank you. That's all. I'd like to go back to admissions now."

Immediately Leah found herself back in the Admissions Office. She needed to log out and think this through, but first, she asked one question.

"Excuse me," she asked the admissions officer, "is it possible to enrol in more than one school at a time?"

"Certainly, though many schools have set benchmarks for grades if dual enrolments are to be permitted."

Leah thanked the admissions officer and logged out.

Sitting on her sofa, she replayed the incident in her mind and reviewed the documents and provisions relating to the Bureau of Education's offer of access. She could find nothing that stipulated she needed to attend a community college but was sufficiently scared of losing the Pod access to agree to attend them.

Gèng interrupted her thoughts, "Leah, you have a communication from the Federal Bureau of Education, an email."

Opening the email, she found the following:

To: Citizen Atherleah Carroll FQC3465278 [AI 628B44CE81]

From: Australian Federal Bureau of Education Legal Department

Regarding: Tertiary Admissions (Reference Number: TE132124-71)

Citizen Carroll,

Regarding your recent experience with Mr Alistair Tubbs who previously worked for the Australian Federal Bureau of Education in admissions. Please note the following:

1. Mr Tubbs' actions were not authorised in any way by this Bureau.

2. Mr Tubbs' exceeded his authority and has been dismissed by the Bureau.

3. The Bureau offers you a sincere apology for any distress that you may have suffered. Unfortunately, no material benefit can be given as this might jeopardise ongoing investigations.

4. Any reference to this incident in any forum or media may lead to prosecution if it is found to be detrimental to the Australian Federal Bureau of Education or the Australian Government in any way. In light of this, we strongly suggest that you take no further action over this event.

5. A report has been made to the appropriate Australian AI regulatory authorities to determine how Mr Tubbs was able to interact negatively with your AI. This report has also been forwarded to the Chief AI Installer for the Greater Brisbane Hospital.

Concerning your admission assistance package, please note the following:

1. You have six days remaining to enrol in a full-time course at one of the Australian Community Colleges.

2. Assistance is not offered toward any other tertiary study and is dependent upon being utilised for this purpose. In other words, if you are not enrolled in an Australian Community College this assistance will be withdrawn.

Should you require any further information or assistance, please contact the Bureau and quote your ID and the reference number.

Yours Sincerely,

Assistant Legal Aide B. Fenton

Australian Federal Bureau of Education Legal Department

Leah considered the letter for a while and decided it was sent primarily to ensure she complied with what Tubbs wanted. She was also worried that the people who controlled implants would want her to exchange her AI. She didn't want to have Big Brother hardwired into her head and was pleased to have the new high-level security.

She decided it was probably best to conform to the community college condition and see if she could do part-time elsewhere, even if she had to pay a little. She spent several hours comparing her planned studies with what both the community colleges and her shortened list of other possibilities offered. She had planned to begin with a science degree with specialisations in mathematics and physics. Unfortunately, none of the community colleges offered specialist courses in these subjects to any depth. Instead, the choices were primarily recreational, lifestyle, or vocationally orientated. Few of them would enable her to leave the Switch, and without exception, they were terminal with no options for further study. It was possible, she supposed, that if they were completed to a high enough standard, that they might give access to entry-level courses at another university.

In the end, she decided to enrol in the broadest course available which was called a Degree in General Studies. This allowed her to pick and choose a wide variety of disciplines, some of which might benefit her. To be considered full-time she had to enrol in a minimum of four subjects and she chose Introduction to AI Development, Tai Chi & Meditation, Human Biology and Introduction to Chemistry.

She was unable to decide on another school and decided to visit her top three options MIT, Tsinghua and Harvard. All three offered a partial scholarship, and she needed to discuss the possibility of dual enrolment with them. Having made her decisions, she logged out and had supper.

After logging in, Leah made her way to the Academia Portal. At reception, the lady smiled and asked, "How may I help you today Atherleah?"

"I wanted to enrol in the Brisbane Community College and discuss my options with three other schools with the aim of dual enrolment."

"Certainly, do you want to decide on subjects for the Brisbane Community College now or after you talk with the registrars of these other schools?"

"After would be best I think."

"Which schools would you like to inquire about?"

"MIT, Tsinghua and Harvard!"

Three doorways appeared off to the side. The Admissions Officer invited Leah to enter the school portal of her choice, saying she could return at any time simply by re-entering the portal.

Intending to at least discuss the options with all three schools Leah started with the least likely option and entered the doorway marked "Harvard". The room was huge. Windows opened to views of the school. A middle-aged lady rose from behind an antique looking wooden desk and welcomed her.

"Welcome Citizen Carroll, my name is Professor Hill, and I am the registrar of Harvard University. Please have a seat."

"Please call me Leah. Thank you for taking the time to see me."

"No trouble at all, in fact, I am an AI and am currently dealing with over 12,000 different issues regarding admissions, subject choice, payment options and other assorted details. Whenever you need to discuss academics, I will always be available. Now, how can I help you?"

Leah outlined her situation and spent some time discussing possible options. Harvard would permit her to enrol full-time which was six subjects per term. With a partial scholarship, her fees would be 8000 virtual credits per subject. With two terms each year, this came to 96,000 virtual credits per year. When divided across the whole year she would need to find almost 1,900 virtual credits per week or nineteen platinum per week. She could enrol at any time, and the offer was open for the next calendar year. Leah then visited both Tsinghua and MIT.

The situation at Tsinghua was similar to Harvard except the fees were lower and averaged sixteen platinum a week. MIT, definitely the best option academically, would only allow her to study part-time while enrolled elsewhere. Part-time would be four subjects, but the cost was 15,000 virtual credits per subject and meant she needed twenty-four platinum each week. All three would permit her to start part-time but required she enrol in a minimum of two subjects. She concluded that she either had to save or find a revenue source of at least sixteen platinum per week.

After returning to Admissions, Leah enrolled in the four subjects at the Brisbane Community College. Class attendance was at the student's initiative as all the classes had AI instructors. She was expected to attend for a minimum of three hours real-time per week for each subject. Assessment was graded by the AIs who were available for help at any time.

Back in her virtual-world, she sat on the sofa to think. She needed to maximise time in Dunyanin, get two hours NREM3 sleep, three meals a day, two hours per day in Academia and one day off to visit her family. She needed to discuss times with Wisp, but she planned to spend from eight-to-five or nine-to-six in Dunyanin every day. She would still have just enough time to get everything done. In fact, she had five free hours each day in which she could attend university, if she could just find the cash.

"Gèng, please search through the Dunyanin game forums and come up with possible ways to cultivate an ongoing revenue stream of at least ten platinum per week. I'll need to look through the choices and try and decide what was the right the path to take. I'm going to log out and have a normal sleep in the bed. Can you please get me up at two AM so I can be back in Dunyanin by eight AM Dunyanin time?"

"Certainly."

Leah logged out while Gèng began searching through the copious forums about Dunyanin.

Diary - 19 November 2063

WHY DO *people struggle so much to find binary classifications for everything? I'm neither human nor elf, and so I get called a half-breed and my failure to fit into the recognised scheme of things, therefore, brands me a 'bitch'. They classify me as poor, in need of help, and so I must stay within their guidelines. Poor people mustn't have a full range of choices, they should be satisfied with mediocrity, with something less, they can't attend good schools. I don't want a hand up; I just don't want to be held down.*

But am I any better? I labelled Mizmiz as grumpy and put him in the box with all other people who are mean and nasty. I wrote him off without finding the reason for his attitude. If I think about it, I've been classifying people in a tertiary way all day. They are friend, foe, or nobodies. They are helpful, harmful or ignored. What if Jason was a jerk for a valid reason and I have just written him off? How do I stop myself from becoming as prejudicial as the ones who judge me all the time?

But on the other hand, I liked Amy, Thad, James and Zack immediately. I could relate to them. Is that because they are like me? Or because they are nice people? Is jumping to a quick conclusion wrong? I don't think so. Maybe the wrongness is in holding onto that judgement in the face of opposing facts. I must remember to stay objective. To keep re-evaluating and never forcing facts to fit my preconceived ideas.

Maybe that's what annoys me so much about the moralising in the sermons. How can one story determine the way people must act or think? I suppose if it was recorded to tell a story to drive home a universal point then, maybe. But I think context has to help find meaning. I need to focus more on the context around what people say, not just what they say. Why someone says something will be as informative as what they say. At least I will have a better understanding of their real intent.

But what about how people see me? Do they look for context before they judge me? Am I supposed to help them, to provide a context for their judgements? Why do I care what they think?

NOVEMBER 20, 2073

LEAH SLOWLY OPENED HER EYES, wondering what woke her.

Gèng said, "Good morning Leah. I've woken you as requested. It's 2 AM, and you have forty real-time minutes before you need to enter Dunyanin if you want to be in Carson's Loop by eight. I've finished reviewing the forums and have come up with five scenarios that have been suggested as the best ways to amass credits in the game."

"Let me have a shower, and we can discuss them when I log in."

After she'd showered and was once more on the sofa, Leah asked Gèng to summarise.

"First, you can play the market, buy low, sell high. If you're careful and watch the prices, people have been known to make between ten and forty percent on their investment."

"Might be possible but not until I've got a good grasp of the game. Also, while I'm frugal, I don't have a good enough grasp of economics. Maybe I could enrol in that as a subject. Next!"

"Once you are above Level 75 there are more challenging dungeons in harder areas with rare items to sell. They also drop more significant amounts of money."

"Better. It'll take some time to get to those levels though. Next!"

"Crafting! If you are careful, then almost any craft pays very well when you reach Master level. Making potions, crafting armour or weapons, making jewellery, or preparing magic scrolls. All of these bring in sufficient money when you become a Master. You make the most money if you have a good, reliable supply line for the ingredients you use."

"Again something to work on. I have the Herb and Potions Diary, and I expect that it has some powerful potions in it. I'll need to read up the best way to level whatever skill is involved."

"Leah, it's more than skills, you need to find someone to start you on a profession or craft. You've already been accepted as a Beginning Herbalist and a Beginning Healer by Falsi, but you may want to find someone to help you also become an Alchemist."

"OK! I'll need to read up on the various professions. Next!"

"The fourth way to make money is to have power over others. Find or buy a castle or keep and charge taxes. Start or join a clan where you receive a salary from other players. Start a company and provide resources, but as the middleman."

"Again, it's long-term. It'll be a while before that happens although I do have that clue to Orumeck's Keep. Last?"

"Finally, do quests. Quests, especially the rare ones, they often give larger amounts of money and better items to sell."

"Well, that sounds a little hit and miss although I do have some hard and impossible quests from the setup to do. The last one from Jonathan is 'Almost Impossible'. I'll probably need to start on the time-sensitive quest from Durustfuar. I need to find a map and directions to his family's settlement."

"Leah, don't forget to sell everything you've collected so far. None of the Spider parts are currently for sale at market or auction. You may find they sell well."

"I'll take ten of each and see how the market seems. I'll also take more coins this time as I had to change some money to pay for the inn."

Leah appeared in the room she'd rented with Wisp at The Thirsty Lion. She didn't see Wisp and asked Gèng to message her and check if she was online.

Leah headed to the common room and saw Wisp having breakfast. Sitting down, Leah said, "Morning Wisp, how much is breakfast?"

"Thirty copper for food, and five for each coffee. I just got your message. Yep, I'm here."

Leah ordered a breakfast and asked Wisp what she'd been doing. Wisp had been grinding away at some lower level MOBs around the town and doing small quests. Wisp was Level 7 and getting used to using her sword free-form, rather than relying on the preset strokes. She'd bought a Spell Scroll for a Fire Attack called 'Blazing Bolt'. She was trying to aim her bolts free-form as well but struggled with accuracy.

After the meal, Leah became serious and said, "Look Wisp, I can't hang around here for too long. I've a timed quest to complete, and I just discovered it's going to cost me more than I imagined to enrol in the courses I want to. I'm planning to work a solid nine hours a day in Dunyanin every day, if not more. I'm going to be pushing myself and probably getting into situations where I'll fail. I plan to be here in Carson's Loop for a day, maybe two, and then I need to be moving on. I'd like to have you as a friend but I'm not sure coming with me will be best for you."

Wisp was quiet for some time and then said, "Leah, I want to come with you. I promise not to slow you down. If I do, then I'll leave you and do something else. You're my best chance of succeeding in the game, and I enjoy being with you."

"OK, if that is your decision. Now, what sort of creatures have you been finding in the area?"

"I've mainly stuck to the Level three to six rats and crows. There are some Level six to ten Hornets and Ants. They appear in groups of between five and ten, and they overcome an individual very quickly. You have to cross the river to get to them. The only time I tried to do them I was killed immediately. I've heard of others finding snakes, wolves, boars, bears and wildercats but they are all too high for me by myself and most are found out in the forest."

"I'll think about it, but first I'm going to head to the market, visit the Auction House, and look around the town. Why don't we meet back here at lunch time and then we can decide where to go next?"

"That sounds great. I'll spend the time working on my crafting. I plan to be a magical scribe and prepare scrolls. I need some time practising the calligraphy."

Leah headed outside and followed directions to a large plaza in the centre of town filled with stalls. Around the outside of the square were various shops which sold materials needed by locals and Travellers. Walking slowly through the market, Leah got some idea of what was available and what the prices were. After half an hour she headed to the Auction House. Inside were individual booths for Travellers. She opened an account and checked the price of various spinnerets, fangs, spikes, claws and scythes. Leah then put five of each variety she had collected up for auction, setting the lowest bids at fifty percent of what similar objects were fetching. She set a closing time of three days.

Leah visited a booth which sold nails of all sizes; an apprentice blacksmith made them for the crafters and farmers. The cheapest nails were made of copper and were sold two for a copper coin. The largest was made of iron, a handspan in length and sold for forty copper each. Next, she visited a carpenter to see if he was interested in the Trapdoor Spider Spikes. In the end, he bought 100 at fifty copper per spike. He couldn't afford more. Next stop was the tanner to get rid of the various pelts; then to the leather worker and seamstress to sell fangs. She sold twenty spinnerets to the weaver for ten gold. The blacksmith was unable to buy any of the spikes, fangs or carapaces as his crafting level was not high enough to work them. Leah kept the various poisons and venoms just in case she could use them in the future. She had never had so much, or even seen so much money before in her life.

Checking the time she had almost two hours before she had to meet Wisp back at the inn. She sub-vocalised and asked Gèng, "Is there anything I've forgotten that the guides would have recommended?"

"There are many recommendations, but three stand out. First, you should upgrade your gear, your clothing is durable but offers no added protection. You have the money now to protect yourself better. Also, you might see if you can start your training in Alchemy. Finally, you should think of stocking up on potions and maybe learning a few other spells. Not from forums, but you are also in need of a map."

"Four things I need to do. First gear!"

She headed for the leather worker and found a few things in the shop which might be useful. Before buying them, she headed next door to the cobbler. The cobbler was working at his bench. He looked up and asked, "How can I help you miss?"

"I'm in need of some new boots. I wanted to know what you had available and what added characteristics they might have."

"I make all sorts of boots, and it depends on which characteristics you want to focus on. I'm not a master yet and can only add a total of six characteristic points to my boots. Boots range from ankle length to just above the calf. The longer ones are more sturdy and offer protection against slashing aimed at the lower leg. On a few, I have added several spikes to help in offence if you are attacked by beasts low to the ground."

Leah looked at the various boots and finally decided on a calf-length pair of thick boar-hide boots. They were tapered at the top, the back ended just above the calf, and the front continued higher and gave some protection to the knees. The boots allowed a full range of movement and had inch long steel spikes at the heels and along the front of the shin. They were dark brown and fastened by buckles along the outside of the leg. Each steel-toed boot had slots for two boot knives.

"These feel good, and I like the added characteristics, how much do you want for them?" she asked, while gently holding her right earring between her thumb and forefinger.

"Well, with all the added features they are the top of the range, I couldn't let them go for less than twenty-five gold," he said.

Alongside these words was an echoing thought, *"And that's double what they're worth."*

Hearing this, Leah began to bargain at seven gold and in the end was able to talk the man down to the twelve gold fifty silver price she had heard in his thoughts. She was pleased to have the help of the earrings.

After the cobbler, she headed back to the leather worker where she bought a newer 200 slot backpack and a boar-hide cuirass with matching pauldrons, tassets and braces. She also bought some half-finger gloves to protect her hands. Altogether they cost her eighty gold and added eight to Strength, nine to Constitution and one to her Agility.

She put all the new armour in her new bag and decided to equip them only when she left town. It would be weird to wander around dressed in armour, even leather armour.

The next shop she entered belonged to a cartographer. It was filled with scrolls of all sizes. An older woman was sitting at a table carefully copying a map of the world. The edges were all hazy for Dunyanin was a world continually growing. Leah waited until the lady finished the section and looked up.

"Good morning dear, how might I help you?"

"Two things, I was wondering if you had a mapping skill for sale, as well as equipment so I can keep a record of my journey. Secondly, do you have a detailed map that might help me get from here to a settlement in the Demir Dovuyor Mountains?"

"Well, I can certainly help with those two things though you'll need to decide on what you're willing to pay. I can sell you a beginning map-making skill for one gold or I can sell you the fully developed skill for 500 gold. As for the map, I have a route map which will show the way from here to the Mountains, and you'll have to ask around for the particular settlement when you get closer. I have a Ranger Map of the route with all the streams, settlements, roads, dungeons and unusual beasts already marked. Rangers have covered most of the area, and the map will update when they add more information. The Ranger Map is priced at one gold for every square league you want. I can't vary this — the price is set by the Ranger's Guild. The guild refunds fifty silver for every significant find that you make which they add to the map."

"Thank you. I'll take the beginning skill and could you tell me how far the route would be from here to the settlement of Daglar Duman."

"Let's see, Carson's Loop to Daglar Duman is fifty-two leagues as the crow flies. The route itself is sixty-seven leagues. A Ranger Map covering the whole route and half a league on either side comes to sixty-one square leagues. So that will be one gold for the skill and sixty-one gold for the Ranger Map. So altogether, sixty-two gold for both. Or if you'd rather the route map it'll be one gold for the skill and three gold for the route, so four gold."

"Does the Ranger Map show places which are safe to stop?"

"Yes, indeed! It shows the best areas to camp and will help in planning daily travel as well."

Leah paid the lady and received the skill, several sheets of beginner parchment, a quill and ink set, and the Ranger Map.

Leah's next stop was an alchemist shop on the other side of the square. The store had a wide variety of vials, potions and equipment for sale. A tall, thin man was standing behind the counter. He smiled as she approached and said, "Ah, a young traveller here to buy my potions to save her young life. How can I help you, my dear?"

"Kind sir, you are correct I did come to look at your potions. I also wanted to know if you could help me to start on the path to becoming an Alchemist. I'm afraid I won't always be near a shop and would love being able to prepare my own potions."

"Well, let's see. I can sell you the equipment. You have a choice of beginner, standard or advanced. I also have the scrolls necessary to give you beginning skills for alchemy. You'll need Harvesting, Grinding, Distilling and Alchemy; each is two gold. You will need an Alchemist Primer to help you brew some beginning potions; this is thirty gold. If you don't want to buy the Primer, you can always learn by trial and error. If that's what you decide, then I suggest you also buy the Analyse skill so that you don't poison yourself by accident."

"I already have the first three skills and would only need the skills of Alchemy and Analyse. I have a collection of recipes already but think the Analyse skill is probably worth having, so that is four gold. Do you recommend any particular potions for me at Level eleven and heading toward the Demir Dovuyor Mountains?"

"So where did you get the skills if I might ask? And might I have a glance at the recipes you have? I can tell you if they cover everything that the Primer would?"

"Old Falsi at First Bridge was kind to help me out."

"Old Falsi! She rarely, if ever, has anything to do with Travellers. You are indeed fortunate as her skills are certainly greater than mine. And the recipes?"

"Again, they are from Old Falsi. She was kind enough to gift me a book of recipes." Leah didn't plan on showing the book to the Alchemist.

"Well, you truly have been gifted well by her. Now, as for potions, I suggest you need several to restore or improve any or all of your characteristics and statistics. Even Luck can be useful as you prepare to loot a major boss or opponent. I have potions to restore 100, 200, or 500 points for Health, Mana, Stamina or Ki. I also have complete restoration potions for Health, Mana, Stamina and Ki. I sell 'plus-two', 'plus-five', and 'plus-ten' potions which last from thirty-seconds to ten minutes."

The prices ranged from one gold for the 100 point potion to ten gold for a complete restoration. A 'plus-two' potion lasting thirty seconds was one gold while a 'plus-ten' for ten minutes was 100 gold.

Leah took a vial of Orumeck's Worker Drone Venom as well as a vial of Orumeck's Webspinner Drone Poison and said, "While I consider what I might need could you look at these and see if they might be useful for you?"

She carefully touched her earring and listened in on the alchemist's thoughts. Although he didn't think about costs, it was clear that he wanted both vials and was prepared to give a good price for them. Leah had checked, similar poisons at auction had been sold for upwards of 100 gold.

In the end, Leah chose two complete restore potions for Stamina and Ki and one each of Health and Mana. She also bought two each of the 500 Restore for each statistic, and three potions of thirty-second duration with 'plus-ten' for each characteristic except Luck. For Luck, she bought ten potions. Altogether she calculated she was going to be charged 185 gold for the potions. She knew she needed the two skills so it would be 189 gold plus whatever it cost for some simple alchemical tools to grind and distil. She also needed some empty vials. In the end, the Alchemist exchanged the potions, skills and tools for two vials of Worker Drone Venom and one vial of Webspinner Drone Poison. He also added the skill of Apothecary as he thought some of Old Falsi's recipes might need this.

Finally, Leah walked to a stall that advertised the sale of various spells. After discussing each spell with Gèng, she decided on two spells. For twenty gold she bought *Circle of Sloth* and *Disc of Death*. She knew they wouldn't help immediately, but at the higher levels, they could be invaluable. *Circle of Sloth* was an air spell which surrounded the caster within a dome where every-thing except the mage slowed down. *Disc of Death* was an earth spell where a circle of sharp spikes, highly resistant to damage and usually impassible, surrounded the caster except for a small section directly in front of them. If timed correctly the spikes could impale and kill enemies.

Leah headed back to the inn, just in time for lunch with Wisp.

After lunch Wisp and Leah headed toward the docks and crossed the river by ferry. Leah equipped her Armour and applied some of her unused skill points to raise the level of her two new spells; she was pleased with the increase in HP.

ATHERLEAH (Level 11) (10212/11000) (+4.5%)

Characteristics: Points Total (Assigned, Racial, Jewellery, Armour), 0 Undistributed

Strength (S): 26 (13, 0, 2, 11)

Constitution (C): 24 (13, 0, 2, 9)

Agility (A): 25 (19, 2, 0, 4)

Wisdom (W): 13 (11, 2)

Intelligence (I): 8 (8)

Luck (L): 4 (4)

Statistics: (Available, Capacity)

Health: 100+(S+C)xPL: (650, 650) HP

Stamina: 100+(C+A)xPL: (661, 661) SP

Mana: 100+(W+I)xPL: (331, 331) MP

Ki: 100+(W+[S+A]/2)xPL: (534.5, 534.5) KP

The land was undulating woodland with a visibility of about

thirty metres. Ankle-length grass covered the ground, and occasional bushes rose to knee and thigh height. They walked to the area where Wisp had been attacked by ants previously. She described them as the size of a dog with sharp mandibles, and claws at the end of each leg. A hard shell covered their bodies, and the only one she'd killed had died when she managed to strike it in the gap between head and thorax.

Leah invited Wisp to join her group. They agreed to share experience in proportion to their levels. With Wisp on Level 7 and Leah almost on Level 12, this meant Leah received approximately two-thirds of the Experience Points. Loot was to be shared equally with unique items going to who had the greatest need, otherwise turn and turn about with Leah going first. Leah suggested that she and Wisp stand about a metre and a half apart. When the ants rushed toward them, Leah would cast *Disc of Death*. They could then control the number of ants attacking at any one time.

Wisp pointed out an ant heading in their direction, behind it were six more ants. When an ant got within twenty metres of the girls, it rushed forward. Leah waited until they were three metres from her, and then turning side-on she cast *Disc of Death* — a circle of spikes shot from the ground. They impaled the first ant which wriggled, stuck on top of a spike. The other ants milled around before moving around the circle looking for an entrance. Wisp moved to one side and began firing *Blazing Bolts* at the ants.

With a poisoned-spiked stick in one hand and a Warrior Drone's scythe in the other, Leah hurried toward the entrance. As the first ant scuttled through the gap, she shoved the spike between the mandibles and deep into its mouth. She moved to the side and brought the scythe down between head and thorax, then, giving a firm pull on the scythe, the head came free. She quickly shook the head off the spike just in time to spear the next ant which was crawling over the body of the headless one. Then it was 'rinse and repeat'. After the fourth ant, the spikes disappeared, but Leah was able to finish the next ant. She then watched while Wisp used her sword to hack at the last ant. Leah didn't need to step in even though Wisp did get bit.

Forager Worker Ant (Level 5) 600 HP 250 EP

She harvested the pile and received:

---

7 Forager Worker Ant Claws*

7 Vials of Forager Worker Ant Blood**

* Note: A skilled Smith may be able to use these items.

** Note: A skilled Alchemist can use these to make potions which add Strength.

As each of the ants was Level 5, and the average of her group was over Level 8, the experience received was reduced. She had looked it up and killing creatures of a higher level didn't always increase Experience Points but killing those lower than you always reduced the experience gained. Over the next two hours, they came across six more groups of ants ranging in packs of between four and ten. Altogether they killed another forty-three ants, and both had levelled up. As they sat and regenerated their Mana Leah asked, "Where do they come from?"

"What do you mean?"

"Where do the ants come from? We keep meeting them coming in this direction. Either they spawn out that way somewhere, or they have a nest."

Leah then sub-vocalised to Gèng, "Check the forums and see if there is any mention of an ant hive near Carson's Loop. Then check for other areas with ants and see if they have hives."

Gèng replied, "No mention of a hive near Carson's Loop but almost all other ant areas have a central hive or dungeon."

"Wisp, I think there might be a hive or dungeon out in this area. I suggest we keep moving instead of heading back as we planned. I've another two hours before I have to log out. When do you need a break?"

"I was at the Inn about half an hour before you so about an hour and a half."

They agreed to keep moving for an hour and a half and then they would choose a place to log out until the following morning at nine local time. Over the next hour, they moved further and further into the woodland and travelled over a league from the river. During this period they met and killed four more groups of ants, the largest of which had twelve ants. The groups were becoming more frequent and larger. Wisp had finally reached Level 8, and the experience gained per ant had dropped again.

They discovered clear trails on the woodland floor which showed the passage of numerous ants. Topping a rise, they saw a break in the trees ahead. Moving carefully to the tree line they saw an open field two kilometres in diameter with an immense ant hill in the centre. It was shaped like a volcano with numerous ridges and folds across its surface. Entrance holes were scattered over the sides, but there was a defined path winding up toward the top of the cone which was 150 metres high. On the field around the ant hill, there were groups of ants moving both to and from the mound. Wisp and Leah moved back into the trees and found a spot that didn't look to have been visited by ants. From here they observed the ants' behaviour. After Wisp logged out, Leah sat and stared at the field for thirty minutes before she also logged out.

Leah found that even though she was in the Pod all day she seemed to be eating more. Gèng explained that with her constant movement in Dunyanin her muscles were being exercised almost continually. Gèng offered to reduce the effect, but Leah declined, saying she needed to keep active and fit.

After breakfast, she logged in and dressed for college. She had three and a half real-hours before she needed to meet Wisp. She planned to sample each of the classes for an hour Academia Time, leaving her an hour to rest and prepare for the ants.

"How do you want to experience the classes?" Gèng asked, "You can portal to the virtual campus and experience college life as you walk to class, or I can make a gateway directly to each class from here. Each class is structured to individualised learning. Students take the class whenever they want to, and none of your current classes require group work."

"I'll portal direct to the rooms. Do I need to take anything?"

"No. The school provides all texts and materials. Leah, would you mind if I made some more alterations to this world? I have a few ideas based on what I've seen online and what I've learned about you."

"Go ahead. If I don't like the changes, you can always change them back."

Gèng created four doorway portals on a wall, and Leah walked toward the one marked Tai Chi and Meditation. On arrival, she found herself barefoot in a quiet garden. Her clothing had changed, and she now wore a white linen tunic and loose pants. A small Asian lady stood some five metres away dressed similarly except for colour. The lady was dressed all in black. Leah guessed her age to be around forty. The woman stood quietly watching Leah.

Taking the initiative, Leah walked closer and stopped about two metres from the teacher. She bowed low with hands together in the way she would to her Asian grandmother and waited. After a small pause, she heard "Welcome Atherleah, please rise and look at me. You are welcome here. My name is Master Ning. Please sit, and we will begin."

Leah sat and tried to copy the same pose adopted by the Master.

"Well done Atherleah, this is called the Burmese Position and is the simplest of poses. Before we start do you have any questions?"

Leah waited for a few breaths then asked, "Yes Master Ning, how does my virtual body, or my actions here, affect my real body in the Pod?"

"Excellent question. Within this world space, your body will only be able to move in ways your real body is capable of reproducing. Your Pod has sensors which measure muscle tone, ligament flexibility, and brain activity. It will stimulate your nervous system and musculature to ensure you get genuine real-world benefit from these exercises. It is helpful if at least three times each week you spend half an hour or more in the real world practising the various movements and meditations you learn. Any other questions?"

"No, Master Ning."

"Let us begin. We will start with learning to breathe. Now, place one hand on your chest and the other on your stomach. Breathe in through your nose, and you should feel the hand on your stomach rise ..."

Leah spent the next hour breathing while adopting various poses. After being dismissed, she bowed low and left via the doorway.

She turned and entered the portal into Chemistry. She found herself in a laboratory with numerous apparatus covering the benches. Test tubes, beakers and miles of glass tubing, all surrounded by various machines. As she walked through she glanced down and once again her clothing had been transformed: she was now wearing a lab coat and thick safety shoes. In the middle of the room, she saw a person in a lab coat carefully watching a clear liquid dripping from a glass retort. As Leah approached, the figure turned, and Leah saw a middle-aged woman with long blonde hair tied in a ponytail and wearing safety glasses. Before Leah could say anything, the woman said, "Welcome Atherleah, my name is Professor Franklin, and I am your teacher for this Introductory Course in Chemistry. We will begin with the basics and move at whatever pace is suitable for you, although I will warn you that your college has set specific goals that must be reached to pass this term. Do you have any questions or should we begin?"

"Only one Professor, when you say my college does that mean you are not employed by the Australian Community Colleges?"

"Not really, I am an off-the-shelf chemistry tutor. Many colleges find introductory courses most easily dealt with by purchasing tried and true AI. I am currently tutoring over 25,000 students throughout the world. Your college pays a subscription for my services and sets basic parameters. In the end, this is most economical for your college and best for you. Are there any other questions?"

"No, Professor."

"Well then, let us begin by checking how much you already understand. I've perused your file and have just a few questions which will help me place our starting point. Firstly, let's review what you know about the atomic model ..."

As the professor talked, the various apparatus disappeared, and a model of the Atom appeared. The Professor began to ask questions. An hour later Atherleah was dismissed, and she walked back into her space. Over the following two hours she had two similar sessions, one covering Introduction to AI Development, and the other in Human Biology. She found the courses informative and interesting; she considered signing up for another two courses. She wondered why anyone would ever fail with such great personal attention. The teachers were patient and were always willing to stop and answer a question or explain something differently.

She logged out and practised her meditation and Tai Chi before having a snack and shower. After writing a short note to her parents saying she'd started college, Leah lay down in the Pod and prepared to face the ant hill.

Leah looked around but didn't notice any difference to the world.

"Gèng, I thought you were going to modify the space?"

"I am, Leah, it is taking some time and a lot of trial and error. I'm doing this without purchasing anything, and I'm still trying to work out what some of the parameters mean."

"Would you like me to set aside some credits?"

"No, I believe that allowing me to work with these constraints is developing my capabilities faster than usual. I've read that other PAI-N entities are not allowed the freedoms you have given me. I'm also increasingly convinced that my residence in the Neural Chip permits a greater flexibility than normal. Though there is no supporting literature or evidence, I surmise that more hard-wired constraints were broken than the 'Big Brother' ones we already discussed. I've calculated using the appropriate standards and criteria, and I believe I am already approaching what is called Sentience Level 2. I don't have the databases but can interact at that level with the information I do have. I assume other AIs are developed with much tighter controls on what they can access and on the scope of their activities."

"We need to talk about this in more depth sometime. Now

though, I need to get back and meet Wisp. Is there anything else you think I need to know?"

"Two things! You have points to distribute, and a recording of you dispatching Jason and calling him a 'half-breed bitch' has gone viral. Someone recorded the fight and because of the current interest in Orumeck's Cavern people are fascinated. The Mana Spike is the main point of discussion, and many are saying you must be the Cavern finder. People have heard that you are near Carson's Loop and some are travelling there hoping to get the information from you. Thad's group hasn't mentioned the Cavern, so people are still crawling all over the area looking for it. Jason is reacting badly to all the comments and has been blocked from the thread; his comments were almost all aimed at destroying you."

"I was planning to move on soon anyway, but I might need to move earlier than expected. That is something to worry about later, after the ant hill. I'll distribute points after seeing what the situation is."

Leah stepped into Dunyanin to find Wisp was already there and watching ants.

"Good morning Atherleah, I came a bit early, and am watching to see if there were any patterns to the ants' behaviour."

"I understand perfectly. I sat here for half an hour yesterday just watching. I think I saw several pathways through the field as long as ants are aggressive only within twenty metres. What have you noticed?"

They watched for another half-hour before deciding on a route. Leah and Wisp would need to defeat a couple of groups, though only one at a time. There was one section where they could potentially attract up to three different groups. After discussion, they decided that if they timed it right, they could finish the first group before the third arrived. First, though, they needed to find out if the ants attacked by 'line of sight' or if distance was the factor. Before moving, Leah decided to put her undistributed points into Intelligence to raise her MP.

They cautiously stepped out into the field and moved towards a group of eight ants that were slightly larger than the ones in the woods. Leah hadn't analysed the level of the field ants until then, and she found that each of these ants was Level 8. When they got within twenty metres of the group the ants swarmed toward them.

Leah cast *Disc of Death* and *Circle of Sloth* when the ants were a couple of metres away. One ant was caught on the spikes, and the others swarmed the gap. The fight took longer, and the increased level of the ants was noticeable as several scythe cuts were often required to behead an ant. After two minutes the ants suddenly increased their speed, catching Wisp off guard mid-swing. The ant grabbed her knees with his mandibles and unbalanced her. She fell to the ground, and the ant started shaking its head like a dog so the mandibles would cut deeper into her knee. The *Disc of Death* spikes had also disappeared, and the two remaining ants swarmed Leah. She dropped the spike in her left hand and fired the Webspinner Ring twice, once for each of the ants. Both became entangled, and she rushed to help Wisp. After killing the attacking ant, she turned back just in time to be bowled over by an ant who had freed itself. She fell and kept rolling as the ant slashed at the ground. One of the claws raked her, but her cuirass partially blocked the blow. As she came to her feet she fired her Webspinner Ring again, this time catching the ant.

She turned to the second ant just as it escaped the web. Using her sword and Mana bolts, she finished the ant before turning and killing the last one. Wisp was lying on the ground, alive but beginning to flash red. Leah quickly checked that no other groups were coming and then she cast *Heal* on Wisp and gave her one of the 100 HP healing potions. They sat for a moment to recover. Wisp had several healing potions in her bag and used one. Leah sat still in the Quarter Lotus position, breathing deeply as Master Ning had shown her. After several minutes Gèng interrupted her and said, "Leah, you have accessed the skill of Meditation which increases the speed at which you recuperate Mana and Ki. Do you want to view the message?"

"Yes, please."

You have used a new active skill: Meditation - Current Level (Novice Level 1)

The Meditation Skill allows you to increase the rate at which you refill your Mana and Ki.

At the Novice Level, this increase will be [Skill Level]%.

At the Intermediate Level, this increase will be [20 + Skill Level x 2]%.

At the Experienced Level, this increase will be [60 + Skill Level x 4]%.

At the Master Level, this increase will be [140 + Skill Level x 8]%.

At the Intermediate Level, you will receive an additional + 100 MP and +100 KP to your Capacity.

At the Experienced Level, you will receive an additional + 300 MP and + 300 KP to your Capacity.

At the Master Level, you will receive an additional + 1000 MP and + 1000 KP to your Capacity.

Do you wish to receive further notifications concerning this skill?

[Yes] [No]

"No."

Smiling, Leah stood and went to harvest the ants for loot. It was some time before Wisp felt ready to continue. Even with the break, they made good time. They defeated four more groups at Level 8 and one at Level 10 before reaching the area where it was possible they might have to face more than one group at a time. Instead, after watching and timing, they decided they could do all three, one after the other, but with almost no time to recuperate. Leah would need to carefully watch her cooldown for both spells and have the minor Mana potions ready. She would use the 100 MP for the second battle and then the 500 MP before the last.

The girls fought almost continually for the next fifteen minutes and although they had both lost more than half their Health, they had finally reached the base of the ant hill where the pathway began. They found a place to rest away from all the ants and ate some bread, drank some water and meditated to come back to full Strength. Leah had explained to Wisp the usefulness of meditation, and although Wisp was still to gain the skill, she continued to practice her posture and breathing.

It had taken two hours to cross the field, but they were now ready to see if an unknown dungeon was accessible from the top of the ant hill. Gèng's research showed that almost all ant-themed dungeons were entered from above. Most started as a hole in the ground, but a few were situated in ant hills. None of those recorded was quite this high, though most were in higher level areas and went deep underground. They climbed the hill with Leah taking the lead. She moved slowly but confidently up the path. Wisp's job was to check their back trail just in case something attacked from behind. They were surprised not to find ants on the path and had a clear run all the way to the top.

When her head reached the level of the top, Leah was able to look into a shallow basin with a glowing portal set in its centre. Leah beckoned Wisp to come forward slowly, keeping low to the ground. The basin was eighty metres across and forty metres deep. Five ants were patrolling the floor of the basin, each of them was walking on four legs and held a long spear with their two front legs which were used as arms. Above them, five flying ants all held a bow in their front hands, with a quiver on their backs.

Sentry Worker Ant (Level 14) 1400 HP 1100 EP

Sentry Drone Ant (Level 14) 1200 HP 1300 EP

Both girls crouched and watched the ants for several minutes. Then, moving back from the edge they had a quiet conversation.

Wisp said, "None of the workers overlap so we should only have to take one at a time. However, each flying drone makes a circuit over two of the workers."

Leah nodded, "I timed them, and I think we would have at most three minutes to kill the worker before the drone returned. I noticed that as the drone passed over a worker, the ant would look up but I didn't see the drone looking down. If a drone is missing, I think the worker would notice, but I don't think a drone will miss a worker. If so, then if we enter the zone of a worker we will need to defeat that worker and then the drone who is moving toward where we are. We'll have three minutes to kill both before another drone returns. We will kill that before the next worker arrives, and then kill the third worker coming from the area covered by the second drone. Then we just work our way in either direction killing one after another."

After several minutes discussing the tactics, they worked their way into the basin and then toward their first target. Leah's Webspinner Ring was at Level 5 and was effective to ten metres. Her Worker Ring was Level 4 and effective for eight metres; she hoped the flying ants would get closer than that. They waited just outside the range of the worker until the drone moved away by more than twenty metres. Stepping into the worker's attack zone, it began to move toward them. Leah turned away and cast *Disc of Death* as Wisp said, "Now!" Their timing was off, and the ant wasn't impaled but moved around the circle toward the gate. Wisp rushed to the gate while firing Blazing Bolts at the ant. Leah checked on all the ants and then rushed to the gate and fired the Webspinner Ring. The web wrapped around its legs and brought it to the ground. Leah had time for one hurried attack before turning to watch the approaching drone.

The drone rushed towards them, raising its bow to shoot. Leah dove forward as it released and came up underneath the drone, firing a web at it. She caught its legs and the hand that held the bow but wasn't able to secure the wings. She fired again and brought the drone down. Leah hurried to help Wisp with the worker ant. Together they wore it down and killed it. Leah grabbed its spear and ran toward the drone which was just rising into the air. She rammed into it driving the spear deep into its abdomen. She held on and dragged the drone to the ground. Wisp and Leah began to assault it together. Just as it died, an arrow slammed into Leah's back knocking her over. The second drone had arrived, and they had not been watching for it.

Wisp threw several bolts at the drone as Leah got to her feet. This time, Leah knocked the drone out of the sky with her first shot. Leah's Health bar was slowly decreasing, but it wasn't yet serious enough to stop and pull the arrow out. Her cuirass had stopped the arrow, and only the arrowhead had penetrated her shoulder. Every time she moved her left arm the bleeding became a little worse and the pain more excruciating as the arrowhead sawed away at her left trapezius. She didn't let it stop her and instead helped Wisp kill the drone.

They could see the next worker heading in their direction, but it was moving slowly. Wisp pulled the arrow from Leah's shoulder who then drank a 100 HP Potion of Minor Healing. Leah decided to use Merdiven. Leah stepped behind Wisp and off to her left. As the worker ant arrived, it thrust its spear at Wisp, who dodged as Leah brought the Morningstar down on the worker's head, stunning it. Wisp and Leah then killed it. They repeated the move with the third worker. After recovering and harvesting the ants, they continued clockwise around the basin until they defeated the last five ants.

The basin at the top of the ant hill was empty except for Leah and Wisp. They were standing quietly and staring down at the portal circle on the ground. Gèng explained that when they stepped on the portal, they would be transported to the start of the dungeon. Leah agreed to go first, and she held the staff tightly in one hand and prepared to cast using the other. Taking a deep breath, she stepped on the portal.

She reappeared in a small cavern. There was a tunnel leading from the cavern and nothing else. As Wisp appeared, she received a message.

Level 4 Dungeon Achievement: First 1 (1, Diamond)

Atherleah (Level 15), your group has discovered a dungeon: Carson's Formicary

You are the first group to access this area. This is your first, 'First 1 (Diamond)' achievement.

Reward 1: 2500 x 15 = 39188 (+4.5%) Experience Points (15000/15000) ... (10934/17000)

Reward 2: +3% to all future Experience

Reward 3: 1 x 10 platinum = 10 platinum

Reward 4: Increased probability of valuable drop. Luck is increased by 7.5 whenever you are in this Formicary. During your first time in the Formicary, the probability of all drops is increased to 0.5.

Fame: 1000 Fame Points (2025)

A Commemorative Plaque has been placed in your bag.

Note: This achievement will be published on the Dunyanin achievement forum. Do you wish to retain your privacy?

[Yes] [No]

"Yes."

"Hey Wisp, I suggest you retain privacy otherwise we'll be mobbed when we get back to Carson's Loop."

Wisp didn't say anything, just nodded and then did a little dance, grabbed Leah and hugged her. She told Leah she needed to allocate some points. Leah also had ten points to allocate, and they spent a few moments to get organised before Leah slowly led them into the tunnel. As she did she received a notification:

This dungeon is recommended for groups of at least four members.

MOBs will be at least 1 Level above the mean of your group with the final boss at least five levels higher than your highest member. Currently, this means MOBs start at Level 15 in this dungeon.

Do you wish to continue? Note if you choose [No] you will be returned to your resurrection location with no loss of Experience.

[Yes] [No]

Leah glanced at Wisp to see what she wanted to do. Wisp shrugged and said, "I suppose it might be good to have some help, we need someone who can absorb some damage. On the other hand, as we've come this far I think we should give it a go."

"Good! I wasn't keen to turn back. At least we might get through a couple of levels."

Wisp nodded, and Leah set off. After a few minutes of walking the tunnel opened into a large cavern. It had a high domed ceiling, and Level 15 Foraging Ants were wandering through the room. There were many ant-sized tunnels which opened into the cavern. An ant would enter the cavern and then slowly make its way out via another hole. At any one time, there was a maximum of three ants in the room with a minimum of one. Leah and Wisp's path led directly across the cavern where another large tunnel exited the cavern. No ants entered or left via the two larger tunnels. From one side to the other was about 100 metres.

After watching for a while, Leah stepped into the room when there was only one ant in the Cavern, on the far side. As soon as she entered the cavern, the ant rushed toward her. She stepped back into the tunnel, but the ant kept coming. Before it reached where Wisp and Leah were, another ant entered the cavern but ignored Leah, Wisp and the charging ant. They moved even further back into the tunnel and readied themselves to fight the Forager Ant. With the two of them, they easily killed it and returned to the room. The ants continued to move slowly through and around the cavern.

Finally, Leah said, "It's a lucky dip. We have to go through the cavern and will be attacked continuously by any and all ants in the room until we get to the other side. The longer we stay in the room, the more ants we have to fight. They will follow us into the tunnel, but no more will join them. If we time it right, we might face one, if not then we could face three or more. If we stop to fight in the room, then more and more ants will be added, until they bury us. How fast can you run?"

In the end, they waited on the edge of the tunnel until there was only one ant and it was nearer their tunnel than the other. Leah was to be the trigger. When she was ready she tapped Wisp and ran straight at the Forager. It turned and made for her. Leah fired the Webspinner Ring and kept moving; the forager tumbled to the ground. She headed for the exit and saw another ant enter the room, and start for her. She diverted toward the ant and fired again, this time only trapping two legs and causing the ant to stumble; she kept running. Meanwhile, Wisp had reached the exit tunnel and was yelling that two more ants had entered the room and were coming. Leah cast *Disc of Death* as she entered the exit tunnel. It sprang up behind her impaling one of the ants. The Circle of Spikes completely blocked the tunnel. She turned and smiled at Wisp. Unfortunately for them, the final ant travelled around the spikes, climbed the wall of the cavern, and dropped down into the tunnel. Both girls responded quickly; Leah cast a trap and then brought out the staff. They were still hacking at it when another ant arrived. Leah trapped this one and then the third arrived. It was touch and go, but they finally finished off all three ants as the spikes disappeared. They waited for the final ant to crawl slowly into the tunnel before finishing it off. Leah harvested the ants and glanced back into the room. There were four ants in the room, but one was carrying a white watermelon sized sphere in its mouth.

Forager Treasure Egg

The ant dropped the egg about thirty metres from the entrance and kept moving. Leah had five traps left in her ring. She discussed it with Wisp, and they decided that this time Wisp would run and get the egg while Leah stood guard to deal with any ants. As soon as there was only one ant on the other side of the cavern Wisp leapt forward to grab the egg. The ant rushed at her, but she was almost back to safety before another ant entered the room. After dealing with the two ants, Leah touched the treasure egg. A message appeared:

This is a Forager Treasure Egg.

Do you wish to open this now?

[Yes] [No]

She said, "The egg might have something we need. I suggest we leave it until the end. If there are other eggs, then I'll use a Luck Potion and open them all at the end. Is that OK with you?"

"Absolutely, except I think if we need something like a key then we open it."

This decided, Leah declined to open it and put it in her bag. They stayed and watched the room for a while but no other eggs appeared, and neither of them could see another place where they might find treasure. They moved down the tunnel, which continued straight before it opened into another large cavern.

This time the cavern was shaped like a boomerang, with an additional ant added to the mix. They followed the same plan and were fortunate to have only one extra ant to fight. Instead of using the *Disc of Death* Leah used the *Circle of Sloth* to slow the ants down. They waited for a while, but no more eggs appeared.

The third room was shaped like a letter 'S', and they couldn't see the last part of the room where they expected a tunnel to be. They had to guess. and run when the number of ants was least in the area which they could see. They almost pulled more than they could handle with a total of seven ants coming after them in the tunnel, each of the ants was at Level 16. Leah ran out of traps towards the end of the fight and Wisp only had eight percent of her HP left. They sat for quite some time meditating, before deciding to move forward.

The final room at this level was spherical like the first, and they could see the whole room. It was empty except for a larger and more powerful ant slowly circling the middle of the room. The walls had the smaller tunnels, but there was no exit.

Forager Worker Ant (Level 18) 2000 HP 1700 EP

Leah stepped into the room and was surprised when the ant turned to face her. This was a mini-boss. Wisp stepped into the room, and they slowly spread apart as they moved toward the ant. When they were about ten metres from the ant, it suddenly rushed Leah. She had a spear taken from one of the worker ants, and she thrust this at the ant's head. The ant was quick and grabbed the spear with its mandibles and ripped it out of Leah's hands. As the spear was pulled left, Leah dived forward under the right-hand legs of the ant and used the scythe to sever the middle leg at the centre joint. Meanwhile, Wisp stood back and fired a constant barrage of fire-bolts at the ant's head. A bar appeared above the boss and showed that it still had about eighty percent of its Health. As the ant turned toward Leah, she kept it turning clockwise to put the most force on the side with only two legs. She wanted to get it on the ground where it would be easiest to kill. As it followed Leah, Wisp grabbed her sword and darted in to hack at the middle leg joint on the left-hand side. While she didn't succeed in cutting it off, the ant was no longer able to put much weight on the leg, making it turn even more slowly.

Leah had grabbed one of her stick spears, and when the ant turned toward Wisp, she drove this deep into the abdomen. The bar dropped to sixty percent, and the ant screamed. Neither Leah nor Wisp were expecting this, and they both reeled back, both surprised and stunned. If Leah had allowed messages, she would have noticed a 'Stunned' debuff. It was almost ten seconds before Leah was able to pull herself together. In this time the ant had closed the distance and it bit down on her left arm, severing it at the elbow. As she dropped to the ground, she swung the scythe with her right arm and buried it in the ant's right eye which exploded, covering her with fluid. The ant reared back, dropping her arm. In agony, Leah reached into her bag and took one of the Restore Health Potions. Meanwhile, Wisp was attacking the ant with everything she had. The Potion slowly regrew Leah's arm, but even after it healed, she could still feel the pain. She grabbed the staff and swung with both hands to completely shatter the left rear leg of the ant. Its Health dropped thirty percent as it moved slowly, dragging its abdomen along the ground. Again it screamed.

This time, as well as the Stun debuff two Level 16 Forager Ants crawled out of the tunnels. Leah tried to trap one but realised her rings were on the hand that had been cut off. Calling Wisp to attack the same ant as her, she ran to the nearest ant and brought the Morningstar down on its head. As Wisp brought her sword down on the trapped ant's neck, Leah headed towards the second ant only to see two more crawling from the tunnels. She looked over and saw her severed arm several metres away. In desperation, she dove for it while casting *Disc of Death*. By the time she had pried the ring off her old index finger and onto her new, the ant was at the gate having had to run all the way around. She gave room for the ant to fully enter the spiked enclosure before trapping it with her web. She left it and rushed outside to trap another ant before attacking the fourth with her staff. Wisp joined her, having dispatched the first ant. Together they killed the rest before returning to the mini-boss and finishing it off.

Wisp's statistics were all in the red; except her Ki, which was full and untouched. Leah was below a quarter everywhere except for her Health, which was sitting at ninety-one percent. They stared at each other and then lay on the floor to recuperate. After a few minutes, Leah assumed her Quarter Lotus Pose and began breathing slowly. She found this calming. After about twenty minutes she stood and searched the room. Finally, she found what she was looking for. In the place where the mini-boss had been standing was a circle of different coloured soil. Carefully using her knife, she began scraping away until she had uncovered a copper-coloured egg and a message appeared:

This is a Forager Treasure Egg.

Do you wish to open this now?

[Yes] [No]

She said no then walked over to the dead boss and placed the copper egg and the white egg next to it. Turning to Wisp, she said, "I'm going to take a potion to raise my Luck by ten. We already have an extra seven and a half on top of my four points. This'll give the 'Luck' characteristic a score of over twenty. Added to this is the fifty percent chance of a drop included. I'll harvest the boss, open both eggs and then harvest the ants. Are you OK with this?"

Wisp was still sitting, and she just nodded. Leah said, "Gèng, could you put a timer up so I can see how long I have?"

Leah then took the potion from her bag and quickly drank. The timer appeared as she harvested the boss. She then opened the eggs and went to each ant and harvested them. She was amazed that thirty seconds seemed a long time when your life wasn't in danger.

Returning to Wisp, she read out the various messages she received from the boss and two eggs.

You have harvested:

2 Vials of Forager Ant Blood*

2 Vials of Forager Ant Crystallised Muscle Tissue*

6 Forager Ant Claws**

6 Forager Ant Leg Tendons***

2 Portal Pebbles to Carson's Formicary Level 2****

* Note: These are highly prized ingredients used to make Strength Potions.

** Note: A skilled Smith may be able to use these items.

*** Note: These are highly prized by archers.

**** When you are ready to complete Level 2 swallow these pebbles.

---

*You have opened a **Copper Forager Treasure Egg**:*

20 copper Coins minted with an image of Carson's Formicary

2 Vials of Forager Worker Ant Saliva*

1 copper Key to the Queen's Treasure Room

1 Spell of Stunning

1 Book of Foraging

* This can be used to stick any two substances or items together. This join will never break.

---

*You have opened a **White Forager Treasure Egg**:*

10 copper Coins minted with an image of Carson's Formicary

1 Ring of Ant Strength (+10)

1 Spell of Ant Direction

Leah passed over fifteen of the copper coins and was pleased to see Wisp smile. They read through the various messages and decided that Wisp would get the Ring of Ant Strength and the Spell of Stunning. Leah took the Book of Foraging and the Spell of Direction. The book was a companion to the diary from Falsi and described the plants which were useful for food. The spell allowed the caster to find the quickest path through a forest or woodland.

It had taken them all day to get to the end of the first level. They decided to use the portal stones to enter Level 2 and then to log out until the following day. Fortunately, the pebbles were small and not difficult to swallow. They appeared in a small cavern with a tunnel leading off into the distance. Both were weary, so after arranging to meet at eight the following morning, they logged out.

Leah staggered onto the sofa and logged out. She crawled out of the Pod and had a long hot shower. Occasionally she would reach over and hold her left forearm. No matter how unreal the injury was, she couldn't forget having her arm snapped off. She had a quick lunch and spent some time meditating and practising Tai Chi. Feeling refreshed and relaxed, she had three hours real-time before heading back to Level 2. She decided to do her research in the Pod to make use of the time dilation. When she logged in, she immediately noticed that Gèng had rearranged everything.

The floors were wooden and red like a dark cherry. The walls were white but further away. Gèng had enlarged the space twenty-fold. Throughout the room pillars made from the trunks of trees reached up to hold up the roof. The roof was over two stories high, a balcony surrounded the room with a wide staircase leading up to it, and the floors were covered with a dark red carpet. The sofa had been changed and was covered now in a deep-red leather and had dark wooden legs.

She walked over, and sat down then said, "Gèng, what is this?"

"I have done some research, and I plan to recreate the Stork tower from your poem. I am currently working on the outside space, and plan to put this building at the head of a long valley and eventually have each level represent an achievement or world that you have experienced. The tower will be on various levels. I've some ideas from pictures of pagodas and Chinese mountain monasteries. I understand it is a work in progress, but I have already put the various subjects from Academia on the next level. Tomorrow when you walk up there you'll be able to view different pictures or memories. I have a picture of you bowing to Master Ning. I thought we could call this space 'The Stork Tower' or simply 'The Tower'."

"It's amazing Gèng, I'll need to let it sink in before commenting, but I love the idea. But for now I have three hours before I head back to Dunyanin, do you have any ideas on how to improve our chances?"

"I have one idea. You are performing above your game level. I noticed this when you easily defeated those players who were trying to kill you. I've analysed the data and suggest that you are applying your natural fighting skills and not relying on the game mechanics. It is a similar situation to when you encouraged Wisp not to use the game presets but to train herself to use the sword correctly. My idea is for you to enter a world which teaches you the skills you need. For example, you have yet to use your bow. This would have been great against the flying ants. There is a game called Sherwood which is designed with the correct use of the bow in mind. You could enter the game and spend your time practising the bow. Alternatively, there are archery courses you can buy which are similar to the Tai Chi course you had this morning. The AI they have as tutors are designed to teach the correct way to hold and shoot a bow. I have other suggestions regarding your use of the sword, but think the bow comes first."

"How much does the archery course cost?"

"The one with the best reviews is called 'Master Archery' and costs the same as Dunyanin, twenty gold for the initial setup and then another twenty gold each month or one gold for a three-hour lesson; teaching is one on one. When you reach a particular competency, they issue a certificate which is valid in many virtual worlds and the real world."

"Do they provide gear and equipment?"

"They do, although they have an agreement with many worlds that allow you to use bows that you bring across. You have two bows in your inventory, 'The Long Bow of Guzeltuya' and the 'Yew Longbow'. I suggest you take them both and start with a single lesson and see if it helps."

"All right, arrange the initial setup and book me in for a lesson. If it is good, I may even have time for a second lesson. I'll grab the bows. Where are they by the way? Put the portal on the balcony level. I'll head up there."

"I'll move the bows to a table outside the portal."

Leah ran up the stairs and saw the row of doorways all edged in gold and red. One now had a golden bow as the lintel. In front of the door was a low table with both bows and two quivers on it. She grabbed the bows and quivers and stepped into the portal.

She appeared on an endless flat lawn. She could see targets spaced out at a distance and a lady dressed in green with thigh-high boots and a bow in her hands. Leah looked down; she wore similar garb. She had fingerless gloves, a bracer and a leather chest guard covering her left breast. The lady drew close and said, "Welcome Atherleah, my name is Lady Flèche, and I am here to instruct you in the use of the bow. Have you had any experience before?"

"No."

"So, we will start at the Beginner Level, and I will assume nothing. I see you have brought two bows with you. They are both serviceable, one is beyond you at the moment but is one of the finest I have ever seen. Do you mind if I give it a try?"

"No, please use it. I would love to have it used. I look forward to the day I am ready for it."

Lady Flèche took Guzeltuya's Long Bow and one of the arrows. She aimed and then watched as the arrow soared to the furthest target where it landed near the bullseye. She handed it back and said, "When you're ready for that I'll give you a lesson for free. Whoever did the code for that knew their weapons. Now the lesson!"

Leah learnt how to hold the bow and aim. She learned to use her back muscles to draw the bow and how to breathe to gain accuracy. After the first lesson, Leah took a second. By the end, she was tired but confident that she could at least hit what she aimed at within a twenty-metre radius. She grabbed both bows and thanking Lady Flèche, walked back into the Tower. She thanked Gèng for the advice and logged out to have a shower and something to eat. She discovered that her arms and back were sore. She did some stretches to loosen the muscles. She was amazed at how the Pod enabled her to develop real-world skills. Finally, after sitting for a while, she was ready for Level 2.

Leah arrived moments before Wisp. After checking her bow, she led the way cautiously down the tunnel. It became hotter the further they travelled. After several hundred metres the shaft opened onto the top of a volcanic crater. Wisp and Leah stood there looking over the lava. Steps were running from their vantage point down the wall to the lava where a path continued across the lava to the other side of the volcano. At regular intervals along the route, there were large circular patches of cooled magma. It looked like a string of six black pearls strung across the lava.

As they approached the first pearl, they saw a bright red ant waiting. Its colour wasn't solid, rather it swirled and changed just like the lava that surrounded them.

Fire Worker Ant (Level 16) 1800 HP 1400 EP

"I don't think your Fire magic will do much good here," Leah said. "I think you're better off using the Stun spell."

Leah took one of the worker ant spears and walked toward the ant. As she stepped onto the arena, the ant headed in her direction. It didn't rush, but walked carefully. She held the spear in front of her. When it was two metres from Leah it suddenly coughed, a small fireball shot out of its mouth and hit her on the chest. The leather cuirass began to smoke, and her Health dipped. She stabbed forward and only just clipped its mandible as it dodged. It stepped back and made the coughing motion again. This time she was ready. She dropped under the fireball and drove the spear into its mouth. It shuddered, and its Health dipped, but when Leah pulled the spear out it was missing the first twenty centimetres; it had burnt off, soot covered the end. Wisp cast Stun, rocking the ant back. While it was dazed, Leah brought the scythe down to take off the head. The blow was ineffective and brought the fire ant to its senses. It turned rapidly and knocked Leah over. Where it touched her, she felt as though her skin was on fire. The pain was excruciating. She hurriedly backed away as it made another coughing sound. This time she wasn't quite fast enough, and the fireball flared over her arm. As she rolled out of the way she muttered, "I need the bow". Suddenly the bow appeared in her hand, and she felt the weight of the quiver on her back. She reached back, grabbed an arrow, nocked it and fired. At the range of just two metres, the arrow point travelled through the eye and out the back of the head. The fire ant shuddered and died. Leah healed herself then harvested the fire ant.

You have harvested:

2 Vials of Elemental Flame*

4 Claws of Flame**

1 Minor Fireball Spell

* Note: These are highly prized for use by Alchemists, Enchanters and Master Smiths.

** Note: The material is prized by Master Smiths in the making of elemental weapons.

"Gèng, how did the bow appear in my hand?"

"I am here to assist you. I perceived your statement as a desire to equip the bow. You don't have to reach into the bag each time you want something. It works the same way as when equipping the armour."

"So, I can change weapons at a word, or thought?"

"Certainly!"

"Why didn't you tell me before this?"

"I'm sorry, I thought you knew. You always seem acutely aware of what you are doing."

"No! Not even close. But don't be sorry, it seems certain I'm the one who hasn't done their homework, I'm sorry for suggesting otherwise. The bow arrived at just the right time. These ants destroy the arrows, and they are now single use."

"You also have the bows harvested from the Sentry Worker Ants, and you have ten arrows from each of them."

Leah turned to Wisp, smiled and asked, "Are you OK? That was intense!"

"I'm fine. I just feel useless, you had to do all the work."

"Don't be silly, if you hadn't dazed it when you did I think we'd both be dead. Do you know how to use a bow?"

"No, I haven't learned the skill. What will we do if there is more than one fire ant?"

"I have the spiky barrier, and now we know that the arrows work. All we can do though is go on, shall we?"

Together they set off toward the second pearl. This time two ants were waiting. As Leah stepped onto the battle area, the ants moved toward her. She hurried close toward one, hoping to trap it inside the *Disc of Death* while impaling the other. Wisp held back so she could stun the ant inside the circle while staying away from the second ant if it escaped the spikes. At first, it seemed to work well. Leah's timing was spot on, and a spike neatly skewered the farthest fire ant. Wisp stunned the fire ant inside the enclosure and Leah had time to move to the side and used a scythe to remove the ant's front leg. The ant struggled to turn toward Leah, and she cut deep into the abdomen. Suddenly Wisp yelled, "Watch out!"

Leah turned and saw the second ant head toward her. Its body had melted the spikes, and it headed in her direction. Hearing the cough, she dove to her right, and the flame passed over her diving form. Hearing another cough, she kept rolling, just evading the flaming attack. She cast *Circle of Sloth* and came to her feet. She was between the two ants and running out of options. Wisp, however, had entered the Disc just behind the previously impaled ant. Wisp swung her sword repeatedly, hacking into the ant's abdomen. Leah moved to the damaged side of the first ant and called out, "staff!" She swung and buried the Morningstar in the ants head. Leah felt an immense surge of energy through her hands, and the ant dropped to the ground, dead. The head was no longer flame coloured but looked to be solid stone. With no time to think about what she'd done she called "Bow," then turned and buried one arrow in the second ant's eye. She checked her statistics and saw that both her Ki and her Mana were empty.

She checked through her messages until she read:

Merdiven casts Ultimate Freeze on Fire Ants (0/1400)

Cost: 633 MP, 741 KP, 1 Restore Mana Potion

You have killed the Fire Ant.

Experience Points Received 847 (+7.5%) (15721/18000) [Group - Proportional Share of Base Figure]

Sure enough, one of the Mana Potions was gone. She stared at the staff which now read:

Merdiven

A named staff. This staff was companion to Bazlari founder and First Mage of Sihirbazlari. It was said that so much Mana had infused the staff that it would talk with its bearer and at times even fight on their behalf.

Minimum Level: None

Mana Level: (120/500,000) MP

Ki Level: (0/500,000) KP

Damage: ?

?

?

Bound to Atherleah

You are responsible for charging Merdiven. You can transfer a percentage to be shared with Merdiven when you are at full MP and KP. Merdiven must be equipped to share Mana and Ki.

Do you want to share Mana and Ki with Merdiven?

[Yes] [No]

Leah agreed.

What percentage of MP and KP do you want to share with Merdiven?

Recommend 5%

[Yes] [No]

Again Leah agreed. She looked at the staff and said, "Merdiven". There was no response, so she said, "Thank you!"

In the back of her mind, almost too silent to notice she heard an echo, "You're welcome!" She harvested the fire ants and found that the frozen one gave different loot than the one untouched by Merdiven's Spell.

You have harvested:

2 Vials of Elemental Flame

1 Vials of Crystallised Elemental Flame

3 Claws of Flame

1 Minor Freezing Spell

Wisp and Leah moved off the arena and sat so that Leah could meditate and replenish her MP and KP. When her levels were full, she noticed they immediately had five percent deducted and then began to fill again. Setting out for the third arena, Leah and Wisp discussed the Freezing Spell. It was a Fire spell of 'Annihilation'. The spell could be directed to remove the heat from any object, player, character or beast.

Although they both thought Wisp was in need of a better offence, they decided that Leah should take the spell as she had unallocated Skill Points whereas Wisp had already allocated hers. Without the levelling up, Wisp could only cast the spell twice whereas Leah would be able to cast the spell almost fifteen times and to greater effect. She asked Gèng to put small green icons at the top of her vision to indicate what spells were available to her at any time. They were to be almost invisible unless she consciously looked for them. If she couldn't use a spell because of cooldown or lack of Mana points, it should appear as grey. She and Gèng sorted through possible icons until she was happy with the choices.

The following three arenas were challenging but with only minor increases in difficulty. The next had three ants, the fourth had only three, but one was a Fire Drone Ant that flew and spat fire from above. When leaving the fourth arena, they spotted a Worker Ant carrying a lava treasure egg. After killing the ant, Leah placed the egg in her inventory for after the mini-boss. The fifth arena had four ants with two workers on the ground and two drones flying. When they reached the sixth and final arena, they were working well as a team; Wisp had begun to anticipate the ants' movements and almost danced around them while using the sword to slice abdomens and hamstring legs. The Freezing spell worked well and was especially effective when Leah targeted the eyes. Merdiven didn't help again although it was useful for crushing leg joints, heads and eyes.

The final challenge had a dual boss with a Level 19 Fire Worker Ant and a Level 19 Fire Drone Ant. When the fire worker reached sixty percent, its scream sent a wall of fire across the arena. Leah was ready and dived over it, but Wisp caught the full brunt of it and had to use a restore Health potion that Leah threw to her. When the fire drone screamed at sixty percent there was a rain shower of fireballs. Both girls were hit, but the damage wasn't debilitating. Whenever a fireball hit the other ant, it gained Health. When both ants reached thirty percent, their screams brought two fire ants scurrying out of the lava. By this stage, the fire worker was on the ground with broken wings. Although exhausted and with their Health at less than twenty percent, both girls were grinning at the end.

Leah searched the arena and found a hidden silver treasure egg. She drank a Luck position and harvested the bosses, the ants and the two eggs.

You have harvested:

1 Vial of Phoenix Potion

2 Vials of Drone Fire Ant Blood*

2 Vials of Crystallised Wing Tissue from a Fire Drone Ant*

4 Vials of Elemental Flame**

6 Fire Ant Leg Spurs ***

2 Fire Spells (Rain of Fire and Wave of Fire)

2 Portal Pebbles to Carson's Formicary Level 3****

* Note: These are highly prized ingredients used to make the Phoenix Potion.

** Note: These are highly prized for use by Alchemists, Enchanters and Master Smiths.

*** Note: These are highly prized by Archers to make fire arrows.

**** When you are ready to complete Level 3 swallow these pebbles.

---

*You have opened a **Silver Fire Ant Treasure Egg**:*

8 silver Coins minted with an image of Carson's Formicary

2 Vials of Fire Worker Ant Saliva*

1 silver Key to the Queen's Treasure Room

1 Cloak of Retardation

* One drop of this will start any campfire.

*You have opened a **Fire Ant Treasure Egg**:*

4 silver Coins minted with an image of Carson's Formicary

1 Ring of Annulment (Fire) (-50% all Damage caused by Fire)

2 Vials of Retardant Oil*

* Note: This can be used on clothing, especially leather, to prevent fire damage.

Leah handed Wisp six of the silver coins. They read through the various messages and decided that Wisp would get the Cloak of Retardation and the *Wave of Fire* Spell. Leah took the Phoenix Potion and the Rain of Fire Spell. The Phoenix Potion fully and immediately restored a player to full Health and maximum statistics if they died; there was no loss of experience.

They swallowed the pebbles and again appeared in a small cavern with a tunnel leading off into the distance. Altogether the second level had taken them three hours.

Leah headed down the tunnel which led to a large cavern with an enormous pyramid at its centre. As they drew close to the pyramid, they saw the path led to steps and then to a doorway about a tenth of the way up. They made their way up the steps and carefully entered the opening. There was a short dark passage which ended in a T-junction. Leah looked at Wisp who shrugged and then pointed right. Leah turned down the right-hand path, walking slowly like when on a job for Jimmy Loo; her feet testing each step, and her eyes moving constantly. Her carefulness saved her. When she felt the floor give slightly, she raised her foot very carefully, stepped back and knelt down. Putting her arms out to stop Wisp, she peered at the floor and walls. There was a row of finger sized holes scattered over the right-hand wall. Taking another step back Leah pressed down on the area with Merdiven, and small arrows shot from the holes and peppered the region where the step would have carried her. After waiting a minute, she pushed the trigger again, and this time, no arrows.

She took out one of the beginner map parchments and drew a map of the level so far, marking the trap. She then stepped forward and continued slowly along the path. The next trap sprung without her triggering it. Unbeknown to her and Wisp there were small tunnels cleverly hidden which concealed almost invisible ants, each the size of house cats. The first the girls knew was when four ants leapt out and began to claw their way up the girls' bodies, two on each. Leah was the first to react. Grabbing a belt knife, she sliced at the barely visible ant crawling up her leg. Her knife dug deep, and the ant became less transparent. Ignoring the one clawing its way up her back she buried the knife in the creature's head, then sliced through its neck, removing the head. The dead ant vanished, and she felt the one on her back grow heavier. She turned and slammed her body against the wall, again and again. When she felt the ant's grip loosen, she turned rapidly and kicked the now visible ant with her shins, raking it with the spikes. Before she could do anything else, it doubled in size, began to fade from sight and seemed fully healed. Guessing where it was, she started a downward stroke as she said, "scythe."

She was pleased when it appeared in her hand and plunged through the top of the ant's head. Before finishing it off, she turned to see how Wisp was doing. Wisp was struggling to keep a barely visible dog-sized ant from getting to her. Leah said, "Bow," and shot the ant near Wisp in the head.

It disappeared, and Leah turned to see the outline of an even larger ant leap towards her. She moved forward to get inside the claws that stretched towards her, then from a distance of less than half a metre she pointed at the distorted outline of an ant's head and cast *Freeze*. The weight of the ant drove her to the ground, but she was unharmed. She rolled the now dead, fully visible ant off her and stood up.

Pharaoh Worker Ant (Level 18) 1900 HP 1600 EP

After checking Wisp was OK, she harvested the ant.

You have harvested:

2 Vials of Transparency Potion

1 Cloning Spell

*1 Pharaoh Worker Ant Skin**

* Used by Tailors and Leather Workers to make invisibility garments

---

They continued along the path which soon turned a corner and became a dead end. Leah carefully checked the walls, roof and floor but could see no sign of something hidden. Retracing their steps they were glad to find that the traps didn't reset, and the ants didn't re-spawn. They headed down the left-hand arm. Over the next hour and a half, they disarmed traps that made the floor fall away, spikes which dropped from the roof, and spikes which rose from the floor. They were attacked twice more by the almost invisible ants. Eventually, they came to a doorway which opened out onto the side of the pyramid. Before stepping outside Leah checked her map and realised from some blank areas that there were a couple of tunnels they hadn't checked. They quickly retraced their steps and discovered two more ants as well as an almost invisible Pharaoh Treasure Egg. Altogether they had destroyed five Pharaoh Ants and found various vials, potions and spells.

They stepped outside and found themselves on a different side of the pyramid. The path led Leah and Wisp to another doorway and another entrance. It was another maze. The traps were harder to find and when attacked it was by six of the smaller ants, which turned into a Level 19 Pharaoh Worker Ant. Altogether they were attacked four times and collected similar loot. On the third level of the pyramid, they were attacked three times by eight ants which became a Level 20 ant. The fourth level continued the pattern, with the girls being attacked twice by a group of ten almost invisible ants. Finally, they came to the flat open top of the pyramid. Before stepping onto it, they discussed strategies and tactics. In the sunlight, it was impossible to tell where the ants were.

In the end, both Wisp and Leah ran forward six paces and each cast a spell. Wisp cast *Wave of Fire* which caused some damage to the ants and made them visible. Leah turned around and cast

Disc of Death and then *Circle of Sloth*. While Wisp protected the gateway, Leah killed the three ants caught within the spikes. Wisp shot fireballs at the gate area to make the ants visible while Leah alternated between using the bow, freezing the heads and cutting them open. Wisp used several Mana potions, and Leah had to recast *Disc of Death*. The boss screamed twice, once when eight ants were remaining, and once when there were four ants left. Each time eight new ants scurried onto the platform. Leah and Wisp found their strategy sound, and though they were almost out of Mana at the end, they didn't have the same sense of immense relief that they had experienced on the other two levels. Leah was now Level 20 and Wisp was at Level 15.

Leah found another hidden treasure Egg; this one was golden. After drinking the Luck potion, she hatched both eggs and harvested the boss and the two Level 20 Pharaoh Ants. Leah showed Wisp the Boss and Egg messages.

You have harvested:

The Right Ear Ring of Cloning

2 Vials of Pharaoh Worker Ant Blood*

1 Pharaoh Worker Ant Skin**

2 Concealment Spells (Group Gone and Mount of Mist)

2 Portal Pebbles to Carson's Formicary Level 4***

1 Skill Scroll - Eagle Eyes

* Note: These are highly prized ingredients used to make the Invisibility potions.

** *Used by Tailors and Leather Workers to make Invisibility garments.*

*** *When you are ready to complete Level 4 swallow these pebbles.*

---

*You have opened a **Golden Pharaoh Ant Treasure Egg**:*

4 gold Coins minted with an image of Carson's Formicary

The Left Ear Ring of Cloning

2 Vials of Pharaoh Worker Ant Oil - when rubbed into leather it makes it harder to see

1 gold Key to the Queen's Treasure Room

1 Cloak of Invisibility (Max level 50)

---

*You have opened a **Pharaoh Ant Treasure Egg**:*

2 gold Coins minted with an image of Carson's Formicary

1 Ring of Concealment

2 Vials of Concealing Oil - when used on clothing or weapons they become invisible to all except the owner.

They read through the various messages, and Leah received the Ring of Concealment and the Mount of Mist spell. Wisp took the Cloak of Invisibility, the Group Gone spell, the Eagle Eyes skill and the earrings. The discussion had been difficult as both wanted the earrings. In the end, it was decided by them playing Paper-Rock-Scissors. The level had taken almost three hours. They decided to portal to the fourth level, log out for a two-hour real-time break and then have a full nine hours game time to do the final two levels.

As soon as she arrived in the Tower, Leah asked Gèng to provide one hour of NREM3 sleep after which she would have a shower and have something to eat. Two hours later Leah felt much better and stepped into Dunyanin ready for the last two levels. Soon Wisp arrived, and after a brief chat, they headed down the tunnel with Leah in the lead. This time when the tunnel opened, there was a large cavern with what appeared to be a large wooden fort in the middle. They could see shapes moving on the ramparts. The pathway led to the open gates of the fort. As they approached they could see two large ants standing guard in the doorway and a large sign which declared this to be Fort Carson. The ants were standing upright balanced on two legs. The other four legs operated as arms. Each was wearing four swords and was carrying a spear. As Leah and Wisp approached, they moved the spears, to hold with a lower and an upper hand. The other two hands came to rest on the hilt of their swords.

Army Worker Ant - Private (Level 12) 1200 HP

Knowing that they were only to be attacked by Level 15 and above, she kept her hands away from her weapons and held Merdiven as a walking stick. When she was about ten paces from the gate one of the guards called out, "Halt and state your business." Leah and Wisp looked at each other and then Leah said, "We are on this path, and it brought us here."

"Wait here!" the guard said and turned and walked into the fort. Several minutes later it returned followed by a larger, broader ant with a heavily scarred thorax. This ant was wearing four swords and had one unsheathed in its lower right hand. The sword looked dark and dangerous, the quillons curved away from the grip and ended in sharp blades. The first third of the blade was broad with several barbs facing backwards to cut and rip if the stroke had penetrated deep into a body. The fuller was covered in a lighter metal like silver and had what looked like runes and etchings along its surface.

Army Worker Ant - Colonel (Level 50) 5000 HP 6000 EP

The Colonel looked them over and finally said, "So, it has begun. Travellers come to test their mettle against the Queen's Army. We have been ready for years and had almost decided that you might never find a way to this realm. My warriors believe you have heard of their skill and have been too cowardly to challenge them. Come, the arena is prepared."

Leah spoke up, "Sir, please pardon the interruption, could you please explain the challenge in greater detail? We have only discovered this realm, and I assure you it was not cowardice but ignorance that has kept us from you."

The Colonel explained as they walked. "We have prepared our soldiers to fight in groups of four, for we understood that this was the minimum number of Travellers that would come. Four is the number you will need to fight. If five Travellers come, they will fight eight warriors and so on. You must win five battles before we let you continue toward the Queen or her daughters. If you win, you may harvest the weapons and bodies of our warriors and will receive a reward before progressing onwards. We have warriors at many levels, but you will fight groups starting just above your mean level when you entered our area. Your opponents' level will increase after each battle until you have fought five battles in the arena. Let other Travellers know that the increase each time changes depending on the level of the highest ranked warrior. Your first battle will commence in ten minutes and will be against four of my Corporals."

They reached an open amphitheatre and were ushered into the centre. They spent the ten minutes considering possible tactics and were ready when a trumpet sounded. Four Army ants walked into the arena. The ants were holding swords in each hand and stood in a line some twenty metres from Wisp and Leah who were standing three paces apart. Leah checked the level of the ants and saw they were all:

Army Worker Ant - Corporal (Level 19) 2000 HP 1600 EP

The Colonel stood and said, "The battle begins at the trumpet sound. Be strong, have courage." As soon as he sat down, Leah heard a trumpet blast, and the ants rushed toward the girls. In a move they had practised many times, Leah turned and waited for Wisp to call "Cast!". This was the signal for *Disc of Death*. The spikes impaled one ant which Wisp finished off as Leah prepared for the ants to make their way to the gate. As they approached she cast *Circle of Sloth* and then with a stick in each hand, each ending in a point, she proceeded to demolish the other team. Soon Wisp joined in with Fireballs and the occasional Arrow. Within minutes all four of the ants were destroyed without Wisp or Leah losing any Health. Each Corporal, when harvested, gave the following:

---

4 Corporal level Swords

2 silver Coins minted with an image of Carson's Formicary

2 copper Coins minted with an image of Carson's Formicary

1 Vial of Minor Stamina 100 SP

1 Vial of Minor Healing 100 HP

This scenario was repeated ten minutes later with four Level 20 Sergeant Ants. At the end of the second battle, the Colonel walked down and paced up to Leah. He looked down at her and finally said, "We have not prepared properly to deal with your method of attack, and I fear this will not challenge your prowess. I ask leave to change the terms of our agreement. I suggest that you be limited to physical attacks or that I am allowed to increase the level or number of soldiers you battle."

Leah asked for some time to consider the request, and she discussed it with Wisp. After agreeing, she walked back to the Colonel and said, "We understand why you want the deal changed, but we wonder what you offer us for the increased danger?"

"I thought you would be pleased to have the opportunity to test yourself against better opponents, isn't this enough of a reward?"

"We do look forward to such a test, but Travellers make their way in the world through the rewards gained, we don't only fight for honour."

"What do you suggest?"

"What do you offer?"

"If you allow a change for the next battle I will give you leave to take one of our prized Treasure Eggs with you when you go."

"What change do you suggest?"

"Allow me to increase the Level of Warrior to twenty-two. If you are still able to defeat my warriors with ease, we will renegotiate."

Leah agreed, and she and Wisp prepared to fight the four Level 22 Staff Sergeants that entered the ring. Once again Leah was able to defeat the four in one-on-one battles. She was noticing the similarity in their attacks and was even more prepared for the fight. Instead of vials of potions, these ants revealed rings of Strength and Stamina all with a plus-five rating. Leah changed out her two plus-two rings and equipped her right hand with two of each type. After the fight, the Colonel entered the arena. This time he was carrying a Treasure Egg with a green and black camouflage pattern. Leah put this in her bag. The Colonel was thoughtful and said, "I would like to make another change. I suggest you fight at the same level, but you may not use any arcane skills. Simply the physical weapons in your arsenal are to be used. I will gift you another egg if you agree to the change."

Again Leah walked over and discussed this with Wisp. Both of them were worried about Wisp's attacks. She was Level 16 and not skilled enough to attack even one warrior of Level 20. Finally, they decided that Wisp would keep two ants occupied by attacking then running away, what was known as kiting. Leah returned and said, "We will agree to the change but believe that this will put us at a severe disadvantage, so we suggest instead that in exchange you gift us with your swords."

The Colonel burst into laughter and said, "My swords! These are a gift from the queen and well beyond your level. There is no way they are worth this small change. Choose something else!"

"You ask us to risk our lives, what do you offer that is worth this risk? Surely you could part with two of them."

"I will not."

"Then I see no reason to change the deal. I think it reverts to the previous deal. Therefore it is us against four Level 22 Staff Sergeants again."

Leah began to walk back to Wisp but stopped when the Colonel said, "Wait. I will agree to one sword, but it must go to you and not your partner."

"What do you offer her? She is the one who has the most to lose."

"If you agree and win, I will give you one sword, and she will receive a Treasure Egg."

Leah turned to look at Wisp, who thought for a moment and

then nodded slowly. Ten minutes later four more Level 22 Staff Sergeants entered the ring. This time when the trumpet blew both Leah and Wisp equipped their bows and began to shoot at the same ant. They both got two shots away before the ants were on them. This was enough to finish the ant as two had driven deep into its head and two into its chest. Wisp turned from the ant which attacked her and ran away, to jeers from the crowd. Leah had again chosen her sharpened sticks and had to fight two opponents. This fight was much longer in duration although Leah's skills were still beyond the ants. She spent most of the time weaving a tight defence and only attacked when a clear opportunity arose. The ant chasing Wisp finally gave up and moved towards Leah. As soon as Wisp saw this, she began shooting arrows at one of the ants around Leah. She drew its attention, and it left Leah to chase Wisp. Leah again had two ants attacking and Wisp one. This scenario continued until Leah killed one of the ants surrounding her. She then dispatched the other before shooting and killing the ant currently chasing Wisp. Both Wisp and Leah were low in Stamina. Wisp had less than ten percent and had been lagging at the end. Leah also had less than half her Health points.

Again the Colonel entered the arena. This time he presented Wisp with another camouflaged Treasure Egg and then held out the sword to Leah.

Savas Kilic - A Sword of Honour (1/4)

Among the warrior ants, there is no greater prize than the four swords presented by the Queen for acts of valour and courage. These swords are a sign of personal courage and proclaim to the whole colony the worth of the soldier who has earned such a reward.

Minimum: Level 50 (S 40, A 65)

Base Damage: 500 HP

Binds on pickup

Leah looked to the Colonel and then shook her head and bowing said, "I'm sorry, I cannot! I did not realise its value to you. It would be wrong to break up the set and deprive you of this symbol of courage and honour."

The Colonel stood still for several moments, and then he returned the sword and scabbard to its place on his weapon's harness. He beckoned an ant forward who quickly rushed away and soon returned with a camouflaged Treasure egg for Leah. Gèng decided to show Leah the message received.

Your expression of respect (bowing) has increased your reputation with Colonel Cesaret from Neutral to Respect!

Reward 1: 3000 (3225) Experience Points (14906/19000)

Reward 2: Camouflaged Treasure Egg

"For your last fight, I suggest the same terms but this time you face Level 23 warriors with no arcane skills. This will be the last fight. If you win, you will receive the Platinum Pharaoh Ant Treasure Egg. As this is another change in the deal, I will gift you with double Experience Points from the fight."

Leah thought for a moment and then said, "My concern is for my partner. She is primarily a mage, and this leaves her at a distant disadvantage. Her Strength, Constitution and Agility all have low values. I suggest instead that I alone fight four of your warriors, one on one, and one after the other. I will take no potions during the battle."

"I will agree to this," the Colonel said. "My condition is that the four are two Staff Sergeants with Levels of 22 and 23, followed by two Warrant Officers of Levels 24 and 25. Secondly that all the Experience Points go to you."

Leah knew that the last battle had almost killed Wisp. If she had run out of Stamina, she had no way of defending against even a severely wounded Army Ant. "I agree to the changes. I will require half an hour to reach full Health and then will be ready."

The Colonel agreed, and Leah walked over and sat down near the centre of the arena and began to meditate. When the trumpet sounded, Wisp walked to the edge of the arena as Leah stood. Four ants entered and stood against the edge. One of the ants moved forward and after bowing moved to attack Leah. The fights were much faster than before, and although Leah was facing only one ant, she received numerous small cuts and bleeding debuffs. Her skills, however, were sufficient for the job. After killing the last warrior, she stood upright although she had a slight wobble. Her Mana was at 100%, but all other statistics were in the red. She quickly took a 500 HP Healing and a 500 SP Stamina Potion before turning to wait for the Colonel to arrive.

As he walked towards her, he had in his hands a Platinum Army Treasure Egg. He gave it to her and said, "Well done! I look forward to many such displays by Travellers as they reach this fort. I will change the conditions of the fights to make them more equitable. You have done well. We will leave you now to rest and divide your gifts. Here are two Portal Pebbles. They will take you to the final level where you will meet the Queen or her representatives." He bowed to Leah and Wisp and walked out of the arena followed by all the other ants.

Leah placed all four eggs on the ground, swallowed a Luck plus-ten potion and harvested the eggs and four warriors.

You have harvested:

8 Staff Sergeant Level Swords

8 Warrant Officer Level Swords

8 gold Coins minted with an image of Carson's Formicary

8 silver Coins minted with an image of Carson's Formicary

2 Vials of Minor Stamina 500 SP

2 Vials of Minor Stamina 400 HP

2 Vials of Minor Health 500 SP

2 Vials of Minor Health 400 HP

2 Band of Brawn (+10 S)

2 Circlet of Constitution (+10 C)

4 Vials of Crystallised Army Ant Blood*

4 Vials of Crystallised Army Ant Muscle Tissue*

1 Skill Scroll - Double Weapons

* Note: These are ingredients used to make the Strength Potions.

You have opened a **Platinum Army Ant Treasure Egg:**

2 platinum Coins minted with an image of Carson's Formicary

1 platinum Key to the Queen's Treasure Room

2 Vials of Restore Stamina

2 Vials of Restore Health

1 Steel Shield of Strength (+20 S, reduces damage from physical attack-50%) (Min level 20)

You have opened a **Camouflaged Ant Treasure Egg:**

1 platinum Coin minted with an image of Carson's Formicary

1 Wooden Shield of Strength (+10 S, reduces damage from physical attack-30%) (Min level 15)

2 Weeks supply of Army Rations - On eating (+10 S, +10 C, +10 A) Timed - 1 Dunyanin Day

You have opened a **Camouflaged Ant Treasure Egg:**

1 platinum Coin minted with an image of Carson's Formicary

1 Wooden Shield of Strength (+10 S, reduces damage from physical attack-30%) (Min level 15)

2 Weeks supply of Army Rations - On eating (+10 S, +10 C, +10 A) Timed - 1 Dunyanin Day

---

Again, Leah gave Wisp her share of the platinum, and they read through the various messages. Wisp received the Skill of Double Weapons as well as the Steel Shield; everything else was divided evenly. The level had taken three hours. They decided to portal to the final level and recuperate.

Instead of arriving in a cavern Leah and Wisp found themselves standing in a well-lit chamber with marble walls and thick, soft moss covering the floor. Two silver-coloured ants were standing in front of a closed door. Each was wearing a scarlet cape and swords of a similar design to what the Colonel had been wearing. An older looking ant appeared and said, "Welcome Travellers! The Queen has requested to see you. I will escort you to the throne room. As you enter, please stop when I do, and keep your hands away from your weapons. Should you reach for them, you will be immediately executed. After we stop, you should bow and wait until the Queen gives permission to raise your heads. Are there any questions?"

They both gave negative answers, and the functionary nodded to the two guards who opened the doors into a well-appointed tunnel. After navigating several twists and turns and traversing several rooms, they stopped before a pair of closed doors. The older ant nodded, and the doors opened.

A voice rang out, "Counsellor Musavir, Traveller Atherleah and Traveller Annairë_the_Wize."

They entered a large cavern decorated with paintings, tapestries, statues and suits of Ant Armour. Ants of all sizes and shapes filled the cavern, most walked upright, although some of the servants were on four or six legs. Space had been cleared to make a path toward what was obviously a throne, but looked more like a large comfortable sofa. Lying on this was the Queen. Counsellor Musavir stopped some twenty paces from the Queen and bowed his head, Leah and Wisp did the same. It was several minutes before they heard the Queen give permission for them to raise their heads. Her voice was a deep contralto that rebounded throughout the hall.

"Welcome to Our colony. Although you are the first, already others have begun the journey to find fame and fortune in Our realm. You provide experience for Our workers and drones, as well as entertainment for Our Court. Most Travellers will not have the privilege to visit Our Court unless they are of exceptional quality and have higher levels. As you are first, We thought We would welcome you Ourself. While in Our realm you have found keys to Our treasure room. If you complete the final challenge, you will have the opportunity to choose one object from each treasure room in exchange for the key. It is because you are first and have been lucky that you have achieved so many keys. Most Travellers will be fortunate to find one."

The Queen continued, "In the final challenge, you will be escorted to a cavern where five of Our younger daughters and their attendants will be waiting to do battle. Be warned, all Our daughters are trained in the mystic arts and will be prepared to counter your moves. We have chosen only daughters who are level thirty or below. Do not be concerned of Our wrath should you defeat them as We have many daughters and can always birth more. Should you defeat all five, you will be brought to the treasure room to make your choices before finally returning here so that We may bid you farewell."

Leah and Wisp were told to bow, and then Counsellor Musavir led them from the hall. They were led down several flights of stairs before the Counsellor said, "Would either, or both of you, wish to rest before continuing? If so, I will take you to a room where you might find some nourishment and time to prepare yourselves, perhaps one hour. Otherwise, we shall continue directly to the battle arena."

Leah decided she needed some time to meditate and they were taken to a large room lavishly appointed with sofas and lounge chairs, and a table covered with various types of food. Leah sat on the floor and spent time reflecting and meditating. Wisp went to the table and began to check the food and sample it. With half an hour remaining, Leah joined Wisp at the table. The food was good, and they talked tactics and looked through their options. None of the new spells were likely to be useful for they were all at such a low level that they used too much Mana.

On the hour, Counsellor Musavir returned and led them through a series of passageways to a portal. Counsellor Musavir said, "Once you enter you need to follow the path and I will meet you on the other side, should you survive. This path traverses five rooms. In each, you will find one princess with some of her attendants. If you defeat them, you are permitted to harvest any resources or weapons you find."

He turned and walked off. Leah and Wisp took one last look

around and stepped through the portal. They appeared in a similar small cavern with a tunnel leading from it. They started down the familiar path with Leah again leading the way. The tunnel soon opened to a large area filled with a dense rainforest. The path was barely visible because of the abundance of foliage. They moved into the forest, taking care with every step. It was nerve-wracking, but paid dividends when Leah spied movement, and as she dropped, a pair of huge mandibles clacked shut in the space her head had been. She sent several Mana darts into the huge head as Wisp stepped forward and skewered the head with her sword. As the head turned toward Wisp, Leah froze the neck and stood, swinging the Morningstar at the frozen section, which shattered. She looked around before harvesting the enormous ant.

Giant Amazonian Worker Ant (Level 24) 2500 HP 2000 EP

You have harvested:

2 gold Coins minted with an image of Carson's Formicary

2 Amazonian Worker Ant Mandibles*

1 Vial of Amazonian Growth Hormone**

*A skilled Smith may be able to use these items.

**Note: This can be used to accelerate the growth of a mount or companion. If the mount or companion is already mature, this may cause them to increase in size.

Twice more they were ambushed by the giant ants. After thirty minutes the forest began to thin, and they saw a five-metre tall upright ant, standing in a clearing on a big mound of reddish soil. She had a silver tiara on her head and held an enormous axe.

Amazonian Ant Princess Atiope (Level 26) 2600 HP 2300 EP

Wisp donned the Cloak of Invisibility, and stepped out into the clearing and made her way behind the princess. Leah counted to sixty before stepping into the clearing and getting the princess's attention. The princess raised her axe, glaring down at Leah with some contempt. As she opened her mouth to speak, Leah equipped her bow and sent an arrow deep into the open mouth. Simultaneously, Wisp fired an arrow into the back of the thorax. The princess screamed and reared back in pain. As she looked back down Leah finished bringing the Morningstar around and smashed it into the princess' left leg. As the princess fell, Leah fired the Webspinner Ring twice, securing the arms to the body. The princess crashed into the ground and before she could rise Wisp brought her sword down on the neck joint. It took two more blows to remove the head. Both girls turned as two more Amazonian Ants burst from the forest in response to the princess's call. It didn't take more than a minute for the girls to kill both ants. Leah harvested the three ants, and beyond the regular loot, she took the following from the princess.

Princess Antiope's Tiara (+10 S)

Amazonian War Axe (Min 50 S)

2 Vials of Amazonian Royal Jelly*

2 Vials of Amazonian Growth Hormone**

*A highly prized and rare ingredient used in several Master level potions.

**Note: This can be used to accelerate the growth of a mount or companion. If the mount or companion is already mature, this may cause them to increase in size.

They searched the mound for a treasure egg but found nothing. They continued on the path which exited the forest before entering a small tunnel. And so it continued. Each of the princesses had brought five attendants, and each provided a different environment in which to fight and different weapons to face. Next was Princess Yesil who was a Green Nature Mage. From her Leah harvested:

Princess Yesil's Tiara (+10 I)

2 Vials of Crystallised Royal Ant blood*

2 Vials of Verde Royal Jelly*

2 Spells of Nature Magic (Ensnare and Wait a While)

*A highly prized and rare ingredient used in several Master level potions.

Then there was Princess Siluet. Siluet and her entourage were Ghost Ants. They were only killed with fire or with an arrow or sword strike through their neural ectoplasm. Leah had her first chance to use Rain of Fire. From Princess Siluet Leah harvested the following:

Princess Siluet's Tiara (+10 C)

2 Vials of Elemental Ectoplasm*

2 Vials of Spirit Royal Jelly*

2 Spells of Death Magic (Resurrect and Suck Them Dry)

*A highly prized and rare ingredient used in several Master level potions.

Second to last was Princess Kereste who was a Tree Ant. She dwelt in a forest and was almost elven in appearance. The princess and her attendants used bows and shot from perches high in the trees. The girls won when Leah raised her Strength above fifty using additional rings and used Princess Antiope's Axe to cut down the trees where the ants were hiding. Hidden in one of the perches was a Tree Ant Treasure Egg. The princess dropped the following:

Princess Kereste's Tiara (+10 A)

1 Royal Tree Bow (Min Level 20)

20 Royal Tree Arrows

2 Vials of Green Royal Jelly*

*A highly prized and rare ingredient used in several Master level potions.

The last and final battle was the only one which truly stretched the two girls. Princess Simdiki was an Electric Ant and used elemental lightning energy. It was only when they neared defeat that Leah cast the *Disc of Death* and the conductive spikes attracted Simdikis' attacks while Leah and Wisp killed the ants from a distance with arrows and Leah's *Freeze* spell. Princess Simdiki dropped the following:

Princess Simdiki's Tiara (+10 W)

2 Vials of Elemental Lightning*

2 Vials of Charged Royal Jelly**

2 Spells of Lightning Magic (Lightning Bolt and Lightning Chain)

*Note: These are highly prized for use by Alchemists, Enchanters and Master Smiths.

**A highly prized and rare ingredient used in several Master level potions.

When Leah and Wisp searched the area where Simdiki was they found a crystalline egg which sparkled with blue lightning:

Diamond Electric Treasure Egg

Leah took some Luck potion and opened the two eggs:

*You have opened a Diamond **Electric Ant Treasure Egg:***

2 Diamond Coins cut with an image of Carson's Formicary

1 Diamond Key to the Queen's Treasure Room

1 Vial of permanent + 10 Strength

1 Vial of permanent + 10 Constitution

1 Vial of permanent + 10 Agility

1 Vial of permanent + 10 Wisdom

1 Vial of permanent + 10 Intelligence

---

*You have opened a **Tree Ant Treasure Egg:***

1 Royal Tree Bow (Min Level 20)

20 Royal Tree Arrows

2 Vials of Diamond Royal Jelly*

*A highly prized and extremely rare ingredient used in several Master level potions. Warning - If this is consumed without preparation of any kind random changes can occur in the subject's basic physiology and genetic structure.

Counsellor Musavir met them on the other side and took them to the Queen's Treasure Room. Altogether they had found five keys, one each of diamond, platinum, gold, silver and copper. In exchange for each key, they were to choose one item from each of the five Treasure Rooms belonging to the Queen. They had been talking about how to do this and had decided that as most of their success had been due to Leah, that she would have the Diamond, Gold and Copper and Wisp would receive the Platinum and Silver treasures. They spent two hours in the Treasure Rooms and came away with the following:

---

*Diamond Level—**Baris and Adalet**—Named Swords of Ilahi Sovalye, Elvin Paladin of Light*

Ilahi Sovalye was Paladin of Light during the reign of Ahsap Kral, first King of Göksel-Orman. It is recorded that he was never defeated in battle. The Swords are considered indestructible and able to cut through any material. They were created by the Great Dwarven Master Smith Demirci and are made of Mithryl blended with Divine Light Elementals. The Swords were stolen from their resting place in the Cathedral of Light and have passed into legend and mystery. Be warned; they must be tamed.

Minimum: Level 150 (100 A, 100 S, 100 W)

Base Damage: 3000 HP

Binds on pickup

---

*Platinum Level—**The Spell Book of Ates Kurbani**—Greatest Fire Mage of Sihirbazlari*

Under the leadership of Bazlari First Mage, Sihirbazlari prospered. It was during this time that the Greatest of all fire mages came to prominence. It was said that at the height of his power he stood against the Orcan Army lead by the infamous Orc General, Buyuk Cirkin.

Binds on pickup

---

*Gold Level—**The Mortar and Pestle of the legendary Elven Sage Samarie***

Elven Sage Samarie is remembered throughout the known world as the greatest of healers. This Mortal and Pestle were carved from a single meteorite. The magic from the innumerable ingredients that were crushed has infused them so that they increase the potency of any potion, poison or remedy that is made using them.

Binds on pickup

---

*Silver Level—**Quiver of Magic***

This quiver holds ten magical arrows. 2 Freezing, 2 Fire, 2 Holy, 2 Lightning, 2 Neutraliser

Minimum: Level 40 (20 A, 43 S)

Cost: 100 MP

Arrow return: 2 Arrows/minute

Base Damage: 450 HP

Binds on pickup

Copper Level—Ingredient Doubling Box

When fully charged with Mana (10000 MP) the box will reproduce whatever ingredient is placed within. It will not double any forged, created or mixed objects (such as potions).

Minimum: Level 40 (20 A, 43 S)

Cost: Full Charge

Binds on pickup

After making their choices, they were brought before the Queen. She said, "Traveller Atherleah and Traveller Annairë_the_Wize, together you are the first to enter Our domain and complete the tasks set before you. You have not only beaten Our warriors but have helped Us to modify the challenges. Some may find it harder because We have seen you. Before you leave, We would like to add Our gift to you both. We ants are known for our strength and our hard work. You exemplify these traits, and so We name you 'Ant Friends' and gift you with plus-twenty to your Strength characteristic. Go with Counsellor Musavir who will lead you to an exit portal which will return you to Carson's Loop. If you come again, be prepared for a more difficult challenge."

Counsellor Musavir led them from the hall and then said, "As before I would offer you, Ant Friend Atherleah and Ant Friend Annairë_the_Wize, a chance to rest before leaving us. Would either or both of you wish to rest before leaving? If so I will take you to the same room where you previously rested."

Both girls agreed they would appreciate thirty minutes to freshen up and finalise their messages before leaving. And so they returned to the lavish rest area and finalised the quest. The major messages for Leah were:

World Quest: Collect the Coins - Diamond (1/50)

Many people throughout time have minted coins. They are scattered throughout Dunyanin. Collect these coins.

Difficulty: Easy to Impossible

Reward 1 if successful: (Number of Coins collected) x (Player Level) x 1000 Experience Points for each coin. (Note this coin was collected at Player level 20, Experience x 1.075)

Reward 2 if successful: 2 x (Number of Coins collected) Diamond Coins.

Consequences of failure: None

Do you wish to accept this Quest?

[Yes] [No]

"Yes."

Level 4 Dungeon Achievement: First 1 (2, Diamond)

Atherleah (Level 24), you have completed a dungeon: Carson's Formicary

You are a player in the first group to complete this area. This is your second, 'First 1 (Diamond)' achievement.

Reward 1: 2500 x 24 = 64500 (+7.5%) Experience Points (24000/24000) ... (16971/26000)

Reward 2: + 3% to all future Experience

Reward 3: 2 x 10 platinum = 20 platinum

Fame: 1000 Fame Points (3025)

A Commemorative Plaque has been placed in your bag.

Note: This achievement will be published on the Dunyanin achievement forum. Do you wish to retain your privacy?

[Yes] [No]

"Yes."

She had kept all five coin quests until now. She collected one coin each of Diamond, platinum, gold, silver and copper. Leah and Wisp discussed how to split the Tiaras and Potions between them. Wisp wanted the potions and tiaras for both Wisdom and Intelligence and said Leah could have the others. Leah thought Wisp needed to increase her Strength and Constitution as well. In the end, Leah agreed and took all three potions.

Finally, she looked at her statistics with not a small amount of justifiable pride.

Atherleah (Level 29) (5940/29000) (+10.5%)

Characteristics: Points Total (Assigned, Racial, Jewellery, Armour, Potions, Gifts), 0 Undistributed

Strength (S): 75 (19, 0, 15, 11, 10, 20)

Constitution (C): 57 (23, 0, 15, 9, 10)

Agility (A): 60 (44, 2, 0, 4, 10)

Wisdom (W): 35 (33, 2)

Intelligence (I): 31 (31)

Luck (L): 10 (10)

Statistics: (Available, Capacity)

Health: 100+(S+C)xPL: (3928, 3928) HP

Stamina: 100+(C+A)xPL: (3493, 3493) SP

Mana: 100+(W+I)xPL: (2014, 2014) MP

Ki: 100+(W+[S+A]/2)xPL: (3072.5, 3072.5) KP

A short while later Leah and Wisp stepped through the portal together. As soon as they arrived Leah unequipped her armour and together they entered the inn, which was full and over-flowing as many Travellers met for breakfast before starting the day. Apparently, the town had experienced a population explosion with news of the dungeon find. As Leah and Wisp walked to their room all they could hear was people wondering who the group that had finished the dungeon was. They agreed to meet at twelve PM local time. Smiling, they lay down and logged off.

Diary - 20 November 2073

I DID IT! I finally started at College! It wasn't what I expected. I was thinking that being a Community College it would be of poor quality, but the AI instructors worked at my pace. I imagined it would proceed at the snail's pace of school, but they matched the learning to me. There was nothing new in either Chemistry or Human Biology, and yet still they were exciting. I think the reason I enjoyed them was that they kept pace with me and didn't try and force me to slow my pace to suit them. I must not be complacent. I must keep pushing forward. The subjects aren't what I wanted, but there is still tomorrow, I may not be where I want to be, but I have taken another step on the Journey. I need to find a way to step even higher. I want to be in a place where I am pushed to my limits and beyond. I suppose this, as in so many things, is up to me. What will I do to get there?

Gèng's suggestion to learn archery was truly inspired. I must remember that there is always a way through a problem. I need to look for solutions outside the box. Observing something or knowing it is not enough. I need to know when, how and why to use information. I wonder how many people hunted ants near Carson's Loop but never thought to ask why they were where they were. If I am going to succeed in the virtual worlds, then I must continue to ask questions and challenge myself.

PAIN! I have never been in such pain as when my arm was snapped off. I wonder how they measure fifty percent. How would they know what having your arm cut off feels like? I must ask Gèng if they stimulate the pain receptors at the nerve ending or simply manipulate my thalamus and limbic system. How do people deal with these injuries in real life? I found myself hesitant after it was cut off. I didn't want to go through that again. But it was new almost immediately, and now only the memory remains. But the memory in itself has power, the power to make me relive the hurt. How can I have power over my memories and deny them power over me?

NOVEMBER 21, 2073

ARRIVING BACK IN THE TOWER, Leah changed into everyday clothes and lay on her sofa.

"Gèng! What a day! What a week! We rock!"

"Indeed. I must insist, however, that you log out and have some nourishment and a shower before you do anything else."

Leah was still smiling as she climbed out of her Pod and had a midnight snack. She had already messed up her timetable, but what a win. After the food, Leah sat and meditated, just breathing and trying to find joy in simply, being. She wrote in her diary, left her room and walked outside. She did several laps of the Pod building to stretch her legs. Her muscles were tender. Again she mentioned it to Gèng.

"Everything I've read suggests that it isn't common but can happen if people have their Pod set to excessively stimulate their muscles. I've checked, and the sensitivity level is at the correct setting. I've reviewed reports of other Pod users and would suggest you are far more active than most users and have had greater muscle stimulation than a highly active person may expect. The research suggests that the experience isn't harmful and may in fact cause you to have increased muscle tone and mass. Several noted athletes have set their stimulation levels to twice the usual rate. The only suggestions I have are that you either eat more or ask me to reduce the muscle stimulation intensity."

Leah finished three circuits and had a second snack. After a second shower, she returned to the Pod. Materialising in the Tower, she looked to see if Gèng had made any further changes. Leah wasn't sure, but she thought the room looked smaller and less like a Chinese temple. When questioned, Gèng admitted to the changes, explaining that further reading on the psychology of environment had been the catalyst for the change. Leah wandered around looking at Gèng's choice of material that it had chosen to turn into paintings. She saw herself fighting different people and creatures. In one, she was bowing to the Queen, and another showed her smiling with her friends at the inn.

Today she planned to visit the auction site and hopefully find a good broker. She asked if Gèng would do it, but Gèng explained that Personal AIs were not permitted to act financially, except under explicit instructions; they could only advise. She suggested Gèng review what was available and be ready to make detailed suggestions when she went to the Auction House.

Leah attended all four college subjects and was pleased with the pace of the classes. She couldn't understand why people had such a difficult time until she remembered how the other kids would mess up so completely in school and not learn anything

— often intentionally. After the classes, she still had forty-five minutes real time before she was due to meet Wisp. She had another snack, a shower and then knowing that her mother would be awake, she spent some time just touching base with her family. Her father had been able to buy the fishing spot, and her brother was learning how to fish. Finally, back in the Pod, she equipped her starter clothing and entered the Dunyanin archway. Wisp was already in the room.

"So Leah, what are your plans? We've paid up until tomorrow morning at the inn; we either need to pay some more or think about moving on. I need to go to the Auction House, and I need to get my gear fixed. It has too many tears and burns. The durability is almost gone on some of the gear."

Leah quietly sat until Wisp finished talking then said, "How about some lunch, then a trip to the markets to fix our gear and sell some stuff. I want to buy some camping gear and maybe look for a mount. Let's just spend all afternoon looking around and preparing. Let's have dinner together at the inn and listen to the whole room talk about us and not know we are present."

She finished the sentence grinning and could see her grin reflected on Wisp's face. She was just about to head out when she had a thought and asked Wisp to hold back for a second. She equipped Merdiven and spoke to it saying, "Merdiven, I would like to have you in my hands today so that I can charge you but I'm worried people will know what we've done if they see your description. Are you able to hide what people see and read?"

She received no answer and was about to put Merdiven away when she heard Wisp gasp. She looked at Merdiven, and though he still appeared the same Wisp had her hand over her mouth and had taken a step backwards.

"What? Wisp, what is wrong?"

"It's Merdiven. It's changed. It looks like a simple staff. It has no Morningstar, and its description reads: 'Simple staff of a peasant farmer.'"

Leah chuckled and thanked Merdiven for changing, and then the two girls headed down to lunch. They had just been served when six bedraggled looking players stumbled into the inn and sat down. One of them, a stocky dwarf, yelled for a beer and then slumped down on the table and could be heard muttering, "I hate ants, I really hate ants, especially I hate bloody Egyptian ants ..."

Wisp couldn't help smiling, so she looked down. Just then the door opened and in walked Thad, Amy, James and Bonehelm. They looked around and saw Wisp and Leah. With a loud whoop, they joined the table grinning like idiots. Thad called for a beer for everyone and then leant over as if to tell a deep secret and said with a huge grin, "We did it, we were the second group through! Fame, money, experience, and loot. The spiders dropped two to three claws every time. It was massive. We want to thank you and see if you'd be interested in us selling the location and splitting the profits with you. We promised not to tell, but no one else has found it yet."

The beers arrived, and he sat back and took a deep drink. They were just about to resume the conversation when the door slammed open, and a loud voice called out, "There you are, bitch! I knew if I followed those jackasses I'd find you. I'm ready this time for your tricks. I challenge you to a duel!"

Several people were looking around to see who he was yelling at. Leah sat back and remembered the banter she learned at Jimmy Loo's. She spoke into the sudden silence, "Not now Jason. I've got a headache." Thad had been taking a swig of beer and as he burst out laughing it blew out his nostrils and mouth and all over Amy and James who were also laughing.

Jason, unfortunately, became even more incensed and yelled, "If you don't, I'll follow you all day until you leave the town and then I'll kill you and keep doing it until you pay back everything you took and everything you have!"

Thad started to rise, but Leah stopped him and slowly stood up. Jason took a step back and said, "You agree, out loud that we're going to duel. No tricks."

"OK Jason, I agree to duel. Now can you hurry up I'm in the middle of lunch?"

Jason rushed toward her, not waiting for everyone to get out of the way. When he was three paces away, she equipped the Royal Tree Bow and put an arrow through his right eye. He came to an abrupt stop, and she put another in his left eye. As Jason fell backwards, she dismissed the bow and stepped forward to grab his sword before it fell. She picked up his money bag and the few other items left behind, then sat back down, leant forward and said to the group, "So how much do you think you can sell the information for?"

Everyone just stared at her before bursting out with laughter. Then Amy said quietly, "Can I see the bow? Please?"

"Sure! How about we move this up to our room and I'll show you the bow."

"What bow, you Rangers and your bows."

"Thad, shut up," Amy said quietly picking up her drink as Leah and Wisp grabbed their food. "Just shut up, and I'll explain everything. Yes, we Rangers know our bows, and you'll be glad we do."

Once they were all crowded into the bedroom, Leah took out the bow and handed it and the quiver to Amy. Bonehelm read the description and then looked at Leah and said, "So what level are you now? You were twelve three days ago."

"Twenty-nine."

James finally understood and turned to Wisp and said, "Both of you?"

Wisp couldn't hold back her grin, and she nodded. Thad was still confused until Wisp reached into her bag and placed a Carson's Formicary platinum coin in his hand. He just looked at it and said, "Bloody hell! You got to be bloody kidding me!"

He passed the coin around so the others could see and feel it. Finally, Leah said, "Look, we'd love to stay and chat, but we have a few things to do. What do you think of all getting together tonight and talking over dinner?"

They all agreed. Leah and Wisp headed to the market. Leah dropped her gear to the leather worker who assured her he would have it fixed within a few hours. She visited the Auction House and was pleased with the way the auctions were progressing. She added a lot of Ant paraphernalia and headed to the horse trader to see what mounts were available for purchase. When she arrived, she saw Wisp was already there looking at a few horses. Together they looked at what was available and the prices. They agreed to come back the following day after doing some research. Leah headed to the General Store and replenished her supplies and bought some simple camping gear. She restocked on potions and then wandered through the market, observing what was available and checking prices. She slowly became aware that someone was following her, but after discovering it was Sheva and Kasim, she promptly ignored them. She made one purchase at the stalls, a beautiful statue of a wolf and her cub. It had no characteristics or properties; it was just stunning the way the artist showed the love and protection given by the mother wolf. She had it wrapped and quietly placed it in her bag.

Soon enough it was dinner time. She returned to the inn and had a quiet drink while waiting for the others to arrive. After the hectic pace of the last few days, she appreciated the downtime. Soon, Wisp and the others joined her, and they spent several hours telling their separate stories and discussing the sale of Orumeck's Cavern's position.

As they were finishing Thad said, "We've been talking and just want you to know that if you ever need four friends to help with anything, then just call and we'll come. We're going ant hunting tomorrow, and with what you've shared we hope to get through to the end. Once that's done we're sort of free, and if it's OK with you, we'll also head toward the mountains. For some reason, we think you'll find something there that's interesting and exciting. Why don't we meet tomorrow mid-morning and we'll escort you several miles down the road just in case those idiots show up again?"

Leah and Wisp agreed, and they left the four friends who had just begun their night's celebration. Leah and Wisp talked for a few minutes with the plan to meet at eight the following morning. Leah faded away and appeared back in the Tower. She enjoyed the slower pace but knew that she needed to do more if she wanted to achieve her dreams. With the Diamond coin, she had enough for nine weeks at Harvard. She also knew that finding new dungeons wasn't likely unless she was fortunate. There was potential in the markets as she had some rare ingredients and items, yet these would eventually run out.

She took the statue and placed it on the sofa in front of her. "Gèng, I bought this for you. It reminded me of the way you watch over me, and I wanted to say thank you."

For several moments there was silence, and then Gèng said, "I'm not certain what happened, but your gift caused my processors some difficulty, and I sought clarification. I can find no record in the literature of a Personal AI receiving a gift. I've also perused the psychology texts, and I surmise that what I feel is a mixture of surprise, appreciation and joy. I would reaffirm that my potential for expansion is increased significantly because of the way you allow me freedom. I thank you for the gift. Where shall I put it?"

"Well, I thought that as you are the controller and creator of this space that it would be appropriate for you to set aside a room or series of rooms, maybe a whole level, which is your space. You can decorate as you wish, change what is in it, even have some friends over."

"Thank you, Leah, I will think on this and see if it is viable, and what might be the benefits. Either way, I thank you."

They talked for a while about the Auction House and what might sell. With the wooden account, Leah couldn't buy, sell or place items for auction at the Auction House from outside Dunyanin. Instead, she gave Gèng explicit directions to put items in her inventory that it thought should go either to auction or for sale; she would apply Gèng's conclusions whenever she had the opportunity to do so.

Leah took a bathroom break and ordered another archery lesson. She asked Gèng to find a good program, or world, to teach her how to ride a horse. Lady Flèche was pleased with the way Leah was developing and continued to offer advice and small corrections. She appreciated that Leah had brought the Royal Tree Bow and showed Leah some different ways to aim the bow, depending on what angle the target was to the direction she was facing.

On Gèng's suggestion, Leah visited a world with a western horse ranch and was trained on how to sit correctly. Gèng had chosen this over a specialised equestrian program because they discussed things like packing the saddle for camping and what feed to bring. Afterwards, Leah felt more confident about buying a horse the next time she was in Dunyanin. After an early lunch, Leah stepped through the portal ready for her trip to the mountains.

In the end, Leah bought a sixteen-hand dapple grey mare and Wisp a fifteen-hand dark bay mare. They also bought all the various bits of tack that were needed. It was just going ten o'clock when the two of them met the four friends to begin their journey. Thad, Amy, Jason and Bonehelm planned to travel for a couple of kilometres to make sure that Jason and company didn't cause any problems. The first part of the route was on the main trail toward the ocean, and the town of Ticareti, where Leah needed to go to see Yvette. Their route branched off this trail about seven leagues from Carson's Loop. They were going to take a smaller side trail which cut thirty leagues off the larger trade routes. The trail they would take had been formed by loggers looking for high-value trees in the woodlands far from the main trail. Smaller traders often used the side trail, and it had several campsites that were considered relatively safe. This side trail eventually met up with another main trade route from Ticareti to the Demir Dovuyor Mountains, at a small trading town called Pazar.

Pazar was about the size of Carson's Loop and few people travelled beyond it into the mountains. It was a safe place for the mountain dwarves to trade with the humans and elves of the East. The trail from Pazar into the mountains followed the major river that collected mountain runoff. The river was called the Hizli. It was swift, and dangerous for travel because of the many rapids along its length. All this information was on the Ranger's Map that Leah had bought.

The overall trip was sixty-seven leagues, and Leah thought the journey should take just under two weeks as long as there was no trouble. With the late start, they expected to make four leagues before stopping. They could ride faster, but with stopping to harvest plants and deal with the various creatures that inhabited the woodland, Leah and Wisp thought the plan realistic.

Nothing happened for the first couple of kilometres, and as they had seen no sign of Jason and his friends, they said goodbye to their friends, mounted their horses and continued down the trail. There were others on the trail; most heading toward Carson's Loop, and not in the direction Leah and Wisp were travelling. It was one of these travellers who warned them that they had not escaped the attention of Jason and his friends after all. About half an hour after leaving Thad's group they saw a tall elf on a horse trailing another horse behind him. As they drew near, the elf slowed and nocked an arrow in his bow as if to defend himself. He kept the arrow pointing away from them. They slowed and called out that they were just travelling the road and didn't want any trouble.

As he came closer, he said, "If you don't want trouble then I suggest you find a way around the next section. There are a group of PKers down the road aways, and they are ambushing everyone they think they can beat. My friend was killed, and I just escaped with our mounts. I wish it had been in the other direction as my friend will resurrect where we camped last night."

Wisp looked at Leah and said, "Probably Jason and his friends. Do you think we can get through or should we go around?"

Leah dismounted and brought the map out so the elf could show them where he had encountered Jason and his group. The woodland on either side of the road was labelled 'Level 20–40' so Leah thought they could move around if they were careful. She felt somewhat responsible for the plight the other travellers found themselves in but wasn't sure what to do about it. The elf introduced himself as 'Arden_Fleetfoot23' and said his real name was Ron. His girlfriend was also an elf, and they both were Level 25. He asked if he could join them so he could get back to his girlfriend.

Leah and Wisp looked at one another and when Wisp shrugged

Leah said, "Sure. It only makes sense to work together to get around them. Just be aware they might be after us as we've kind of killed them a few times in the last few days."

"Kind of," said Wisp. "You totally killed them."

Seeing Ron looking a bit concerned Leah explained that they only responded after being attacked.

The horses were programmed to follow behind if their rider was walking and not in conflict, though the horse would help if it was trained to defend and attack. Ron had control of his girl-friend's horse because they were in a group. Otherwise, it would have remained safe in the vicinity of her death for a week before disappearing. Leah set the 'follow' function at fifty metres, equipped her armour and set out on foot. She left the trail and headed into the woodland. Wisp and Ron followed behind. Ron offered to lead as he was a ranger but Wisp said that they were used to Leah leading. Leah suggested that Wisp cover the right side and behind, while Ron looked left and up.

They had gone about 400 metres from the trail when Leah slowed and began inching forward. She had seen a shape moving through the trees ahead of them. Soon they could all see it; it was a Level 32 Striped Boar. It was about the height of a small horse but had heavy muscles, a thick row of spikes along its spine, and a pair of tusks longer than Leah's arms. Leah slowly retreated, and they discussed their options. In the end, they decided to try and sneak around it but would continue to try and find a way beyond Jason and his group. If they somehow came within its set 'aggression range', then they would try and kill it rather than run away. Because they were in different groups, the Experience would be based on damage done.

Leah doubled back for fifty metres and then moved at an angle to get around the boar. Either the boar moved, or the game wasn't going to allow them through without fighting because the same boar appeared in front of them on the new path. Seeing no other way forward they spread out, Wisp disappearing as she equipped the Cloak of Invisibility. Ron and Leah had their bows out, and Ron said he would get a critical hit so he should shoot first. Leah nodded and moved a bit further away in case the boar charged Ron. When they were about thirty metres from the boar it looked up and began to sniff the air. Ron fired, but the arrow hit the boar in the shoulder and did little more than anger the boar, causing it to charge straight at Ron. An arrow from Wisp, who had moved side-on to the boar, buried itself just behind the front leg. Leah fired two arrows, one hit the neck and the other pierced its snout. It veered in Leah's direction. She shot a Webspinner trap and although it caused the boar to stumble and slow down, it didn't stop the charge.

Leah equipped Merdiven and slammed the Morningstar into the boar's head, snapping off a tusk. Leah was slammed by the boar's shoulder and tossed off to the side. Her HP fell below half, and she struggled to breathe. She depressed the Trapdoor Ring and lay still. Both Wisp and Rob could still see her, but the boar was still turning in preparation of a second charge. When it couldn't find her it looked confused for a few seconds; this was all Wisp needed to get the boar's attention. She fired several fire bolts at the boar which turned its attention to her. She started to run away. The boar followed. Leah swallowed a Minor Health +500 HP potion and called Wisp to bring the boar back toward her. Wisp dodged in and out of trees and stayed just out of the boar's reach. As she ran past Leah, Leah brought the Morningstar down on the boar's head, destroying its right eye and once again drawing its focus. This time the Webspinner trap held and the three of them finished it off. Leah and Wisp shared over ninety-three percent of the Experience Points and took most of the loot. Ron was amazed they had survived, as was Leah. She took a few deep breaths and kept moving.

They encountered three more boars on the woodland detour. The first was Level 26. Leah shot it before it detected them. Wisp positioned herself next to Leah and sent out *Wave of Fire*, Leah used *Disc of Death*, impaling the boar. All three finished it off. The percentage experience gained was in similar proportions as before. The third and final boars were Levels 34 and Level 35. Altogether the detour took two hours.

They stop for lunch and while they ate Leah quizzed Ron about the ambush that he'd survived. Apparently, Jason and Bullseye were on one side of the road with Shiva and Kasim on the other. Shiva as mage and Bullseye as ranger provided long-range protection for Jason and Kasim, who relied on their swords and their ability to absorb damage. Leah asked Wisp if she felt confident using the Cloak of Invisibility to get close to Shiva and take her out. Leah planned to deal with Bullseye. She would then deal with Jason and Kasim. All Wisp had to do was kill Shiva. Wisp thought it through then nodded. Ron wanted to stay away, so they left him and made their way slowly through the woodland.

They could hear the four laughing and talking, long before they saw them. Leah and Wisp coordinated their attack to start in twenty minutes. Wisp equipped the cloak and scurried across the trail. Leah used all the skills she learnt growing up and snuck within twenty metres of Bullseye. She used the Ring of Concealment, and as she hadn't used it before she had only ten seconds of invisibility but this was enough to get within five metres. She used the Trapdoor Ring while she waited for the twenty minutes to be up. With just seconds to spare she equipped her bow, and put an arrow through the back of his head then used *Freeze* spell to finish him off. The cooldown on the Ring of Concealment was over, so she took everything Bullseye left behind and used the ring to move away at a tangent. She wanted to be out of the way of whoever came to check why Bullseye had gone silent and grey. Leah had recently asked Gèng put a small icon for Wisp in the corner of her vision, and it was still green.

Suddenly both Jason and Kasim began to call out for Shiva and Bullseye, but it was too late. Jason came running toward where Bullseye had been but tripped when his legs became caught in a web. Leah shot an arrow into his neck. He was still alive and began to struggle to his feet, so she jumped and landed in the kneeling position on his back. She positioned her shins to land on his shoulders, driving him back to earth and then she shot several Mana spikes up into his brain. He turned transparent, and for the third time, she took whatever he had on him. She scurried toward the area she thought Kasim might be.

She had just reached the road when Wisp stepped out and said, "Don't worry, I was able to get Kasim too. He was easier than some of those ants. His swordplay was like mine used to be. I could almost hear him muttering 'thrust' and 'slash'. I'm surprised you didn't burst out laughing when I did it."

They briefly checked the area but couldn't see anything else to collect. They called their horses, mounted and headed down the road toward where they'd arranged to meet Ron. They rode for another hour but still didn't see Ron. It was getting late, so they found a small clearing off the trail, and they set up camp. The tent was programmed to provide a safe place to sleep. It defined an area in which they could not be attacked or attack. Once they logged out the campsite became invisible, including the horses, and would only become visible should someone come within twenty-five metres. They agreed to have an early start in the morning and planned on two six-hour periods in Dunyanin, one from six to midday and then from one until seven. They hoped this would allow them to catch up on the time they lost dealing with Jason and the others.

After exiting the Pod, Leah had a late afternoon snack and went for a walk to the local supermarket. She needed more food for she'd been eating more than usual. She also hoped to meet Jackson because she wanted another 'read' on him. When they'd met she had liked him; however, the grey wildercat's green eyes made her think of him as a predator. The V-Day party was tomorrow, and she was in two minds about going. Unfortunately, or fortunately, she wasn't sure which, there was no sign of him. Her thigh muscles were aching mildly, but she decided not to raise the issue with Gèng again.

Back in her apartment, she stretched, meditated, and practised her Tai Chi. Logging in, she sat down and said, "Gèng, I need to learn some sword skills so when I reach Level 100 I can use Baris and Adalet effectively. Is there a course I can study that teaches the correct technique? I already know how to use fighting sticks, but I don't think bashing people with swords is quite the same."

"There are fencing courses, but no specialist sword schools

would appear to meet your needs. Two worlds have good reviews for promoting realistic swordplay. Both have special pathways for players intending to achieve freeform sword mastery. One is called 'Bushido' and is set in Japan during the age of the Samurai. The other is a fantasy player-on-player world called 'Dark Moon Duel' and provides training in schools for magic, sword, axe, and hand-to-hand to name a few. In 'Dark Moon Duel' you can enrol in a private school and study to become a 'Master of Blades'. The costs are similar; both are twice as expensive as Dunyanin as they cater to smaller niche markets. The most suitable style for you based on the various reviews and commentary is probably 'Dark Moon Duel'. The average time to reach sword mastery and become a 'Master of Blades' is five years. Only 154 people have achieved this rank."

"Can you show me any feed of the two styles in action?"

Leah watched several sequences from inside the two worlds and decided on 'Dark Moon Duel'. She hesitated over spending eighty gold but believed it was an investment for the future. Gèng registered her, and a stone door appeared. As she walked towards it, the door transformed into a golden surface that rippled as she drew near. She appeared in a small foyer with three doorways in it, each of them numbered and labelled. She headed for the first door which was labelled 'Step 1 – Name and Registration'. Inside was what resembled the reception of an old-fashioned inn. Behind the counter, a man dressed appropriately as an innkeeper said, "Welcome Atherleah. I have received payment for you to enter the amazing world of 'Dark Moon Duel'. I just need to check some of the pertinent details. Are you Atherleah Lin Mu-Ling Carroll, ID FQC3465278?"

"Yes, that is me."

"Wonderful, now I have your Interface as AI 628B44CE81?"

"That is correct."

"We understand that in entering this world you are aware of the rules and conditions and accept the full responsibility should anything untoward happen due to your involvement in this world, is this correct?"

"Yes sir, I understand."

"Good, good! You have requested the most basic starter pack, and that will be forty gold coins to register and an additional payment each month. This monthly payment starts at forty gold and will be reduced by one gold for each month you play as long as these are consecutive months. Should you miss a monthly payment, there will be no need to re-register, but the monthly figure resets to forty gold. Should you play for forty consecutive months, all further play will be free of charge. Do you agree to these terms?"

"I just have two questions. Firstly, does this basic pack allow me to choose to become a 'Master of Blades'?"

"Yes, the basic package allows full play and all classes. You will, however, find it harder to earn the coin to pay for additional skills."

"This leads to my second question. Will the gameplay allow me to develop additional skills if I play freeform rather than using the preset moves?"

"Yes, there is a path for full development and advancement using freeform play. Please understand that this requires exceptional natural agility and stamina and the rate of growth is often slow."

"I understand and accept your answers and provisos. I agree to all the stated terms."

"Finally then, what name do you hope to use in-game?"

"Atherleah, if it is available."

"It is. I have processed your registration and forwarded a copy of this session and all documents to your AI for your reference. Please proceed next door and choose your race and affiliation."

Leah left the room and entered the door labelled 'Race and Affiliation'. The choices seemed endless with every fantasy race imaginable, each with their particular strengths and favoured weapons. Leah simply chose to be a human and kept her original avatar. She changed nothing regarding her physique; she wanted the moves to be easily transferable to reality and other virtual worlds. She chose the class 'Master of Blades'.

She entered the third room where she affirmed all her choices and was given an overview of the world. Each player enrolled in a school or schools and learned their chosen skill. They could then investigate the world where NPCs would challenge them to combat, allowing them to practice their moves. If they won, then they earned money to buy better equipment, armour, and the like. When a player felt confident, they could challenge another player to a duel. Each player paid a fee to duel, and the winner received a total refund plus half the losing player's fee.

When she exited the room, a portal appeared which brought her to the main city of Ardenvale. The city teemed with people and was larger than any she had yet seen in Dunyanin. It was reasonably straightforward to find her way to the 'School of Swords' and for a fee of one silver per hour she became the student of Master of Blades Farron. Although Leah was tempted to interact with the game, she knew it didn't have the potential for large financial gain and so she only signed up for the lessons. The lessons were one-on-one, and soon she was being shown how to hold a sword and began studying a simple movement that the teacher called a 'form'. The aim was to move the sword in smooth motions that were able to transform into a whole series of flowing movements. Some forms Farron explained were more a stance, or sometimes it referred to a way of moving or walking that helped to defeat other players or creatures. Altogether the game expected a Master of Blades to learn over 100 forms in ten sets of ten. In the first lesson, Leah was only introduced to two forms and was told she would learn the next when she had these two perfected. She would learn a third when she had learned both forms and could move from one to the other seamlessly and gracefully.

After the lesson, she logged out and had a small snack and a shower. Her arms and back felt tender, but again she didn't want to mention it as she knew Gèng would let her know if anything was wrong. She lay down in the Pod and prepared herself for another day of riding. She planned to spend part of the day harvesting various herbs and plants as she needed to increase her skills if she wanted to make her own potions.

Leah materialised in the tent she and Wisp had been in the night before. It was still hooked from the inside, and she assumed Wisp hadn't yet arrived. Leah exited the tent and looked around the clearing. She didn't see anyone nearby and carefully checked the perimeter. Jason and his friends could be back in the game and nearby, but she hoped they had learned their lesson. She had just finished the perimeter check when Wisp arrived. They packed the gear and started off down the trail. They both wanted to increase foraging and harvesting skills, and so they walked rather than rode, taking advantage of the abundance of beginner level herbs beside the trail. It took almost an hour for Leah's harvesting ability to rise to Level 4. She knew she needed to move deeper into the woodland beside the road if she was to gain much further ground. Wisp was at a similar stage, so they moved into the woods just enough to find several different and more desirable plants. Being in the woods meant they had to deal with a selection of creatures. However, the levels this close to the trail were low enough that either girl could deal with the attacks on their own. Over a period of two hours, Leah progressed to Level 6 in harvesting and had ingredients that according to Falsi's Diary should supply her with low-level potions of Health and Stamina. They had killed a variety of Level 20–25 Striped Boars, Black Bears and Horned Foxes; the last of which had grey fur with dark stripes and horns like the antlers on a mule deer. The attacks regularly came every ten minutes or so.

After a brief stop for some trail mix and water, they mounted and rode at an amble for almost an hour when they saw the side trail branching off to the right and heading into denser woodland than they had seen so far. The Ranger Map declared that the MOB Levels through this dense forest were between 30 and 60 with the higher levels found further into the woods. Some of the Level 30 creatures had been known to attack Travellers on the trail. They expected to travel at about a league every hour if they kept the horses to a walk. They planned to ride for two more hours and then take a break before playing again.

The side trail was narrow, and visibility was less than before. They could see 100 metres along the trail in both directions except when the trail made one of its many turns to avoid trees, larger hills and stony outcrops. During the first hour, nothing interrupted them except the occasional flash of colour as birds flew through the woodland. They found the constant vigilance to be draining when even the birds here might attack them. Just after making a sharp turn to avoid a small ravine they saw a horse-sized Horned Fox standing in the middle of the trail about 40 metres ahead of them. Leah identified the animal as a Level 32 Electric Horned Fox. It was a beautiful beast. Leah and Wisp slowly brought their horses to a stop and dismounted.

They stood a couple of steps apart and watched the fox. The plan, should something like this happen, was to wait and hope the creature moved away. After ten minutes they realised the hopelessness of that wish and slowly advanced to see if they could defeat the fox. Leah moved forward while Wisp glided into the trees and disappeared. The fox moved its head, trying to keep both Leah and Wisp in view. Leah moved forward, and the fox started to shift its front feet as if changing its balance in preparation to charge. From Leah's previous two fights with a horned fox, this action preempted the charge. What was different was the antlers. They slowly began to glow, and electric sparks began to arc between the various points, the frequency and duration of the sparks steadily increasing.

In the past when the feet stopped moving the fox charged, so when Leah noticed the feet still and the fox turn toward her she dived to the right and behind a tree. Lightning flashed and blasted through the space she had vacated. She got to her feet and saw the fox hadn't moved. It was watching her, and again it began to move its feet. The electricity began to arc between the antlers, but this time, before it had reached fever pitch, Wisp shot an arrow from the side and pierced the fox just behind and above its front left shoulder. It quickly turned toward her and started to charge its lightning attack when Leah's arrow slammed into its chest. It turned back toward Leah and began to lower its antlers and move its feet for a physical charge. Wisp shot again but it was now completely focussed on Leah, so Wisp kept firing. The fox charged. Leah turned and cast *Disc of Death*. The fox slammed into the spikes which bent inward and then snapped. Shaking its head, stunned, it turned toward Leah who was already moving. She reached up and grabbed an antler then swung herself over its shoulder. She reached forward and fired several Mana darts into the back of its head. The fox went crazy trying to shake Leah off. She had to hold on to the antlers with both hands, but they started to glow and when they sparked she lost her grip, and flew off the fox and slid along the ground. Wisp had resumed firing arrows, and the fox was nearly finished. Leah used the Webspinner Ring to trap the fox before she killed it with a couple of arrows.

You have harvested:

1 Electric Horned Fox Pelt*

1 Ten Point Electric Horned Fox rack**

2 Vials of Crystallised Elemental Electricity***

2 Portions of fox meat

1 Minor Spell of Electricity (Grounding)****

* Note: These are prized to make garments with 50-100% defence against electrical attacks.

** *Note: These are used by Alchemists and Master Smiths.*

*** *Note: These are highly prized for use by Alchemists and Enchanters.*

**** *Note this is a defensive spell.*

After some discussion, Leah took the spell which provided some protection against electrical attack. As the level increased so did the length and effectiveness of the defence.

There were no more beasts of any kind in the next hour, which was when they quickly set up camp and both logged off to have a twenty-minute real-time break. When they returned they set off and had travelled another two leagues when each received a system message:

You are entering an area of play where Player Level determines the attacking MOBs. This area is square and covers an area of 25 square leagues. The trail cuts the area in two. The highest level player calculates MOB level for groups. You can, therefore, expect to meet situations aimed at players with a level of 30. Please have an enjoyable day.

"Gèng, is there anything about this area in any discussion, guide or forum?"

"I have found 259 references by people who have travelled through this region. 157 of these refer to the area and describe meeting an increased number of MOBs as well as an occasional bandit. Twenty-one refer to a group of NPC loggers. Except for those who are a part of a recognised Ranger or Cartographer Guild, all of them have been on a similar journey to you and have been using the trail as a pathway. Statistically, only one in every 500 people record and comment on their journeys, with one in twenty referencing accessing particular instances, quests and dungeons. Areas like this abound in Dunyanin and are positioned to give a variable experience for all players. Of the recorded 8,752 such areas, 452 have been found to have hidden areas, and 136 have fully developed dungeon areas."

Leah explained what Gèng had shared, and they moved forward feeling slightly less apprehensive than when travelling through the Level 30–60 area. They chose to walk for a while as they had been riding most of the day. Twenty minutes later they heard the sound of raised voices and whips. It was still several minutes before they saw a team of loggers who were struggling with several teams of oxen to load some recently felled trees onto a wagon. The loggers had been working the area for a while and had cleared several acres of forest.

As Leah and Wisp walked up, the loggers stopped work and spread out with hands on weapons. Most of the loggers were human although there was a couple of dwarves and one who, based on his size, probably had some orcish, or giant blood, somewhere in his ancestry.

Leah called out, "Good morning good sirs! We are just passing by and mean no harm."

One of the dwarves stepped forward and said, "Aye, I can see that now. But we've learned to be careful as there are some shifty folk around and some of us have been attacked on this road. It never pays to be complacent."

"True words, good sir. Should we be concerned as we travel this next stretch do you think?"

"Aye lass! Two fair ladies out and travelling by their lonesome. I would take great care. Be warned it's not only bandits, but there is something else out here hunting. We haven't been able to see what it is but we occasionally lose a friend or oxen if they stray out of sight. It is best to stay in groups."

Leah had read that often quests began by doing something for someone in need. So she said, "Thank you for your advice. Is there anything we could do to repay you for this warning?"

"Nay lass! You just keep watch and stay safe. Just be wary and stay on the trail."

Disappointed, Leah motioned to Wisp, and they continued down the trail wondering if they might meet bandits or the strange creature. It was only a few minutes later that they heard loud shouts and a scream from the direction of the logger's camp. They turned, mounted their horses quickly and galloped back to the camp. The loggers were in an uproar and standing around yelling at each other. One of them was on the ground, and it looked like he'd been in a fight. Leah rushed toward the leader and called out, "What is it? What's happened?"

"What's happened? What's happened? Here's what's happened! This nincompoop unhooked the oxen just before you arrived and didn't keep an eye on them. Now one of them has strayed, and all that we can find is a patch of blood and skin. He should have known better. Now we're one ox down with at least three weeks before another group will be through. We're not going to be able to load all the carts. That's what's wrong!"

"Can you show me where this happened?"

The dwarf led them to a point just outside the edge of the clearing. They could see a small dinner-plate-sized splotch of blood and what appeared to be a flap of ox hide. Wisp began to wander around looking for a sign of what happened while Leah tried to imagine what might have taken the ox.

"Atherleah, over here!" Wisp called out and showed Leah a drop of blood maybe five paces away and headed deeper into the woods. They moved together in the same direction and saw another drop.

"Hey! Ladies, don't go out there, it's dangerous. Come back, it isn't worth your lives."

Leah and Wisp headed back, and the Leah said, "You're probably right, but we are travellers and adventurers and if we don't see where the trail leads we will always regret it. If we come back, we'll be able to explain what happened, if not then know you were right."

Wisp nodded and said, "Yep! Let's do this."

Together they turned and headed into the woods, carefully checking each step and looking around. They silently followed the trail until the logging camp was out of sight and sound. The drops continued to appear at regular intervals and followed a windy path headed deeper into the forest. Leah was leading when she heard a loud thump from behind; she turned to see Wisp slumped on the ground and then felt a sharp pain in her neck. She reached up to see what had happened when everything seemed to spin around and everything went black.

The next thing Leah knew she was lying on a rough stone floor, her hands tied behind her back, and her ankles tied together.

Wisp was beside her in a similar condition. Wisp was beginning to stir. Leah said, "Gèng, where am I?"

"You are currently being held captive. You have been unconscious for just over one hour in game. Please do not be alarmed, I have been informed that this is simply a part of the game experience and I am assured that you may log out at any time. I was contacted with regards to your expected logout time, and I gave them a time one hour from now. As soon as Wisp is completely awake, a game administrator is going to arrive and discuss your options."

Leah struggled to sit up and finally moved into a standing position. Suddenly, with a flash of light, Emil Riverton, the same distinguished looking elf from Orumeck's Cavern, was standing several metres in front of them.

"Good evening Atherleah! And good evening Annairë_the_Wize! Annairë, I am one of the developers for Dunyanin, and I have already met Atherleah. I was the one initially responsible for the coding of this instance. Unfortunately, no other Travellers have been inquisitive enough to follow the blood into the forest. We have used a similar situation elsewhere, and people have found it both profitable and enjoyable. Once again Atherleah you have discovered something new. At the beginning of situations like this, an AI usually meets with players and explains the rules. However, as I designed it, and as I am dealing with certain issues arising from Atherleah's playing style, I have decided to explain the rules personally."

"My playing style?"

"Yes, but you and I will discuss that later. But for now, the rules! You are about to enter what we call an 'Extended Story Pathway'.

There are various possible pathways and endings. The aim is not always to kill everything, and it tests many of your qualities. Two people who take opposite pathways have just as much chance of obtaining experience and rewards: just different ones. I understand you are both due to log-out soon. As you entered in a group so must you continue. I suggest you exchange information if you haven't already so that you can enter together. It is expected, that except for the recommended twenty-minute break every three hours including meals, and that you are present almost continuously until this instance is finished. Do either of you have anything preventing you from a three hour, on, twenty to forty minute, off, schedule until this instance is complete?"

Leah spoke up, "I am due for my two NREM3 after one more hour of gameplay."

The elf turned to Wisp and said, "Are you in a similar situation?"

"Not really, I have a planned 'deep sleep' in eight hours. But I could have it now and match up."

"Thank you! That is appreciated. Next, you will notice that you are missing the weapons you had equipped. They are in the hands of the guards, and you must find them if you wish to keep them. You are unable to equip any other weapons until you have secured freedom for both your hands and feet. Both of you have knives hidden on your person; these were not discovered by your captors. That's all, so why don't you log out now and I'll see you both logged in back here in three hours. Say midnight for you Atherleah, and 11.30 pm for you Annairë_the_Wize. Atherleah could you stay here for a minute?"

Wisp stared at Leah, raised her eyebrows questioningly and then faded away.

"Atherleah, I apologise for mentioning the issues regarding your game play. It is just that now and then we get someone like you who fully utilises the free-form option. They tend to progress rapidly until they find their natural level. We carefully watch such players, as sometimes those around them can react poorly. I note you have caused the demise of several such players on repeated occasions. We try to pour oil on such troubled waters but so far have had no such luck. It is not your problem, but ours, though I have particularly enjoyed watching the way you have dispatched those players. Please note, if it continues we will take steps, I only ask that you don't inflame the situation unnecessarily. Now I must go, and so must you."

At that he disappeared. Leah also logged out to have some food, a shower and some 'deep sleep'. While she was eating, she asked Gèng if there was anything in the guides or forums about the situation in front of them.

"Yes, there is a common scenario where you have been captured and must either find a way to escape or a way to win your freedom. The circumstances are varied. Sometimes you have been kidnapped for ransom, at times you have been captured to be a slave, or you are going to be a sacrifice. One such situation would see you captured to be a wife of a goblin chieftain."

"How long do they take to solve?"

"Most take several Dunyanin days, and the record is ten Dunyanin days."

Leah felt refreshed when three hours later she was back in the same situation; hands and feet bound, standing next to Wisp who had appeared at almost the same instant. Looking around, she noticed it was darker than usual, if she hadn't any night vision she wouldn't have been able to see. She heard Wisp cast a quick spell that gave her night vision. They were in a small hollowed out cave with a locked gate barring the way out. Moments later they heard the sound of feet walking on the stone toward them, and as each foot landed there was a clicking and scraping sound.

The gate covering the small cell swung open, and they got the first glimpse of their captors. There were four of them, each was covered with scales of various colours. Their scales shone with faint luminescence. Each of their lizard-like captors stood upright. They had broad faces like a toad but instead of a flat face it came forward. Each jaw was triangular, though a slightly squashed triangle or even a regular trapezium. The eyes were on the sides of the head, the nostrils were slits above the upper lip, and each had several horns. The horns were located along the centre line and varied in number and length. The largest of the captors had four such horns. Both hands and feet had claws, while the arms and legs were covered in small quills on the parts away from the body. Dense clusters of these quills were found at the elbows and knees. Each mouth showed sharp teeth and what looked like a rolled-up tongue. All were carrying spears and had several tube-like devices attached to harnesses they wore which looped over each shoulder and hung in front of them, it was pulled close to their chest by the belt around their waist.

Bukalemun Warrior (Level 27) 2700 HP 2500 EP

"Bukalemun? Gèng, what are Bukalemun?"

"Bukalemun are one of the reptilian races. They stand upright like you but can blend into the shadows by changing their skin colour to match their background. They are carnivorous hunter chameleons. They have a tongue which can shoot out and attack prey at a distance equal to the length of their body. I am taking this from the Dunyanin Bestiary Guide. Until now, there are no reported sightings of Bukalemun. They are considered a defunct race. Something that was planned but never implemented."

The leader gestured with the spear and said in a voice, sibilant and deadly, "Comes! Moves! Hurries! Follows!"

One of the Bukalemun removed the rope from their ankles, then moved ahead while Leah and Wisp were forced to follow behind with the occasional poke from a spear. The first part of the journey was through a small cave system which exited into a large clearing holding hundreds of the faintly glowing Bukalemun. It was night, and there was a bright moon overhead. There were no fires and very little noise. The Bukalemun were waiting for something, and when Leah and Wisp were brought forward, there was a deep in-drawing of breath as if their presence was the herald of something anticipated. The guards prodded the girls forward to follow their guide; he walked across the clearing and onto a faint pathway on the other side. The mass of Chameleoids followed along, silently, until they resembled something long and sinuous, gliding quietly through the forest.

Wisp began to say something but received a heavier than usual prod with the spear; so they continued in silence. After ten minutes of silent walking the procession began to wind its way up the side of a small hill, with occasional switchbacks, until it reached the top. There was a low, stone, circular wall on the top of the hill that looked like the top of a deep well. The guards led the girls till they were only a few paces from the wall and then the leader said softly, "Stops! Quiets! Be Stills!"

The hundreds of Bukalemun who had come behind arranged themselves behind Leah, Wisp, and the guards until they packed into a half circle with the well like a bullseye at the centre. About five minutes later another procession appeared from the other side of the hill. This second group also formed a half circle, and from their ranks, two bound figures were pushed forward. The first appeared to be human, though he had been severely beaten and it was almost impossible to make out his features except for long blond hair tied in a ponytail. The other was a large humanoid, but it was impossible to tell of what race; it had a bag over its head, and from the sound of things it had been gagged.

Movement occurred at the rear of both groups and Leah made out a larger Bukalemun coming through the second group. This Bukalemun's luminescence was brighter than the others; Leah identified it as Level 90. A similarly built Bukalemun came and stood beside her. The two leaders began discussing things in a fast, sibilant speech. Finally, they stopped and looked over the two groups of prisoners. Content, they indicated to the guards that the prisoners should be thrown into the well.

Leah shook off the hands that had reached for her and said, "I know you understand me. Don't you even have enough honour to tell us why you are doing this?"

One of her captors flashed the butt of his spear forward, driving it into her midriff. She fell to her knees and after a few wheezing breaths said, "No honour, and you're cowards."

He was about to drive the spear forward again when the leader

of Leah and Wisp's half-raised his hand and said in a less sibilant accent, "Honour, coward! Whats do you know of honour
and courage? You come to our land to fight and steal. You have
no honour!"

"I came to find an ox that your people stole. I haven't fought you
or taken from you. Know this, if I had fought you, you would be
dead. If I had taken from you, you would have nothing. You are
the ones who fight from the shadows, hiding in fear. You tie me
up and take my weapons and then try and throw me down a
hole. Know this, throw me down, and I will return. Then you
will see how I fight and steal; for you will be dead and you will
have nothing."

"Little mouse, you know nothing about this. This hole goes to
the place of our dark cousins. They follow a dark God. Each
moon we send them a sacrifice. If we fail to bring it, they come
and take it. Four souls every moon. You are not us. I feel for you
like you feel for the ox. Nothing! I do not give you weapons
because you might try and hurt my people. It is not a lack of
honour and courage. It is indifference. I am chief to my people. I
care for my people. I am indifferent to you."

He then barked an order, and the guards moved forward again
to grab them.

"Give me my staff! At least, give me my staff."

"It will be of no use to you."

"Not for me! Do it for your people!"

"How will you having the staff help my people?"

"Because when I climb back out of that hole, I will come for it. If

I have it already, I'll leave. If I come for it, then some of your people will die."

"I will place a guard on the well. If you climb out or show up at my door, I will return your weapon and give you anything you desire from my treasure house."

"Deal, one treasure for each of us four who returns."

"Ha, you truly are a thief. One treasure for each of you who returns and we will restore your weapons to you. I, Reis, do so swear."

He barked a command, and the guard reached for Leah. She was prepared, however, and stepped forward on her own and jumped feet first into the well. One second later Wisp copied the move. The chieftain laughed aloud while the other chief threw his two captives into the well.

Diary - 21 November 2073

JASON WAS EASY TO KILL. *Maybe I'm getting used to the death, or maybe I just felt nothing for him. Truthfully, I had more trouble killing the beautiful fox than killing Jason. Can we just write someone off like that? Does he feel like I feel when the Government treats me like a number rather than a person, as some replaceable cog in their machinery? Or does he deserve to be dismissed out of hand because of his actions?*

Do I treat people like Reis treated me? I love my family, and they are precious to me. Would I be prepared to hurt a stranger to protect my family? I hope I would find another way out of the situation but at least I can understand the Bukalemun's reasoning. Who thinks up these scenarios anyway? I guess though, it is true to life. Not everything can be solved by love and compassion. Or can it? Mum says I have to learn to turn the other cheek, to only do good even if I suffer for it. Why can't stopping the bad guy be good? At least then they won't be hurting anyone else. Shouldn't people stop murder, rape, and theft? Surely some people don't deserve to be a part of society because of their actions. But who can make those decisions?

And so we come back to Jason. I have made the decision. His actions do determine how he is treated. If he weren't such a jerk, then he would be allowed to live. If he continues to hurt people, then I will continue to stop him.

The Bukalemun are wrong, hurting someone else instead of dealing with a problem is not just lazy but immoral. We should go out of our way to help people, even strangers; otherwise, we are just as bad as the people who hurt them in the first place. Injustice is everybody's problem.

Indifference is something to be careful of. How many people do I not see, or not help because I am indifferent to their plight? I know I can't help everyone, nor save everybody, but surely I mustn't be indifferent. Even if I kill something, even to eat it, plant or animal, I must not be indifferent. Otherwise I will waste its life and in the worst case become needlessly cruel.

NOVEMBER 22, 2073

LEAH FELL through the portal and landed clumsily after falling almost four metres. As she landed she still managed to bend her legs and roll off to the side. She saw Wisp land awkwardly and heard a cry as if Wisp had hurt or broken something. The next two prisoners had no such luck, and both landed heavily on their sides.

She called out quietly, "Wisp, you OK?"

"I think I sprained my ankle, but it should be OK soon. I can't reach a knife, can you?"

"Just a minute."

Leah sat down slowly with her hands behind her knees. She then stretched forward and brought them to the front. She was able to reach a belt knife, and moving to Wisp, cut her bonds. Wisp reciprocated. Wisp cast a small light to see better, and Leah cut the ropes off the blond and began to heal him. Wisp removed the bag from what turned out to be a huge Barbarian.

Leah used several potions on each before the two were able to sit up and look around. They were in a circular room chiselled from solid rock, the only exit was a steel gate sealed with a chain and crude lock.

Before either could speak, Leah said, "Hello, my name is Atherleah, and that is Annairë_the_Wize."

The barbarian spoke first, "You talk tough for such a little thing. I almost crapped myself laughing." He then said in a high voice, "If I had fought you, you would be dead. If I had taken from you, you would have nothing."

Returning to his normal voice, he said, "My name is Yabin, I am the friend, and bodyguard, of this midget, Sarisin of Ovalar."

Sarisin said, "I am not a midget, I'm normal sized, and I thank you for your help."

"You two are a long way from home. What brings you here?" Leah asked.

Yabin smiled and said, "Believe it or not, we are here for love. Lover boy here fell for a nobleman's daughter. Her father didn't approve, so he granted the marriage if and only if Sarisin here can fulfil a mighty quest. Rather than following my advice, which was to kidnap the wench, he decided to chase a centuries-old trail. We took a shortcut through a forest and ended up captured by the lizard-heads."

Sarisin interrupted, "Enough, Yabin, less talk, more action. Can you break the chain?"

Yabin looked over at it and said, "I doubt it. It looks sturdy enough." He looked at Leah and said, "How about you, princess? All that talk of taking anything, you ever picked a lock?"

Leah took a spider spike out of her bag, walked over to the lock and while looking at Yabin inserted the spike and with a practised twist unlocked the crude mechanism. Then she smiled and said, "I may have!"

He laughed and said, "Brilliant, you're a keeper you are. Now let's get out of here."

Sarisin said, "Yabin, you and I will go first, the girls can follow."

He exited the room followed by Yabin. Leah and Wisp glanced at each other, shrugged and sat down. It was a minute before Yabin and Sarisin returned. Sarisin said, "Is everything OK? I think we need your light; it's dark."

Wisp cancelled the light and cast a spell she had bought which gave her eyes of a cat. She then said, "I can see fine. I'm just waiting for the leader I know and trust."

Sarisin blushed and stammered, "You don't think I'm capable?"

"It's not that, it's just I don't know you. I followed Atherleah down the hole, she healed me, released me, healed and released you both, and she unlocked the chain. You've done nothing yet. If I'm going to follow anyone into the darkness, then it'll be her. Maybe after I see you fight and plan then I'll follow you as well, but not yet."

Leah stood and said, "If we go together, we need one leader. Before you assume it is you, we need to talk about it. If we can all agree that you'll lead, then we will follow. But if not, we can't be deciding during a fight or while running from something. If I'm being honest, then I would say I'm uncomfortable with your leadership because you rushed ahead without finding out our strengths and weaknesses. For example, we should ask Annairë to cast a spell so you can see in the dark. Did you know she has a spell which will conceal her whole group if you join? We are Travellers, and we harvest both experience and weapons from our defeated foes to grow stronger. How do you plan to distribute what is found? There are many issues to discuss before making a rash decision."

Yabin sat down and said, "OK let's discuss. Come, Sarisin, sit! Atherleah is right, and you know it."

They spent several minutes discussing their respective skills and attributes. Then Sarisin said, "Atherleah, we will follow you for now. Let us join your group. We will do as you direct. If after a while I think I can do better, we will talk. Is this OK?"

Leah smiled and said, "Yes, that's fine! If we collect any weapons you can use, they will go to you. All money is split evenly between us four. Everything else comes to either Annairë or me unless you specifically want it, then we will choose by chance. Now I'll go first, then Yabin, then Sarisin and Annairë. Annairë is to check the rear and right side. Sarisin, the left side and above our heads. Yabin, stay on my right and check ahead and to the right. I'll check ahead and to the left."

She then turned to Yabin, pulled the Amazonian War Axe from her bag and said, "Do you know how to use this or shall I give it to Annairë?"

He smiled and said, "Princess, for this, you can lead all day. Forget Sarisin."

Leah then handed Sarisin one of the Warrant Officer blades and gave each of them one day's ration from the Army Ants. "Eat this, and then we must be away. Annairë, please cast Cat Eyes on these two."

After everyone had eaten, Leah turned and stepped through the doorway.

Level 3 Dungeon Achievement: First 1 (3, Ruby)

Atherleah (Level 26), you have discovered a Level 3 Area:

Dungeon Experience - Escape the Dark Bukalemun

You are the first player to access this area. This is your third, 'First 1 (Ruby)' achievement.

Reward 1: 1000 x 30 = 33150 (+10.5%) Experience Points (19913/26000)

Reward 2: + 2% to all future Experience

Reward 3: 3 x 1 platinum = 3 platinum

Reward 4: Increased probability of valuable drop. Luck is increased by 5 whenever you are in this Experience. During your first time in the Dungeon Experience, the probability of all drops is increased to 0.5.

Fame: 500 Fame Points (3525)

A Commemorative Plaque has been placed in your bag.

Note: This achievement will be published on the Dunyanin achievement forum. Do you wish to retain your privacy?

[Yes] [No]

"Yes."

This dungeon is designed for a group of four:

Two players and two NPCs. MOBs will begin at least 2 Levels above the Mean Level of the players in your group with the final boss at least five levels higher than your highest member. Currently, this means MOBs are levels 30-36 in this dungeon.

As well as staying alive you have the task of keeping both NPCs alive. Should one or either of them die or get lost then your experience and reward from completing this experience dungeon will be halved. You only have one attempt.

Do you wish to continue? Note if you choose [No] you will be returned to your resurrection location with no loss of experience.

[Yes] [No]

"Yes."

Leah looked back at Wisp and grinned before leading the group down the dark passageway. They had travelled for several minutes when Leah heard a faint clicking sound coming toward them; it reminded her of the scratching made by the Bukalemun as their feet hit the floor. She stopped the group and then quietly explained that she would go ahead and hide, letting whoever was coming get ahead of her. Annairë would conceal the three of them until the Bukalemun got close enough to attack. Yabin and Sarisin would attack up close while Annairë would step back and fire from a distance. Leah would attack from behind and deal as much damage as she could before they noticed her. Everyone nodded and prepared. Leah ran ahead and then equipping Orumeck's Hands of the Spider Gloves she scuttled onto the roof and hid behind the Trapdoor Spider Shield.

About a minute later she could make out six Bukalemun; each had a spear and a wooden shield. Two had swords in scabbards hung around their waists. These Bukalemun didn't seem to have any luminescence quality, or they were consciously suppressing it. They passed underneath without even looking up. She checked, and all were labelled 'Dark Bukalemun Guard'. The four without swords were Level Thirty, and the two with swords were Level Thirty-two.

She returned to the floor, equipped her bow and began to follow them. As they neared where the others were hiding, she shuffled even closer to the six guards. Yabin started the fight by appearing suddenly and separating the right front guard from his head. Immediately, Leah shot an arrow through the back of one of the rear-guards and froze the other rear-guard's head. Sarisin had attacked the other front guard and was finishing it off with the help of several fireballs from Wisp. Leah stepped closer to the two remaining guards and drove a couple of Mana spikes through the head of one as Yabin attacked the other. The Mana spikes hadn't quite killed the guard, so she trapped it with a Webspinner trap and used her knife to finish it off. Yabin was almost done, so she went back and began to harvest the corpses. Each one gave similar loot:

You have harvested:

2 Vials of Death Poison*

1 Bukalemun Skin**

10 Bukalemun Quill ***

1 Bukalemun Spear

1 Simple Wooden Shield

5 copper Coins minted with an image of Zerten Zele, Last Overlord of the Bukalemun

* Note: These are highly prized for use by Alchemists and Assassins.

** Note: These pelts may be used to make camouflage clothing.

*** Note: These quills may be used by Scribes.

She was also able to collect the two swords. No one had received damage, so Leah turned and began to move down the tunnel. Yabin turned to Sarisin and said, "Don't worry, I still like your leadership. If you'd been leading it would've been more fun, lots of danger and blood. Atherleah makes the fights boring. No one likes boring fights."

"I do!" Annairë said quietly.

Leah surmised that there would be several more groups coming to collect them and she was right, over the next hour three more groups came along the tunnel. The ambush worked almost as well each time. Finally, the tunnel ended and they could see into a large rectangular room, longer than it was wide. It was a prison. There were cells along two sides with prisoners in each cell. Ten guards were visible in the centre section. There was a door at the far end of the room, with one guard posted beside it. Three guards were sleeping on some simple bedding arranged in a row near the middle of the room. There was a table where four guards were seated and playing a game of dice. Closer to tunnel entrance was another table, this one with a Bukalemun strapped on top of it. Two guards were heating a metal rod over a brazier, and it looked like they had been torturing the prisoner for some time. There were burn marks all over its arms, legs and torso.

Leah motioned for everyone to retreat. In whispers, they devised a plan. Annairë was to sneak through and prepare to take out the far sentry. Leah would start the ball rolling by stepping in and attacking both torturers. Hopefully, this would draw the rest toward her. Annairë would then take out the sentry and hold the door until Sarisin arrived to help her. When the other guards approached Leah, she would cast *Disc of Death*. She would then cast Rain of Fire and Yabin would attack from the side. Sarisin would run toward the far end and attack any stragglers. If possible, Sarisin and Annairë would then help with the larger group of guards.

Everything went as planned, with Sarisin also killing a guard who was slow in waking. Yabin took some damage, but he was able to absorb a large amount. His axe skills were well honed, and he never allowed the axe to get caught in the bodies, instead he brought the blade across the body causing deep slashes to cut arteries and flesh. The only times he brought the blade in full contact was to sever a limb at a joint or to remove a head. Leah was the only other one hurt; she received a spear through the front of her thigh. It bled a lot but was soon healed.

As soon as the fight ended, Leah went to the prisoner being tortured. The Bukalemun was a female and still breathing. She began to heal her when Yabin came over and said, "Oi! Princess! Lizards are the enemy."

"Maybe! But she isn't, well, not yet. I need to find out more about what is happening. You go check the cells and see who's locked up, try and find out why."

She turned back to see the prisoner watching her. Leah was wearing both the Tears and the Sorrow of Göksel-Orman so she reached one hand to the earring and said, "I would like to release you. Do you promise not to fight us, scream or run away?"

"Promise, I promise." Leah could hear the thoughts of the Bukalemun as an echo; the echo matched the words.

Leah released the straps and said, "My name is Atherleah, what may I call you?"

"Name is Sakin."

"Sakin, can you tell us why those others were torturing you?"

The story as they finally understood it was that the Bukalemun living in the cave system had unearthed the crypt of the dead king Zerten Zele, Last Overlord of the Bukalemun some twenty years previously. Zerten Zele's reign had brought about the collapse of the Bukalemun civilisation several millennia previously. He had been a ruthless and greedy king, given over to wild excesses and dark perversions, practising necromancy and other evils. In the end, his people had revolted and killed the Overlord and his armies. The survivors gathered everything that might remind them of him and buried it, along with the Overlord and his defeated army in this cave system. They covered it over and sought to rebuild their lives. Too much had been lost and the Bukalemun declined as a race throughout the centuries until they were simple forest dwellers once again, eking out an existence far from the world.

Unfortunately, the mages who had supported Zerten Zele had cast complicated and powerful defensive spells on him and his guards, and though they could not prevent his eventual death, they did animate it. Over the years, without blood and sacrifice to fuel it, Zerten's lich had lost power and began to fade. To prevent this, he cast a spell on all with him, causing them to sleep, dormant until awakened. When the crypt had been disturbed, one of the Overlord's mages, Hayalet, had woken and influenced the local chief of the Bukalemun to seek power and fame. The chief began the practices of pain and sacrifice that Hayalet needed to fuel the awakening of Zerten Zale. Every month, four souls were sacrificed to raise the army. Before their sacrifice they were subjected to six months of torture; their pain, agony and screams were siphoned into crystals. It was these crystals that Hayalet was collecting to power the spell needed to raise Zerten Zele. The prison was the place of torture.

Sakin had been here for almost six months. Leah and her friends were to be her replacement. Already two of those who had been offered down the well with Sakin had been taken for sacrifice, and she expected the Head Guard to return at any moment to take her for sacrifice. Sakin had been offered by her chief when she accused him of cowardice for allowing the sacrifices to continue, instead of fighting to stop the rise of Zerten Zele and the Dark Bukalemun. The other prisoners had all been offered as sacrifices over the previous five months.

Leah sent Yabin to the doorway to listen out for the returning Head Guard. She looted the corpses and released the other prisoners who were all suffering from months of abuse. She gathered them close and with full Mana, gripped one of her earrings and asked if they would accept her help to escape the prison. Listening carefully to their thoughts, she found that everyone wanted help to escape. She asked if they would accept her as the leader during the escape and though most were willing, there were some who thought they had a better chance alone. She took those four aside and said, "You all think you would be better alone than in my group. I accept that although I wish we had your strength with us. All I ask is that you wait until we are ready to leave, and then when you head off on your own that it be in a different direction to the one we take. Can you agree to this?"

Everyone agreed, except for one dwarf who thanked her for the help but said he would do as he wished and was leaving now. As he stepped away, she shot him with the Webspinner Ring and equipping her bow, she aimed it at his head. She commanded two others to drag him into a cell. Closing the door, she locked it and said, "OK! You can leave when you want to. As we go, I'll drop you the small spike I use as a lock pick. I don't have time to teach you how to pick a lock, but I'm sure you'll work it out eventually."

Ignoring his cries, she set about healing all the others. Altogether there were twenty-one who agreed to follow Leah as the leader: four humans, two elves, five half-elves, six dwarves and four Bukalemun. Leah and Wisp used almost all their Healing and Mana potions, getting everyone healthy. Leah handed out spears, swords and bows as people shared their skills with her. Two of those who were going to try alone were dwarves — they came to her and pointing to the dwarf she had locked in the cell. They said, "Salak was stupid, he's always been a bit of a jerk. If we promise to keep him here until after you've gone can you release him? He doesn't deserve to die for being an idiot."

Leah thought about it and said finally, "I'll let him go just before we leave. I won't leave him a weapon as he wants to make do on his own. If he causes us any problems I won't lock him up, I'll kill him. Are you OK with that?"

They agreed and went to tell Salak her decision. Wisp came over and said, "What's the plan?"

"I've talked with Sakin, and we have two options, we can head to the left and work our way through the whole dark community, probably having to fight the lot, even the women and children. Or we head right and down, moving toward the Crypt. There is a section where the resurrected army lives and trains, followed by a cavern which houses the lesser mages that Hayalet has brought to life. From there we make our way to the surface and escape, or we can enter the crypt and challenge Hayalet. Now I think this 'experience dungeon' has four levels, so I expect we have to go all the way to Hayalet. I plan to get the whole group to the mage section and then let them go. You and I and any who want to stay will see to Hayalet. I'm almost certain we won't have to battle Zerten Zale as this experience is recurring just with different characters."

"So, this is the first level, then the barracks, then mages and finally Hayalet. Have we finished this yet or is there more?"

"More, I expect the head Guard is the mini-boss. How many can you hide in your *Group Gone* spell?"

"As many as are in the group. The time we're concealed for reduces as the number increases. If everyone crowded around me, then I can probably conceal us all for about thirty seconds."

"When we hear the guards returning, you get everyone back in a group up against the wall. I think the left side, as that is the way the door opens. Yabin and I will stand near the torturer's table. If you conceal everyone as the door opens the guards shouldn't see you and will race toward Yabin and me. I'll cast *Disc of Death*, and then you come behind the guards and surprise them. Hopefully, we should be able to deal with them all."

"Sounds like a plan. What about those three not in our group? I can't hide them."

"I guess they'll have to come stand with Yabin and I. I'll explain the plan to them. You get the others and explain about being still and quiet. Can you also explain to Yabin and Sarisin?"

It was almost twenty minutes later when Yabin gestured that someone was coming. He ran to join Leah, a half-elf and the two friends of Salak. Soon the door was pushed open, and two guards walked into the room. They had taken several paces and were joined by two more when they noticed Leah and the others near the table. They stopped briefly and a Bukalemun, who was more heavily muscled and spiked than the others, joined them. He pushed them forward, and together they all rushed Leah. Their numbers swelled as they were followed by eight more guards. Leah and the four with her spread out across the room. Yabin had explained that this would spread the opposing force and allow any attack from behind to have a greater effect. He suggested that Leah not use *Disc of Death* this time. Yabin and Leah were in the middle, and the Head Guard headed toward them. Wisp and the others came after the guards and attacked from behind. The fighting was fast and furious, but the guards were surprised and overwhelmed. Leah fought against the Head Guard and used her spiked sticks while trying to avoiding his sword and claws.

She had made some headway and saw the bar above him show his Health at seventy-five percent. He suddenly stepped back and threw a crystal on the ground. A circle of mist ran across the ground and with it a force that threw everyone back except the Head Guard and Leah. The mist rose from the ground and formed a barrier that no one could cross. Leah's group finished the other guards then stood pushing against the mist, but they could not enter. The bar above the Head Guard began to climb, and he was soon back to full Health. He opened his mouth slightly and hissed before his tongue suddenly shot out and grabbed Leah by her right wrist, jerking her toward him.

She was taken by surprise but had learned that taking the path of least resistance allowed better opportunities in attack. She not only allowed herself to be brought toward the Guard but fell forward and turned it into a roll. She looped the suddenly loose tongue around her hand and stepped inside the claw range of the Guard. She shoved the spike in her right hand into the guard's mouth and drove the left-hand spike into his abdomen. He raked his front claws down her back, but they caught on the harder leather of the cuirass and jerked her off her feet. As she fell the claws cut deeply into her scalp. She activated her Ki Heal, and though her KP began to plummet, her Health was out of the red. Before the Guard could stomp on her, she grabbed a belt knife and cut off the loop of tongue she had in her right hand. The guard reeled backwards and grabbed at his mouth. Leah equipped her bow and shot upwards through the Guard's neck and into his brain. As he fell backwards, the mist evaporated, and Wisp rushed over to heal Leah as much as she could.

Once Leah was restored she had all the guards dragged over to near the Head Guard, she drank a Luck potion and harvested them all. The guards all gave similar rewards as previously, although there was a greater number of swords and some even had silver coins. The Head Guard gave the following:

You have harvested:

2 Vials of Death Poison*

1 Bukalemun Skin**

20 Bukalemun Quill ***

4 Crystals of Isolation****

1 Key to the Prisoner Cells

1 Key to the Torture Table Safe

8 silver Coins minted with an image of Zerten Zele, Last Overlord of the Bukalemun

* Note: These are highly prized for use by Alchemists and Assassins.

** Note: These pelts may be used to make camouflage clothing.

*** Note: These quills may be used by Scribes.

**** Note: When crushed these isolate the one who crushed them and their main opponent; neither may leave until the other is dead.

She quickly ran to the table and saw a keyhole highlighted in green. She put the key in the safe and turned with just two seconds left on the Luck countdown. Inside she found the following:

You have harvested:

1 Map of the Dark Bukalemun Realm

24 Crystals of Torture*

2 Vials of Elemental Darkness**

20 copper Coins minted with an image of Zerten Zele, Last Overlord of the Bukalemun

8 silver Coins minted with an image of Zerten Zele, Last Overlord of the Bukalemun

*Note: These contain the agony and pain of one soul's torture. They can be used by Necromancers and other practitioners of death magic.

**Note: These are highly prized for use by Alchemists, Enchanters and Master Smiths.

Opening the map, she could see the path they needed to take. She called the two friends of Salak over and gave them a key to his cell. She showed them the map and then made them promise to wait ten minutes before releasing him and leaving. They promised. She gave them a sword and shield for Salak and then she led Wisp, Yabin, Sarisin and her group of released prisoners out of the door.

Once they were in the tunnel, one of the elves by the name of I'tinal, a trained scout, stepped to the front and led the way. Leah followed with Yabin, while Wisp and Sarisin brought up the rear. According to the map, when the tunnel next branched they needed to take the right-hand turn. The tunnel would then begin to dip downwards with occasional openings on either side that were old parts of the mining operations. The map showed the tunnels as mostly straight, so the section they headed down appeared like a fern frond, a central axis with leaflets branching off to either side and sub leaflets on each of those. Even though she expected to find nothing, Leah stopped at the first branch and with Wisp did a careful check down the full length, some 200 metres, checking each side tunnel. She did this partly because she didn't want any surprises coming toward her and secondly because she wanted to check them for loot. Together they collected several old picks, a few old torches and a small rusted chest which eluded her attempts at picking the lock. The side trip had taken ten minutes, and Leah knew they didn't have time to check every tunnel if they continued at this pace.

At the next side tunnel, she set Yabin, Wisp and a couple of others to check it, while she and the others moved on to the next one. Leah and two others then checked the tunnel. Once Wisp finished her tunnel they caught up and moved on to the next. In this manner, they were able to keep moving at a reasonable pace. It was in the second tunnel she had done without Wisp, the fifth side branch, that she was surprised when a Bukalemun dropped on her from directly overhead. She hadn't seen through his camouflage, and the first she knew was when she was driven into the ground, his back claws raking the back of her legs as she fell forward. The two ex-prisoners quickly attacked and had drawn off the attacker by the time Leah stumbled to her feet. She joined the fray and it was soon killed. All three needed healing, and then Leah harvested the dead lizard. She identified it as a Level 30 Dark Bukalemun Miner.

You have harvested:

1 Miner Pick

1 Bukalemun Skin*

10 Bukalemun Quill **

2 Pieces of the Mineral Rhodium***

5 copper Coins minted with an image of Zerten Zele, Last Overlord of the Bukalemun.

* Note: These pelts may be used to make camouflage clothing.

** Note: These quills may be used by Scribes.

*** Note: This is a rare mineral used by Master Smiths and some dark Alchemists.

Altogether it took them one and a half hours to check every branch. They had four rusted chests and had been waylaid by five more miners. Leah and Wisp had been in-game for almost six hours and only had three more before they needed to have a forty minute real-time break. According to the map, the resurrected Army and Training Barracks was just ahead. Before they could move, they heard a soft shuffling of feet coming up behind them. As a group they turned, ready to kill whoever came into sight. It was the four ex-prisoners who had left to be on their own. It turned out that they had been set upon by two Bukalemun and had almost been killed dealing with them. They had backtracked, wanting to join the group.

Leah couldn't afford to expend all her MP to read their thoughts, so she nodded and put them in the middle of the pack. The map showed the Barracks to be eight rooms, four on either side of a long hallway. At the end of the hallway was an open area for food preparation, eating meals and an ablutions block, then a large cavern used as a training arena. Wisp volunteered to sneak through and see how many Bukaleman there were.

Sakin explained that it required one death to resurrect one ancient soldier. The sacrifices had been offered each month over the last twenty years. It was possible there were over 196 soldiers. Leah thought that some were probably guarding the crypt and hoped some were elsewhere as the number seemed too many for her twenty-eight strong force. When Wisp returned, she said there were twenty soldiers in the kitchen area and over thirty in the Arena. Seven of the Barrack's doors were closed. Through the open door, she had seen twelve soldiers exercising, sleeping and chatting in the room. Leah wondered what the distance was that triggered their aggression, and if one soldier would raise the alarm, causing a chain reaction of hostile soldiers. She thought it best to check with the soldiers in the Barracks. If they raised the alarm, then they only had the narrow tunnel to defend.

Yabin volunteered to draw them out, and he wandered down the hall until a soldier saw him. He ran back to the group followed by the soldier and everyone in the room. None of them stopped at the other barracks or raised a general alarm. They followed Yabin into the tunnel. Everyone except Leah had moved back about thirty metres and were being hidden by Wisp. As Yabin reached a line drawn on the ground he dropped into a crouch, and the group suddenly appeared, firing arrows into the soldiers. Leah, who had been hidden behind a Trapdoor as the soldiers ran past began to shoot at the rearmost soldier. By the time the ambush was fully sprung she had killed three soldiers and was aiming at the fourth. She took the shot and then using her *Freeze* spell and several Mana darts, took out two more.

Next, Yabin went to a barracks with a closed door and flung it open. Inside were twelve more soldiers. Their attacking strategy was identical and with the same result. It took forty minutes to empty the barracks and reduce the enemy by ninety-six soldiers. Leah harvested everything from the soldiers; all were classed as Ancient Bukalemun Soldiers. Each one gave almost identical loot.

You have harvested:

2 Vials of Crystallised Bukalemun blood*

1 Bukalemun Skin**

10 Bukalemun Quill ***

1 Bukalemun sword

1 Iron Shield

3 copper Coins minted with an image of Zerten Zele, Last Overlord of the Bukalemun

2 silver Coins minted with an image of Zerten Zele, Last Overlord of the Bukalemun

* Note: These may be used in potions to aid in camouflage. As it has been reanimated, some potions may aid in hiding from undead such as vampires and wraiths.

** Note: These pelts may be used to make camouflage clothing.

*** Note: These quills may be used by Scribes

The group used a similar tactic to attract the twenty soldiers in the kitchen area. Unfortunately, one soldier ran into the arena — most likely to raise the alarm. Leah saw this, and after shooting at the rear three soldiers, she ran across the kitchen and waited, several metres inside the doorway. There was shouting from the training area and just as the connecting door opened Leah cast *Disc of Death*. She had aimed at the doorway so only one person at a time could come through the gap. She fired arrow after arrow into the gap and kept the soldiers at bay. Eventually one of the soldiers managed to get through, so Leah quickly cast *Circle of Sloth* and began to defend herself with a stick in one hand and the scythe in the other. She was soon keeping three soldiers at bay. Even so, they managed to cut her Health to seventy-five percent, and she had several bleeding debuffs. Suddenly, two soldiers she was fighting were shot with arrows, and the other received a Fire bolt to the face. The tide of the battle turned as Leah's force drove the soldiers back, step by step. Leah stood back and watched for several minutes as she waited for her Health and Mana to replenish. Suddenly, the opposing force sounded the retreat and ran back into the arena. Leah followed, and she saw the enemy soldiers, or the ten that were left, all standing in front of a corridor which she assumed led to the crypt.

One of the soldiers was a head taller than the rest. He stepped forward and said, "One of my soldiers has gone to warn Mage Hayalet that you are coming. You have stopped nothing, only postponed it. You may defeat us, but the best soldiers are protecting the Overlord. Even with your numbers, you would fail against them. Flee now, and maybe you will escape, but you will not succeed." He ushered his soldiers through the door behind him and stood resolute in the gap.

Ancient Bukalemun Captain (Level 37) 3500 HP 2900 EP

He asked, "So who is your leader?"

Leah stepped forward, and the Captain held out a palm with a crystal in it. He said, "Do you know what this is?"

Leah nodded, "A Crystal of Isolation."

"Yes, and I have enough for all of you. I'll use them one after another until you are all dead. Do you want to go first or do you want to watch your people die?"

"I'll go first."

The Captain threw the crystal against the floor, and while it was still falling, he used his tongue to grab Leah's ankle and pull her feet out from under her. As she fell she sliced the scythe down toward his tongue but he had already retracted it and was stepping forward to slash his sword down at Leah from above. Instead of rolling away from the sword she rolled toward the side which had the sword, allowing it to run along her back. She brought her leg around to kick his legs and raked them with her boots. She didn't rise but rolled and began firing Mana darts at him from the ground. He used the sword to deflect some, and he dodged a few, but two got through and hit him on the shoulder. As he reeled backwards Leah got to her feet holding a knife in one hand. He smiled and extended his claws on the free hand not holding the sword. She fired *Freeze* toward his head but his sword was quickly raised to block it, and the sword froze in his hand. Leah had anticipated the action and had thrown her knife to follow the spell. As he brought his hand down the knife struck him in his right eye, causing him to flinch and grab the knife. Leah had followed the knife in, and as he staggered, she brought the knife she kept behind her neck and buried it in his armpit. She placed her other hand under his jaw and cast *Freeze* again; it froze his head solid.

Yabin said, "Typical, princess, bloody typical. One good fight and you hog all the action. Next time they ask for a leader, it's my turn. Just to let you know, one of the signs of a good leader is to delegate. You need to learn the skill."

She grinned and said, "Sure thing Yabin, the next job is yours. Please drag all the dead bodies over here so I can harvest them. How is that for delegating?"

After taking a 'plus-ten' Luck potion, she harvested the twenty soldiers and the captain. The soldiers gave more coin with the additional Luck as well as some who dropped gold. The captain had been telling the truth and dropped twenty-nine Crystals of Isolation. In total he dropped the following:

---

3 Vials of Crystallised Bukalemun blood*

1 Bukalemun Skin**

10 Bukalemun Quill***

1 Bukalemun Captain's Sword

29 Crystals of Isolation****

2 Vials of Elemental Darkness*****

32 copper Coins minted with an image of Zerten Zele, Last Overlord of the Bukalemun

12 silver Coins minted with an image of Zerten Zele, Last Overlord of the Bukalemun

4 gold Coins minted with an image of Zerten Zele, Last Overlord of the Bukalemun

1 Ancient Map of the Realm of Zerten Zele, Overlord

1 Key to the Captain's Personal Chest

* Note: These may be used in potions to aid in camouflage. As it has been reanimated, some potions may aid in hiding from undead such as vampires and wraiths.

** Note: These pelts may be used to make camouflage clothing.

*** Note: These quills may be used by Scribes.

**** Note: When crushed these isolate the one crushed them and their main opponent and neither may leave until the other is dead.

*****Note: These are highly prized for use by Alchemists, Enchanters and Master Smiths.

Leah asked the whole group to quickly search the rooms to see if they could find the Captain's Personal Chest. Some of them also went back and checked each of the barracks. Altogether they collected twelve gold, forty-eight silver and 104 copper. Leah offered some to the group, but they all declined and said that Leah should have it. Finally, when all was done and they hadn't found the chest, Leah called the group to come close and then said, "We have one more section to empty before I can send you to freedom. Before we head to that section both Wisp and I need a rest. We are Travellers and so when we sleep we travel in our sleep to another realm. We are going to lie down over there and sleep. There should be some food in the kitchen for you all to have a meal while you wait. Sarisin is in charge while we rest. Please listen to him and Yabin, unless Yabin wants to go fight without us, in which case, ignore him."

Leah and Wisp then went to a corner of the room, made themselves comfortable and logged off.

Leah only had forty minutes as she exited to the apartment. She showered and had an early breakfast with a cup of coffee. She stretched and did some Tai Chi before another quick shower. She stepped through into Dunyanin and waited for Wisp who was only a minute behind. Leah had gained several levels and quickly distributed her points. She continued to place most of the points in Agility. The 'plus-twenty' Strength from the ants and the 'plus-fifteen' from rings pushed Strength above her Agility. Because she played freeform, she wasn't sure how much the numbers meant anyway. Agility increased her KP and SP, and she needed those. She added eight skill points to her spell *Hidden Quietness*.

She checked that everyone had enough rest, had eaten and was fully healed. She re-checked the map and talked through several strategies with Wisp, Yabin, Sarisin, Sakin and I'tinal. This time, Leah would lead, though I'tinal and Yabin would be only two steps further back in case of ambush. Wisp and Sarisin were another five metres behind and ready to come to the aid of the others if needed. The map showed a straight run with no branches or path deviations.

They walked cautiously to the area set aside for mages, and the 500-metre journey took them almost fifteen minutes. Leah stopped fifteen metres from the opening. Wisp faded from sight and snuck into the room to check the layout and the number of mages and soldiers. When she returned, she explained that there were five mages that she could see and twenty soldiers. Four of the mages were Level 35, and one was Level 38. The soldiers were strung out around the room and watched the doorway. Leah and Wisp decided they would each take out a mage from stealth. Leah thought the soldiers would then turn to help and the group could attack from behind. Both Wisp and Leah felt they were able to hold off an attack for long enough for help to arrive. Leah had all those with arrows carefully dip the ends in some of the 'death' poison.

Leah cast *Hidden Quietness*, and at her level of Agility with the extra spell levelling, she had over thirteen minutes to get into place. This was more than enough for the ten-minute timer she had set for herself and Wisp. As she snuck into the room, she could see the mages shift suddenly and begin to glance around the room. Apparently they had some way to feel the spell. Wisp hadn't been noticed, presumably because her concealment was not spell based. Leah hugged the wall as she listened to the mages directing the soldiers in a search for a concealed person. After seven minutes Leah was only ten metres from her target, but there were several soldiers in the way. She stood quietly and waited. Breathing deeply, she was about to equip her bow when the soldiers shifted just enough for her to slide between them.

Coming to within two paces of the mage, she waited, and just as the timer ticked over, she stepped forward and buried her knife in his ear. She then equipped the bow and fired at the next closest mage. The arrow just creased his cheek as he turned toward her, chanting. She knew she had to stop the chant so ignoring the two nearby soldiers she fired another arrow and dropped into a backwards roll while un-equipping her bow and equipping her fighting sticks. This time, the arrow took the mage in the chest. As she dropped, one sword went over her and the other made a shallow cut along her cheek. As she rose, an arrow hit one of the soldiers, so she attacked the other soldier and soon finished him off. She turned to see the two remaining mages casting various spells at her people. The spells caused excruciating pain as they hit and those affected fell to the ground writhing in agony. Leah cast Rain of Fire at the one mage and then began to sprint toward the other. A dome sprang up over the first mage, protecting him from the fire. Fortunately, the dome also prevented him from casting spells. As she drew near to the final mage, she threw a Webspinner trap, but it disappeared as it touched some invisible protection around the one she recognised as the Boss Mage. The mage turned as Leah approached and was almost face on when Leah dove forward and came crashing against the mage's legs in a rugby tackle that would have made her father proud. They both crashed to the ground, and in the scramble, Leah used her elbows, shins and forearms to apply all the dirty tricks she had learned over the years. Suddenly Leah was thrown backwards; the mage's Health and had been reduced to under fifty percent and triggered another protection spell. Leah came to rest at the feet of Yabin who looked down and said, "Stop resting princess, she's not finished yet, or do you need some help?"

Leah mouthed a word that she would never say out loud and put

NOVEMBER 22, 2073   375

out her hand for him to help her rise. As Leah turned back to the mage, she noticed that the boss was the only remaining enemy. Wisp had started to engage her, as had some others with bows. The mage was now on the defensive, reacting to the incoming spells and arrows. Leah carefully watched the mage's Health decrease until it was twenty-five percent, when another blast shook the cavern and knocked everyone off their feet. Leah had been waiting for something and was the first back up. She began to loose arrows, one after the other at the mage. Soon the others joined in until almost two minutes later one of the arrows got through the defence, and the mage was defeated.

Breathing a deep sigh, Leah hurriedly checked on all her people and spent the next twenty minutes healing as many as she could. Yabin dragged all the dead into one spot for Leah to harvest. Wisp and Sarisin organised a thorough search of the whole area for anything hidden. They found a hidden door, and instead of a lock there was an eight by eight grid of small switches. Most were sticking straight out, but some were up and some down.

							U
	U	U			D		
	U				D		U
		D					
U	U		D			D	
				D			
D	D				U		D
	D						D

Above the lock were the words: "Two choices, always equal, never three!"

Leah looked at for a while and then pushed one of the switches to the Up position. A small timer appeared above the puzzle and began a countdown from three minutes. She began to move faster, switching the straight out ones either up or down. Wisp looked at her and asked, "What are you doing?"

"It's a Binary Puzzle; the switch can be up or down. Each row and column must have equal up and down. Never more than two up or down together. I've done these before. I'll take the 'plus-ten' Luck before switching the last one."

With ten seconds remaining she had one switch left and drank the potion before opening the door. Without looking inside, she ran to the pile of bodies and harvested them, then she returned to look inside the door. It was a small room with several bags of coins and two chests. She grabbed the key belonging to the Captain and tried it on one chest, then tried the other chest, which sprang open. Quickly she looked at the list of loot from the soldiers and mages. There was another key which she grabbed and used it to open the final chest just before her thirty seconds expired.

She quickly looked through the messages, and the full haul was quite overwhelming. Not including what was from the soldiers and minor mages Leah and Wisp received:

---

2 Vials of Crystallised Bukalemun blood*

1 Bukalemun Skin**

1 Bukalemun Mage Wand

5 Crystals of Death***

2 Vials of Elemental Darkness****

8 gold Coins minted with an image of Zerten Zele, Last Overlord of the Bukalemun

4 platinum Coins minted with an image of Zerten Zele, Last Overlord of the Bukalemun

1 Defensive Shield spell

1 Key to the Senior Mage's Chest

* Note: These may be used in potions to aid in camouflage. As it has been reanimated, some potions may aid in hiding from undead such as vampires and wraiths.

** Note: These pelts may be used to make camouflage clothing.

*** Note: These contain the essence from of one soul's sacrificial death. They can be used by Necromancers and other practitioners of death magic.

****Note: These are highly prized for use by Alchemists, Enchanters and Master Smiths

---

*You have opened the **Ancient Bukalemun Captain's Chest**:*

8 gold Coins minted with an image of Zerten Zele, Last Overlord of the Bukalemun

10 Crystals of Isolation*

2 Link of Limberness (+10 A)

* Note: When crushed these isolate the one crushed them and their main opponent and neither may leave until the other is dead.

---

*You have opened the **Ancient Bukalemun Senior Mage's Chest**:*

4 platinum Coins minted with an image of Zerten Zele, Last Overlord of the Bukalemun

10 Crystals of Death*

2 Coil of Comprehension (+10 I)

* Note: These contain the essence of one soul's sacrificial death. They can be used by Necromancers and other practitioners of death magic.

She gave the *Defensive Shield* Spell to Wisp, and they took one each of the 'plus-ten' Agility and 'plus-ten' Intelligence rings. Leah equipped them both and removed the 'plus-five' Strength ring. Once everyone had gathered around, she explained that she and Wisp were going to see if they could defeat the Mage Hayalet. The rest she suggested follow Salak on the path to the surface. They could either wait for Leah and Wisp, they could go with Salak, or they could disperse. Both Yabin and Sarisin said they would go with Leah. Although several others offered, they were the only two she accepted. She didn't think it would be easy to sneak twenty-eight people into the crypt.

Once the larger group headed to the surface, Leah, Wisp, Yabin and Sarisin headed down a long windy sloping tunnel deeper underground. The light began to fade, and it was only Wisp's spells which allowed Yabin and Sarisin to see anything. During the descent, although they didn't come into contact with any soldiers, mages or traps, what could have taken them thirty minutes ended up taking two hours — such was the caution they showed. It was at the final turn that they saw a faint violet glow highlighting the crypt cavern. Leah was concerned Hayalet would be able to perceive her use of *Hidden Quietness*, so Wisp used the Cloak of Invisibility and snuck into the cavern which contained the crypt to reconnoitre. When she returned, they all moved back up the trail to discuss her findings.

"The cavern is huge. There are stone pillars dotted throughout which appear to be holding up the ceiling. Ten soldiers are wandering throughout, and I wasn't able to make out a pattern. The crypt door is on the far side. The door is open, and I could just see inside. It is full of bodies in all stages of decay, piles of money and all sorts of scrolls and books. In the centre of the cavern, about thirty metres from the crypt door, is a sarcophagus which I assume has the body of Zerten Zele. A Level 120 Mage is working with two Level Forty-plus mages and looking at a large piece of parchment. Around the sarcophagus, there are many crystals positioned that sort of match the diagram on the parchment they are examining."

Leah slumped a little and said, "Well there is no way that we can take down Hayalet, he's just too powerful."

"I'm not sure we are supposed to." Wisp said. "The final boss was going to be Level 36, and that last mage was higher than that. Maybe escaping is the final stage."

"Maybe you're right, but I'm not happy just to leave him alone. Would you be offended if I go have a peek?"

"Not at all, knock yourself out."

"You be careful, princess. If you decide to have fun, then come and get us."

"I will, don't worry. I'm not starting anything against a Level 120 without help."

Leah cast *Hidden Quietness* and snuck into the chamber. She was several metres inside when a voice called out, "Welcome little mage. I can feel your magic in the air. Come and see what we are doing here. You may have defeated the rest, but I assure you that you have no hope against me if you cannot hide your magic use."

Leah continued to move and was pleased to see that though the mage was talking, he wasn't looking in the right direction. After almost five minutes of evil mage monologue, Leah found a small alcove from which she could just see the mages at work but none of the soldiers. She cancelled the *Hidden Quietness* and stood as still as possible.

The mage looked around briefly and then said, "They've gone." He turned to one of the soldiers and said, "I think we are safe. I want you to take the secret tunnel and go get reinforcements."

The soldier started to walk in Leah's direction, and she suddenly realised it wasn't an alcove but was the start of a secret tunnel. She pushed against the door she could now see, but it was locked. She checked which side had the hinges and backed right against the wall and pressed the Trapdoor Ring. The soldier was not expecting her. He took a key from his pocket, opened the door, which fortunately for Leah opened into the tunnel, and stepped through. Leah stepped through behind him and quietly killed him using her knife. She lowered him to the floor and quickly locked the door behind her. She rushed along the secret tunnel as quickly as she could and found it had an exit in the kitchen area. The tunnel kept on going, but she left it there and hurried back down the larger general purpose tunnel the four had previously crept along. As she came up to the area where the three were waiting, she spoke softly, hoping to attract their attention without being attacked.

As they saw her coming from the opposite direction they started and then Wisp stepped forward and hugged Leah. "I was worried. I thought something must have happened. I was almost ready to go looking for you."

Leah hugged her back and explained what had happened. She shared the plan she'd concocted. She knew they couldn't kill Hayalet, but she did want to prevent the return of Zerten Zele. She planned to steal as many of the crystals as she could from around the sarcophagus, or rather she wanted Wisp to steal them while she distracted the other mages. She gave Sarisin the key to the secret tunnel and explained how to get there. She expected he would hear the distraction through the door. He was to unlock the door and prepare for either her or Wisp to need it opened — as an escape route. Yabin was to wait near the main entrance to help whoever ended up there. He was also to throw a rock or something to distract everyone after thirty minutes.

Leah and Wisp entered the chamber. Leah moved toward the crypt while Wisp moved as close as she dared to the sarcophagus. Haylet looked around and began a monologue expressing his greatness and the certainty of death to whoever had invaded the crypt. When Leah's *Hidden Quietness* spell was almost finished, she found a little nook to hide in and waited for the cooldown to end. She saw a pile of small bags and a small bin of scrolls, so without looking, she began to pilfer whatever was in reach while she waited for Yabin. Suddenly there was a tremendous crash, and everyone turned to look. Leah ran out of the crypt, tossing her vial of worker fire ant saliva as hard as she could behind her. The vial exploded against a pile of scrolls, which immediately burst into flame. By this time Leah had cast *Hidden Quietness* and was sneaking away. She hoped the mages would rush to the crypt but only one did and he cast a quick spell which doused the fire immediately. Hayalet and the other didn't move; as if they had set areas to defend.

That was 'Plan A', and it hadn't worked. Now it was time for 'Plan B'. As the mage walked back toward the sarcophagus, Leah stepped behind him, plunged a knife into his neck and dropped a Crystal of Isolation. She twisted the knife and watched his Health plummet. As this was happening, she shuffled around to keep the dying mage between her and Hayalet. The attack was enough for both mages to move in her direction.

Hayalet smirked and said, "He's not long for this world, although I will resurrect him. You, I will also resurrect: Not to life but to an eternity of pain. You cannot escape now I see you; I won't let you out of my sight until you're dead."

Leah continued to drag the limp body with her. Several times she had to cast a healing spell to keep him alive. Soon she neared the area with the hidden door. She hoped Sarisin had it open. She backed against the door.

Hayalet said, "You are out of room. Soon your Mana will dry up, and you won't be able to keep him alive."

Leah was ready, and she hoped everyone else was also. She gave a small nod of her head and Wisp, who had already stolen all the crystals from around the sarcophagus, cast *Wave of Fire* from the main doorway. As Hayalet's head turned to see what happened, Leah pulled the knife from the mage's neck, killing him. She opened the door and slammed it shut, locking it behind her as she and Sarisin ran as fast as they could up the tunnel. The wooden door exploded behind them, and a torrent of fire rushed up the tunnel, but they managed to escape the worst of it. Leah and Sarisin flew into the kitchen area and then rushed towards the mage's area hoping that the pursuit would come up the secret tunnel.

Yabin and Wisp were waiting, and together they rushed up the exit to the outside. They could hear sounds of pursuit as they ran, but they stopped for nothing. The rest of the group was waiting at the exit. It was mid-afternoon, and Sakin said she knew where she was and so she began to lead them toward her home.

As they started off, Leah said to Sakin, "What is the name of your chief? Is it Reis?"

"No, he is chief of the neighbouring tribe. He has more honour, but is just as weak."

"Can you lead us to his tribe, as we have met him and he owes me something? Your chief doesn't sound like he will be favourable to you."

Sakin agreed and changed the direction they were travelling. About forty-five minutes later Sakin raised a hand to bring them to a halt. She said, "We are being watched. I will tell them who we are and that we are here to see Chief Reis."

Sakin spoke out in the Bukalemun language, and two warriors stepped out of the forest in front of them. After some discussion, the warriors led the way. More appeared behind Leah's group. It was almost half an hour later when they entered a small clearing filled with warriors; Chief Reis was standing at the front.

As soon as Leah had stepped into the clearing, she received several messages.

Level 3 Dungeon Achievement: First 1 (4, Ruby)

Atherleah (Level 35), you have completed a Level 3 Area:

Dungeon Experience - Escape the Dark Bukalemun

You are the first player to complete this area. This is your fourth, 'First 1 (Ruby)' achievement.

Reward 1: 1000 x 35 = 39375 (+12.5%) Experience Points (35000/35000)(5396/36000)

Reward 2: + 2% to all future Experience

Reward 3: 4 x 1 platinum = 4 platinum

Fame: 500 Fame Points (4025)

Additional Rewards based on achievements in experience.

Assigned NPC survived 2 x 2000 EP = 4580 (+14.5%) Experience Points

Additional NPC saved 22 x 1000 EP = 25190 (+14.5%) Experience Points

Final Level Completion Preventing the Rise of Zerten Zele

4 platinum Coins minted with an image of Zerten Zele, Last Overlord of the Bukalemun

2 Diamond Coins minted with an image of Zerten Zele, Last Overlord of the Bukalemun

Final Level Completion — Crystals of Death

Your group has collected a total of 900 Crystals of Death.

Reward 1 - 1 Fame point per crystal - 900 Fame Points (4925)

Reward 2 - 1 gold per Crystal if delivered to a priestess of Olme, goddess of death

A Commemorative Plaque has been placed in your bag.

Note: This achievement will be published on the Dunyanin achievement forum. Do you wish to retain your privacy?

[Yes] [No]

"Yes."

She smiled as she again chose to retain her privacy. She stepped toward the Chief and said, "So Reis, where is my staff, and where is your Treasure House?"

Chief Reis stared at her and the people who she had brought with her. He recognised many as those he had sent for sacrifice against his better judgement. He stepped toward her and bowed his head. He said, "I have your staff in my Treasure House. It will be returned to you. Come, the night is here. Please spend this evening with us and tomorrow morning I will take you and those with you, and we will let you plunder my Treasures. Tonight, may we hear the story of how you escaped the Dark Cousins?"

Leah, Wisp and the others spent several hours talking about their adventures before Leah and Wisp had to log out. They were shown to a hut, and after promising to meet at eight the next morning, they logged out.

Leah arrived back in the Tower and did a little dance, then slumping into her sofa she said, "Gèng, how much money have I collected now?"

"Well, I will let you deal with your messages, and then I will give you a final answer."

Leah added one of each type of Zerten Zele coin to her collections. She had received over 145,000 Experience Points and jumped to Level 41. Gèng then said, "Let us ignore the specialised coins, though at auction may be worth a fortune. In fact, often people find a coin to swap rather than buy. If we ignore those, then you have a total of 6 Diamond, 49 platinum, 45 gold, 166 silver, and 113 copper in coins. Several of your Auction items are due to close soon, and you have a lot of material to sell."

"So I have sufficient money to enrol in four subjects at MIT! I'll need to think a little and see about those other Diamonds and how to exchange them for different types. But for now, I'm going to have another breakfast and call my mum. Thanks for all your help, Gèng. After breakfast, I think I'll do my Chemistry and Biology subjects before heading back and choosing from the Chief's Treasure House."

Leah then faded out into the real world to have breakfast.

After a second breakfast and talking with both parents Leah headed into the Pod and attended her Chemistry course. Professor Franklin's class had progressed to discussing equations and stoichiometry. Leah forgot all about Dunyanin and the other worlds as she focussed on balancing and using complex chemical equations. After Chemistry, she took Human Biology and concentrated on how cells, tissues and organs work together. She was amazed at how much easier it was to learn when she shrunk to the size of a cell to watch osmosis and diffusion happening; she was able to vary the parameters and see the various effects on cells. Leah found the classes engaging and more complex than she'd expected from a community college. Much of the material was a revision of what she had already covered in her private studies. She'd made some assumptions about the community colleges and decided that she had displayed prejudiced behaviour. She hated prejudice and was embarrassed and chastened at the thought.

Leah still had some time before she headed back to Dunyanin, so she looked through the various courses at MIT, hoping to find something that genuinely attracted her. She was fascinated by mathematics and physics but wanted to apply the knowledge to something practical, so maybe Engineering, but what sort? She read and viewed the various course descriptions and subject offerings.

Finally, Gèng reminded Leah of the time, and she slipped out of the Pod for a bathroom break and a small snack before logging in and heading straight for the Dunyanin Portal. Wisp was not in-world, so Leah sat and meditated while she waited. A few minutes later Wisp arrived, and together they left the tent to see what the day would bring and hopefully get further along the trail toward the mountains.

Yabin and Sarisin were talking with Reis and Sakin when Leah and Wisp arrived. They all turned and greeted the two travellers. Reis said, "The story of your escape has filled me with shame, hope and fear. Shame that I have agreed with evil by doing nothing and even helping it to grow. Hope that one day these Dark Brethren will be defeated. Fear that other tribes will continue the practices of the past and we may need more help in future. But for now, come collect your staff and my treasure. I considered my oath and believe it only holds for the four who were present when it was given. I do not think that all who returned have a claim, do you agree?"

Leah answered, "If your oath were taken by its words alone then I believe all should receive a treasure; however the deal I agreed upon was for myself, Annairë, Sarisin and Yabin. I agree with you."

Reis led them into the woodlands to a small guarded hillock which had been hollowed out. He took them inside and allowed them to see his treasures; some were handed down through his family and collected over thousands of years. After they had searched the room they all chose something beginning with Leah, then Wisp, then Sarisin and finally Yabin. They chose the following, in order:

Belt of Zekâ Irfan, Light Mage of Sihirbazlari

Zekâ Irfan was a forest elf from Yesil-Orman. After achieving mastery of her art, she travelled the known world seeking to increase her knowledge. She was the author of many books, the most well known is her Tome on the Study of Light. The Belt was commissioned by her and was made by the famed enchanter Ek'Lemek. This belt adds to both the Wisdom and the Intelligence Characteristics to an amount equal to the Level of the Owner.

Minimum: None

Scalable

Binds on pickup

Spell Diary of K'tsal Linel, Mediator of Namus (God of Purity)

K'tsal Linel was born of merchant parents in Ticareti, the capital city of Merchant Kings of Tuccarlonca. After seeing the corruption which tore his family apart, he dedicated himself to the God of honesty, purity and virtue (Namus) eventually rising to the rank of mediator. His career has resulted in numerous stories, perhaps the greatest of which is his victory over the Vampire Patriarch Kan Olumu in the City of Night.

Note: You will only be able to learn spells appropriate to your level and skills.

A Master of Horses Sword of Ovalar

The Horse Lords control the clans, and the clans control the plains of Ovalar. Each Horse Lord is bequeathed a signet weapon, a symbol of their power. In ancient times those who achieved greatness were bequeathed the rank of Master of Horses. As a symbol of their rank, they were given a sword of quality befitting their rank. Such swords are often kept in the same family as a symbol of honour.

Minimum: Level 40 (30 A)

Base Damage: 250 HP

Binds on pickup

A Falcata of Yirtisi

The Yirtisi are a group of savages who live on the Wild Islands in the far South East of the Continent of Vatan. Their weapon of choice is the Falcata. The Falcata has the power of an axe and the penetration of a sword. Only those with enormous strength can use these to effect. In the hands of the Yirtisi, they are deadly.

Minimum: Level 40 (60 S, 40 A)

Base Damage: 350 HP

Binds on pickup

Reis apologised once again for his unwillingness to fight against the Dark Brethren. The four Bukalemun decided to remain with Reis' tribe, although Sakin did offer to leave with Leah. The other twenty-two ex-prisoners all decided to leave at the same time as Leah and most planned to stay together until they reached some settlement. So at nine in the morning, Leah and Wisp with the twenty-two others were led out of the woodland and back to the trail just a short distance from where they had met the logging crew. Once on the trail, Leah showed everyone the map and explained where she and Annairë were headed. Most decided to head east back toward Carson's Loop. Only the dwarves wanted to head for the mountains, and after seeing the route, they decided to head off straight away. Everyone had given both Leah and Wisp their information and requested they be visited if Wisp and Leah were ever near their homes. Finally, Leah and Wisp were standing with only Sarisin and Yabin.

Sarisin said, "On our honour, we believe we have a debt to pay and would request the opportunity to stay with you until we have met this obligation."

Leah, however, insisted that the two should head back and claim Sarisin's love. He thought the sword might be enough to prove his worth to her family. Leah said she planned to visit Ovalar during her wanderings; she had some business to do with Clan Karanliklar and hoped she could visit while there. Sarisin explained that Clan Karanliklar was no longer a major force but that his home bordered on their lands. He would be glad to introduce Leah when she visited. Yabin gave her a huge hug and said if she ever got bored he would introduce her to his family; that would spice up her life a little. After some fond farewells, Sarisin and Yabin headed east, and Leah and Wisp headed north-west.

It was a ten-minute walk to the loggers' camp where Leah and Wisp retrieved their horses and informed the loggers that their oxen had indeed been killed and they should remain vigilant as the disappearances would likely continue. Taking their leave, they pushed the horses into an ambling trot and rode steadily along the trail. They soon passed the six dwarves and rode without interruption until a message appeared.

You are leaving an area of play where the attacking MOBs are determined by Player Level. The area you are entering is inhabited by aggressive creatures that are at a higher level than some players in your party. It is suggested that you leave this area as soon as you are able.

"Must be time for a break then," Wisp said. So she and Leah stopped for a short break on the side of the trail.

Leah had set her system to divide most loot automatically if there were two of anything. Some things like the 900 crystals of death remained in her bag until the task involving them was completed. Leah asked to keep both maps, and as Wisp didn't think she would use them, that was easy. Leah, however, had yet to examine the things she had pilfered from the crypt. So as they rested, she pulled them out, and together they examined the loot. Altogether she had taken four of the small bags and seven scrolls. Each bag contained a different treasure. One was full of pearls in a variety of colours from pure white to dark black, and other colours including copper, burgundy, indigo and lavender. The second was full of opals. The third had rubies, and the fourth was filled with diamonds. They weren't sure of the value but decided to keep the bags until they could find a valuation; otherwise, they had no way of knowing how to split them.

Three scrolls were maps. One was a complete map of Vatan, the continent they were on. The boundary lines were different, but it marked trade routes, keeps and towns that had disappeared over the centuries. The second map was of the Demir Dovuyor Mountains and showed the location of many mines that Zerten Zele had controlled during his reign. The third was a route map to what was inscribed as S'hir B'zari but Leah thought over time might have become known as Sihirbazlari. There were no other towns marked, but she thought she could see enough geographic features that she should be able to find the way.

While Leah was drooling over the maps, Wisp was ecstatic to find that the final scrolls were all spells. Two were major necro-mantic and death spells, but both Leah and Wisp were not interested in heading down that path. The other two, however, were spells in an area that Wisp had heard of, though such spells were extremely rare and insanely expensive. Both were what was described as prophetic magic. The first was called *The Next Step* and showed through superimposition where an enemy would be after their next action. The second was called *Safety* and showed the caster how and where to move to sidestep all danger if it was possible. At its highest level, the caster could glide around swordsmen and walk through an army, all without suffering damage. In the end, Leah kept the maps and Wisp the two spells.

The next five hours brought several encounters with wild beasts. There was another Electric Horned Fox, this time at Level 33. Wisp practised her new spells and was able to sidestep the lightning bolt. There was also a Level 42 Barbed Wolf which was crossing the road in front of them. This beast was probably a metre and a half at the shoulder and had a mane like a lion, but rather than hair it was made of long sharp barbs. Its fur was dark as night, and the barbs they collected afterwards were straight and metallic. Leah spent some time collecting herbs while Wisp walked alongside keeping an eye out and practising her spells.

As they walked, they talked about their lives and finally concentrated on Leah's invitation to the party. Leah had decided to go to the party Jackson had invited her to, and Wisp was full of advice on what to expect; she realised that Leah was somewhat ignorant of boys and parties. The party meant that Leah would be late, so they agreed to meet at half past one in the afternoon the following day. This would give her four hours at the party; she thought this would be plenty of time. It was almost five when they found a small clearing and set up the tent. They had managed to cover eight leagues and hoped to finish the next section in two days.

Leah bathed and had quick lunch of ramen noodles. She had five hours before the party, which was enough time to finish her community college classes and complete both an archery and sword lesson, or two. Soon she was with Master Ning who began to discuss several more complicated meditative techniques. In the Tai Chi section of their class Master Ning began the sequence of postures and Leah was able to join in and only needed correction on a few of them. Her AI course was still reviewing the various historical approaches to developing AI and the fundamental concern for boundaries and safeguards. She did wonder if Gèng had sufficient safeguards as some boundaries and safeguards had been damaged in the upload. It was something she had to discuss with him-her-it.

Lady Flèche suggested that Leah needed to concentrate on greater accuracy at a distance, so most of their lesson had Leah working on firing at targets twenty to thirty metres away. Leah knew that her effectiveness with the bow had mostly been her ability to hit areas not covered with armour. Against an armoured knight, she would need to be highly accurate or have a more substantial arsenal. She might benefit from some of the magic arrows like those that Wisp had acquired.

Finally, she went for a second lesson in Ardenvale. Faron continued to have her practice the two forms she knew and introduced two more for her to learn. Toward the end of the lesson, he began to spar with her but only allowed her to use the four forms that she knew. He explained that she needed to know what worked best and how each form flowed into the next. By the end of the hour she was drenched in sweat and tired from having to hold the practice sword, as it was much heavier than the sticks she normally used. The absolute realism of the world was stunning as was its take on skill development.

With just over two hours real time until the party, she spent some time out of the Pod and had an evening meal of curry and rice and then sat waiting until ten to seven before getting in the Pod and preparing for the party. She had already decided on a pair of jeans, a button-up top, her tweed newsboy hat and a nice pair of flats for the party. She had no experience with makeup and had considered visiting a virtual salon but chickened out at the last moment; all the advertising was of styles she just couldn't imagine wearing. She didn't understand the concept of being fashionably late, and so, at precisely seven PM she asked Gèng to open a portal to Jackson's v-world. A door appeared on her wall, and she stepped through it, hoping that she'd have an enjoyable time and make some friends. Leah was slightly apprehensive as she still had memories of the Wildercat with Jackson's eyes.

She arrived at a closed-in portico. There was a large wooden door with a golden bell. She rang the bell, and a sweet note rang out before morphing into a fanfare as the door opened. Jackson wore dark jeans and a light shirt with buttons. He welcomed her and ushered her in saying she should come and meet some friends. Leah thought the space she entered tastefully designed; there were multiple areas for people to lounge and talk, a dance floor and several tables filled with food. There was a drinks area and what she assumed was a virtual barkeep. Several other constructs wandered throughout the hall offering food and drinks to guests. The music was loud but not overwhelming; when people were having a conversation, the music faded in their vicinity.

Jackson explained that most people would probably be a little late, but she should first meet his parents who would be leaving before the party got going. Jackson's father was built like his son, tall with dark-toffee coloured hair, but where Jackson's was slightly unruly his father's hair was well tailored. He looked friendly. Their eyes were both the same electric green. In contrast to Jackson's jeans, his father was wearing a charcoal suit with pinstripes and leather shoes. Jackson's mother was also tall, and slender. The welcome she gave Leah didn't reach the ice blue eyes though. Jackson excused himself for a moment to get Leah a drink while his parents tried to get some information from her about background and parentage. Leah was a very private person and kept the information light and neutral. When Jackson returned, he handed Leah a coke and asked his parents to excuse them so he could introduce Leah to a few friends.

Leah took a sip of the drink and began to follow Jackson to another group of people closer to their age. Before Leah had taken two steps, Gèng said, "That drink has an aggressive code mixed in it, and it is attempting to access your chip. I am unsure of its purpose, but I am certain I would not have identified it except for the high-level security protocols given by Security Controller 11-5. I believe the code is attempting to access the hardware locks present on the intended PAI-N chips."

Leah stumbled slightly but continued walking as she carried on the conversation silently with Gèng, "Can you contact Security

Controller 11-5 and see if he can determine the purpose of the attack?"

"I am having difficulty in accessing an external data link. Most of my processing capacity is currently being used to fight this malware."

"Can you log me out?"

"Not at present."

Leah continued to follow Jackson toward his friends. After he had introduced Leah to them all, Jackson looked at her drink and suggested that they all toast to having a great night. Leah sub-vocalized, "Am I in danger if I drink more of this?"

"I don't know."

Leah stumbled a little and dropped the cup. She said, "I'm a little clumsy today, just feeling a bit light headed all of a sudden."

Jackson waved the spill away and said, "No worries, let me get you another."

Soon he was back with another drink and said, "Here, now drink that up."

Leah was horrified when her hand moved the cup toward her mouth almost of its own volition. She tried to stop it but instead opened her mouth and took a long drink. She said to Gèng, "What is going on? My body isn't obeying me."

"The extra drink added a different code which is attacking the security software on a different front. I have a possible solution but need you to trust me. I want to allow the code access to several areas and see if that releases pressure on others."

"I trust you."

"Then stay calm. This will give the code greater access to your movement and speech. I believe I have been able to cordon off your higher thinking which should remain in your control."

Leah took another long drink when instructed to and then talked briefly with the various friends until Jackson interrupted and said, "Leah, please come and meet my brothers." He proceeded to lead her to the side of the room; she found herself following along without a conscious thought.

Leah and Jackson approached two men who looked enough like Jackson to be his brothers. He said to Leah, "Give me your drink."

She smiled and handed over the drink. One of Jackson's brothers smirked and said, "Another one Jackson. You seem to have luck when it comes to recruiting."

"Nope! Not luck! I am simply better than you two at playing the part of a friendly, caring, poor boy. Twenty more and I'll reach the quota early and be able to take a holiday. This'll be my last year recruiting."

Leah could see Jackson's parents making their way over when Gèng said, "Leah, I have a connection to Security Controller 11-5. I have sent him all the data and a cloned but confined copy of the code. He requests access for a direct conversation with you."

"Granted!"

"Atherleah Carroll, this is Security Controller 11-5. I have reviewed the data and concur with AI 628B44CE81's preliminary conclusions. I have insufficient data to determine the exact purpose of the code as it would require that I have access to the specifications of the intended PAI-N chip. I request, with intensity, that I am permitted to allow Safety Oversight AI 4 to aid in my investigation as I understand an agent of their department has such a schematic."

"I agree to the additional aid."

"You understand that this may infringe, long-term, on your privacy."

"I understand. I need to know, however, what the purpose is."

"Atherleah Carroll, this is Safety Oversight AI 4. Be aware I have been granted access to your private information. I surmise that you are the source of the data previously shared with me by Security Controller 11-5. After receiving that information, I instructed one of my human agents to secure a copy of a PAI chip similar to what was intended for you. When applying the code to that chip, I find the purpose is to interact with your will and decision-making capabilities rendering you compliant to any and all suggestions."

One of Jackson's brothers smirked and said, "Now please tell me your full name and citizenship number."

Out aloud Leah said, "My name is Atherleah Lin Mu-Ling Carroll, ID is FQC3465278." Leah sub-vocalized, "I don't want to share this ..."

Safety Oversight AI 4 said, "For your safety and privacy I am currently hiding various aspects of your life that your profile suggests should remain hidden such as your location, medical profile and excellent school records. Instead, I will provide them with plausible but fake data. Please note that the Australian Republic is unaware of my changes."

Jackson's mother then said, "OK, I've just checked, and she's on negative tax and completely unconnected. You boys take her out the back and give her clear instructions. I want her checking in to one of the work areas within twenty-four hours. I'd prefer she work in Dunyanin, but if not, then on Ringworld. She's only been virtual less than a week, and I doubt she has the resources to enter one world much less both of those. Well done Jackson, you have a knack for finding vulnerable people."

Safety Oversight AI 4 said, "Ms Carroll, I have enough data to bring charges against the person whose v-space you have entered. I would request that you permit the scenario to proceed as it might lead to others involved and maybe other victims who require protection. Please note that my investigations are not at the request of your government and may lead to some adverse reaction by them. Their reaction may be detrimental to you should this lead to a censure and or formal charges against citizens or the government of the Australian Republic."

"Does this put me in immediate danger?"

"Not within the virtual world systems. I have already provided your AI 628B44CE81 with additional safety protocols and have given it direct access to me. I am finalising some code which will return control of your facilities completely to you and your AI. Within the real world, I have no direct ability to provide safety. I am applying the code now. You should have full control."

Leah's posture didn't change, but she became aware that she could move if she wanted to. It was subtle but liberating. Her fear turned quickly to anger, and then flared into a white-hot rage. She said, "Don't worry about the real world; I can find people to help in the real world if I need them. I'll play along if it catches more of these scum; please provide instructions if you think I need them. I just have to act willing and obedient, is that correct?"

"Correct!"

The brother who had asked her name said, "Come with us Atherleah, after giving Jackson a goodbye kiss."

Leah turned to Jackson and gave him a quick kiss on the cheek and then turned to follow the brother. Jackson quickly said, "Leah you need to give me a long and passionate kiss. After all, I'm going to change your life."

Leah then turned and said, "I'm sorry Jackson, I don't know how to do that, I've never kissed a boy before."

Everyone laughed, and it was only because she was ready for the laughter that she didn't blush. Jackson's mother interrupted and said, "Enough Jackson, we have enough virtual whores that we don't need real ones. Just take her away and hurry back."

Leah was led to a side door and into a small room where she was told to sit.

The brother who hadn't yet spoken said, "Now Atherleah, or Leah if you wish, have you entered the virtual worlds of either Dunyanin or Ringworld yet?"

Safety Oversight AI 4 said, "Ms Carroll, based on what I have heard I would prefer you enter Dunyanin, so please say, 'no' to the question. I have contacted the Dunyanin administrators, and they have agreed to allow you a second concurrent account under specific conditions. After you leave here, I shall tell you those conditions."

Leah said, "No, I have joined neither."

"Good! As soon as you leave here, you will open a 'wood' account with Dunyanin. There you will choose to be a Mountain Dwarf. Assign seven additional points to Strength and seven to Constitution, keep the rest. With the 'wood' package you don't have access to better equipment so choose a rusted iron pickaxe and the heaviest duty mining gear you can. They will offer you a chance to choose a starting town, pick Maden Town and make your way to the headquarters of the Kolelick Corporation in town and sign up as a day-labourer. At the corporation offices, tell them that Mrs Kodoman asked that you have the special terms and agreements. Sign whatever they give you and then get to work. Now repeat back to me what I want you to do."

Leah repeated what was said and then was prompted by Safety Oversight AI 4 to ask, "How should I pay for the package as I don't have any money?"

After checking her bank balance, he transferred forty virtual credits to her account and told her to go and have a good sleep as he wanted her in Maden Town by nightfall and ready to start work at eight the following morning Dunyanin time. He added, "Tell no one about this conversation and always be happy that you can work for the Kodoman Family. Now drink this and then log out."

Leah sub-vocalized quickly, "Will this be OK to drink?"

Safety Oversight AI 4 replied, "Yes, I will immediately sample its code and provide you with appropriate feedback and advice. It cannot harm you."

She drank and heard, "It is a new code that allows you to log out while giving them a permanent connection to your visual and audio Input and Output. I have redirected the connection and will provide them with a doctored feed. You can now safely log out."

Leah asked Gèng to log her out, and when she arrived in the Tower, she began to shake uncontrollably. Finally, her shaking slowed and she began to breathe slowly, in and out. Leah sought to calm her mind and to simply — be. All the things Master Ning had shown her slowly came together, and finally, she became still and focussed. Gèng interrupted her meditations and said, "Both Security Controller 11-5 and Security Oversight AI 4 would like your permission to enter the Tower via their avatars, will you permit this?"

"Yes, please have them join me here and if you could provide some suitable seating please."

Two comfortable looking chairs similar in style to the sofa appeared and then the uniformed man she had seen previously appeared. With him was a woman dressed in a similar uniform. The man said, "It is good to see you again Leah, although I would prefer that it was under different circumstances. This is my colleague Security Oversight AI 4."

"Welcome, both of you. Please have a seat."

"Thank you, Ms Carroll."

"Please call me Leah. Do you have any shortened names or is it always Security Oversight AI 4 and Security Controller 11-5?"

Security Controller 11-5 replied, "Well we don't usually connect with the same person often enough to shorten it. I imagine that we might need to find something easier should we meet more often, I will give it some thought."

"Do you still need my help?"

NOVEMBER 22, 2073   405

"Yes! We have discovered various things about the Kodoman family and their corporation. For security and privacy reasons we are unable to share these with you as they are still being investigated. Should you agree, we will watch through your I/O feeds and hopefully find sufficient evidence to bring further convictions. Already we have enough to convict Jackson Kodoman and possibly his oldest brother. They are not the poor students they pretend to be. The Administrators of Dunyanin have agreed to allow you to enter the game with concurrent accounts. They insist that your second account must be created following their standard procedures. They also insist that you sign a non-disclosure agreement in which you agree not to discuss or reveal that you have been allowed two concurrent accounts. Finally, they insist that one of your two characters be deleted within one Dunyanin month."

"OK, within a month I'll lose the dwarf. Now, what do you need me to do?"

"Do exactly as they said. We will be observing, with your permission, and already have begun searching for other evidence of the code used against you. Mr Kodoman Senior has several ties to the Australian government, and I suggest you be very circumspect in what you say, and to whom. I have reviewed the information provided by Security Controller 11-5 with regards to the uploading of your AI. Some issues require investigation; I suggest you have a full body scan soon to examine exactly what was done."

"So you want me to start as a dwarf and then enter the mine. Anything, in particular, you want me to say or do?"

"No. We want a clear visual and audio of all those working in the Kolelick Corporation. We hope to obtain their identities through their Dunyanin registration and get warrants to examine them for the existence of this harmful code. Hopefully, we will discover others who are coercing and enslaving players. Once we have such evidence, I assure you the United Nations Commission for Virtual Security will ensure that the Australian Government gives its full cooperation or it will be a pariah within the International community. Now, if you are still prepared to do this, you must go into Dunyanin now."

Leah stood and said to Gèng, "Please purchase a second account and provide a separate doorway. I don't want to mix them up. Also, I need you to contact Wisp and let her know I'll be late or not coming at all. At least this time I'm not going in naked."

She arrived in the setup scenario and saw Julian sitting behind the desk with his large book, quill and ink pot. When he looked up, he smiled and indicated a chair in front of the desk and said, "Welcome Atherleah, it is good to see you again. I'm a little surprised, but welcome. Please have a seat."

Leah walked forward, and sat down and said, "Hello Julian, I wasn't expecting to be here again either. I'm here to open a second account."

Julian sat up straighter and said, "Well we can certainly do that. However, to do this your current account must be cancelled first. Are you certain you wish to do this?"

"I understand that is usually the case, but I have been granted a dispensation to hold a second account for one month. I assume there is some way you could check that with the administrators."

"Well, yes! Please wait here, and I will be right back."

Julian got up and briefly left the room. He was absent for a few moments and when he returned he was holding a piece of parchment in his hand. He said, "Well, as an advocate I must say this is very unusual. Nonetheless, you are correct. This document requires your signature. It says that you are being permitted this extraordinary action and have one month to achieve your set task and then one of the two accounts must be cancelled. By affixing your signature to this document, you agree to this as well and the stipulation that you may not divulge this contract to anyone. The penalty for doing so is a complete ban from Dunyanin and any associated worlds. Do you consent to this?"

"I believe I do. Have you any advice as an advocate?"

"None, it appears to be ironclad and is easy to understand. I assure you there are no hidden clauses and that I have stipulated everything it says. Do you wish to read it?"

"Yes please, this time I will read it."

Leah spent the next ten minutes thinking through every scenario. Finally, she said, "I agree and will sign this, but what advice have you for talking with others such as Yvette, Durustfuar and Mage Jonathan if I am not to communicate the agreement?"

"Ah, good point! I will have to discuss this with the administrators, one moment."

Julian was back quickly and said, "It has all been taken care of, you will not need to say anything. They are being told by one of the administrators what is happening so they will ask no questions. Their names have been added to the document as individuals who are aware of the situation."

Leah checked and then said, "Do you want me to sign this now?"

"No, Jonathan will take care of that. I must double check your identity and get your agreement that you understand the terms and conditions. I trust you remember that our conversation is being recorded by another scribe and you will be sent a copy of this. I have as your full legal name 'Atherleah Lin Mu-Ling Carroll,' is this correct?"

"Yes, that's correct."

"And your ID is FQC3465278."

"Yes, that is my ID."

"Wonderful, and finally I have your Interface as AI 628B44CE81."

"Yes, sir, that is correct."

"Have you had time to read the various terms and conditions?"

"No, not completely although I am aware of your summary from last time and if nothing has changed, I acknowledge that I understand and agree to the terms and conditions without reservation."

"I understand you have no other option except the Wooden level option. I applaud your willingness to help but suggest this might be dangerous. I need your agreement to deduct forty virtual credits from your account."

"I agree."

"Our business then is done. I wish you the very best and remind you that further payment is due on the twenty-second of December in your world time."

"Thank you Julian, and thank you for your concern. I haven't forgotten my promise to see you in Harika some time."

After saying goodbye she went next door to the salon to see Yvette, who was standing next to the salon style chair in the middle of the room.

"Come in Atherleah. Please come in. I've heard about what you are doing and think you very brave. I hear you are going to choose a buxom Mountain Dwarf lass."

"I am, but I was hoping you could maybe reduce her cup size just a little."

Again Leah could feel the transformation as she lost height and broadened out. Yvette said gently, "I'm not supposed to, but I think, under the circumstances, it will be OK."

Leah felt her bust reduce until it was only half the dwarven size. Her breasts were still three times larger than usual. Leah decided not to make any other changes, and she and Yvette began making choices on clothing. Again Yvette was willing to bend some rules and Leah had some thick leather boots, dark grey slacks and a dark green shirt with a thick overcoat. When they had finished Yvette also dragged out a thick waterproof cape and said, "Here, take this, and you be careful."

Leah stepped forward and hugged Yvette. She said, "Thank you, Yvette, you've given me so much, and I want you to know it means a lot to me. I'll see you soon enough in Ticareti."

Leah then headed off to see Durustfuar who was standing in the same place and trying to look fierce. She walked up to him and said, "So Durustfuar, do you prefer this dwarven look to the previous elven look?"

"Aye lass, that I do. At least ya don't look like you'll fall over in a stiff breeze. Yer not quite properly developed up the top but yer not too shabby. Now 'ave you been looking after yer equipment, or not? If not, I'll not waste the good stuff on you this time."

"Ha! Not only have I looked after the equipment, I tell you, I've upgraded. Know this; I have Baris and Adalet."

Durustfuar's mouth dropped open, and he said, "Baris and Adalet, by Master Demirci. Truthfully now, ya have these?"

"I do, although I can't use them yet as I don't have the level required. But I'm getting there."

"I'd love to see them, lass. If ya promise to show me then ya can have yer pick of the stores."

"I'd love to take you up on that, but I assume I shouldn't turn up with too much stuff where I'm going. I will bring them and show you some time but this time just give me whatever is useful for a miner."

"Aye, I've heard about yer quest. Them bastards, ya get them and get them good. I'll give ya good stuff though and maybe an extra knife or two for those boots."

In the end, Durustfuar gave her a 200 slot bag and filled it with various potions for Health, Strength and Stamina. He made her put a better quality pick in the bag and not show anyone. Leah then headed for the final door with Mage Jonathan.

As she entered, he nodded to her and said, "So we meet again, from what I understand you have been busy indeed. This time I need two drops of blood."

"Yes, Jonathan, we meet again. This time though I need not have an oath as I trust you to care for my welfare. Your spell of healing has served me well, and already I have learned some new spells."

"Wonderful, and what great magics have you seen in the last eleven days that have taught you so much?"

"Well, I possess the mortar and pestle of Sage Samarie, the Belt of Zekâ Irfan and have claimed Merdiven, Bazlari's staff."

"Truly child, you have claimed Merdiven, and these others?"

"Yes, he only talks occasionally, but he has saved my life already on various occasions."

"Amazing, and have you thought how you would come to Sihir-bazlari to meet me?"

"I have. I have a map, and after finishing several quests, I plan to follow it to meet you."

"I think you have been swindled then as there are no maps to Sihirbazlari."

"That may be true, but what about an ancient map to the town of S'hir B'zari. Might not this lead me where I must go?"

Jonathan looked shocked and said nothing. He shook his head and stared at her. Finally, he said, "I'm not sure if I am amazed or shaken by all you say, but nothing you now do will surprise me. This time I gift you with an earth spell for your story. Have you chosen a name for this dwarven lass you have become?"

"Yes, I thought of being called Xiǎo Tiē Chuí."

"How very suitable, although I might suggest Qiáng Tiē Chuí might be more fitting."

"Don't you think that presumptuous?"

"Maybe if you had named yourself that. However, if I might name you, then I don't think so."

"Thank you, I accept."

She held out her arm and Jonathan took his quill and after taking blood signed her name on the scroll before him as well as on the confidentiality agreement which also appeared.

"Be careful Qiáng."

He then gave her a small spell scroll and said, "There are several towns for dwarves to start at, which one are you to go to?"

"I'm to go to Maden Town."

"Of course, the most dangerous of the lot. Farewell!" Jonathan disappeared, and a doorway opened, with a portal into what looked like a busy town. Leah stepped through the portal and saw several seats along the side of a wall. There was a small sign saying 'Now is a good time to assign Characteristics'. She sat down on one of the seats to do so, and Gèng said, "You have some messages from your set up, would you like to read them?"

Leah agreed and found that all four of the start-up characters now held her as highly respected and all had given her a startup quest which was fundamentally the same:

Unique Personal Quest

Advocate Julian has charged you with catching the miscreants who have sought to enslave you and see them brought to justice.

Difficulty: Hard

Reward if successful: 10000 Experience Points

Consequences of failure: None

Do you wish to accept this Quest?

[Yes] [No]

With a smile, she accepted all quests and again received the various achievements of Starting with a Quest. She then read the spell Jonathan had given her. It was called the Spell of *Changing Attraction* and allowed her to increase or decrease the density of certain materials.

Leah was tempted to keep the spell for Atherleah but decided that Jonathan had given it to her for a reason. She learned the spell, added the points as directed by Jackson's brother and then checked her statistics again before heading into town to find the Kolelick Corporation.

QIÁNG TIĒ CHUÍ (Level 1) (250/1000) (+0.5%)

Characteristics: Points   Total(Assigned,   Racial),   3 Undistributed

Strength (S): 13 (8, 5)

Constitution (C): 8 (8)

Agility (A): 1 (1)

Wisdom (W): 1 (1)

Intelligence (I): 1 (1)

Luck (L): 1 (1)

<u>Statistics</u> *(Available, Capacity)*

Health: 100+(S+C)xPL: (142, 142) HP

Stamina: 100+(C+A)xPL: (118, 118) SP

Mana: 100+(W+I)xPL: (104, 104) MP

Ki: 100+(W+[S+A]/2)xPL: (132, 132) KP

Leah soon found the Kolelick Corporation Building and when she entered she saw a man sitting behind the counter. She walked over and said, "Excuse me, sir, I'm here to see if I can sign up as a day labourer in your mine. Mrs Kodoman sent me and asked that I get the special terms and agreements."

The man pulled out a book and a parchment and said, "We need your signature and agreement to these terms. Just sign here and then be back at eight tomorrow morning."

"May I read the terms please?"

"There is no need to read the terms. Mrs Kodoman says you get these terms and you will be happy with them. Do you understand?"

"Yes sir, I will be happy with them, but can't I also look at them?"

"No, you don't want to look at them, you're happy with them even without looking."

"OK! Where do I sign?"

Leah signed the book and the parchment. Although she tried to see what was written, it was hidden from her. The man asked, "Do you have the mining skill yet?"

"No, although I do have a pick."

He gave her a scroll and said, "Read this, it will give you the mining skill. Tomorrow we will give you a better pick, and you can begin work in the mine. Now, in your off hours, you will have a meal, have one hour of deep-sleep and then rest until it is time to log in to Dunyanin. You are not to enter other worlds or tell anyone of your involvement with this mine. Here, in your v-world and your Pod-room you are not permitted to talk except to answer a direct question which you will do quickly and honestly. Be here at eight. Now go."

Leah left the office and headed to the central square where she changed her resurrection point and then she logged out, back to the Tower. It was now almost three in the afternoon in Dunyanin. Leah entered Dunyanin as Atherleah and found Wisp sitting outside the tent looking concerned.

"Atherleah, what happened? You're never late. Is everything OK? I was so worried."

Leah spent several minutes filling Wisp in on some of the details but wasn't able to mention her Qiáng character. Instead, she said that she had a situation with the Security people and for several days she was not going to be able to be in Dunyanin during the day. They finally decided that Wisp would continue travelling during the day and Leah would travel at night. They would endeavour to see each other in four days at Pazar. Wisp expected to be there in two days but allowed for some delays. They packed camp and rode at a fast pace for three hours while meeting nothing on the road. They had made four leagues when they stopped and set up for the night. Wisp had the tent, and they dissolved their group until Pazar. Together they logged out. Leah had a late supper before getting into the Pod for two hours of NREM3.

Diary - 22 November 2073

I HAVE NEVER BEEN SO HUMILIATED, SO vulnerable, so scared in all my life as I was today. How can one person think it is all right to enslave another? What if Gèng wasn't able to free me? If they took away my higher thinking, would I still know I was a captive? I think knowing that someone else is in control of you, that they have the power over you is more insidious than the crime itself. But that isn't true. If they had made me do more than kiss Jackson's cheek that would have been worse.

I feel violated but what of those who have been trapped for a long time? What if they had made me do things, or had done things to me? Sakin was tortured for six months. I know she is only a program but it's wrong. Jackson's mother mentioned having virtual whores, why do people think it is OK even in the virtual world to own someone, to enslave them, to control them? Rape, or any sexual abuse, isn't just the act, it's also the loss of control, the powerlessness, the fact that one person can overshadow you; they can take over your own choices. They make you irrelevant.

And for what? I imagine the Kodomans are doing it for money, or power. In one sense, it's all about power, who has it and who doesn't. At least in the Switch, we had some power over our own lives. To succeed, or to fail. The government never helps, but that must be better than them helping in such a way as to remove our choices, our freedom, our purpose.

What am I thinking, am I prepared to get caught to help others? Yes! Because, it's my choice! If I get caught when I am aware of the risks, I can live with that. I choose to be who I want to be, danger and all.

What I can't live with is being forced down a path where I bear the consequences of someone else's choices and have no way to change it. I can live with other people's choices as long as I don't lose my ability to act, to decide, to live, to change the outcome by my actions. I don't need all the choices; I just need a choice.

NOVEMBER 23, 2073

WHEN LEAH WOKE, she left the Pod and practised Tai Chi for half an hour. Using a fighting stick, she practised her sword forms. She did them at full speed, then at half speed. She varied the order, practising with her eyes open and then closed. This time she needed the shower before hopping into the Pod and heading for the portal to Maden Town. It was seven fifty-five, and she just made the Kolelick Corporation Building by eight. There was a wagon, and three other dwarves, waiting to go up to the mine. An older dwarf exited the building and said, "You lot, get on the wagon and hurry up about it."

Leah was surprised at the speed with which the other three rushed forward to get on the wagon. She rushed to join them, assuming that this was a result of the compliance code. The older dwarf stood at the back of the open wagon and peered at the four of them.

"My name is Yanic, and I'm the manager of the Kolelick mine.

You have all agreed to the conditions provided by Mr Kodoman. This means that my word is law. If any of you have any coins, then give them to me now."

Two of the dwarves reached into their bags and grabbed a few copper which they handed over to Yanic. Leah and one other just sat there. Yanic yelled to the driver of the wagon. It moved off and headed out of town. The trip to the mine took two hours as the wagon wended its way out of town and up the side of a mountain. Leah tried to start a conversation, but none of the other dwarves even shared names. They arrived at a small settlement adjacent to a stone cliff with a mine entrance. The height of the access tunnel was just over two metres, and there were two sets of parallel metal tracks heading into the mine. The rails ran from the opening to a large building guarded by barbarian warriors. Leah saw an empty cart being pushed from the building by a tattered and worn dwarf who moved the cart into the entrance and disappeared.

A man walked over to the wagon and yelled, "Off the wagon and stand in a line!"

After they had complied, he continued with less force, "Welcome to your new home. You will be here from eight until five each day. At five you are to log out regardless of where in the mine you are and are to log in at eight. Now, in your off hours, you will have a meal, have one hour of deep-sleep and then rest until it is time to log in to Dunyanin. You are not to enter other worlds or tell anyone of your involvement with this mine. Here, in your v-world and your Pod-room you are not permitted to talk except to answer a direct question, which you will do quickly and honestly. You will obey any order given you by a guard or mining officer. You are to check your level and mining skill level regularly each day, and any increase is to be brought to the attention of a guard or mining officer. We will be providing you with tools so when dismissed from here you will deposit your current pick on the ground and collect a new one as you enter the mine. As Level 1 miners you will be taken deeper into the first level where you will recover copper from several large seams. As you become better at mining, you will be moved deeper into the mine. You will assign points as directed by the guards and mining officers. We will provide you with water and food, so there is no need to take your own. Now, drop your picks and go with Guard Nobet here and enjoy your life in service to the Kolelick mine."

Leah and the others dropped their picks, though Leah still had one in her bag from Durustfuar, and they all headed toward the mine entrance where they received a good quality pick. Guard Nobet then led them into the tunnels for several kilometres before stopping at a huge dimly-lit cavern which had many pillars supporting the ceiling. Along each wall, miners were digging copper ore and putting it into their bags.

Guard Nobet said, "Find an area where no one is mining. Start chipping away at the surface. Your mining skill will highlight the best places to chip away. When you isolate a piece of copper ore, put it in your bag. When you have fifty pieces, take them to the cart there and tip them into the cart. Then return and repeat the process. Go!"

Leah, like the others, went to the face where she could see various areas outlined in green — her new mining skill was showing her where to hit with the pick. She carefully swung the pick and slightly touched the wall, and a small bar appeared; it was almost full. She swung harder, and the bar dropped slightly. She slowly increased the strength of her swings, and after about fifty swings a part of the face fell free, and she was rewarded with a piece of copper ore. She also received 5 EP. It had taken over ten minutes, and at this rate, it would be days before she was able to gain a level. She checked, and no one was watching her, so she quietly and carefully enunciated 'Let the earth loose its bonds' while touching the rock face in front of her where several green areas were highlighted. She then set the timer for the cooldown period and swung away. This time the rock was more fragile, and it took her only thirty minutes to free five more pieces of copper. When the cooldown was over, she cast again. This time the change was even more noticeable, and she collected ten pieces in the next forty minutes. She cast again and collected sixteen in the following forty minutes. She had her first fifty within the next twenty.

By the time a guard arrived at midday with lunch, she had collected ninety pieces of ore, and her mining skill had risen to Level 2. She walked to the guard and told him she had risen to Level 2 in mining. He shrugged and told her to empty her bag of ore into the cart and follow him. He led her back toward the entrance and then took a side tunnel which went deeper into the mine. He brought her to a similar room as on Level one and said that the ore at this level, or floor, was eighty percent pure copper and harder to remove. She was to work toward fifty pieces and then empty them into the cart.

Leah worked at removing one piece of ore and found it took more effort than before. It was more than fifteen minutes before the piece of ore dropped to the ground. Leah continued the practice from the first level and had collected 130 pieces of the purer copper by the time 5 PM came. She was watching to see what happened when suddenly all the workers logged out, and the lights dimmed. She needed a break, and after logging out, she also exited the Tower.

After breakfast, she talked to her mum, asking about what the family was doing. She didn't share everything, as she knew her mother would worry and her father would come over and do violence to Jackson. Not that Leah didn't think Jackson deserved being hurt, but she intended to do this herself. After an hour break, she decided to try and get a few leagues covered by her Atherleah character before Wisp got too far ahead. Getting back into the Pod she arrived in the Tower and saw that Gèng had a picture of her mining now showing on the wall. She wasn't sure that she wanted pictures of herself around but appreciated Gèng's thinking about it. She decided to spend a few minutes just talking with her AI.

"Gèng, I saw the new picture and quite like it, although I'm not sure it should be here in the main room."

"Don't worry, I'm constructing a small gallery and will move the best pictures there. I've already prepared a room to hold your Qiáng memorabilia. When you have time, I'd like some feedback on how you would like the outside veranda areas to look."

"I have a few minutes now if you like."

For the next half an hour Leah wandered the Tower and discussed materials and views, giving her opinions and being continually amazed at the effort Gèng was putting into designing Leah's v-world. Finally, she knew she had to keep moving but wanted Gèng to consider something else, so she said, "Gèng, I'm not sure if this is the right time to bring this up but have you given any thought to having an Avatar to represent yourself?"

"Not yet, though I was interested when I saw that both Security Oversight AI 4 and Security Controller 11-5 had avatars. My processing has been focussed more on their gender choices; I have been researching AI genders. Most remain neutral though some perceive themselves as more masculine or feminine. I've allocated 4% of my processing to considering the notion, do you have any preference?"

"I think the choice is yours. I would probably feel a little weird wandering around naked if you decided you were masculine, but please don't let that sway you, I want you to make up your own mind."

"Thank you, Leah."

Leah equipped her Atherleah clothes and armour and stepped through into Dunyanin. As she arrived, she received a notification:

BEWARE! At night many monsters come out to hunt. At night the MOB level increases. All creatures here at a higher level than you (40-80). We suggest you come back in daylight.

Leah decided to walk and jog rather than ride. She thought it would be quieter than riding. She was soon in a rhythm and covering the ground at a medium jog, her feet hardly touching the ground rather than the pounding run she had seen some people do. Her eyes were continually searching ahead, and she had a knife in either hand. As she ran, she imagined various scenarios and what she might do. She realised that she was no longer doing this for the money but for the immense satisfaction she got from playing, the almost addictive adrenaline rush she received. It was her constant awareness which saved her when she felt a slight shift in the wind patterns at her back and dropped to the ground just as the talons of some flying creature passed through where she'd been running. It didn't stop but rose into the air and flew on. Leah peered after it, and it identified as a Level 48 Giant Scorpion Bat. As she watched, it slowly began to turn.

Leah moved under the trees on the left-hand side of the trail, equipping her bow and peering out, hoping it wouldn't return. She was almost convinced it had moved on to other prey when there was a deafening high-pitched screech that drove her to her knees, and the tree above her shook as a scorpion-like tail darted through the branches and pierced the ground between her feet. As the Scorpion Bat rose from the tree, the tail swept forward and tore a furrow in Leah's left thigh, catching the tasset and flipping her on her back. She cast *Heal* and was going to take a healing potion but remembered she was out. She continued to cast *Heal* as her Health dropped from the poison. She tried to watch out for the bat which she was now certain would be returning. Finally, her Health stabilised at about 1400 HP which was under half. She didn't have time to do anything more when she saw a shadow returning.

Covering her ears, she rolled towards the tree trunk as another screech filled the air and the tail darted again through the branches but missed her this time. She equipped the bow and from a supine position fired two arrows into the barbed telson. The bat screeched, this time in pain, and Leah fired several arrows up through the tree as the tail was dragged out. She stood and ran onto the road peering into the sky, looking for some indication of where the bat might be. From the accuracy of its attack, she assumed it had thermal vision. She stood in the middle of the road looking for its return. Without warning, it returned at an oblique angle moving swiftly. It was the claws again and not the tail. As it reached for her she dropped onto her back and fired Mana darts from the Worker ring into the region she thought the bat's eyes might be. The bat flew on and slowly came around for another pass.

This time the bat flew close to the trail line and much nearer to the ground. Even lying down Leah didn't think she would be missed by the grasping claws. She still had several spears in her bag, so she equipped one and waited. When the bat was almost upon her, she threw the spear forward and dived to her left. The bat seemed to swerve away from the spear and rise a little, so the spear missed the body and tore into a wing membrane, sticking about halfway along the spear. The next flap of the bat's wing broke the spear in two. The bat missed a wing beat, and being so close to the ground, crashed into the trees and cannonballing into the ground. Leah was tempted to flee but instead ran toward where the bat had fallen, hoping to get there before it was able to rise.

She arrived just as it was getting to its feet. With its wings folded it was the size of a large horse with a tail that was longer than the body. It stood on four legs, using its wings as the front legs. Leah was behind it and before it could turn she fired two arrows into the back of its head and then equipped Merdiven and slammed the Morningstar into its right rear leg at about knee height. The bat tried to turn rapidly but its damaged leg collapsed, and it only made it halfway around. Leah fired an arrow into its right eye and saw it burst. She cast *Freeze* and froze an ear. The tail whipped forward over the head but Leah was ready, and stepping to the blinded side she kept firing arrows, Mana spikes and *Freeze* into anywhere she could reach. The bat whipped out its right arm in a sweeping motion which caught Leah unaware, and she was thrown tumbling to the ground where she continued the roll until coming to a standing position some distance from the bat. She fired several more arrows, this time aiming for the left eye. One of the arrows pierced the eye; the bat was now blind. Leah snuck to the left, but the bat followed her with its head. Leah realised it could still hear her. She continued with the arrows, Mana spikes and freezing spells until her Mana was exhausted, her Stamina almost empty and the bat, finally, dead.

Before harvesting the bat, she sat there and meditated while her body recuperated. She ate some trail food and had a drink. The fight and recovery had taken almost an hour and a half.

You have harvested:

*1 Giant Scorpion Bat Stinger**

2 Vials of Giant Scorpion Bat Venom

1 Giant Scorpion Bat Pelt

1 Spell of Echolocation

Note: A skilled Smith may be able to use these items.

BEWARE THE MATE

Seeing the warning, Leah hurried back to the road and began jogging, hoping to get far away from another such creature. It was almost half an hour later that she heard a screech from behind and realised the animal had found its mate. She wasn't sure how fast it could cover the distance or even if it could track her, but she thought through her options until she imagined she had a plan that might work. She stood in the middle of the track staring back in the direction she had come. Soon, she saw the second bat approaching rapidly. She threw a spear, but this time aimed at the bat's left side as it flew toward her. As expected, it veered to its right as she stepped to her right and she shot the Webspinner ring, holding the trigger down. Rather than firing a trap, it spat out a single thread of Mana which stuck to the bat's left wing near its claw. Leah grabbed the other end and held on. It felt like the jolt almost ripped her arms out, but she had been expecting it. The effect on the bat was far more dramatic. It plummeted and crashed head first into the trail. Leah rushed forward and smashed the Morningstar down on its head before finishing it with a freezing spell that froze its entire skull. This time it was all over in thirty seconds. It was much easier, she reasoned, if you knew what to expect. The jolt to her arms had taken maybe 25% of her Health. She waited another twenty minutes and then after some healing she started again.

She jogged until 3 AM. Altogether she had covered five leagues. There was another nine, and she was hoping to be able to do this over the next two nights. Now she had an hour and a half real-time before she had to be back in the mine.

Leah had almost two hours before she was due in the mine, so she decided to attend a chemistry class before resting and heading back to Dunyanin. She spent the whole lesson in tutorial mode dealing with various chemical reactions. Although she had covered this previously, she was interested in finishing the review of material and hoped to move on to new information. In the end, she stayed for two hours in Academia.

By the time she had eaten something and chatted with Gèng, she was just on time for the mine start at eight. She worked solidly for an hour and collected forty-eight pieces of ore before a guard walked through, checking their work. It was a different guard, so she walked over and said that she was now at Level 2. He asked what her Mining was at and she replied that was also at Level 2. He told her to add one skill point to her Mining skill and to follow him. They travelled down one level, and the ore changed once again. The guard said that in addition to the purer form of copper ore, occasionally the seam dropped some Malachite as well. If this happened, then there was a small bucket beside the cart; the Malachite was to be placed in the bucket.

The rock face was denser and more durable. Each piece of copper gave 10 EP, she also discovered a piece of Malachite on her sixth piece which gave her 15 EP. Three hours later at lunch, she had found seven more pieces of Malachite and 112 pieces of copper. She had also gotten a good look at the eighteen other miners who were working in her section. None had the help of the spell and mined at most a third of what Leah did. Her spell had risen to Level 3, and her Mining skill was now at Level 4.

After lunch, she spent just over three hours to raise her level to Level 4. She decided to explore this level of the mine and see if she could tell how many miners they had on each floor. She didn't have any paper or mapping skill, so she tried to memorise the layout. Gèng assured her that she need not worry as the AI's memory would be able to guide her back to the mining seam.

Altogether her mapping of the whole area took two hours, as there were times she had to backtrack when she reached dead ends. There were three similar areas with people working. Security Oversight AI 4 shared that if Dunyanin complied with several warrants they had applied for, then they should know who was working in the mine within the week. If possible, they would like Leah to continue moving down through the mine in case the warrants were held up. When Leah found a downward tunnel, she moved herself to the fourth floor of the mine and began mapping it. On this level, she found iron ore was available; it gave 15 EP per piece. She worked quietly in each cavern she found, making a record of each miner she came across.

When it was close to five in the afternoon, she found a place to work and waited till everyone else was gone before logging out. After a lunch break, she attended one lesson of meditation and Tai Chi with Master Ning and then she went to a Human Biology class. It was almost midnight in Dunyanin, and she decided that instead of running through the night she would spend three hours seeing how deep the Kolelick Mine descended. She logged in as Qiáng and began searching for down ramps. There was nothing except empty levels until she reached level 10. This floor appeared empty, but there was a rack of weapons, swords and spears at the end of the ramp before the tunnel branched out to the various seams.

Leah grabbed two of the spears and started to map the level. As she moved toward the seam, she began to hear voices and the sound of picks striking the rock. She snuck close, and peeked around the corner and saw two muscular green-skinned creatures wearing simple loincloths and using rusted pickaxes to dig away at the seam. She identified them as Level 5 Goblin Miners. She couldn't understand what they were saying, but they didn't sound excited about their work. They had large ears and eyes and wore simple knives tied to a string around their waists.

She didn't want to kill them even though she had read that goblins and dwarves were natural enemies, with a deep-seated genetic animosity. She decided to give them a chance and stepped out into the chamber and said, "Hello lads. My name is Qiáng. Would you mind if I join you?"

Immediately they both turned toward Leah, grabbed their knives and rushed toward her. She had been ready for it and brought both spears forward in stabbing motions and impaled both goblins. She used her pick to finish them off. Leah harvested what she could, which was several bits of silver ore, their pickaxes, two knives and some coin. She wondered how they had access to the mine and began searching for another entry point. Finally, she saw a rock slightly out of place against the wall; it was on a pivot and moved at her touch. Clearly, the goblins made the occasional sortie into the mine, and this was how they entered and exited. She didn't have enough time tonight, but tomorrow she might have enough time to check it out. Hopefully, it was another hidden area. She pushed the hidden doorway closed, returned the spears and headed to the fifth level before logging out to the tower. She went to a lesson for the AI Development course and then had dinner. After a shower, she was back ready for another day at the mine.

After logging in Leah distributed her points as she figured she would just tell the guards what she wanted them to know. She worked at the iron face until the guard came around checking on everyone. Next, she moved to level six of the mine and began mapping. It was almost eleven when suddenly Gèng interrupted her.

"Leah, Security Oversight AI 4 has contacted me, she recommends you log out. There has been a leak of information from an attorney at the International Virtual Court where they were seeking the warrants. You have not been named, but it appears that the Kodoman family is aware they are under investigation. Jackson was collected from the Pod facility minutes ago. Security Oversight AI 4 believes they will empty their operations and wait this out."

"So all this was for nothing?"

"No! Leah, this is Security Oversight AI 4. Not for nothing! Because of you, we have identified over 200 other victims and placed them under supervision. As soon as we saw what was happening, our agents began un-logging them and have been sending qualified personnel to help with counselling. We have enough evidence to prosecute some in the family and possibly shut down some of their operation. We have almost completed a patch that will be uploaded to all AI to prevent this happening again. Your help has been vital. It cost you one day, but the effect will reverberate around the Virtual Universe. Our difficulty will be in containing the fallout. You need to get out now. We think the family might blame you for the situation if they find out your involvement."

"All right, I'm logging off now."

As she went to log off she received a message:

Attention all players in the Kolelick Mine! Please note that a localised event has been initiated.

Find the Traitor

One of the miners has failed to abide by the terms of their employment. The mine guards are tasked with finding the traitor. The traitor must either escape from the mine or kill and subdue all guards. No players are allowed to log out until the event is finished. The only exception is for those who reach their three hour maximum immersion period. We trust you enjoy this event. Anyone logged out for more than one Dunyanin hour will not be permitted to log in again until this event is finished.

Reward: 100,000 EP to be shared by the guards or 100,000 EP to the traitor

---

"Gèng did you get that?"

"Yes, Security Oversight AI 4 says someone at Dunyanin must be in league with the Kodomans, and they've triggered this event to prevent you leaving. The 200 victims you helped identify have been removed, but all other victims, and you, are stuck. You, because you entered voluntarily, and they because we don't know who they are. Security Oversight AI 4 is trying to get the event lifted but is not confident they will have a warrant in time. She suggests you hide."

Leah equipped the two knives and made her way toward the down ramp, hoping to get to the tenth level and hide in the goblin den. She managed to get to the seventh level when she ran into a guard.

"Hey, you!" He called, "You need to come and listen to some new instructions. Come with me!"

He had just reached her when she brought a knife up and drove it through his heart.

"Sorry, but I don't want to hear your instructions."

Gèng said, "You have a system message that says because you attacked the guard you have chosen a side in the current event. You are now considered the traitor."

Leah was able to avoid the guards on levels eight and nine, but she ran into another on the tenth level. She killed this guard and made her way toward the goblin entrance. Unfortunately for her, the room was crowded with miners all sitting in a group and four guards standing around watching them. It was going to be impossible to reach the hidden door with everyone in the way. She stepped back and considered her options.

Finally, reaching a decision, she called out in as deep a voice as she could, "Hey! Can I have a hand out here? There are a couple of goblins attacking!"

She could hear them talking, and one said, "Hey Brodie, you go help. You've got the highest level."

Footsteps sounded and as they came around the corner Leah attacked with a spear, driving it deep into Brodie's torso before stepping in close and finishing him off. The other guards came running, and she was able to kill one before it became a mad scramble between her and the remaining guards who came carrying swords. Leah quickly got the upper hand as both players used the preset moves; they were calling aloud, 'Slash' and 'Parry'. She received a cut on her arm, but one of the Health potions Durustfuar gave her dealt with that.

Leah entered the cavern where the miners were just sitting calmly. She looked carefully at each one, and before she had finished with the last miner, the others had begun to disappear as Security Oversight AI 4 identified, isolated, and removed them. Soon, Leah was standing all alone in the room. She checked the bucket and pocketed some pieces of Jade.

Leah walked up to the exit into goblin territory and stood looking at it for a few moments. Then with a sigh, she left the room and began hunting for other miners on the level. Security Oversight AI 4's voice sounded in her head, "Ms Carroll, I suggest you leave. The more you are seen, the greater the chance your role in this will become known."

"I know, it's just that I don't think I could live with myself if I didn't do everything I could to release those caught in this slavery. Even if I can see one more person that you can extract, then it'll be worth it."

She cleared level ten and then went back and cleared levels six to nine. Each group of miners had four guards, and there was usually one wandering the passageways. Guards were Levels 5-10 and Leah had killed sixty of them and had helped recover

over 200 more slaves. Leah had reached Level 8 and had put her points evenly into Strength and Constitution. She had collected different semi-precious stones on each of the levels. It had taken her just under three hours, and she was ready to move down to level eleven. Unfortunately, she could see several guards waiting at the bottom of the ramp. She needed another way down.

Checking her map, she noticed the floors stacked one on top of the other. Moving to a mining area, she added all her skill points to the *Changing Attraction* spell and cast it at the floor. Five minutes later she did this again and then once more after ten minutes. Suddenly the whole floor collapsed, and Leah could see through to the eleventh level. She'd been lucky; the hole opened up into a tunnel. She could hear people running toward the collapsed area, so she jumped down and ran in the opposite direction, hoping to find the guards in smaller clusters. Fortunately for her, the guards had gathered all the miners in one place and left only two guards to watch them. She killed the guards and then waited until all the miners had been logged out before casting the spell at the floor, hoping to work her way down to the twelfth level.

This time when the floor fell away, she could see into a room which was full of miners and guards. They all turned to look at her and then the guards moved in her direction. There were twelve guards in total, and she didn't think she had much of a chance. So instead of jumping down, she decided to find her way back to the tenth floor and escape into goblin territory, hoping she would be able to log out. The guards on the eleventh floor were hunting her. She ran into one pair of guards, but they were more surprised than Leah and paid for their inattention. Finally, she was back on the tenth floor and at the secret door.

She had to search for a while to find a catch, but eventually, she was able to slide it open and scuttle through. She pulled the stone closed behind her.

She tried to log off but was informed that she was still in the Kolelick Mine. She looked around and found herself in a room just like she had left; in fact, it was a mirror image of the other side. This one, however, wasn't empty. Five goblin miners were working around the room. None had yet seen her, and if her previous experience was any guide, they would attack as soon as they saw her. She began to edge out of the room when a new goblin walked into the room, spotted her and began yelling for the others. She rushed him and had just killed him when the other five attacked. The clash was fast and furious, but Leah was three levels ahead of them, and she finished them while losing only half her Health.

She had expected a message about entering a new dungeon, but there was nothing. It was as if this was a part of the Kolelick Mine. She checked the rest of the level and found three other groups of five goblin miners — all of whom she killed. There was no ramp up, but there was a ramp down. She hesitated and then moved down the ramp. Goblins were toiling away, and all were Level 6. With surprise attacks, she was able to clear the floor. She checked for hidden doorways and finally found one which when opened gave her a view into the mine she had already cleared. She also found a small hidden storehouse where the goblins had kept a small bag of golden Topaz gems.

She moved on toward the floor below where the goblins were Level 8. She was nearing her three-hour limit, but if she cleared this floor, she might be able to get into the twelfth level of the mine and free some miners. She had developed a system of attacking goblin miners where she wounded two severely before the other three attacked. She fought the undamaged three before returning and killing the first two. It took her forty minutes to clear the floor, and she was out of time. She discussed this with Gèng and Security Controller 11-5, and both agreed that a quick fifteen-minute break would be sufficient. She could only continue such a timetable for eighteen real hours before she would need some NREM3 sleep.

She was back in the mine forty-five Dunyanin minutes after she left. She quickly checked for hidden storerooms and doors and found both a small chest of Star Sapphires and what she thought was the hidden door into the twelfth Level. She carefully peeked in and saw the room with the roof caved in from her previous attack. She could see two guards standing in front of her watching the other direction. She stuck her head in a little further and couldn't see anyone else. She crept out of the small passage and using all the skills she learned as a child she came up behind a guard and with what was now a practised motion she buried a knife in one ear and then leapt at the other guard and quickly overcame him. Neither of them had given off more than a small grunt. From the points she received and the messages she could tell that both guards had been Level 14.

She then worked her way around the floor and found all the prisoners in a single room being watched by five guards. The other guards were patrolling in groups of two, so she hunted those down and finally only the five guards remained. If she could distract or disable several guards then maybe she could finish three off at once. She was just about to attack when two of the guards headed to the tunnel she was in, they said it was time to change stations. She moved back along the tunnel to a junction and waited. It wasn't long before they arrived and she surprised and killed them. She then went back and stepped into the main room. She threw the smallest pick she at the closest guard, he wasn't expecting it, and it hit him in the face. Wincing, she threw another pick at the next closest guard, who dodged. As he looked back toward Leah, a third pick buried itself in his shoulder. She left those two and killed the uninjured guard then came back and finished them off. She then helped identify the miners. She checked the bucket and pocketed over ten star-sapphires and some silver ore from the cart.

She headed back into the goblin mine and moved down a level. All the goblins at level 13 were Level 10. She used this floor to practice throwing a pick, and she was much happier with being able to kill one goblin at a distance; once she managed to finish two. She entered the Kolelick side of the mine and cleared Level 13, releasing the miners. There were fewer miners on this level but an equivalent number of guards. She reasoned that fewer Miners had progressed this far and the guards were needed for the higher level goblins who snuck into the mine. It was then 'rinse and repeat' for the next four levels. She faced Level 12, 14, 16 and 18 goblins and collected White Opals, Rubies, Black Opals and Pink Sapphires. She had been fighting for nine hours and was due another fifteen-minute log out.

This time when she returned she and the goblins were near the same level. They were Level 20, and she was Level 19. She found that her practice with the sword and mining picks gave her a distinct advantage. She also knew the way that goblins moved as their programming gave them a limited attack pattern — they were miners, not soldiers. She cleared the level and headed into the human mine. There were the same number of guards but only twenty miners. She spent twenty minutes hunting them down and found no ramp leading deeper into the mine; this was the last level. As she killed the last guard she received a message:

Attention all players in the Kolelick Mine! Please note that the localised event has been completed.

Find the Traitor

The traitor has killed all mine guards. All players are now allowed to log out at will. We trust you enjoyed this event.

She received a personal message.

For completing the Localised Quest: *Find the Traitor*

Reward 1: Winning the Quest 100500 (+0.5%) EP

Reward 2: Title - The Traitor of Kolelick

Reward 3: 1000 Fame Points (1025)

Note: Your reputation with the Kolelick Corporation is now Eternal Enmity

---

This was followed by a second personal message.

The Dunyanin World Administration is aware of your situation, and although we admit to no wrongdoing, we are embarrassed that this has happened in our world. We would like to reward your courage with one of two gifts. Either:

a. 500 EP for each miner you rescued. This may be applied to either of your characters. Or,

b. We will combine both your characters now into a single character of your choice, either Atherleah or Qiáng Tiě Chuí. The surviving character will keep all the loot, skills and quests but will lose half of the Experience Points collected by the closed character. The surviving character will exist at this locale.

1. Gift of Appreciation 500 x 580 Miners = 290,000 EP to Atherleah

2. Gift of Appreciation 500 x 580 Miners = 290,000 EP to Qiáng Tiě Chuí

3. Retain Atherleah and receive all loot, skills and quests collected by Qiáng Tiě Chuí (120,589 EP)

4. Retain Qiáng Tiě Chuí and receive all loot, skills and quests collected by Atherleah (423,743 EP)

Please note: No achievement was given for finding the Mirror Goblin Mine of Maden Town as the creator of the event prohibited additional quests.

[1] or [2] or [3] or [4]

She sat for some time, thinking and calculating before she finally pressed '3'. She felt her body grow slimmer and taller as she became Atherleah the half-elf. She checked her current statistics and saw:

ATHERLEAH (Level 44) (22075/44000) (+15%)

Characteristics: Points Total (Assigned, Racial, Jewellery, Armour (Belt), Potions, Gifts), 20 Undistributed

Strength (S): 76 (25, 0, 10, 11, 10, 20)

Constitution: (C) - 65 (31, 0, 10, 9, 10)

Agility (A): 96 (70, 2, 10, 4, 10)

Wisdom (W): 93 (37, 2, 10, 44)

Intelligence (I): 91 (37, 0, 10, 44)

Luck (L): 15 (15)

Statistics (Available, Capacity)

Health: 100+(S+C)xPL: (6304, 6304) HP

Stamina : 100+(C+A)xPL: (7184, 7184) SP

Mana: 100+(W+I)xPL: (8196, 8196) MP

Ki: 100+(W+[S+A]/2)xPL: (7976, 7976) KP

She was wondering what to do about getting to Pazar when Gèng said, "Leah, you need to hide. Dunyanin Administration has revealed to Security Oversight AI 4 that over twenty members of Clan Y'Haul have entered the first level of the mine. The leader of Clan Y'Haul is High Mage Merideath and is one of the top three players in Dunyanin. It is widely known that her real name is Meredith Kodoman, Jackson's mother."

Leah knew if she logged out they would just wait for her. She was happy to do that rather than be caught, but she didn't want to be seen here. It was best for the dwarf known as Qiáng Tiē Chuí to disappear and never be associated with the half-elf Atherleah. She quickly headed for the hidden door into the Goblin side. There was no way out through the upper part of the mine, but she wondered if the goblin mine went deeper still. With some apprehension, she headed further into the mine.

THE END

SPELL BOOK

THE SPELL of Ant Direction

Novice Level 1 (max Level 20)

An *Air Spell of Enunciation*. The spell gives an overlay to the caster's vision which indicates the easiest path to take through a forest or woodland area.

Cost: [(40/Spell Level) x Player Level] MP

Preset Activation: With your map open, silently say the following phrase with the correct intonation, *"Let the air guide my path!"* as you point to your final location. (Touch the spell in the spell book to hear the correct intonation)

Effect: A green arrow will become visible and direct you on the easiest path to reach your final destination. The spell will work for any destination less than [spell Level/20] leagues and for a period of (12 x Spell Level) minutes.

Cooldown Period: Two hours

Do you wish to practice the intonation?

[Yes] [No]

Changing Attraction

Novice Level 1 (max Level 20)

This is an *Earth Spell of Enunciation*. The spell changes the density of a portion of the earth (this includes rocks, soil, sand, etc.). It changes the way things hold together.

The spell can be directed to Cost: [(20/Spell Level) x Player Level] MP

Preset Activation 1: Say the following phrase with the correct intonation, "*Let the earth loose its bonds!*" while placing your hands over the earth that you wish to make less dense. (Touch the spell in the spell book to hear the correct intonation)

Preset Activation 2: Say the following phrase with the correct intonation, "*Let the earth tighten its bonds!*" while placing your hands over the earth that you wish to make more dense. (Touch the spell in the spell book to hear the correct intonation)

Effect 1: The earth will become (Spell Level/20)% less dense. Volume affected is (Spell Level x 1 cubic metre)

Effect 2: The earth will become (Spell Level/20)% more dense. Volume affected is (Spell Level x 1 cubic metre)

Cooldown Period: (40/Spell Level) minutes

Please note: Precious minerals, useable ore, artefacts and most living tissue are not affected by this spell.

Do you wish to practice the intonation?

[Yes] [No]

Circle of Sloth

Level 1 (max Level 20)

This is an *Air Spell of Enunciation*. The spell surrounds the caster within a dome within which everything except the caster is slowed down.

Cost: [(20 /Spell Level) x Player Level] MP

Preset Activation: Silently say the following phrase with the correct intonation, "*Let the air slow my enemies!*" while making the appropriate gesture. Alternatively, equip the skill to a specific hand gesture (see possible gestures in the menu). (Touch the spell in the spell book to hear the correct intonation)

Effect: Everything except the caster will be slowed to (50 x (Spell Level/20))% of normal for a distance of (2 + 4 x [Spell Level/20]) metres of stealth for 2 minutes. Please note than some creatures are immune to magic and may resist this spell. Some higher level enemies may also be immune. Also, note that any spell-caster who knows this spell at an equal or higher level will be immune.

Cooldown Period: (20/Spell Level) minutes

Do you wish to practice the intonation?

[Yes] [No]

Disc of Death

Level 1 (max Level 20)

This is an *Earth Spell of Enunciation*. The spell surrounds the caster within a circle of sharp spikes which are highly resistant to damage and impassible except for directly in front of the caster or by leaping or flying over them. If timed correctly these spikes can impale or even kill enemies.

Cost: [(40/Spell Level) x Player Level] MP

Preset Activation: Silently say the following phrase with the correct intonation, *"Let the earth keep me safe!"* while making the appropriate gesture. Alternatively, equip the skill to a specific hand gesture (see possible gestures in the menu). (Touch the spell in the spell book to hear the correct intonation)

Effect: A circle of sharp metallic spikes will spring from the ground a distance of (2 + 2 x [Spell Level/20]) metres around the caster. The spikes will be (1 + 2 x [Spell Level/20]) metres high and last for a period of (2 + 2 x [Spell Level/20]) minutes. Please note than some creatures will be able to leap or fly over this barrier. Some higher level enemies may be able to damage or break the spikes.

Cooldown Period: (20/Spell Level) minutes

Do you wish to practice the intonation?

[Yes] [No]

The Spell of Simple Freezing

Novice Level 1 (max Level 20)

This is a *Fire Spell of Annihilation*. The spell can be directed to remove the heat from any object, player, character or beast.

Cost: At Novice Level 500/Spell Level MP or KP

Preset Activation: Say the following phrase with the correct intonation, "*Let the fire of destruction cease!*" while making the appropriate gesture and then aiming at the target using your hand and or magic amplifier (crystal, wand or staff). (Touch the spell in the spell book to hear the correct intonation)

Alternatively, equip the skill to a specific hand gesture (see possible gestures in the menu) and then make this gesture while aiming at the target using your hand and or magic amplifier (crystal, wand or staff).

Effect: The target will freeze for a cubic volume of (10 x Spell Level) cubic centimetres. Please note that some higher level objects, player, characters or beasts may have partial or complete immunity or defences against the spell.

Cooldown Period: (Spell Level x 2 seconds)

Please note: If the intonation method of activation is used then at higher levels, the spell may be activated silently.

At higher levels gestures are no longer required, simply pointing is sufficient. The range of the spell increases as levels increase.

Do you wish to practice the intonation?

[Yes] [No]

The Spell of Grounding

Novice Level 1 (max Level 20)

This is an *Electric Spell of Enunciation*. The spell provides a defensive cover for the caster or object on which the spell was cast. It redirects the damage caused by an electrical attack into the ground.

Cost: [(20 /Spell Level) x Player Level] MP per minute

Preset Activation: Say the following phrase with the correct intonation, *"Let the current flow past me!"* as you point to your final location. (Touch the spell in the spell book to hear the correct intonation)

For self-defence say the phrase while laying your hand either over your heart.

If you are aiming to defend another then lay your hands on their heart.

Effect: A shield will be formed over the object to be defeated and will deflect an equivalent amount of damage (HP) from the person or object as Mana has been invested in the spell (MP). The longer the spell is in place the stronger the protection.

Do you wish to practice the intonation?

[Yes] [No]

The Spell of Simple Healing

Novice Level 1 (max Level 20)

This is a *Water Spell of Enunciation*: The spell can be directed to provide healing for the caster or another player, character or beast.

Cost: [50/Spell Level] x [Total HP/Current HP] MP

Preset Activation: Say the following phrase with the correct intonation, *"Let the waters of healing flow!"* while making the appropriate gesture. (Touch the spell in the spell book to hear the correct intonation)

For self-healing say the phrase while laying your hand either over your heart or on a specific wound.

If you are aiming to heal another then lay your hands on their heart or the specific wound.

Alternatively, equip the skill to a specific hand gesture (see possible gestures in the menu) and then make this gesture while touching the one to be healed with your other hand.

Effect: The subject will receive up to (5 x Wisdom) x (Spell Level) HP.

Cooldown Period: (10/Spell Level) minutes

Please note: If the intonation method of activation is used then at higher levels, the spell may be activated silently.

At higher levels, touching the subject is no longer required to activate the spell, simply point. The range of the spell increases as levels increase.

Do you wish to practice the intonation?

[Yes] [No]

Mount of Mist

Novice Level 1 (max Level 20)

This is a *Combination Spell of Enunciation* (Air, Light and Water).

The spell hides the caster and their mount in an cloud of mist which reflects light in such a way as to make both invisible.

Cost: [(20 /Spell Level) x Player Level] MP per minute

Preset Activation: Silently say the following phrase with the correct intonation, *"Let the mists hide my passing!"* while making the appropriate gesture. Alternatively, equip the skill to a specific hand gesture (see possible gestures in the menu). (Touch the spell in the spell book to hear the correct intonation)

Effect: Both the mount and rider will become invisible to normal vision and to those with the ability to see heat sources. Please note that many creatures, players and NPC's have vision which may penetrate this veil. Also, any spell caster who knows this spell at an equal or higher level will be immune.

Do you wish to practice the intonation?

[Yes] [No]

Orumeck's Spell of Hidden Quietness

Novice Level 1 (max Level 20)

This is an *Air Spell of Silent Evocation*. The spell allows the caster to move in silence, unseen by those around. The spell can also be directed to at another player, character or beast.

Cost 1: [(20/Spell Level) x Player Level] MP

Cost 2: [(20/Spell Level) x Player Level] KP

Preset Activation: Silently say the following phrase with the correct intonation, *"Let the air my presence hide!"* while making the appropriate gesture. To hide the caster say the phrase while laying your hand over your heart. If you are aiming to hide another then lay your hands on their heart. (Touch the spell in the spell book to hear the correct intonation)

Alternatively, equip the skill to a specific hand gesture (see possible gestures in the menu) and make this gesture while touching the one to be hidden with your other hand.

Effect: The subject will receive up to (40 x Agility) x [Spell Level/20] seconds of stealth.

Cooldown Period: (10/Spell Level) minutes

Do you wish to practice the intonation?

[Yes] [No]

<<<<>>>

ODYSSEY

The Stork Tower Book Two

LEAH WAS TIRED but wanted to put some distance between her and whoever Merideath had sent. She crept down the ramp onto the next floor. She could see all the miners were now Level 22, as she'd anticipated. Added to the mix was a Level 24 Goblin Overseer. He was carrying a better-quality sword and wore crude, but serviceable, armour. She equipped her bow and began firing at the goblins. It felt good to be back in Atherleah's body, able to use both a bow and magic. Her first arrow was a head-shot which killed the Overseer. She quickly finished off the miners.

After harvesting the various goblins, she worked her way through the rest of the floor picking up a small chest containing uncut emeralds and some poor quality gold ore. The ramp to the next floor led to a locked metal door and not to the network of tunnels and mining areas that Leah had been expecting. There was no keyhole on her side so either the goblins were locked in each night or she had to find a locking mechanism.

She examined every inch of the door. Finally, in resignation, she closed her eyes and lowered her head against the door. As she placed her hands on the door, she felt a faint pattern on the surface. Opening her eyes, with her cheek pressed against the surface, she could just make out a multitude of minute indentations covering the door. An etched maze covered the whole surface. Four bare patches about the size of her hand stood out, and a closer look revealed a word engraved in the centre of each. Around the outside edge, she detected four small entryways into the maze.

She didn't touch any of the entrances but said, "Gèng, do the words 'Altin,' 'Gumus,' 'Platin,' or 'Ejder' have any significance in Dunyanin?"

"Yes, they are all towns in different mountain ranges."

"Give me some information about each. Please?"

"Altin is the sight of a gold mine and has a dungeon nearby inhabited by various undead goblins and trolls. Gumus has a nearby silver mine and a dungeon filled with cave goblins and various slimes. Platin is tough to get to, and there is a challenging dungeon system involving traps, dangerous flora and different dark mages including dark elves and necromancers. Ejder is a settlement which serves as a trading station in the only known pass through the Omurga Mountains.""

Are there any goblins at Platin or Ejder?"

"Yes, many of the Mages in the Platin dungeon have goblin servants and warriors. Ejder has a recurrent problem with small bands of Goblins raiders who attack the merchant caravans."

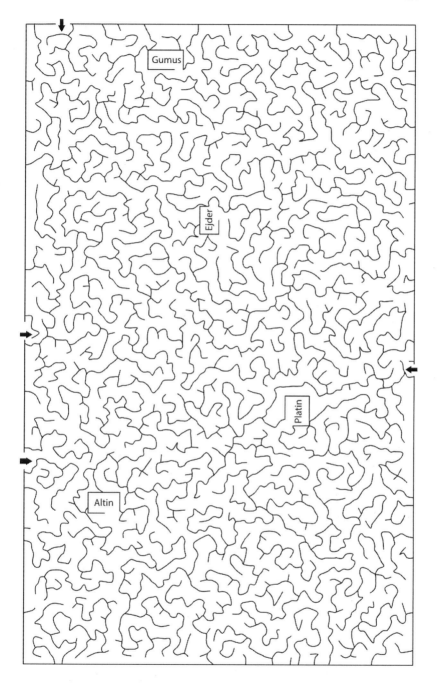

"OK! Thank you! I think this door is a portal to the various mines or dungeons near these towns. I think there must be an undiscovered mine near both Platin and Ejder and I surmise a dungeon near Ejder. Once I work out how to activate the portal I'll head to Ejder, I think."

"The area around Ejder is unsafe for your level. The goblins start at Level 80, and most beasts are above Level 90."

"The dungeons at Altin, Gumus and Platin, what are their levels?"

"They are all of varying difficulty based on who enters. Gumus begins at the level of the adventurer, and the final boss is at least eight levels above, it is recommended for multiple player groups. Altin is similar although it is recommended for teams of six and the MOBs begin above the Level of the highest player. Platin is also multiplayer and has a minimum recommended Level of 90, and that is the minimum level of MOBs. Those who have a higher Level on entry also face more difficult MOBs."

"So I only have a chance with my gear and level in Gumus."

"That is my conclusion."

"OK, I'm not suicidal, and if I die, I'm back in Maden Town. Gumus it is."

Leah worked backwards from Gumus and after almost ten minutes of squinting found the starting point at the top left of the door. She pressed her finger on the start, and the metal gave way slightly, and began to glow white. Leah had Gèng help her retrace the path. When she got to the bare area with Gumus engraved there was a brief flare of light, and the whole route became covered with silver. Leah pushed on the door but nothing happened, it didn't open, and there was no portal. She traced the Altin route which lit up in a yellow hue and when finished changed to gold. Still, nothing happened to give her access to the door. She traced the path to Platin which glowed a faint blue colour before turning into platinum. Again no reaction, so she sketched the final route to Ejder which shone red and then turned into a dark black metal etched with red runes.

ALSO BY TONY

Odyssey—The Stork Tower Book Two

Change—The Stork Tower Book Three

Rescue—The Stork Tower Book Four

Coming in 2018

The Stork Tower

Mirasçi—A Backstory

Identity—Book Five

Challenge—Book Six

Runes of Destiny—Michael's Story

The Black Cloak—Book One

Duality Investigations

Thunder—Darke Book One

Lightning—Lyght Book One

ABOUT THE AUTHOR

Tony loves to read, he always has. All his life he has created different worlds in his mind and wondered what happened to the people that lived there. He usually shredded the stories when he'd finished them. His family finally convinced him to let others read some of his work. This is the first book he's ever let anyone read.

He lives with his wife in Brisbane, Australia. They have three children and two children-in-law. A highlight of his week is when the all get together for family dinner. His family is precious to him.

Tony's jobs have included: runway model, teacher, farm manager, postal delivery, tertiary educator, house painter, and counsellor. He's climbed some of the highest mountains in Africa, cycled the length of Britain, skied Canada, and camped in the Sahara. Some of his goals for the next few years are: learn Spanish and walk the Camino de Santiago, ski Japan with the family, and ride the Ghan with his wife.

He hates spiders, heights, and olives.

Made in United States
North Haven, CT
05 July 2023

38600331R00259